IT'S HARD TO FIND GOOD HELP

X-ray laser weapons were never intended for use in atmosphere, which absorbs X-rays and therefore reduces their range to almost nothing. But "almost nothing" was precisely the range involved within the hangar bay.

Within an enclosed space—even one of this size—the crackling roar as tunnels of vacuum were drilled through air was deafening. One of the gunners sent a rapid-fire series of X-ray pulses down the line of guards, who simply exploded into pinkish-gray mist at the touch of energies beyond any ever intended for antipersonnel use.

The other laser fired at the glassed-in control mezzanine that overhung the hangar bay. It exploded outward in a sheet of flame and a shower of debris.

Andrew ran down the ramp to where Morales lay. Gallivan was cutting open her left sleeve to expose the ugly laser burn. Reislon came immediately behind.

"I thought this might be useful," the Lokar remarked as he applied pain-deadening antiradiation salve from a tube in a first-aid kit, then slapped on a seal that restored the light-duty vac suit's integrity.

"Kozlowski!" Andrew shouted to a first-class petty officer. "Get the weapons distributed to everyone. You, and the rest of Section One, will come with me and Reislon. Now get Lieutenant Morales inside to sick bay."

"Like hell." Morales struggled to her feet. "I'm coming, Captain."

"As am I," said Gallivan.

"God damn it, this i[s] insubordination! I could ha[ve]

BAEN BOOKS
BY STEVE WHITE
✿ ✿ ✿

Blood of the Heroes
The Prometheus Project
Demon's Gate
Forge of the Titans
Eagle Against the Stars
Wolf Among the Stars
Prince of Sunset
The Disinherited
Legacy
Debt of Ages
St. Antony's Fire
Sunset of the Gods (forthcoming)

The Starfire Series:
by David Weber & Steve White
Crusade
In Death Ground
The Stars at War
Insurrection
The Shiva Option
The Stars at War II

by Steve White & Shirley Meier
Exodus

by Steve White & Charles E. Gannon
Extremis

To order these and all Baen titles in e-book form,
go to www.baenebooks.com

WOLF AMONG THE STARS

★ ★ ★

STEVE WHITE

BAEN

WOLF AMONG THE STARS

This is a work of fiction. All the characters and events portrayed in this book are fictional, and any resemblance to real people or incidents is purely coincidental.

Copyright © 2011 by Steve White

All rights reserved, including the right to reproduce this book or portions thereof in any form.

A Baen Book

Baen Publishing Enterprises
P.O. Box 1403
Riverdale, NY 10471
www.baen.com

ISBN: 978-1-4516-3843-1

Cover art by Kurt Miller

First Baen paperback printing, October 2012

Distributed by Simon & Schuster
1230 Avenue of the Americas
New York, NY 10020

Library of Congress Cataloging-in-Publication Data: 2011032764

Printed in the United States of America

10 9 8 7 6 5 4 3 2 1

CHAPTER ONE

NATHAN ARNSTEIN'S LIFE was not an especially long one, but it spanned a great deal of eventful history, some of which he himself made.

He was born in 2011, in what still called itself the United States of America, although it had only a few years to go before the Earth First Party would seize power and rob that name of all it had once meant.

He was nine years old when the Lokaron ships appeared in Earth's sky and began dictating trade treaties. His father, a naval officer sidelined by lack of Party connections (and under constant suspicion for being Jewish), was a sympathizer of the Eaglemen, the secret organization of American junior military officers dedicated to the restoration of the Constitution and the expulsion of the extraterrestrials.

He was nineteen years old in the epochal year when the Earth First Party was overthrown, Earth narrowly saved from devastation at the hands of the Lokaron *gevah* of Gev-Rogov, and the Confederated Nations of Earth formed.

He was twenty-eight, and a junior officer in the United States component of the new CNE Navy, when he distinguished himself in action against the Islamic jihadist diehards in the last flareup of resistance to the new order.

He was thirty-seven, and one of the rising stars of the CNEN, when he was sent to the planet Harath-Asor to study state-of-the-art galactic military technology at the feet of humanity's Lokaron allies of Gev-Harath. He learned his lessons well, and later thought of applications of them that had never occurred to the self-satisfied Lokaron military establishments.

He was fifty-five, and an admiral, when he settled an old score at the Battle of Upsilon Lupus, annihilating the fleet of Gev-Rogov and forcing a Lokaron power—for the first time in the history of the galaxy's dominant race—to sit across a peace table from non-Lokaron. And nothing would ever be the same again.

He was fifty-nine, and nearing retirement, when he was named to the prestigious post of director of the CNEN Academy.

He was sixty-three when his chief of staff found him with his brains blown out.

"Is the director in, Midori?"

"Yes, Captain Roark. Just one moment, please." The secretary turned aside to make the adjustments necessary to admit even those who, like the chief of staff, had automatic access to Admiral Arnstein's inner sanctum. It gave Andrew Roark a moment to glance through the transparency behind her desk. It was a view that would have been breathtaking even if one hadn't known its history.

The Academy was perched on the edge of the rim wall of a vast impact crater, with North America's Rocky Mountains circling it in the distance. The crater was, beyond comparison, the youngest of its kind on Earth, and the elements had not had time to smooth out its brutal contours. Only four and a half decades ago, in fact, part of the Rockies had stood here: Cheyenne Mountain, in whose depths the headquarters of the United States military had been buried, safe even from nuclear bombs. But not safe from a deep-penetrator kinetic weapon like the nickel-iron asteroid that the Lokaron of Gev-Rogov had accelerated, using a titanic mass driver, into a high-velocity trajectory that had intersected Earth at this point just before dawn on a never-to-be-forgotten autumn day in 2030, decapitating Earth's defenses and inflicting ecological wounds that had taken years to heal. It had been meant to be a mere preliminary to the saturation neutron-bombing that would have left the planet a lifeless tabula rasa to be reseeded for Rogovon colonization. That had been stopped by the Lokaron of Gev-Harath, and by two humans who had nearly died doing it.

Everyone knew all this. But Andrew Roark knew it better than most, for those two humans, Ben Roark and Katy Doyle, had given birth to him four years later.

Afterward, the Confederated Nations of Earth had

placed its space-navy academy here, using Lokaron nanotechnology to sculpt the rim wall into terraces and buildings in an architectural style incorporating all of mankind's major traditions, looking out over the crater's floor of congealed magma. Those who studied here could never for a moment forget their service's reason for existence, which could be distilled into two words: *never again*.

"You can go in, Captain," said the secretary, interrupting his thoughts.

"Thanks." He proceeded through the door to her left and into a short corridor. He had long since ceased to notice the slight tingle as he stepped through the invisible curtain of stationary guardian nanobots. The security wasn't excessive, for the Director was a far more important individual than the commandants of the service academies of the last century had been. In the CNEN, his authority extended to a wide range of advanced training functions in many locales, including the hyper-prestigious Strategic College, through which the elite of the Navy's leadership must pass.

Andrew came to the final door, which slid open as it sensed his genetic signature. The director's private office was a spacious one, understatedly elegant, the walls hung with honors. A shelf to the right bore models of ships he had commanded, including CNS *Revenge*, his appropriately named flagship at Upsilon Lupus. To the left was a holo-display tank that would have done credit to a capital ship's bridge. Behind the expansive desk, a wide transparency gave an unequaled view of the crater, including the pylon that rose at its exact center, inscribed with the names of those—worthy and otherwise—who had died in the Cheyenne Mountain strike.

Andrew Roark had seen the office a thousand times. Its familiarity explained why a detectable fraction of a second passed before that which was behind the desk registered on his brain, despite the stench of death that immediately hit his nostrils.

Admiral Arnstein still had a pistol clenched in his hand—a standard M-3 gauss weapon, Andrew automatically noted. It used an electromagnetic pulse (not energetic enough to have set off the alarm system) to accelerate a high-density 3mm bullet to a muzzle velocity of 2,000 meters per second with a crack as it broke the sound barrier (not loud enough to have penetrated the sound-proofing of the multiple doors). It had a full-automatic capability, but it appeared only one shot had been fired; Roark now saw the hole, with a radiating pattern of cracks, where it had struck the right-hand wall. Unlike the needlelike metal slivers fired by civilian gauss weapons, such a projectile at such a velocity resulted in massive hydrostatic overpressure as it passed through a human head, causing the brain to explode outward, blowing out the top of the skull. Admiral Arnstein was slumped face down on the desk, and Roark was looking directly into such a cavity. There was blood and fallen brain tissue everywhere around the body; some of it had stuck to the ceiling.

Modern medicine, drawing on Lokaron technology, could perform what would have been thought miracles of tissue and organ regeneration only half a century before. But nothing could be done about a destroyed brain. The admiral could, of course, be cloned. But the clone would not be the man under whom Andrew had served at Upsilon Lupus; it would be another man with identical genetic makeup, doomed to early aging and death as a result of having been produced from postembryonic cells taken from an adult body. Such use of cloning was interdicted by both law and custom.

All this flashed through Andrew's mind in a second, before the onset of nausea brought him out of shock. He sternly clamped his jaw shut and said *"No!"* to his stomach. Then he raised his left arm and spoke into his wrist communicator in a voice whose steadiness surprised him. "This is Captain Roark. Security to the director's office!" Then he stumbled forward, reminding himself not to touch anything. The scene must be left scrupulously undisturbed for the investigators.

He walked gingerly around the desk, looking for a suicide note. There was none. But a little plastic case of the kind used to hold datachips caught his eye. He looked more closely at it: it was marked with a tiny black symbol . . . and, for the second time since entering the office, he froze into immobility. There could be no mistake: it was a silhouette of a dog . . . or, more likely, a wolf.

For a few seconds, he thought very hard.

He heard a commotion outside. He reached a decision. He scooped up the case, put it in his pocket barely in time, then smoothed out his features and turned to face the security detail.

CHAPTER TWO

AS FAR BACK as the turn of the century, with even the youngest of the World War II veterans nearing their eighties, Arlington National Cemetery had been growing overcrowded. Later, new ground had become available after the ruling Earth First Party's ceremonial razing of the adjacent Pentagon. But that ground, too, had filled up, and by now it was a standing joke that one had to be a general or an admiral to get in.

Ben Roark's military service had consisted of a hitch in the Navy in his youth. But in his case they made an exception.

He had died at eighty-eight, not a great age in this day of Lokaron-derived biotechnology. But he had been in his forties before he'd had access to any of that—and it had barely been enough to save his life after what his body had endured, flying a Lokaron space fighter in a forlorn hope that had actually succeeded.

The morticians had wanted to fix up the areas of smooth, shiny burn tissue, the better for viewing by a funeral party that included the president of the United States and the president-general of the Confederated Nations of Earth, among others. But Katy Doyle-Roark had refused to permit it.

Now she sat, not shedding the tears she had already shed in full, barely noticing the raw winter breeze that blew in off the Potomac as she stared at the coffin and listened to the skirl of the bagpipes.

Out of the corner of her eye, she became aware of a blue six-digited hand (two opposable thumbs on opposite sides of four fingers, all very long and extremely dexterous) moving back and forth, gradually coming into time with the pipes. She turned and looked up at the profile of the tall, thin biped who sat beside her. His face—one always thought of a Lokaron transmitter as a "he"—wore an expression that was perfectly recognizable under all the alienness as one of dawning realization.

"They're playing a *tune!*" he exclaimed. Katy's translator earpiece conveyed his tone of excited discovery perfectly.

"You're not the first to have that reaction to bagpipes," she admitted. "These are the *good* ones though: the Irish ones, distinguished from the Scottish one by having one less drone."

Svyatog'Korth looked blank. *Again, far from the first,* Katy thought ruefully. She had no difficulty reading his expressions, after decades of practice.

Most humans would have looked at his hairless head

and seen simply a Lokar, with large, convoluted ears, slit-pupiled yellow eyes, skull ridge running down to where it formed a bony protection for the nasal orifice, and nearly lipless mouth that, when opened, revealed serrated ridges that performed the same function as human teeth for a race of omnivores with more strongly carnivorous tendencies than *Homo sapiens*. They also would have taken his light-blue skin for granted, for it was characteristic of Gev-Harath, the Lokaron *gevah* that was humanity's closest trading partner, and its offshoot Gev-Tizath which had first discovered Earth fifty-four years earlier.

Katy, however, knew better than most that each *gevah* (most often translated simply as "nation") was in fact a subspecies, descended from Lokaron colonists genetically engineered to suit a world. Only Gev-Lokarath, the *gevah* occupying the original homeworld of the species, represented the original Lokaron genotype, narrower of features and build, and bluish-white of satiny skin. Certain other subspecies diverged from this far more than that of Gev-Harath. Gev-Rogov, for instance. Designed for a planet whose gravity was almost equal to Earth's, the Rogovon were characterized by a body build that was squat and stocky on Lokaron standards—not very unlike tall humans, in fact—and a green skin tone. It was a Lokaron genotype with which humans were familiar.

Oh, yes, thought Katy, *very familiar. And the object of a hate that may endure as long as there is a human alive in the universe.*

Then the honor guard fired the salute with old-fashioned nitrocellulose-burning rifles, causing Svyatog to jump slightly, and the president and president-general presented her with the folded flags of the USA and the CNE. And it was over. She got to her feet unaided, despite her eighty-three years—more easily, in fact, than Svyatog. The Lokar was an old Earth hand, but also inescapably a product of a 0.72 g planet . . . besides which he, too, wasn't getting any younger. She paused for a last look at the gravesite into which her husband's remains had just been lowered, and at the waiting, vacant plot beside it.

Not just yet! she thought tartly.

"Thank you for coming, Svyatog," she said to her alien companion as they walked away, oblivious to the curious glances they drew. "It would have meant a great deal to him."

"Of course I came." With the automatism of long experience, Katy mentally edited out the high-pitched sounds produced by Svyatog's vocal apparatus and heard only the—dare one say it?—inhumanly perfect English produced by the translation software. "It was a stroke of good fortune that I happened to be here on Earth, on *hovah* business."

"Yes, of course. I forgot to congratulate you. And," she teased, "we humans should be flattered to rate the personal attention of the new executive director of Hov-Korth."

Svyatog gave a hand gesture that, in his culture, denoted insincerely self-deprecatory denial. "Executive director" was a pale translation, and Katy had often thought that human history offered a far better one: *tai-pan*.

Early twenty-first-century humans had found it hard to adjust to the fact that the Lokaron were not a monolithic politico-economic unity. That was how super-advanced space aliens had always been visualized: sometimes as an evil empire and sometimes as a goody-two-shoes democratic federation, depending on what hobbyhorse the individual science-fiction author was riding, but always as a single polity. And that was how the Lokaron had initially represented themselves, lest the humans should get any ideas about "comparison shopping." When the truth had come to light, the aliens' division into sovereign *gevahon* had been hard enough to get used to. Still harder was the fact that a *gevah* was not the kind of centralized bureaucratic state that several generations of humans had been taught to regard as the most "advanced" form of social organization. It was more like the seventeenth-century Dutch Republic, with the real power in the hands of the *hovahon*, or merchant houses. (Gev-Rogov was an exception, but the other Lokaron had always regarded the Rogovon as rather backward.) And Hov-Korth was the most influential *hovah* of Gev-Harath, the richest and most powerful *gevah* of the galaxy's dominant race.

When Svyatog'Korth, holder of no governmental office, had been introduced to the two human presidents earlier in the day, he had been just too properly deferential for words. But no one had been under any illusions as to which of the three beings counted for most in the larger scheme of things.

"Yes, I'm glad you could come," Katy repeated as they entered the parking lot. An edge of bitterness came into her voice. "Not everyone could."

Svyatog looked down at her from his seven-foot-plus height. He knew humans better than almost any other Lokar, and this human in particular. "Andrew," he stated rather than asked.

Katy nodded and did not meet his eyes. "He said there was something going on out at the Academy that made it impossible for him to get away, even for this. And he couldn't explain what it was." She sighed. "I suppose I ought to understand how sometimes. . . ." Her voice trailed off as an air-car swooped down with a faint hum of gravitics and settled onto the asphalt. It clamshelled open, and the driver emerged: a strongly built early-middle-aged man with short sandy hair, dressed in the CNE Navy's winter greatcoat of dark green edged with black and gold, bearing a captain's insignia of four small starbursts. His gray eyes looked around anxiously.

"Andy!" Katy called out in joy.

"Mom!" They embraced, and he looked around at the stragglers of the dispersing crowd. "It's over, isn't it? Oh, God, Mom, I'm so sorry!"

"Don't worry about it. We'll visit the grave together later. You remember Svyatog'Korth, don't you?"

"Of course. Thank you for coming, sir." Andrew Roark had known the Lokar as an occasional visitor during his youth and had always regarded him with awe as a tangible link with the heroic past, in which Svyatog had saved Andrew's parents from certain death—twice, in the case of his mother. Arguably, he had done the same thing for this world of Earth.

"As I told your mother, I was fortunate to be on Earth at the right time. And it is good to see you after so many years, Captain Roark. I have followed your career with great interest, ever since your distinguished service at Upsilon Lupus." Svyatog's alien eyes flickered from one human to the other, and then back again, and understanding flickered in their amber depths. He hitched his fur-collared cloak around his neck against the cold. (The Lokaron found the attitude of modern humans toward fur-wearing disingenuous if not hypocritical, coming from a race with such a bloodthirsty history.) "But now urgent affairs call me away, and I'm sure the two of you have much to talk about—hopefully, Katy, not including any complaints about Captain Roark's failure to marry and present you with grandchildren, of which I'm sure he has grown even more weary than I have."

Katy spluttered with mock indignation, and Andrew gave a laugh that was clearly pro forma. Svyatog's eyes gave the two of them another appraising glance, and then he was gone, walking with the careful steps of age and high gravity toward a large, ornate Lokaron air-car.

The towering alien was barely out of earshot when Andrew turned to his mother. "I didn't tell you why I was detained at the Academy—"

"It's all right, dear. I know you weren't allowed to talk about it."

"And I'm still not. But I'm going to anyway." He drew a deep breath. "Admiral Arnstein is dead."

"*What?*" Katy stared at him round-eyed for a second, then her head slumped and she glanced back toward the grave site she had just departed. "Jesus! It seems like all the good ones are going!" Then she drew a deep breath and took control of herself. "But why hasn't it been in the news? How did he die?"

"Suicide." Andrew met his mother's incredulous stare and nodded grimly. "That's why they're covering it up."

"Suicide! I can't believe it! Are you sure?"

"Trust me, it's true. You see, I was the one who found him. That's why they've held me for the investigation. I was lucky to get away as soon as I did. And I'm still under orders to keep it under wraps."

"I can imagine." Her greenish-hazel eyes sharpened as the shock of what she'd heard wore off. "But if you're not supposed to talk about it, why are you telling me all this?"

"Because I've got to talk to someone. You're the only one I know I can trust—and it doesn't hurt that you've still got debts you can call in from people in the American and CNE governments."

Her eyes sharpened still further. "There's more to this than you've told me."

"Yes, quite a lot." Andrew glanced around nervously, making sure there was no one in earshot. And there was no reason for any ranged audio pickups to be focused on this place. "As I said, I was the first one on the scene. And . . . I took something from it."

"You *what*?"

"I know, I know," he said miserably. "And I would never have considered doing it, except . . ." He looked around again, then reached into a pocket of his greatcoat. "I found this on his desk, beside his body." He opened his hand, revealing the little datachip case marked with the odd silhouette. He let her stare at it for a second or two before clasping his hand and putting it back in his pocket.

She met his eyes. "The Black Wolf Society! So they *are* for real!"

"And, it would seem, connected in some way with Admiral Arnstein. Connected, perhaps, in some way that caused him to find it necessary to do away with himself."

She stared. Clearly, she hadn't allowed herself to think this far ahead. Roark sympathized. He'd had more time than she for doing some very hard thinking.

But she recovered quickly, which he knew shouldn't surprise him. He sometimes had to remind himself that in her youth his mother had been involved in intelligence work. One such operation had left her, by the human medical definition of the time, dead. It had been the beginning of her association with Svyatog, who had been responsible for both her death and her rebirth.

"Now I understand why you didn't leave this where it was, and why you don't turn it over to the Internal Investigations Division now," she said levelly. "If Arnstein was involved, then there's no telling how high it's gone, or how deep. Naturally you've run the chip on your own computer."

"Of course. And, of course, it's in code—and not one I recognize. Not that it would help much if I did recognize it. It takes a full-time expert to read this stuff. Naturally, the Navy has some very sophisticated codebreaking computers—"

"But you can't exactly use them for this, can you?" She shook her head. "Andy, I think this is something too big for us."

"I know. And I have no right to involve you. But as I said before: I have no way of knowing who I can trust. The only place I could think to turn was to you and Dad. And now . . ." He glanced toward the endless rows of headstones, which had just gained a new fellow, and his misery deepened.

Katy followed his glance, and she found she had a few unshed tears left after all.

"Well," she said, a little too briskly, "let's at least get out of this wind. I've got a hotel room here in Arlington. You're on leave, I suppose?"

"Yes—indefinite leave. They let me go after all the questioning. But I'm supposed to keep the IID appraised of my movements."

"And coming here was a perfectly natural thing to do. All right. Going home with me to Colorado tomorrow will also be perfectly natural. It's pretty isolated there. We'll be able to consider our options."

"All right. But before we go. . ."

"Of course, dear."

They turned and walked toward the freshly dug grave.

CHAPTER THREE

THE FOLLOWING DAY, they took a suborbital transport from Washington to Denver, where Katy's air-car was waiting. Then they headed west, to Andrew Roark's boyhood home. It was a clear winter day, and the sunlight gleamed blindingly on snow-capped peaks that rose over pine-clothed lower slopes.

Some people who'd known Ben Roark had found it surprising that he had chosen the Colorado Rockies as a retirement locale. Somewhere in the West Indies would have seemed more in character: the Caymans, where he had spent some time before the unforgettable events of 2030, or perhaps Jamaica, whose rum he had always appreciated—appreciated to excess, as some might have said. But Andrew thought he understood what had been going through his parents' minds when they'd chosen this place, in the spectacularly mountainous heart of their country that had then been in the process of reclaiming the soul it had seemingly lost.

Now he was surer of that than ever, as the air-car passed over the throat-hurtingly beautiful valley that held the Maroon Bells-Snowmass Wilderness Area and the town of Aspen. They continued on over the sun-gleaming upland lakes and beyond, where the trees that gave the town its name—now, alas, denuded of the soft golden autumn foliage they had worn a month ago—covered the lower slopes beneath a brutally rugged crag. At the foot of that mountain, and seeming to belong there, was the rambling stone-and-timber house he hadn't seen in far too long.

After they landed and settled in, he got a fire going in the massive stone fireplace at one end of the cathedral-ceilinged great room, flanked by windows that gave a panoramic view of the ranges to the west, while Katy mixed drinks. Then they accessed the datachip. The fire, unheeded, burned low while they studied the readout.

"Can you make anything at all of this gibberish?" Katy finally asked. "I know you're not a crypto specialist, but—"

"No, I'm not. But I've had some basic familiarization. And, as a souvenir of that course, I've got some elementary codebreaking software that my own computer can run."

"Any luck with it?"

"Very little. It helps to have some idea of what you're looking for. So I've tried a few of the codebreaking software, and broken a few words."

"Surely you can build on that."

"Not when it isn't a straight alphabet-based code. I'm sure this could be broken—there's no such thing as an unbreakable code, although various people throughout history have thought they had one. But all I've been able to do is establish that certain words do occur in this stuff. One is Admiral Arnstein's name."

"No surprise," Katy put in.

"Another is 'Black Wolf Society.' I don't suppose that should be a surprise either."

"I suppose not. But I'm still having trouble adjusting to the idea that it really exists. Well, no, I guess there's never really been any doubt as to its existence. But like everybody else, I've always assumed that it's just a crime syndicate, and that the wilder stories about it are just media sensationalism. Sort of like the Sicilian Mafia in the last century. But now I have to wonder."

"In addition to those, I ran through anything I could think of that had any connection with Admiral Arnstein. I got occurrences of quite a few of them, but most were pretty innocuous and useless: words like 'Academy' and 'Earth' and so forth. But a couple of my longer shots paid off." Andrew paused significantly. "One was 'Kogurche.'"

Katy looked up sharply. "Well, after all, that was the system in Lupus where our confrontation with Gev-Rogov began in 2057, leading to the war a decade later. So I suppose it's not too surprising."

"No, it isn't. But I've saved the best for last." Andrew gave another unconsciously dramatic pause. "'Admiral Valdes.'"

Katy looked up sharply. "What made you include *him* in your search?"

"Nothing, specifically. I just threw into the pot the names of all the prominent people I could think of who've been associated with Admiral Arnstein. And four years ago, Valdes went through the Strategic College—older and more senior in rank than most people are when they start it, but he was a special protégé of Admiral Arnstein, who had just taken charge of the Academy. He was grooming Valdes for Chief of Space Operations. He was bitterly disappointed when Valdes abruptly retired—"

"—And went into CNE politics, where he's had a meteoric rise," Katy finished for him, not troubling to keep the distaste out of her voice. "So, this is all you've got?"

"I'm afraid so. And I don't know who else I can trust to go to for advice—or, for that matter, who would have anything to offer."

Silence fell, and stayed fallen for a while. Then Katy visibly reached a decision. She looked her son in the eye. "There might be one person. You see, your father knew Valdes. He met him . . . oh, it must have been more than ten years ago, because it was before the war. And he was always very reticent about what they said to each other."

"Really? I never knew that. But . . ." Andrew trailed to an awkward halt. "Uh, but what good does that do us now? I mean . . . that is . . . well, Dad is . . ."

Katy smiled. "Don't worry. I haven't lost my marbles yet. There's something else you don't know. A few years ago, when we were having to face the fact that your father didn't have very much longer to live, Svyatog came here on one of his visits and presented us with a gift. At first, we were reluctant to accept it—and only partly because it was extravagantly expensive, not that that's any object to Svyatog. But we finally did, while your father was still mentally alert." She held his eyes. "It was a full set of state-of-the-art uploading equipment, with all the accessories, including the ability to project an all-senses virtual image, not just a voice."

It took several heartbeats before what Andrew had heard registered on him. Several more passed before he could speak. "Are you saying that Dad is . . . ?"

Katy nodded gravely. "Yes, he is. So am I, incidentally, just for future reference." Her lips quirked upward in a smile of almost invisible brevity. Then she sighed, and her eyes strayed to the mountains outside the windows. "I haven't accessed it yet. I think it will be a while before I do—before I *can*. But you may want to do it now, if you feel up to it."

Andrew sank back in his chair and tried to sort out his feelings.

What was antiseptically called "uploading"—copying a brain's memories through a painless but lengthy combination of external scanners and probing nanomachines, and storing them digitally—was fairly new technology even to the Lokaron. At first, its inventors had thought they were on the brink of being able to transfer those memories to the brain of a clone of the brain's owner, thus achieving a kind of serial immortality. That dream (nightmare, as some might have said) had proven illusory. The process took finite time, during which an organic brain, unlike a passive piece of neural-net software, could not accept such an imprinting.

That digital program *could*, however, be installed in a

computer—a very special, very powerful, very complex, and very expensive computer. The multi-terabyte software then became self-aware, able to run whatever other programs were available to the computer, including those allowing it to communicate interactively.

The technology had been completely unavailable to humans before the advent of a fully open and equal trading relationship with Gev-Harath. Even now, it found few customers on Earth. Its hideous expense was only part of the reason. Most humans were only a few generations away from belief in ghosts, and for them there was something flesh-crawlingly unnatural about it.

"So," Andrew temporized, "is he . . . I mean, is *it* here?"

"Yes. We had the computer installed in the basement. Do you want to see it?"

Andrew wasn't absolutely sure he did, but he could not refuse. He followed his mother down the dimly lit stairs.

The basement was as he remembered, and the computer wasn't as big as he had expected. In fact it was desktop-sized, and while it had the unmistakable look of Lokaron industrial nanotech, it held nothing foreign to Andrew's experience. As Admiral Arnstein's chief of staff, he had dealt with hardware just as advanced as this. And the keyboard interface was positively old-fashioned.

Katy sat down in a perfectly ordinary swivel chair and booted the system. The holographically projected monitor screen appeared in midair, and as Katy began to bring up programs, Andrew saw Lokaron ideographs. He was familiar with them—of necessity, in his line of work—but his mother had spent years among the Lokaron, and she worked at a speed that made them flash by too rapidly for him to read. Finally she nodded, stood up, and took from the desk a perfectly standard-looking Lokaron virtual-reality headset manufactured for the human market: a light openwork helmet. She held it out to her son and spoke with great steadiness.

"As I've said, I'm not ready for this. I'm not certain I ever will be, but I imagine I will, someday. Just not yet. Besides, I hardly even need it. You see, I still have him here. I'll look at some chair, or step around a corner, and it's as though he's there. We were married a long time, you know."

"I know," her son echoed faintly.

"So if we're to try this approach to getting the answers we need, you're going to have to be the one to do it. It's not fair, but there it is. If you don't feel you can—"

"No, I'll do it. On some level, I even *want* to do it." He reached out and took the headset.

Katy smiled, as though at the confirmation of something she'd more than half expected. "It's all set up. All you have to do is put on the headset and speak a greeting. It's programmed to recognize your voice pattern. I'll be upstairs." And she was gone.

Andrew held the headset in his hands. He was hardly unfamiliar with it. Since Lokaron technology had become common on Earth—even manufactured there, within certain limits—the use of shared VR hookups had become a common means of communication. Indeed, it had probably attained acceptance more easily than it had among the Lokaron themselves, whose upper crust still regarded it as just a bit *arriviste*.

Yes, he had used it often enough. But the people he'd used it with had been alive. And they hadn't been his father.

He drew a deep breath, sat down in front of the computer's video pickup, and put the practically weightless latticework frame over his head.

As always, there was no pain or any other physical sensation as the direct neural induction took hold. There was only the usual indescribable wavering and fading of the senses . . .

He was sitting in the familiar study upstairs, in a chair whose armrests were upholstered in authentic leather, which was showing its age—he could feel that, under his fingers. Across from him, Ben Roark sat in the chair that had always been his favorite. There was a fire going in the fireplace, and he could feel the heat on his face. The wood must have been damp, judging from the slight smoky smell. Svyatog, as Katy had indicated, had spared no expense.

"Hello, Dad," he said, almost choking on his knowledge that what he was addressing was really software.

Ben Roark looked up. He looked essentially the same as he had the last time Andrew Roark had seen him in the flesh. The programming must have been done in the summer, for his bald scalp looked slightly sunburned. (Svyatog, trying to be helpful, had once told him that baldness in humans was, from the Lokaron perspective, rather an improvement. It hadn't helped.) He smiled the crooked smile that was the only sort of smile the reconstruction of his face allowed. Andrew was glad that reconstruction had been left as he remembered it, not edited out to leave the unravaged youthful face that he had never seen save in old photos.

"Hello, Andy. Since we're talking like this, I gather that I'm . . . well, you know . . ."

"Yes, Dad, you are." Andrew had never felt more inadequate in his life.

His father seemed to sigh. "Yes, of course. Is your mother . . . ?"

"She's fine. She just doesn't quite feel ready yet for . . . this."

"I understand." Another sigh, then a businesslike look. "You've got me at sort of a disadvantage. I don't know whether we saw each other after the uploading, while I was still alive."

"No, we didn't. I was away a lot."

"Yes, I know." Was there a faint hint of resentment at the infrequency of a busy son's visits?

"And recently, I haven't been able to get away from the Academy at all. In fact . . . well, I missed your memorial service. I hated that, but I couldn't help it. You see, something has happened—and I need your help." Andrew launched into his story. He was not interrupted—not even software this sophisticated would do that. It was the first false note, for his father would have had no scruples about breaking in with questions.

"And so that's where we stand," he concluded. "The connection with Admiral Valdes is the only thing we have to go on. And Mom said you knew him, back before the war."

"I truly wish I could help you, Andy. But it's barely accurate to say I knew him. I had a couple of conversations with him, that was all. He was a captain then, and a fair-haired boy of Arnstein's. It was in 2064, two years before the war—which, incidentally, he seemed to *know* was going to happen."

"Well, the rivalry between us and Gev-Rogov in Lupus and Sagittarius had been a potential problem for years, although relations seemed to be improving. And then came the destabilization of Kogurche after the assassination of the system's ruler in 2057, which the Rogovon tried to blame on us—and, for a fact, it worked to our advantage in terms of human penetration of the system. So I suppose it was a fairly safe bet at that time that war was coming."

"Yes. But he talked about it as though it were an accomplished fact. Odd. He also talked very matter-of-factly about what he intended to do after it was over. In fact, I got the impression that he regarded his whole CNE Navy career as preparation for the political career that was to follow. A distinguished war record would help no end, you see. In the same way, he intended to go through the Strategic College simply because it's become almost a rite of passage for the power elite, what with all the connections you make there."

"What, exactly, did the two of you talk about in those couple of conversations, Dad? It sounds like he was very forthright with you."

"Well, at first he was fulsomely flattering of me—"

"Thus proving that he didn't know you very well."

The upload flashed an appreciative grin that was entirely in character—eerily so, in fact. "Yeah, well, after going on at length about my alleged prestige—"

(*Not just alleged*, Andrew thought—but didn't say, for he knew any accurate copy of his father's mind would react to that with a snort as derisive as the original's.)

"—he finally got down to business. He wanted me to lend my name to his political agenda. He hinted at various advantages to me—as if I hadn't been too old to care. And he played on my reasons for regarding Gov-Rogov as an implacable enemy. But when he set forth his program for doing something about it . . . well, it was as though he just didn't understand why we had overthrown the old Earth First Party. They had wanted a totalitarian hermit kingdom, while he wanted a totalitarian empire—and I doubt if anybody ever got rich on the difference!" The sentient software reined itself in. "Sorry. I didn't mean to get carried away. Anyway, I told him as politely as possible that I wasn't interested, even though he indicated that he could count on the support of Nathan Arnstein, a man who I respected more than all but a very few I've ever known."

Andrew seized on that last point. "Yes, so did I. And now, as I've told you, he's dead by his own hand. I'm trying to find out what drove him to that—now more than ever, since what you've told me makes me even more certain that it's somehow tied into Valdes's ambitions, in addition to being connected to the Black Wolf Society. Can't you tell me anything else that might help me? Maybe just something else from that same period of time, with any kind of connection with Arnstein or Valdes or the Black Wolf Society?"

The virtual brow of Ben Roark furrowed as the software scanned data. "There's just one possibility, but I doubt if it will help you. As you know, I'd kept up some informal contacts within the Intelligence community. I won't go into the details, but around the same time—just before the war, in other words—I became aware through those contacts of a Lokaron agent named Reislon'Sygnath, working for Gev-Harath . . . and specifically for Hov-Korth."

Andrew nodded his understanding. The largely still family owned Lokaron merchant houses had turned most military functions over to the *gevah* "national" governments. Indeed, it was one of those governments' primary reasons for existence. But the *hovahon* kept the Intelligence function for themselves—they had too many secrets. And Hov-Korth, the preeminent *hovah* of them all, had the most secrets and maintained the most extensive espionage network in the known galaxy. It shared most of its findings with the Gev-Harath military, of course. The exceptions implicit in that *most* constituted one of the inherent weaknesses in the Lokaron militaries that Nathan Arnstein had spotted early in his career. Andrew shied away from that thought, with its freight of attendant grief.

"I'm impressed," he said. "Just by the fact that CNE Intelligence had uncovered the identity of a Hov-Korth agent."

"It isn't really so surprising. You see . . . Well, this is supposed to be a graveyard secret. But I don't guess that's a stopper in my case . . ." The image let the thought trail off, with an ironic lift of eyebrow.

My God! thought Andrew. *The software actually has a sense of humor! But of course it does—my father's sense of humor.*

"Anyway," Ben Roark's digital ghost went on briskly, "what I'm not supposed to be telling you is that Reislon wasn't just working for Hov-Korth. He was also working for us."

In the midst of his shock, Andrew found room to wonder why he was even surprised. Earth's history held no shortage of spies who had sold themselves to more than one side. And in this case, it didn't even involve overt disloyalty: Gev-Harath had been officially neutral in Earth's war with Gev-Rogov, while barely troubling to conceal its sympathy for its human protégés.

But in all those examples from Earth's history, everyone concerned had been human. It wasn't quite the same.

"Was this Reislon'Sygnath acting with his bosses' knowledge?" Andrew asked. "I mean, considering how his ultimate boss Svyatog'Korth felt about Gev-Rogov. . . ."

"Shrewd guess, but to my knowledge the answer is no. I doubt if Svyatog was prepared to be *that* un-neutral. Reislon was playing his own game—or, rather, games. We could never figure out all the dimensions of what he was up to. I doubt if anybody could have." The expression on the virtual face of Ben Roark reflected the respect of a good spook for a great one.

"Did you ever actually talk to him?"

"Oh, no. His contacts with us were, as you might imagine, extremely discreet, indirect, multilayered, and what have you. And I wasn't even officially in the game by then. No, everything I know is from conversations with people who were actually involved—or people who had talked to them. So you see, all I have to offer is hearsay.

That's why I was hesitant to offer it at all. But there was one common theme that emerged pretty clearly from all of it: Reislon took the Black Wolf Society seriously—and he was worried about it."

"How do you know this?"

"The clincher came that very year, 2064. Without going into the details, our people got part of the text of a report by Reislon to Svyatog. Only a fragment, mind you. But he was passing on a warning for the future, and the context made it clear he was talking about the Black Wolf Society."

"And two years after that, the war broke out," Andrew said thoughtfully.

"And shortly after it broke out, Reislon vanished."

"Vanished? You mean he stopped working for us?"

"I mean he dropped from sight altogether. As far as we were able to determine, Hov-Korth also lost sight of him." A wry smile. "After the Battle of Upsilon Lupus, while the peace talks were going on and you were still out-system with Arnstein's fleet, Svyatog happened to be on Earth, and he dropped in on us. It was all I could do not to ask him if he knew anything about what had happened to Reislon. But of course we couldn't let him know that Reislon had been playing a double game—assuming he didn't already know it. So I kept my mouth shut. Being less than frank with Svyatog didn't sit too well with me; as you know, he is more than a friend to me and your mother. But . . . well, nobody ever said the spook game is a nice one."

"Svyatog is on Earth now," Andrew mused.

The copy of his father's mind produced a sharp look.

"Remember, the same considerations still apply. Officially, we never even knew Reislon existed. You can't spill the beans to Svyatog by asking about him."

"Does it really matter anymore? I mean, the war ended seven years ago, and Gev-Harath—especially Hov-Korth—have always been our friends."

"You know better than that! The security classification of this information hadn't been lifted at the time I was uploaded, and I doubt if it's been lifted now. I don't know what the possible consequences of blowing it now would be, and you don't know, either. When we start letting individuals decide for themselves when security restrictions no longer make sense or need to be obeyed, people's lives get put in jeopardy!"

And how, exactly, are you going to stop me . . . Dad? But of course Andrew didn't say that. For one thing, he had to admit to himself that the upload had been quoting Intelligence gospel. "Well, I can ask him in general terms if he can shed any light on the Black Wolf Society, can't I? Maybe he'll be willing to share information derived from Reislon without revealing its source."

"Maybe—but just be careful." The expression on the ravaged face abruptly softened. "I'm a pompous old hypocrite, you know. I've already violated security by telling you all this. Even if you were cleared for it—which you're not, even as Admiral Arnstein's chief of staff—you don't have a need to know. At least not what officialdom would define as one. But—"

"But you were never one to give a damn about what officialdom thought, were you? If you had been, the history of the last four and a half decades would have been very different. And don't accuse me of flattering you. At this stage of the game, what would be the point?"

The image actually goggled at him. "By God! You really *are* an SOB, aren't you? I guess I must have done something right!" And the image grinned.

Andrew grinned back. But then he sobered as he remembered something that had been bothering him. "Uh, I suppose I ought to . . . sign off now. But what is the effect? I mean, how will you . . . ?"

"Don't worry about it, son. I'll just go to sleep. Actually, not even that. You see, I don't dream. Probably just as well."

CHAPTER FOUR

THE "ENCLAVE"—the extraterritorial compound in Northern Virginia that the Lokaron had demanded as one element of the treaties they had dictated to the American government in 2020—had been largely destroyed in the course of the events of 2030, after which it would have been irrelevant anyway. Nowadays, the governments of the *gevahon* maintained normal diplomatic relations with the CNE, while the *hovahon* operated principal and branch offices in accordance with the laws of Earth's various nations, as permitted under the new treaties.

Hov-Korth's headquarters, however, was practically a mini-Enclave in itself, without the extraterritoriality. Located in Rockland County, New York, as close to Manhattan as availability of real estate permitted, it was built in the vaguely *Arabian Nights*-reminiscent Lokaron architectural style, clustering around a central tower whose slender, soaring elongation was possible only to the nanotech-produced materials the aliens had introduced to Earth.

Andrew Roark arrived by ground car in the midst of a winter storm that had grounded all air-cars. An elevator powered by a very minimal application of the reactionless propulsion that drove Lokaron spacecraft took him swiftly up a transparent shaft through which he watched a landscape whose bleakness matched his mood. That landscape receded farther and farther below as he rose to the highest levels, to the suite of offices that had been put at the disposal of the Executive Director while he was on Earth. A live functionary—always a status symbol among the Lokaron—met him as he emerged from the elevator. Trained to read the signs, he recognized a primary male, subjugated along with the females in traditional transmitter-dominated Lokaron societies, although that was changing in modern times, as was reflected by the fact that this one wore the standard "business suit" of loose sleeveless robe over double-breasted tunic.

"Greetings, Captain Roark. The executive director is expecting you. Follow me, please." He led the way along hallways of softly luminous jadelike materials for which English held no names, through gently tingling curtains of hovering security nanobots into the innermost office.

"Ah, Captain Roark!" greeted Svyatog from behind an extensive desk whose capabilities were completely unobtrusive. "Or may I call you Andrew?"

"Of course, sir." They had no difficulty understanding each other. Andrew's skull held a translator implant like

Svyatog's, not generally available on Earth but standard issue for CNEN officers whose ranks and duties involved Lokaron contacts. "Thank you for seeing me on such short notice."

"It is no trouble. I was glad to be able to oblige your mother when she called and indicated that you wished to see me . . . on private business." The amber alien eyes glanced significantly at the visitor's civilian clothes.

"That's correct, sir. I'm not here in my capacity as a Confederated Nations officer. In fact, I'm currently on indefinite leave." Actually, he had no business being here at all. He had informed the IID he was going to New York to settle some paperwork involving his father's estate—and had in fact gone there by verifiable public transport, and then rented the ground car. He could only hope that he wasn't under actual surveillance, in which case he would have some explaining to do.

"I will of course assist you in any way I can," said Svyatog graciously. He touched a control on his desk. "Please take a seat."

Andrew looked behind him, at the previously empty space where an invisible, impalpable cloud of lighter-than-air nanobots had silently coalesced into a chair. He sternly told himself that it wasn't magic, although as cutting-edge Lokaron technology it might as well have been. He sat down gingerly, not fully believing in the chair's solidity until he felt it. It adjusted its contours to him, which didn't exactly aid his efforts to compose his thoughts. Neither did the fact that he was addressing one of the wealthiest beings in the known galaxy.

"I've come to you, sir, to ask for any information you

can give me—within the bounds of propriety, of course—on certain matters. The circumstances are rather delicate, so I'll have to ask that our conversation remain confidential. I'll also ask that you not inquire about my motives."

Svyatog's mouth stretched slightly while remaining closed. Andrew recognized a Lokaron smile. "Would this, by any chance, be related to Admiral Arnstein's death?"

Andrew stared, openmouthed. "I don't suppose I should even be surprised," he finally managed. "Given the intelligence resources at your command."

"You flatter me. I gather you have not had an opportunity to view this morning's news."

"No, I haven't. You mean they've gone public with it?"

Instead of answering, Svyatog manipulated other concealed controls, and a holographically projected display appeared in midair over the desk.

"Yesterday," a well-known news announcer intoned, "the Confederated Nations lost one of its heroes. Naval authorities have announced the sudden and untimely death of Admiral Nathan Arnstein. The cause of death is still under investigation. Admiral Arnstein will be best remembered for stopping Gev-Rogov's aggression in its tracks in 2067 with his great victory at—"

Andrew had stopped listening. *Yesterday? Cause of death under investigation?* The thoughts echoed through his incredulous mind.

Svyatog, with half a century of experience at reading human faces, gave Andrew an expressionless regard as he turned off the recording. "Actually, your initial assumption about Hov-Korth's intelligence apparatus was not entirely unfounded. We have reason to believe that Admiral

Arnstein in fact died several days ago, and that your government has been sitting on it, as I believe the expression goes. Of course, I will not ask you to compromise yourself by giving me confirmation of that."

"Besides, you don't really need my confirmation, do you?" Andrew reached a hasty but unequivocal decision. "Nevertheless, I'll tell you that your sources are correct as far as they go. In return, I'll ask you if you have any information on the Black Wolf Society, dating from the period just before the war."

For a few heartbeats the slit-pupiled eyes that humans found to be the most disturbing Lokaron feature regarded Andrew in silence. When Svyatog finally spoke, the translator implant conveyed his expressionlessness. "Why do you suppose we would have information on what is essentially an internal human matter?"

"You have information on most things. And if the stories about the Black Wolf are true, it isn't just a crime syndicate of no interest to anyone except human law enforcement agencies. With its strident human expansionism, its influence could have a destabilizing effect that would be bound to impact the interests of Hov-Korth."

Had Svyatog been human, Andrew would have sworn he was affecting an air of casual interest. "Have you had the opportunity to access your late father's upload?"

Andrew did his best to equal the old Lokar's expressionlessness. He knew he was skirting the edges of revealing Reislon'Sygnath's double game. He decided on an approach that could do no harm if Svyatog was, in fact, already aware of that game. "Yes, I have. I'm sure I needn't pretend that I didn't put these and other questions to him.

He was able to give me certain vague hints, based on contacts he had maintained in the Confederated Nations intelligence community after his retirement. But nothing really useful. Which is why I'm here today."

Over the decades, Svyatog had picked up certain human mannerisms. One was steepling his fingers—twelve altogether, in his case—and peering over them. He now leaned back and did so. "I did, in fact, receive a report on the subject during the period to which you refer, from one of our agents—a very important agent, who reported directly to me. I have never known quite what to make of it, since the agent in question turned out to be playing a double game."

Andrew held his breath and ordered himself not to mention the name Reislon'Sygnath.

"This was not known to us at the time he submitted the report," Svyatog went on. "It was not until just after the war ended that we became aware that he had been simultaneously working for Gev-Rogov."

Afterward, Andrew had the leisure to congratulate himself for the complete expressionlessness he enforced on his features. At the time, he could only wonder how his father's upload would react to the news that Reislon had been a *triple* agent.

"We were quite prepared to 'play' him, as I believe your own intelligence community puts it, in an effort to exploit his Rogovon contacts. But he dropped from sight after the war. We would of course be very interested in any information as to who his current employers might be." Svyatog paused significantly, but Andrew maintained his poker face. "At any rate," Svyatog resumed, "I was obliged to take his report seriously, despite its inherent improbability and its author's duplicity, because I had independent knowledge of its sources."

"What were those?"

"First I must give you a little background. Before a Gev-Tizath expedition discovered you, we had never encountered any non-Lokaron races above a Bronze Age technological level. As a result, we had fallen into the fallacy of equating 'non-Lokaron' with 'primitive.' I fear this engendered certain attitudes and assumptions that caused us to miscalculate in your case. At any rate, your uniqueness naturally aroused interest. During the 2040s and early 2050s, according to your dating system, the study of human cultures enjoyed a certain fad among the intelligentsia of Gev-Harath and Gev-Tizath."

"Yes, I seem to recall reading that we got a number of curious visitors then."

"One of them was an extremely wealthy Tizathon amateur named Persath'Loven. He began to publish his findings in 2050. At that time, his work was considered quite sound. But subsequently, he wandered into some dubious byways. In particular, he took an interest in the doctrines of the Imperial Temple of the Star Lords. Indeed, his next two works reflected . . . Ah, did you say something?"

Andrew choked down his smothered laugh and took a deep breath. "No, sir. Sorry to interrupt. But . . . did you say the *Imperial Temple of the Star Lords*? They're crackpots—a fringe group!" He took another breath. "You must understand that back in the middle of the last century, when people were expecting the world to end in a nuclear holocaust, one form the general hysteria took was sightings of supposed extraterrestrial spaceships: unidentified flying objects, or 'flying saucers,' as they were called. One offshoot of this was the notion that the saucers had visited us thousands of years ago and started humans on the road to civilization. Every impressive relic of ancient times—the Pyramids, Stonehenge, the Easter Island statues, you name it—was attributed to godlike beings from the stars."

"Odd that humans would assume their own ancestors incapable of such works," Svyatog observed mildly.

"Not if you know humans! It was all a substitute for religion. But then, in 2020, the ships from Gev-Tizath actually appeared, and the flying-saucer believers announced that they'd been vindicated."

"But the Tizathon carefully explained that neither they nor any other Lokaron had been observing Earth for decades before that, or at any previous time."

"Yes, and as a result all the nonsense died down—but only for a while. Shortly before the time you're talking about, around 2040, a con artist named Sebastian Gruber rummaged up the 'ancient astronauts' theory, complete with all its bogus archaeology and mythology and linguistics, and added a new twist: the ancient astronauts were *humans*, who colonized Earth. We today on Earth are a surviving remnant of a prehistoric human galactic empire!"

"But is there not conclusive evidence that your species evolved on Earth?"

"Sure. But many people have never wanted to accept that, and still don't. By denying evolution, Gruber roped in a whole new category of suckers."

"And what supposedly became of this human interstellar empire?" Svyatog sounded intrigued.

"Ah, that was Gruber's masterstroke. It seems the empire fell because it strayed from the true religion—which he, Gruber, had rediscovered and revived. At the same time he left open the possibility that the empire—reformed and chastened—is still out there somewhere, and may return." Andrew chuckled. "You can see why all this was so appealing. It relegated you Lokaron to the status of Johnny-come-latelys. And if the empire *does* come back, then the members of the Imperial Temple of the Star Lords that Gruber founded will enjoy special favor for having kept the faith. No question about it, he was a genius in his way. He died twenty years ago, but the Imperial Temple is still going strong—and, as I understand, since his death it's been run by genuine true believers. To quote a human named P. T. Barnum—although he went to his grave denying he had ever said it—there's a sucker born every minute."

"But I understand that the Imperial Temple has sponsored research into evidence of prehistoric extra-terrestrial manifestations on Earth, and elsewhere in the Sol system."

"Oh, yes. Gruber realized he wasn't going to be able to go on forever milking the stuff he had plagiarized from Von Däniken and Hoagland and others. So he financed some splashy expeditions and claimed anything they dug up, however ambiguous, as proof. All in keeping with the intellectual traditions of this school of thought, if you can call it that."

"No doubt. Nevertheless, as you have intimated, the

Imperial Temple reflected at least an undercurrent of anti-Lokaron sentiment. This made it worth our while to investigate. The agent of whom I previously spoke made it his business to do so, and in the process made the acquaintance of Persath'Loven in the mid-2050s. It was also at this time that . . ." Svyatog hesitated. "This is not general knowledge, and I rely on your discretion. In 2055, a military vessel from Gev-Harath that was paying a courtesy call on this system spotted a formation of unidentified spacecraft—only briefly, for they almost immediately withdrew into the concealment of what seemed to be some very sophisticated cloaking technology. It was naturally assumed that they were experimental craft of yours, but our intelligence agencies were unable to discover any evidence of this." A Lokaron smile. "Your mention of 'unidentified flying objects' in the last century naturally reminded me of this incident."

"It's news to me, sir. And I have a very high security clearance." *But not necessarily a need to know,* Andrew mentally hedged. But he was quite certain that the CNE possessed no cloaking technology capable of spoofing the Harathon space navy's cutting-edge sensors as thoroughly as Svyatog implied.

"The year after that, Persath published his last work about Earth. Most found it to be somewhat incoherent, verging on paranoia. Immediately after that, he returned home to Tizath-Asor, where he diverted his personal fortune into secretive researches into some odd byways of physics. Apparently he is still so occupied.

"We might have looked more deeply into the matter. But the following year, in 2057, came the destabilization of the Kogurche system, and our intelligence resources—including the agent to whom I alluded earlier—were diverted to the developing crisis there. Two years before your war with Gev-Rogov broke out, that agent submitted his highly enigmatic report on the Black Wolf Society. We were puzzled, but his disappearance just after the war prevented us from pursuing the matter."

"You must have been even more puzzled when you learned he had been betraying you to Gev-Rogov," Andrew ventured.

"'Betraying' is too strong a word. He did remarkably good service for us during that period, and we have never found any evidence that he acted directly against our interests. Rather, he seems to have felt that working for the Rogovon was not incompatible with working for us. Or perhaps it would be truer to say that he considered both to be compatible with his own agenda."

And presumably he felt the same way about working for Earth. Aloud, Andrew asked, "And you have no idea where he vanished to after the war?"

"No." Was there just a slight hesitation in Svyatog's reply? "Our last verified sighting of him was in the Kogurche system."

"Then, sir, it would seem that my most promising line of inquiry would be this Persath'Loven, who you say is now back in his home system of Tizath-Asor."

"That would seem to be the case." Svyatog rose to his feet, indicating that the interview was at an end—yet another human gesture he had picked up. "I am sorry I was not able to be more helpful."

Andrew also rose. "To the contrary, sir, you've been

most helpful, as you always have to my family. I suppose my next stop should be the Tizathon embassy, to obtain a visa." He inclined his head—handshaking was not a Lokaron custom—and departed.

CHAPTER FIVE

THE GEV-TIZATH EMBASSY, like all the embassies of the *gevahon* under the new treaties, was in Washington. It made no legal sense—the Confederated Nations of Earth made its capital in Geneva. But it had just worked out that way, in the tumultuous transition period just after 2030. Nowadays, correcting matters would have been more trouble than it was worth. Geographical location meant less and less in today's global village.

Andrew arrived at the relatively new air-car annex of Reagan National Airport (it had been restored to that name after the overthrow of the Earth First Party) in an acute state of nerves. At some point, his failure to report in to the IID would trickle down through the bureaucracy and there would be pointed questions. For now, he was relying on the general flap over Admiral Arnstein's death to bury relative trivialities like the tardy movement reports of a certain officer, at the bottom of what was still commonly referred to as the "in basket."

By the time he drove his rented ground car into the compound of the embassy, in an area of cleared former slum in the northeastern quarter of the District, he had stopped worrying about it, thereby clearing his mind for an infinitely greater worry: how he was going to justify a little side jaunt to Tizath-Asor.

The winter storm in New York had bypassed this latitude, and it was sunny and merely chilly as he parked in a side lot that served the wing of the embassy devoted to the issuance of visas. Getting out and crossing the wide expanse, he saw no Lokaron in evidence and only a few other humans coming and going. Most were obvious business types—no surprise, as the *hovahon* of Gev-Tizath had many dealings here. But there was one exception: a tall, slender woman striding purposefully across the lot, clad in a sensibly warm dark-maroon business suit but for some indefinable reason seeming to be working in a different world from all the purchasing agents, lawyers, and others hurrying by.

She was bareheaded, allowing her long dark hair to toss in the breeze. Her features were well-marked, her complexion light olive, her nose an aquiline curve, her lips somewhat full but firmly held in a straight, determined line. It was a striking face . . . and one which Andrew felt looked somehow familiar, even though he was certain he'd never met her.

He was still wondering about it when a black, fully enclosed, quasi-military style air-car dropped out of the sky so suddenly that the displaced air almost blew him off his feet. He stumbled to one knee.

At first it didn't even register, thanks to its sheer unexpectedness and flagrant illegality. Air-cars were inherently more dangerous than ground cars, and anyway by the end of the previous century it had become painfully obvious to anyone who drove the highways that all too many humans lack an adequate sense of relative motion in even *two* dimensions, much less three. So licenses to operate air-cars were harder to obtain, leading to a revival of the occupation of chauffeur, and they were banned altogether from densely urbanized areas. He decided this one must, in keeping with its overall appearance, have cloaking technology normally unavailable to civilians, to have slipped by the police.

He looked around. People were either running in panic or stunned into immobility. Then a cry wrenched his attention back to the young woman, whom he had momentarily forgotten. The air-car had landed as close to her as it could without actually hitting her, and the ground-pressure effect of its drive had knocked her to the ground. Before it even settled onto its landing jacks, its doors clamshelled open. Two men dressed in ninjalike head-to-toe black leaped out and grasped her.

She screamed, struggling like a wildcat.

That scream brought Andrew to his feet. He launched himself at the two attackers, whose backs were to him as they held on to the woman, one to each arm.

A whole series of desk jobs had intervened since his training in unarmed combat. But he had tried to keep up with refresher courses, and these days forty-one was not as creaky an age as it had once been. He managed a quite creditable flying side-kick that connected with the small of one attacker's back, sending him staggering into the other.

Andrew landed on his feet with a balance that would have left him feeling smug at any other time. At this moment, his only thought was to grab the young woman by the wrist and pull her away from her two off-balance erstwhile captors.

"This way!" he yelled, with no particular plan except to get her to his ground car. She caught on at once, gripped his wrist as tightly as he was gripping hers, and sprinted in that direction with him . . . and suddenly went limp and became dead weight.

He spun around in time to see her slump to the pavement. Behind her, a third black-clad figure had leaned out of the air-car and was pointing the weapon that Andrew knew had brought her down: a standard M65-A-3 laser rifle, highly illegal for civilians to possess. At least Andrew knew it had brought her down alive, for there had been none of the pinkish-gray explosion of instantly superheated bodily fluids that marked the full-power use of a weapon-grade laser on a human target. So it was set on its stun function, powering down the laser to a mere guide-beam that ionized the air for the passage of an electrical charge.

Then the gunman swung the weapon toward him, and with his right hand made an adjustment that Andrew recognized as switching the setting.

Before he could make a futile attempt to evade a weapon that struck at the speed of light, he heard a somehow familiar voice from inside the air-car. "Take him, too." The gunman made a reverse adjustment . . . and Andrew lost consciousness in a brief agony of electric shock.

Almost twenty years ago, as part of the climax of the Academy's survival training, Andrew had been hit with a laser stunner. Now the miserable sensations of awakening from it—the splitting headache, the tremulous feebleness of the muscles, the residual nerve pains—all came roaring back as he struggled up to an unwelcome consciousness.

After a while he felt able to take an interest in his surroundings.

He was in a dimly lit, starkly featureless enclosed space with insufficient headroom for a tall man to stand up straight under the metal-raftered ceiling. It was completely nondescript, but a sensation of movement and a faint hum of grav repulsion enabled him to identify it as the cargo hold of an air carrier—a large cousin of air-cars, widely used for economy and quietness whenever the tearing speed of suborbital transports was not needed.

The only interesting thing in view in the semidarkness was the woman, still dressed as he had last seen her, and unbound as he now noticed he himself was. She sat on the deck, hugging her knees and regarding him with what seemed to be clear eyes.

"How long have you been awake?" he asked.

"Only a few minutes," she replied, which irrationally made him feel better, even though he knew it was only natural that she should have recovered first, being younger. "Thanks for trying to help me."

"Not very effectively." He tried to sit up, only to subside with a spinning head. "Do you have any idea who has grabbed us, or what this is all about?"

"I have a pretty good idea what it's about, at least in very general terms. But I haven't a clue as to who these people are. That was one of the things I was there at the Gev-Tizath embassy trying to find out—which, I'm sure, was why I was snatched."

The reply didn't make a great deal of sense to Andrew. He sat up, with rather more success this time. "Maybe we'd better start with the basics. My name is Andrew Roark."

"I'm Rachael Arnstein."

It took some fraction of a second for the name to register. Then he simply stared. "Arnstein? You mean—?"

"Yes." Her voice held the faint sigh of someone who has had to answer the same question too many times. "I'm Admiral Nathan Arnstein's daughter."

All at once, it came back to him. He had always been accustomed to think of the admiral as simply unmarried, but he had known of an earlier marriage, ending in divorce but producing one child. Now he recalled certain photographs on the Admiral's desk, of a dark-haired girl at various ages . . .

"Well, we have a connection of sorts. I was your father's chief of staff."

It was her turn to stare. "Why, yes, I remember him mentioning . . . Then you're the son of . . . ?"

"Yes." As soon as it was out of his mouth, he realized the same sigh had crept into his voice that hers had held. A twinkle in her eyes confirmed it.

"Well," he said, perhaps a little too briskly, "you still haven't explained what you were doing in the Gev-Tizath embassy's parking lot."

The twinkle died abruptly. "Because I'm determined to find out the truth about my father's death. You've heard the news stories about it, I suppose."

"Yes. I'm sorry." Andrew left it at that, unsure as yet how much of what he knew, if any, he should reveal.

"Well, then, you know that those reports were strangely vague about the cause of death. I have reason to believe that the government's official announcement covered that up, and a lot of other things as well, including the actual date of his death."

"Why do you think that?" Andrew asked carefully.

"Lots of reasons. I live in San Francisco, but he and I stayed in touch pretty regularly. He had seemed not quite himself for a while, and then I stopped hearing from him altogether." A sudden thought seemed to occur to her. "But you were his chief of staff! You must know the truth!"

Andrew was desperately searching for a way to deflect the question when an overhead hatch opened, admitting a flood of light that dazzled their dark-adapted eyes. A ladder extruded itself, and a figure descended, silhouetted against the glare. It was a male figure, well-built in a compact way but short enough not to have to stoop due to the low ceiling.

"Are you two all right?" he asked in a deep baritone voice which only the incongruous setting prevented Andrew from instantly recognizing.

"Yes, we seem to be," he replied, disarmed by the voice's apparently sincere concern.

"Under the circumstances," Rachel Arnstein added tartly.

The man moved forward slightly, out of the glare from the hatch, and his features became more visible. All at once, Andrew recognized that familiar voice.

Rachel regained the power of speech before he did. "You!" she gasped.

Rear Admiral Franklin Ivanovitch Valdes y Kurita, CNEN (ret.), smiled the trademark smile that had captivated so much of the Confederated Nations' electorate. The face that formed the smile somehow blended the features of all the elements of his name—four of the most influential ethnic elements of the CNE—without being in any way bland or average. Indeed, with its square jaw and high cheekbones, it epitomized a kind of universal ideal of reassuring masculine strength. And he also embodied the history of the CNE, for his family had been wiped out in the Islamic insurgency of 2039, leaving him—a boy of ten with little besides the records of his birth—to rise without any advantages through the ranks of the Navy.

It was, Andrew had often thought, as though nature and chance had conspired to produce a man ideally suited for an inevitable rise to the CNE's political apex. And so it was proving to be.

The CNE's Legislative Assembly was apportioned according to a formula that allocated each nation a number of delegates based on a three-way compromise among population, the fiction of equal sovereignty, and a complex calculation that was popularly known (to the teeth-clenched fury of those nations that were not its beneficiaries) as the "civilization factor." Each nation then chose its delegates by popular election. Valdes had just been elected from the United States, of which he had, at some point in his past, become a naturalized citizen. He was being widely touted as a coming man—the next president-general, an office elected according to an equally complex electoral formula under which his array of birthright constituencies was advantageous. Indeed, the pundits were starting to use the word "inevitability" in connection with his name.

Now he smiled his well-known smile. "I had that 'under the circumstances' coming, Ms. Arnstein. I deeply apologize for the methods used by my men. They mean well, but I'm afraid we're dealing with extremely limited rocket-scientist potential." He turned to Andrew. "My apologies to you also, Captain Roark. I imagine the sudden change of plan occasioned by your unanticipated appearance confused them."

Andrew shook his head to clear it of a fog of unreality. "You know who we are, then. So why have we been kidnapped?"

"Please! At most, you've been taken into temporary protective custody."

"An extralegal form of it," Andrew interjected.

"And, as I indicated, there was never any intention of taking you at all," Valdes continued with no indication of having heard. "But when you unexpectedly showed up . . . well, we just had to adapt to circumstances."

Sheer irritation completed the clearing of Andrew's head. "You still haven't explained why you found it necessary to abduct Ms. Arnstein in the first place."

"Again, that's too strong a word. I had learned—never

mind how—of Ms. Arnstein's quest to learn the truth about her father's death. By the way, Ms. Arnstein, please accept my sincere condolences. And . . . if I may ask, how did your inquiries happen to lead you to the Gev-Tizath embassy?"

"I learned that Father had been in communication with a certain Tizathon scholar." Rachel suddenly seemed to clamp shut a barrier of caution, and Andrew silently released his breath. "Beyond that, I'd rather not say at this time."

"Very well. But I must impress upon you that I am not motivated by idle curiosity. You see . . . well, there's no good way to say this, but I happen to know that your father was murdered. And I have reason to believe I know why— but not by whom. That's what I'm trying to find out, but my inquiries have to be outside official channels because I don't know who can and can't be trusted."

The very last vestiges of disorientation drained from Andrew like water from a broken jug, for he had just learned two very important points of data. *Valdes is lying. And he doesn't know that I know he's lying—otherwise he wouldn't have spoken the lie to Rachel in my hearing. All of which means that, from this moment on, I'd better play my cards very close to my chest.*

And the game he must play had acquired yet another level of complexity. Rachel—for whom he had, for reasons as immemorial as they were irrational, come to feel protective—did *not* know Valdes was lying. Nor did she know what Andrew knew about the real circumstances of her father's death, and the knowledge might shatter her.

Yes . . . very close to my chest indeed.

Rachel leaned forward, trembling with a complex mixture of emotions. "Murdered? Are you sure? But who—?"

"As I say, I don't know exactly who. But I'm fairly sure I know the motive for this heinous act." Valdes's eyes—large, and so dark a brown as to be almost literally black—took on a hypnotic intensity. "Your father, Ms. Arnstein, was about to declare openly in favor of my candidacy for the president-generalcy of the Confederated Nations of Earth. That was why he had to be silenced by my enemies!"

"He hadn't said anything to me about this declaration," said Rachel dubiously.

"And," Andrew trusted himself to add, "it would hardly have been appropriate, as he was still on active duty."

"Well, of course he intended to wait until after his retirement—which, as you know, was imminent—to go public with it. But I solemnly assure you that he had come to see, as I have, that we stand at a unique turning point in human history—no, the history of all life in the galaxy! At such a moment, human destiny can't be entrusted to business-as-usual hack politicians! Your late father, Captain Roark, had also come to see this. Unfortunately, he died before he could say so publicly."

Another lie, Andrew filed away.

But Valdes was in full tilt. "The Lokaron were the first to master high technology, including the secret of interstellar travel. That head start enabled them to spread their multitudes across the stars. But now their greed has been their downfall, because they've sold their technology to us and thus lost that advantage. The war with Gev-Rogov made this clear for all who have eyes to see. Given technological parity, or near parity, we handed them their asses! Humanity is the natural ruling race of the galaxy. Lokaron population numbers mean nothing, any more than did the population numbers of the Persian and Roman and Chinese empires when younger, more vigorous peoples burst in on them and shattered their decadent, fossilized structures, opening up unimagined new possibilities.

"But we were robbed of the full fruits of our victory. The established Lokaron powers that brokered the peace settlement saw to that. All at once, their traditional rivalries with Gev-Rogov were forgotten, when they realized that the unthinkable had happened and Lokaron had been humbled by non-Lokaron for the first time in history. That couldn't be permitted. The lesson is clear: the Lokaron will always close ranks around their own when the chips are down. It's an illusion to think we can join in the traditional Lokaron political and economic games as an equal player. They'll never allow that. We can rely on no one but ourselves.

"Unfortunately, our current leadership can't see beyond the short-term profits from dealing with the doomed Lokaron mercantile system. That's the limit of their vision. If we are to seize this unrepeatable moment, we must be unified under a strong leader who won't let commercial money-grubbing or constitutional nit-picking stand in the way of the imperatives of racial destiny!"

And who, I wonder, might that *be?* thought Andrew.

The strange thing, he reflected, was that even though he had heard all this before—Valdes's speeches were hard to miss on the news—and had always considered it claptrap, he now found himself, on a certain level, being caught up against his will in the oratorical flow. Not that he took it seriously . . . but he could see how others might. Was it some subliminal quality of Valdes's voice? Or was it that Valdes was speaking to something deep in the recesses of the human soul, some dark need that today's prosperous libertarian democracy did not satisfy?

"Uh, sir," he ventured, "isn't this a lot like what the old Earth First Party—which my parents fought to overthrow—used to say? I mean, they were opposed to free-market economics, and particularly to doing business with the Lokaron, and—"

"Don't confuse me and my supporters with that gang of pathetic losers, Captain! They wanted the human race to crawl back into its womb and pretend the universe wasn't there. I want us to go forth boldly into the universe and claim—no, *seize*—our rightful place among the stars. But that kind of boldness terrifies the bean-counters who run the CNE, and their fear makes them desperate.

"Now you understand why I'm investigating Admiral Arnstein's death on my own. I want to be able to present an airtight case before I go public. For this reason, Ms. Arnstein, I couldn't allow you to reveal whatever you may have learned prematurely. So you see, I was acting for your own protection. But I also admit to a degree of self-interest, for we can perhaps pool our findings to our mutual benefit." Valdes gave Andrew a speculative look. "Perhaps the same applies to you, Captain. You still haven't said what brought you to the Tizathon embassy. Do you, perhaps, also have an interest in uncovering the truth about your old commander's death?"

Andrew forced his features into an expressionless mask behind which he thought furiously.

He's lying, and he doesn't know that I know he's lying, he thought once again. *He's looking for something. All this talk about the Admiral being murdered is just an excuse for that search . . . and, in all probability, a way of tricking Rachel into leading him to whatever it is.*

And the fact that he's going to the trouble of trying to trick her must mean he needs help.

So . . . if I play along and make him think I can also be of use to him . . .

"Actually, sir," he said carefully, "I do have reason to suspect there's more to Admiral Arnstein's death than is being officially admitted—and he was a man I admired tremendously. I was going to obtain a visa to go to Tizath-Asor because I want to pursue the only lead I have."

"And what lead is that?" asked Valdes with what Andrew could have sworn was controlled avidity.

"Hardly a lead at all, sir. Just some vague remarks by the admiral—and also by my father—concerning a certain Tizathon researcher who spent some time on Earth back in the Forties and Fifties."

"Yes!" Rachel's eagerness practically blazed from her. "This was why I was going to the Gev-Tizath embassy. That's the one I mentioned before. Father spoke of him."

Andrew's shock—he had only invented the connection between Admiral Arnstein and Persath'Loven on the spur of the moment, hardly expecting to have his imaginary link confirmed—lasted for just a moment. He knew that if he did not break in at this instant, Rachel might very well blurt out Persath's name to Valdes. And, for reasons his forebrain still hadn't formulated, instinct told him that might be a very bad thing indeed.

And an equally strong instinct told him that he needed to offer Valdes one more item of bait.

"Also, sir," he said hastily, just as Rachel was opening her mouth, "my father mentioned, in the same connection, a Gev-Harath intelligence operative who may have had contacts with this same researcher." Out of the corner of his eye, Andrew saw from Rachel's expression that this was new to her . . . and had served to silence her, at least temporarily. He could also see that Valdes was not even troubling to conceal his interest.

"Hmm . . . Perhaps I need to look into it further."

"Actually, sir, I'm thinking I might be in a better position to pursue this. Given some of my acquaintances with my father's old colleagues, and some of the in-depth background I soaked up from him . . . Well, if you could let me proceed to Gev-Tizath as I had intended . . . and maybe even use your influence and contacts to smooth my way . . ."

"In exchange for which you would of course be willing to share your findings with me," said Valdes dryly.

"Of course," Andrew echoed, mentally crossing his fingers. "For one thing, I'm currently on indefinite leave, but I'm supposed to report and account for my movements."

"I think you can leave that to me."

"I'm going too!" blurted Rachel.

Andrew endeavored to put the gravitas of officialdom into his voice. "I don't think that would be a good idea, Ms. Arnstein. I couldn't be responsible for your comfort or safety—and I would be able to function more effectively if I weren't having to try to do so."

"You're not responsible for me in any case, Captain Roark! And as a free citizen I don't need your permission to go to Tizath-Asor!" Rachel turned to Valdes. "Besides, I have some leads of my own. I can be useful to the investigation."

Valdes considered. "She may have a point, Captain. I believe I'll arrange for transportation for both of you to Tizath-Asor. I'll also provide you with a contact there. The two of you might generate a certain synergy."

That's not all we might generate, Andrew groaned inwardly.

CHAPTER SIX

THE BLUENESS FADED from the sky beyond the shuttle's viewports and the untwinkling stars of airless space emerged like innumerable tiny jewels strewn across black velvet.

Valdes had been as good as his word. There had been no problem about visas and passage had been booked for Andrew and Rachel Arnstein to Tizath-Asor aboard the *Star Wanderer*, pride of Spinward, Earth's premier shipping line. Now the great interstellar ship appeared and grew in the view-forward.

"There's the *Star Wanderer*," Andrew said. His attempt to make conversation was not notable for success. Rachel, who sat across the aisle from him in an attitude of tilt-nosed aloofness, gave no acknowledgment save a short nod as the shuttle continued on with the same gentle acceleration its drive core, converting the angular momentum of atomic spin directly into linear thrust, had imparted ever since takeoff. Alas, it was not magic; it still produced sensible acceleration. But at least it required none of the brutal g-forces of the last century's spacecraft that had needed to worry about reaction mass.

After the first Lokaron had arrived from Gev-Tizath forty-four years earlier, Earth's physicists had gone into deep denial. Reactionless drives had been almost the least of it. Far worse had been the aliens' apparent ability to cross the interstellar gulfs in less time than general relativity allowed for, from the standpoint of observers at each end of the journey—and the same amount of time as perceived by the journeyers themselves.

The Lokaron had been compassionate enough to assure them that, yes, Einstein had been right . . . as far as he went. Their ships didn't really transgress the sacrosanct lightspeed limit. They merely avoided it by means of a higher dimension—"overspace"—in which points congruent to locations in normal space were only relatively short distances apart, and in which space drives worked normally. All one had to do was enter and leave overspace— a multidimensional tunneling in spacetime known as "transition," possible only in a gravity field of less than 0.0001 standard Earth G.

And there was the rub. A ship could achieve transition for itself, but only if it carried a massive, energy-intensive generator. Exploration ships and warships did precisely that. But no such ship could earn its keep in the mercantile world of the Lokaron. Fortunately, the same effect could also be produced *externally* to its generating machinery— the "transition gate." That machinery was even more massive and energy-intensive than the ship-mounted transition engines. But once in place it paid for itself innumerable times over, for it could be used by any ship that could reach it. It was, in fact, what made interstellar commerce economically viable, and as such it formed the basis of the Lokaron-created interstellar order.

The shuttle gradually slowed to a near-halt relative to the mammoth interstellar ship. It eased through a nonmaterial atmosphere screen and settled onto a cavernous hangar deck. A queasy moment passed before the great ship's artificial gravity clamped gently down on them. They emerged, and most of the new arrivals, including Rachel, looked slightly apprehensive at having nothing material between them and the vacuum of space. They had all been assured that the atmosphere screen— an application of the same technology that allowed shipboard artificial gravity—was impermeable to atmospheric gasses while permitting the slow passage of massive objects like spacecraft. Still . . .

They were given no time to let it prey on their minds, but were ushered to their cabins. Andrew and Rachel had been assigned quarters on different levels . . . which, he reflected, was probably just as well. He was still getting settled in when the intercom announced departure from orbit. There was only a momentary flutter in weight; the ship followed the standard "aft-equals-down" design philosophy, and the artificial gravity released its hold just as the drive commenced its steady one-gee acceleration. Andrew went on unpacking. Watching Earth recede in the view-aft was no novelty to him.

Later, he went to the lounge for dinner. (The ship was

still keeping Earth's Eastern Standard Time for benefit of its newly arrived passengers but would gradually shift away from it in the course of the voyage so as to eventually conform to the destination planet of Tizath-Asor, thus avoiding a drastic form of "jet lag"; it was yet another way of making interstellar passenger travel practical.) There, the large overhead dome-shaped viewscreen showed the view-aft for the edification of the diners. He spotted Rachel Arnstein, alone at a table, her eyes glued to the shrinking Earth.

"May I join you?" he asked with what he thought was unexceptionable diffidence.

She started. "Oh. Yes. Sure." But her eyes kept going back to the viewsreen. "I suppose this is old hat for you."

"Pretty much," he acknowledged. "But probably not for most of our fellow passengers, from the look of them."

"No. I notice they're all human."

"That's right. The Spinward Line has yet to provide accommodations acclimatized for Lokaron passengers. Even if it had, they'd probably be amused at the thought of traveling aboard a non-Lokaron shipping line—the first such shipping line in the known galaxy. In fact, I imagine the idea would be too amusing to even seem unpatriotic."

"They still look down on us, don't they?"

"In a way—most of them. The wiser ones know better." Andrew thought of Svyatog. "You can't blame them, I suppose, given their history; before us, they'd never encountered anybody above the level of pyramid builders. But now, at least, the traditional patronizing attitudes are tempered by a certain respect."

"Since the war with Gev-Rogov," she finished the thought for him. *The war you fought in*, she seemed about to add. But then a steward (live human; the Spinward Line spared no expense) approached, and the moment passed in the flurry of choosing drinks and ordering dinner. The menu held nothing strange or exotic about it, which was hardly surprising given Spinward's exclusively human clientele.

"So," said Rachel as a conversation reopener, "I gather that we're going to take about three days to reach the CNE transition gate."

"That's right. It orbits just inside the asteroid belt, which is as deep in the sun's gravity well as it can be and still function. But we're in luck; it's only about thirty degrees ahead of Earth, so at a steady one-g acceleration that's about how long it should take, even with some maneuvering adjustments that have to be made at the end." He laughed. "We could have done it in less time if we'd used the Harathon gate—it's trailing Earth by just a little, so we would only have had to kill our relative velocity. But that would have meant paying a toll. And besides, it's a matter of prestige. Constructing a transition gate was the greatest project the human race had undertaken since the formation of the CNE—it took a public-private partnership involving Spinward and the other infant space lines, as well as the CNE government. And now we use it whenever possible, instead of the Harathon and Tizathon ones, out of pride as well as toll-avoidance."

Their drinks arrived and they clinked glasses—chablis for her, bourbon and branch water for him—as though to formalize the breaking of the ice. Andrew reminded himself that he must never lose sight of the multilayered game he was playing.

"Listen," Rachel said impulsively after the first sip, "I really do appreciate what you tried to do for me back in Washington. And I know you don't want me along on this trip. But I promise I'll—"

"No, no. You were perfectly right, and I was probably being too stuffy. I'm still curious, though, as to what made you so certain that the official reports of your father's death were less than candid. You mentioned something about him 'not seeming himself.'"

"That began before I happened to find out about his being in communication with this Tizathon researcher . . . You mentioned that you knew of him, too. Persath'Loven, was that his name?"

"That's right," said Andrew, who had expected to have to worm the name out of her. *Was I ever so candid and artless?* he wondered. *Probably not.*

"Well, he seemed terribly upset to know I had found out—as though the knowledge might put me in some kind of danger. It was afterwards that he stopped communicating. That hurt." Rachel's expression reflected that remembered pain. "I wasn't completely honest when I said he and I stayed in touch pretty regularly. That was only so after I'd moved away from Mother—their divorce had been pretty bitter, you see—and gotten established in San Francisco—I'm a graphic designer. So it was like I was losing something I'd only just gained."

Dinner was served. The conversation frayed out into inconsequentialities—which was fine with Andrew, who didn't want to risk pushing too hard. But over coffee he

managed to steer the subject to their encounter with
Valdes, then spoke with what he hoped wasn't overdone
casualness. "You know, when I asked him if his views
weren't a lot like that of the old Earth First Party, I almost
wanted to ask if they weren't also like those of the Black
Wolf Society."

"Huh? Aren't they a crime syndicate?"

"On one level. But they also push an ideology that is
expansionist and human-supremacist and, if not anti-
Lokaron in general, certainly anti-Rogovon. In fact, their
name comes from the constellation Lupus—the Wolf.
There, and in Sagittarius, is where our interests have
come into conflict with Gev-Rogov's. The Black Wolf's
goal is to drive the Rogovon out of that constellation
entirely."

"I never knew that about their name."

"Not many people do." Andrew made his voice even
more casual. "Did your father ever mention them?"

She gave him a sharp glance and spoke with a certain
abruptness. "No. Why should he have?"

"Oh, no reason." Andrew changed the subject as
quickly as he could without seeming obvious about it.

A little less than three Earth-days later they sat in the
lounge to watch the transition, pressed down into their
recliners by the sudden, stomach-lurching surge as the
ship was pulled into the nonmaterial hole in space-time.
This time the dome above them showed the view-forward,
and the stars ahead seemed to flow sternward and merge
into a tunnel of light that streamed through the spectrum
before vanishing into a well of blackness—the utter,

disturbing blackness of overspace, into which the tiny blue dot of Earth had preceded it—in a secondary screen that showed the view-aft. It was a sensory experience that not even Andrew had ever really grown used to.

The rest of the voyage was uneventful. *Star Wanderer*, built by and for humans, was no more alien-seeming than its cuisine. They couldn't even watch the stars while in overspace, and all external viewscreens were deactivated after transition to guard the passengers' emotional equilibrium from the sight of the indescribable nothingness that lay outside the hull. There were various recreational and entertainment facilities available, and as time went by Andrew felt that a thaw was beginning to creep into his association with Rachel.

"Listen," she said in one unguarded moment, "I'm sorry if I seemed to snap at you that first night after departure, at dinner."

"You mean when I asked if your father had ever mentioned the Black Wolf Society?"

"Right. I'm sure you're just pursuing every possible lead. But . . . well, I had a friend once, shortly after I'd first moved to San Francisco. He got hooked on drugs— relatively harmless ones at first, or so he thought. But then one led to another, right up to brainbloom."

Andrew didn't trust himself to speak. He knew of the utterly illegal designer drug. It produced an explosive enhancement of creativity—for a while. But then . . .

"Dead?" he finally queried.

"That would be better. He might as well be anencephalic. But his brain still produces EEG readings, so they can't legally pull the plug on him. He's just a mass of flesh, hooked up to a machine." She shook herself and spoke a little too briskly. "The police are certain that the Black Wolf Society is behind distribution of the stuff, but they haven't been able to prove anything. Confidentially, one of them told me they're swimming against a very strong tide of influence at high places."

And when I mentioned your father's name in the same sentence with them . . . "You're right," Andrew said quickly. "I was just speculating at random." He steered the conversation into safer channels. The subject never came up again.

Andrew discovered that his travels hadn't really prepared him for Tizath-Asor, when they emerged from overspace at one of its transition gates. He had been to Harath-Asor, home of Earth's closest Lokaron associates and origin of Tizath-Asor's original settlers. There, he had been struck—as had so many others, including his parents, the first humans to see it—by the strange contrast between the overwhelming presence of transcendent technology and the ancientness of the world itself, with its worn-down landscapes, its enigmatic cyclopean ruins of an extinct pre-Lokaron race, its long days . . . and, in its deep-blue sky, the great orange sun whose tidal pull had produced those long days by slowing its rotation over the eons.

There was none of that here. Tizath-Asor was younger than Earth, and its sun was a G2v like Sol. It still held oceans that covered three-quarters of its surface, even though its surface gravity was only slightly higher than the 0.72 Terran G its Harathon colonists had evolved under.

Those colonists had required so little genetic engineering that the two subspecies could still interbreed normally, as was not the case with either of them and the Lokarathon of the species' homeworld, who represented the original Lokaron genotype—or with the Rogovon, or any of the other gengineered Lokaron subspecies.

They proceeded inward from the transition gate through the crowded spacelanes, passing awesome space habitats, titanic powersats, streaming convoys of ore carriers, and all the rest of what had to be expected in the capital system of a major Lokaron *gevah*. But as a secondary colony of Gev-Harath, this was a relatively young *gevah*, and as they approached the planet (reassuringly Earthlike despite its smaller size), its night side wasn't the almost unbroken dazzlement of city lights Andrew had seen on Harath-Asor. There was, however, the same thread—impossibly thin for its straightness—extending three diameters out from a point on the planet's equator. Most of the metropolitan Lokaron worlds still had orbital towers utilizing materials technology even now beyond Earth's horizon, for reactionless drives were a more recent development than the capability of overspace transition. But nowadays such towers were merely tourist attractions. *Star Wanderer* proceeded to a low-orbit space station where Spinward Line had leased facilities, and shuttles waited to waft them down to the surface in today's cheap, quiet way.

They disembarked, emerging from a tube connecting *Star Wanderer* with the station. There was no fluctuation in weight, for gravity, like the diurnal cycle, had gradually been adjusted to the destination planet's values in the course of the voyage. As they entered the cavernous lobby, a human stepped forth to greet them. He was youngish, short and slender, with straight black hair and regular dark features that reflected an indefinable blend of ethnic origins. Andrew thought he might as well as have had "gofer" tattooed on his forehead.

"Captain Roark? Ms. Arnstein? I'm Amletto Leong, with the CNE embassy to Gev-Tizath. But," he quickly added, "I'm not here in any official capacity. As part of our latest courier run from Earth—which beat you here by a few days—we got a request from Assemblyman Valdes to extend you any assistance we could. Naturally, we try to accommodate such requests from members of the Legislative Assembly whenever possible. So the ambassador asked me to do whatever I legitimately can for you."

Translation: the bureaucrats are already sucking up to the man they sense will be the next president-general. "Thank you," Andrew said aloud. "I suppose our first need is planetside accommodations and transportation."

"*Separate* accommodations," Rachel put in primly.

"Already taken care of." Leong smiled. "I think you'll find the accommodations comfortable. Certain Tizathon hotels have gotten quite good about catering to human requirements. They can even give you Earth-normal gravity if you choose. Personally, I enjoy the local version. And an air-car will be available whenever you need it."

"I'm overwhelmed," Rachel remarked. "I just hope I'm not equally overwhelmed by the bills."

"Not to worry," said Leong with an airy gesture. "That's been taken care of. Assemblyman Valdes assured us he'd reimburse us for all expenses."

"Thank you," said Andrew, somewhat inadequately. *This is above and beyond*, he thought, and Rachel's expression made it clear she was thinking the same thing. *Of course, the other side of the coin is that everything we do is going to be reported back to Valdes. But there's nothing I can do about that, and given the time lag I don't need to worry about it for now.* "Our next request is going to be for an introduction to see a certain Persath'Loven."

Leong's out-of-character sharp look was smoothed over almost too quickly to be noticed. He pursed his lips. "That could be a little more difficult. How much do you know about him?"

"Only that he spent some time on Earth back in the late Forties and early Fifties, studying Earth's cultures and history, and that he published some books on the subject."

"Yes." Leong nodded. "He's a type that has pretty much vanished on Earth: the super-wealthy dilettante. In fact, he almost fits into an even older type from Earth's past: a 'remittance man,' but on a fairly grandiose scale, because he's a collateral relation of one of the established *hovathon* of Gev-Tizath. Incidentally, he's a primary male rather than a transmitter, which isn't as much of a social disability as it would have once been—Gev-Tizath is pretty progressive that way. But you get the general idea. He had an obscene amount of unearned wealth with which to pursue his interests."

"Still," Andrew persisted, "I understand some of his works on human studies were well-regarded."

"True. The earlier ones. He's actually rather brilliant,

in an undisciplined, unfocused sort of way. But afterward . . . well, he seems to have fallen under the influence of certain mystical human cranks—the Imperial Temple of the Star Lords, they call themselves—and his later writings verged on sheer hysteria."

"And now he's back here on Tizath-Asor?"

"Yes. After his return from Earth he began to pour his money into an obsessive study of some very odd—some would almost say occult—aspects of physics. The whole business is actually very mysterious . . . which has added to its popular appeal and, I gather, even increased sales of his earlier books, making him even richer." Leong chuckled. "But the point is, he's very eccentric and has the resources to protect his privacy. He hardly ever sees anyone—even fellow Lokaron, let alone humans."

"Tell him," said Rachel, "that I'm the daughter of Admiral Nathan Arnstein, who has died under suspicious circumstances."

"You might also mention that I was Admiral Arnstein's chief of staff, and I, too, have reason to believe that the circumstances surrounding his death were questionable." Andrew paused, trying to decide how much he should reveal. He wanted to mention the Black Wolf Society, but he still wasn't ready to trust Valdes, with whom Leong was obviously associated, if only indirectly.

"Hmm." Leong stroked his chin. "This might make him more amenable to your request. I'll see what I can do. But for now, let's get you through the local customs— that's all handled here in the station—and then to your shuttle. I'll show you to your hotel."

CHAPTER SEVEN

THEIR HOTEL WAS AN OCTAGONAL TOWER that had seemed rapier-slim from above but whose true dimensions were now obvious as they stared up and up its vertiginous side until it vanished in the midsummer haze.

The interior, organized around a vast central well whose ceiling could not be seen, combined immense mass with the soaring, infinity-aspiring etherealness made possible by nanotech-manufactured (grown?) materials—a defining quality of Lokaron architecture, and one that could be only dimly glimpsed in their structures on Earth. Here it was on full display, and Rachel gasped when they first walked in.

They remained there for two of the 27.8-hour local days while Leong brought them periodic cautiously optimistic progress reports on his attempts to make arrangements with Persath'Loven. In the meantime he arranged guided jaunts for them over the environs. Those environs consisted, for miles around in every direction, of mind-numbing cityscape, if possible even more stunning at night, when it was ablaze with light. Night and day, the sky was crisscrossed with a traffic pattern of air-cars, moving with a computer-enforced orderliness that explained the willingness of the local authorities (unlike those of Earth) to allow them over urban areas. But after their first few jaunts, Andrew and Rachel began to wonder if there were any *other* sorts of areas on Tizath-Asor.

They learned better when Leong finally arrived on the third morning with good news.

He met them in an alcove off their hotel's central nave (the word came more naturally to mind than "lobby" in these cathedral-like vastnesses). "Persath'Loven has finally stopped dithering," he announced with obvious self-satisfaction. "He's agreed to see you—I almost said 'grant you an audience,' after listening to the way he put it! You can go out to his estate this afternoon."

"*We* can go there?" Rachel queried. "Does that mean you're not going with us?" Andrew silently hoped that was exactly what it meant.

"That's right." Leong took on a miffed look. "He doesn't altogether approve of the CNE government. Just an extreme form of the traditional Lokaron attitude, I suppose; they don't even trust their *own* governments, if you can call the *gevahon* 'governments.' But don't worry about finding your way. You'll be using public transportation—a lot faster than air-cars, by the way. You see, Persath also doesn't approve of air-cars over his property."

"What does he approve of?" Rachel asked dryly.

"Not very much."

The public transportation in question proved to involve a continent-wide network of subterranean tunnels that had been evacuated in the true sense of the word. In the absence of air resistance, small passenger capsules could quickly accelerate to great speeds and decelerate just as quickly, with carefully balanced artificial-gravity fields protecting the passengers from any sensations stronger than those experienced in old-fashioned elevators on Earth. Nevertheless, Andrew and Rachel stayed in the cushy (though, of course, overlarge) seats of the private capsule Leong had arranged for them and watched the wraparound-screen simulacrum that created the illusion they were flying above the surface rather than under it. Only a machismo that he would have been the first to identify as archaic made Andrew maintain jaw-clenched silence and not echo Rachel's gasps and occasional squeaks as they appeared to flash at insanely recklesss speeds through the dense cityscape.

"The Lokaron are probably used to it," he thought fit to reassure her.

"They probably enjoy it," she corrected. "I even think I'm starting to."

It became easier to enjoy once they left the towers of the city behind. The agribusiness that must be required to feed Tizath-Asor was clearly elsewhere, for they traversed an increasingly hilly parklike landscape where suburbs nestled, partially concealed by the summer foliage of unfamiliar trees. The vegetation, Andrew thought, must reflect a blend of the local ecology and imports brought by the colonists from Harath-Asor. He also reminded himself that on a Lokaron world as highly developed as this one, open space was the prerogative of the very rich, so "suburbs" did not carry the middle-class connotation that it did on Earth.

Soon even these fell behind, and they proceeded up a valley at whose far end the sea could be glimpsed—a bay beyond which, farther inland (very much further than it seemed, Andrew was sure), another city raised its towers through the haze halfway to the zenith. But immediately before them, perched on a cliffside above the bay in what humans would have considered a dramatic setting, was what Andrew recognized as a very extensive private Lokaron dwelling—a compound, really, given the number of utilitarian outbuildings that sat in jarring contrast to the grand villa.

Hmm, he thought. *Persath must be* really *eccentric.*

The Lokaron had evolved on Lokarath-Asor, a small, dry world with seas (glorified salt-water lakes, really) rather than oceans. They had felt right at home on Harath-Asor. Even the Tizathon, gengineered for an ocean planet like this one, didn't live on the seaside by choice. They saw nothing picturesque or romantic about it, only the chance of storm damage. They found it impossible to understand why oceanfront property commanded higher-than-normal prices on Earth.

So Persath's choice of what would have been prime human real estate could only have been motivated by a desire to assure his privacy in what his fellow Tizathon would consider a remote, unattractive locale. *Besides which,* thought Andrew, recalling that Persath was no fool, *he probably got it on the cheap.*

As they neared the villa the screen shut off, abandoning the pretense that the capsule was aloft. They came to a seemingly gentle halt, and the capsule opened to reveal an underground reception room. Andrew recalled Leong's explanation that someone as rich as Persath rated an individual transit system "address," but one strictly controlled by privacy protocols. Had Persath not consented to release that address, the capsule would never have stopped here.

They stepped out into the reception room, an oblong white-tiled expanse lit by afternoon sun slanting through light-wells behind trickling fountains at each end. It was not at all what Andrew would have expected. He reminded himself that this was no more typical of Tizath-Asor's housing than some Gilded Age plutocrat's Newport "cottage" would have typified that of late nineteenth-century America. It also occurred to him that the dry-planet-evolved Lokaron would naturally see fountains as a prime form of conspicuous consumption, even though here on Tizath-Asor they really weren't all that extravagant.

The wall opposite the capsule egress held a doorway. They paused before it and gave their names in response to a robotic inquiry that Rachel understood, having been given a relatively bulky exterior equivalent of Andrew's translator implant, which she wore as an earpiece. The door slid silently open, and the artificial voice directed them to a platform that lifted them up to ground level, where they followed a series of dimly lit hallways to a large vaulted chamber where they were told to wait. They tried to make themselves comfortable on chairs too high for Andrew's feet, much less Rachel's, to reach the floor.

Persath kept them waiting, which gave Andrew time to examine the chamber. Its walls were devoid of ornamentation, but it was filled with computer equipment, tables bearing unfamiliar devices, cabinets, shelves piled high with hard copy. It seemed cluttered even to a human, so it must have been inconveniently so for the larger Lokaron. Andrew knew the Lokaron well enough to recognize the appearance of disorganization and disarray as genuine. Even across the gulf of species and cultures, he knew the study or workroom of an eccentric scholar or researcher when he saw it.

The tedium of waiting was beginning to wear on them when an old-fashioned door swung open and a Lokar of the Tizathon subspecies came bustling in. To anyone who knew what to look for, he was an obvious primary male, even more gracile than the transmitters and with certain more subtle indicia. He was, Andrew recalled, middle-aged for a Lokar, and he was beginning to show the usual signs of aging. His attitude of jittery distraction transcended races and worlds.

"I am Persath'Loven," he announced without preamble. The translator gave him the kind of high tenor English it always seemed to consider appropriate for primary males.

Andrew stepped forward, remembering not to offer his hand. "Thank you for seeing us, sir. I am—"

"I am well aware of who you are." The software reproduced peevishness to perfection. "I hope *you* are aware that this visit is most, yes, *most* inconvenient! But I doubt if you have any conception of the importance of the work you are interrupting."

"We have no wish to take up any more of your valuable time than necessary, sir. We only hoped you could assist us in—"

"Again, I am quite aware of why you are here. It was explained to me by various *gevah* functionaries whom your embassy had somehow enlisted on your behalf. Pressure, yes, *pressure* was brought to bear on me to see you!" Having gotten this off his bony chest, Persath calmed down slightly. "It is true that I communicated with Admiral Arnstein recently, and I regret to hear of his death. But I know nothing about it. I cannot help you." He gave every indication of believing he had discharged his duty and began to turn toward the door.

"We hardly expected you to have any direct knowledge concerning Admiral Arnstein's death," Andrew said hastily. "We only thought you might be able to shed new light on certain background information."

"How could I possibly do that?" Persath's peevishness was back full force, and he was practically twitching with eagerness to leave.

Andrew drew a breath and took the plunge. "Well, in view of your association with the Imperial Temple of the Star Lords . . ."

The effect on Persath was remarkable. He started as though from an electric shock and stared at Andrew with yellow slit-pupiled eyes grown huge. Andrew made himself hold those eyes with his own, without a side-glance at the look of puzzled surprise he was certain he must be getting from Rachel.

"Whatever do you mean?" Persath finally spluttered. (The translator software could even do a splutter.) "I was never 'associated' with that human pseudo-religious cult, as you imply. Admittedly, I inquired as to their beliefs while I was on Earth, as part of my inquiries into the possible prehistoric roots of certain human folk legends. But I came to the conclusion that their doctrines were the purest claptrap. I thought I had made this clear in my last published work on the subject, to the satisfaction of all discerning minds!"

"Perhaps my mind is insufficiently discerning, sir. But there was an additional link between you and the Imperial Temple . . . or, if you will, a mutual associate. During your time on Earth you were acquainted with a Harathon intelligence agent working for Hov-Korth, by the name of Reislon'Sygnath."

This time Andrew couldn't help but see Rachel's jaw-dropping reaction to a name he hadn't mentioned in her and Valdes's presence. To his relief, she at least kept quiet (for now) about the various items of information he had been withholding from her. And Persath, even if his knowledge of human body language had been sufficient to recognize her astonishment, was in no condition to notice it. He shakily lowered himself into a chair, continuing to stare at Andrew.

"How did you learn that name?"

"Never mind. The point is, there was some kind of three-way connection between you and him and the Imperial Temple. Furthermore, I believe the connection somehow involved the Black Wolf Society." Andrew stopped and waited for Persath's indignant denial of this bluff, which didn't even rise to the level of a hunch.

Instead, something seemed to break inside the elderly Lokar. He slumped in his chair, and if Andrew had been looking at a human he would have sworn that he was seeing a kind of relief that a long-held secret no longer need be kept.

"How widely is all this known?" The translator put it into a normal tone, but Persath's actual voice was the rasping rattle of a Lokaron whisper.

"Very few know it besides ourselves." Andrew deemed *very few* more prudent than *no one*, even though Persath didn't seem inclined to, or particularly capable of, violence. "And those few are keeping it in strict confidence. But you will understand why we need your help in tying all these strings together, so we can evaluate their relevance to Admiral Arnstein's death." He wanted very much to nudge Persath further by mentioning that he knew of a connection between Admiral Arnstein and the Black Wolf Society, but he didn't think Rachel was ready for that just yet, and he already had quite enough explaining to do about things he hadn't told her.

Persath began to speak, first in a slow monotone, then more rapidly, as though his words were flowing through a breached dam.

"Yes, I do know Reislon'Sygnath. I met him on Earth in 2056." (As usual, the translator software effortlessly did the mathematics of conversion to Earth years.) "He sought me out because of our mutual interest in the Imperial Temple. I, as you know, had been studying it in the course of writing my final book on Earth's protohistory; he was investigating it on behalf of Hov-Korth because of the anti-Lokaron attitudes implicit in its doctrines, although he was rapidly coming to the conclusion that it was an apolitical organization of harmless cranks."

"Yes, so his then-boss Svyatog'Korth told me," Andrew said with a nod. Persath didn't really need to know about his relationship with the executive director of Hov-Korth, but he thought it might be worth mentioning for any added prestige it might impart to him. Rachel continued to hold her peace, although he could tell it wasn't getting any easier for her.

"At the time we met, I was in a somewhat agitated frame of mind, and as a result I must admit that I was indiscreet. You see, earlier that year the leaders of the Imperial Temple had, after much hesitation and repeated entreaties on my part, consented to show me the most secret object in their possession—an object which they regarded as constituting the final proof of their beliefs."

Andrew and Rachel hardly dared speak.

"As you know," Persath seemed to digress, "the Imperial Temple has sponsored archaeological work, generally of questionable value. In 2055, one such expedition was working on the fourth planet of the Sol system."

"Mars," said Rachel automatically. "It's a lifeless little world, pretty much ignored since the interstellar frontier opened to us."

"But it used to be the setting for a lot of romantic fiction," Andrew put in. "And for a lot of dingbat theories."

"It was in the latter capacity that the Imperial Temple found it of interest. They wished to investigate a region known as Cydonia, which they believed to be the site of certain pyramids and a gigantic sculpted human-like face."

Rachel recovered before Andrew. "But . . . but even before the end of the twentieth century it was known that those pyramids and that face were just tricks of shadows in the photos taken by an early space probe!"

"The leaders of the Imperial Temple persuaded themselves that the powers-that-be had tampered with the photographs to cover up artifacts that would prove the existence of the prehistoric human galactic empire."

Why am I even surprised? Andrew sighed to himself. Now that he thought about it, he dimly recalled the Cydonia expedition of 2055, when he had been twenty-two, and the stony silence from the Imperial Temple that had followed it.

"At any rate," Persath continued, "the expedition went to Mars and was encountering disappointing results, when something unexpected happened. A spacecraft performed a crash landing not far from their camp."

Andrew was instantly alert. "I've never read anything about a crash on Mars, then or at any other time."

"Neither has anyone else outside the Imperial Temple. As you have pointed out, Mars is generally disregarded by modern humans. No one observed the crash except the Cydonia expedition. Receiving no reply to their attempts at radio contact, they set out across the desert in search of survivors.

"The attempt at an emergency landing had not been a success. The craft was wrecked beyond reconstruction, but it was a wholly unfamiliar design. And only one body was found. Even that one was barely recognizable . . . but it was inarguably human."

"*Human?*" Andrew and Rachel exclaimed in unison. Persath continued, ignoring them.

"Only one other item of interest was recovered: a

device in operable condition, which seemed miraculous until it became clear that it was built to extraordinary standards of indestructibility. Its nature and purpose were a mystery, but after a great deal of careful tinkering, it produced a kind of almost undetectably brief dimensional distortion which seemed to defy all knowledge and experience. They immediately ceased any further experimentation, the results of which were unforeseeable and potentially disastrous. Instead, they took the body and the device and returned forthwith to Earth, where they reported in deepest secrecy to the leaders of the Imperial Temple.

"To those leaders, this was confirmation of their most cherished hope: the ancient human interstellar empire that colonized Earth must still be in existence somewhere and is even now reconnoitering the Sol system, so its second coming is surely imminent." Andrew wondered if the translator software had used that turn of phrase with malice aforethought.

"But," Rachel wanted to know, "if they believe this, then why haven't they made the evidence known, and publicly congratulated themselves on having been vindicated?"

"They fear that the body and the device, if revealed, will be destroyed or somehow falsified by the large and powerful conspiracy they believe seeks to discredit their doctrines. Also, they are not at all sure they *want* to convert the rest of the human race. It would rob them of the privileged position they expect to enjoy when the empire returns."

Yeah, Andrew reminded himself, *Sebastian Gruber had died the year before that, and the true believers had* taken over the Imperial Temple. If he *had still been around*, he would have milked this for every nickel it was worth.

"So they're just sitting on their precious secret," said Rachel.

"Not entirely. After I had worked my way sufficiently into their confidence, they kept dropping broad hints to me. I suspect they couldn't help wanting to 'prove' to a Lokar that humanity had preceded us in interstellar space. They may also have reasoned that, as a Lokar, I would have no motive to make the secret generally known—rather the contrary. At any rate, they finally let themselves be persuaded to show me the body and the device, and even demonstrate the latter.

"I did my best to be respectfully noncommittal and not reveal my stupefaction. There was no disputing the human body—and, using instrumentation more sophisticated than any available to my hosts, I was able to determine that the momentary effect produced by the device was even more unfathomable than they found it. I did not for a moment take the Imperial Temple's interpretation seriously. But what *was* the explanation?

"You will now understand my agitation when I talked to Reislon'Sygnath shortly thereafter. I tried to restrain myself, but the hints I let slip seemed to pique his interest."

I'll bet they did, thought Andrew, cudgeling his memory and doing some mental arithmetic. *As a Harathon intelligence operative on Earth, he naturally knew about the Harathon warship's sighting of mysterious spacecraft in the solar system in 2055—the same year as the Cydonia crash. Persath, as a Tizathon civilian, wouldn't have known about that.*

"At the same time, I hastily finished my last book about Earth, in a state of mind which I must admit may have affected its quality. I then returned here to Tizath-Asor and since then have diverted my resources into trying to interpret the readings I obtained from the device and, if possible, ascertain its purpose. I have attracted some eminent, yes, *eminent* physicists, although their ideas are perhaps a bit too advanced for the hidebound scientific establishment. They and I have developed some promising, yes, *promising* leads." Persath was himself again, and Rachel and Andrew waited expectantly for him to elaborate. But he seemed to bring himself up short as though on a leash of caution and resumed his narrative. "Then, around 2060 or shortly thereafter, imagine my surprise when I received a visit from Reislon'Sygnath."

"But," said Andrew, "I was under the impression that he had been reassigned to the Lupus frontier by that time."

"Indeed he had. The assassination of the Kogurche system's ruler in 2057, and the subsequent charge by Gev-Rogov that humans were responsible, had destabilized that region of space, and the Harathon—particularly Hov-Korth, with its special relationship with the CNE—were sufficiently concerned to send their best intelligence operatives. In the matter of the assassination, Reislon had come to smell a rat." Andrew's respect for the translator software went up another notch. "He became convinced that the Rogovon accusations were not entirely unfounded, but that the humans in question represented not the CNE government but the Black Wolf Society, which wished to incite a war. What's more, in the course of his investigation he had uncovered indications that the Black Wolf Society was exhibiting an interest in the Imperial Temple. This last caused him to recall his earlier conversations with me, and he put two and two together. He then arranged a leave of absence and came here to Tizath-Asor to take counsel with me.

"At this point my inhibitions dissolved and I told him everything I knew. We agreed that the Black Wolf's curiosity about the Imperial Temple could have but one cause."

"I have reason to believe," said Andrew carefully, "that shortly after this, in 2064, Reislon communicated a vaguely worded warning about the Black Wolf Society to his superiors in Hov-Korth and then dropped from sight after the war."

"The vague wording was doubtless a result of my entreaties to him to be discreet and conceal my identity, which must have placed definite limits on his use of the information I had given him. And as for him dropping from sight . . ." Persath took on what Andrew's acquaintance with the Lokaron told him was a look of sly caution. "Yes. The human-Rogovon war broke out in 2066, despite his best efforts, for he was deeply concerned with averting it."

"Was he?" Andrew left it at that, not mentioning that Reislon had been working for both sides of that war simultaneously, in addition to his official employers. He didn't even try to relate Reislon's triple game and his antiwar sentiments to each other, for his head was spinning with the implications. There would be time for that when he had more information.

"Yes, although I was never entirely clear on why. And

afterward, disgusted, he vanished . . . as far as most were concerned."

"But not you," Rachel stated rather than asked, before Andrew could.

Persath stood up slowly and looked down on them from Lokaron height. "Reislon and I are working toward, if not the same goal, then goals which are not incompatible."

"So are we," Andrew risked saying.

"Especially," Rachel added, "in light of your recent communication with my father. I can't believe that was unconnected with all this. Coincidence isn't that hard-working."

"You are correct. Your father contacted me because he had been contacted by Reislon." Rachel drew in a hissing breath, but said nothing. "I told him little he had not already heard from Reislon. It is my sincere hope that whatever knowledge I imparted to him had no connection with his death."

His suicide, Andrew mentally amended.

"You too are correct," Persath told Andrew. "The three of us are now linked in this—as is Reislon, although he does not know it as yet. There is only one solution: we must consult with him."

"You know where he is?" Andrew asked.

"Yes—but I would rather not say. The fewer who know, the better. We will use my personal ship to go to him. I suggest you return to your lodgings and prepare yourselves. I will communicate with you directly, rather than through your embassy—and I must insist that you not involve them."

"No argument," Andrew muttered.

CHAPTER EIGHT

THE GREAT INTERSTELLAR LINERS, freighters, and men-of-war were strictly orbit-to-orbit ships, built in space and never touching a planetary surface, where their weight would have wrecked them. The consequent economies of lightweight construction more than made up for the inconvenience of surface-to-orbit interface via shuttles.

However, given reactionless drives and transition gates, there was no reason why a surface-to-surface vessel could not be given interstellar capability if money was no object, as it was not to Persath'Loven.

He sent word to their hotel as promised, with instructions for meeting him at the private-vessel annex of the city's spaceport. They packed some basic necessities, and Rachel met Andrew in his room.

"Do you realize how many gender stereotypes you're shattering, being ready before me?" asked Andrew, looking up from the packing process he still hadn't completed.

"Dinosaur!" She stuck out her tongue. "I just wonder how Leong is going to react when he finds out we're gone."

"Have a stroke, I imagine," Andrew predicted, going on with his packing.

"I hope not. He's been helpful, after all, and . . . and what, exactly, is *that*?"

There was no apology in Andrew's voice as he held up the weapon he had been about to toss into his bag. "It's called an M-3 gauss pistol—a standard Navy sidearm." *With which your father spattered his brains over his office*, flashed through his mind, only to be sternly suppressed. "It has a number of highly desirable qualities. One is that it's manufactured entirely from materials that can get past ordinary customs scanners, which is why I was able to bring it from Earth without having to answer any awkward questions. Another is that it can be used inside a space vehicle without jeopardizing hull integrity."

"But . . . do you really expect to need it?"

"I have no way of knowing what to expect. So I've done my best to be prepared for all eventualities."

She held his eyes with hers—eyes oddly at variance with her overall appearance, for they were that curious light shade that could seem blue or gray or green depending on the lighting. Some unacknowledged Cossack ancestor who had gotten in a bit of raping in the course of a pogrom, Andrew imagined.

"You know a lot that you're not telling me," she finally said. "That was obvious from some of the things you said to Persath. I kept my mouth shut at the time because I didn't want to queer the deal. For that, I think you owe me one. I wish you'd take me into your confidence. And *please* don't give me any military chickenshit about 'need to know.'"

"It's actually not as chickenshit as it may seem. More often than not it operates for the protection of the person lacking a need to know. As you'll recall, I told you I can't be responsible for your safety. That doesn't mean I'm eager to expose you to potential danger unnecessarily."

"All right. I'll accept that for now. But sooner or later I'm going to want to know everything you know."

"Yes, I know you will." Andrew did know it, and he dreaded it so much that he was still in denial about the prospect. A glance at the clock saved him. "And now it's time to get up to the landing flange and meet the air-car Persath is sending."

Persath hadn't wanted them to use public transportation, in which the two humans would have attracted attention, and Andrew wasn't quite prepared to write this off as paranoia. So an air-car awaited them, piloted by a completely uncommunicative Lokaron chauffeur. (Tizathon law required air-cars over urban areas to be under sentient control as well as being hooked into the computerized traffic-control network.) He took them over the seemingly endless alien cityscape until the towers thinned out and the extensive open expanse of the spaceport appeared. They passed beyond the vast commercial facilities for ground-to-orbit shuttles and finally came to rest alongside the private vessels of the super-rich.

One of the things Andrew had always found appealing about the Lokaron (at least those of Gev-Harath and cultures derived from it, like Gev-Tizath) was that they didn't make any sophomoric noises about having "outgrown ornamentation." The vessels that stretched away into the distance were inherently attractive, with the streamlined look of ships intended for atmospheric transit. But that look had been enhanced with a dazzling variety of colorful designs programmed into their liquid-crystal skins, giving them almost an enameled appearance, pleasingly "retro" to human eyes. Some of the color combinations seemed gaudy, but Persath's ship was tastefully understated: mostly medium-gray, with a decorative pattern of sweeping lines in gleaming dark green lined with sliver trim.

Persath was waiting alongside it and dismissed the chauffeur. His jitters were manifest. "Good. You are here. We have clearance. Let us proceed immediately."

The interior lived up to their expectations of luxury. It was organized around a kind of saloon from which one could look directly up a half flight of steps to the control bridge, where Persath now seated himself.

"No crew, Persath?" inquired Rachel.

"No organic one." Persath didn't look up from the control panel, and his irritability would have been obvious even if the translator hadn't reproduced it. "The ship is almost entirely automated, and I am qualified to perform those piloting functions which are not. And now, please prepare yourselves for takeoff."

The preparations were not as elaborate as might have

been supposed, for the ship, unlike the ground-to-orbit shuttles with their brief flight times, had a complex system of compensating artificial-gravity fields that gave it a ventral-equals-down orientation and largely cancelled out the feeling of movement. This enabled its reactionless drive—quite powerful relative to the mass it had to push—to pile on an acceleration that quickly brought them to one of Tizath-Asor's transition gates. (Even among the Lokaron wealthy, private individuals simply did not own ships with their own transition engines.)

Once the kaleidoscopic tunnel of light had vanished into infinity astern, leaving them in featureless blackness, Andrew turned to their host. "All right, Perath. We're in overspace now, and as we all know that means we're cut off from the normal universe with no possibility of communication. So could you please gratify our curiosity about our destination?"

"I suppose it can do no harm," Persath conceded with no good grace. "We are bound for the Kogurche system."

"The Kogurche system?" echoed Rachel. She sounded as stunned as Andrew felt at the mention of the system in Lupus that had been the proximate cause of the late unpleasantness between Gev-Rogov and the CNE.

"I believe that is what I said." Persath did not look up from the controls, with which he was peevishly preoccupied. "I assure you that this vessel, with its high thrust-to-mass ratio, will get us there in a reasonable length of time."

"But are you saying that Reislon'Sygnath has been there all this time?" Andrew couldn't keep the incredulity out of his voice.

"No. He moves around. But he spends a fair amount

of time there, and I have excellent reason to believe it is his current locale." Persath's eyes were still on the instruments.

"But what's he doing there? And how is he able to operate there undetected nowadays? And—"

"The answers will become apparent in due time." Persath finally looked up. "I suggest that at the moment we have more immediate concerns."

"Such as?"

"A vessel passed through the transition gate after we did. This ship mounts military-grade detectors, by which I can ascertain that the other ship has matched our course, far enough behind us to be beyond the range of ordinary civilian detectors. In short, we are being followed."

Earth had been the first non-Lokaron world ever found to have made the twin breakthroughs of the scientific and industrial revolutions. To fit it into their edifice of comfortable assumptions of superiority, the Lokaron had been forced to devise elaborate theories assuring themselves that it was an unrepeatable freak.

Then, a decade after the tumultuous events of 2030, explorers from Gev-Rogov had discovered the Kogurche system. The Lokaron had been picking up the pieces of their theories ever since.

They tried to tell themselves that it was a matter of chance, for Kogurche was an unusual system. In the first place, it had a binary star: a G0v primary component with an M2v red dwarf in an orbit which, while quite eccentric, hadn't prevented the formation of planets around either component. Those planets formed a tightly organized system around the central star, and masses and orbits had fallen into a pattern that made terraforming a more practical proposition than it had ever been in the Sol system. (As one human wag had remarked, it was as though Mars and Venus had traded orbits.) Furthermore, the secondary star had a "hot Jupiter"—a gas giant planet that had formed and then migrated inward to take up a very close orbit. This phenomenon, which even the Lokaron hadn't entirely accounted for, occurred with unfortunate frequency in planetary systems—unfortunate because in the course of its inward spiral, the gas giant destroyed any planets that might have formed in the star's liquid-water zone. But in the case of Kogurche B this was no loss, as a red-dwarf star was unlikely to have had a life-bearing planet. And the result was a wide region of orbiting planetary rubble almost as dense and resource-rich as Sol's asteroid belt had once been imagined to be.

All of this had made spaceflight a more attractive proposition for the Kogurin—compact bipeds averaging four and a half feet tall, an advantage when coping with the dismal mass ratios of chemical rockets—than it had ever been for humans. They had first ventured into orbit when their overall technological level had approximated that of Earth in the 1930s, and by the time it had reached the equivalent of the late twentieth century (which had taken them longer, as they had lacked the driving force of hot and cold ideological wars), they had a bustling interplanetary commerce, powered by a variety of fission rockets, ion drives, Orion drives, and other forms of nuclear propulsion from which, for various reasons, they had not flinched as late twentieth-century humanity had.

They had even established a very slow but self-sustaining importation of raw materials from Kogurche B.

At the same time, their society had gradually been overtaken by toxic sociological byproducts analogous to those that had produced the dominance of the Earth First Party. The Kogurin equivalent of the EFP hadn't been able to abandon space travel, which had become basic to the economy. But it could and did freeze technology before the computer revolution could take place, resulting in something which, to human eyes, bore an uncanny resemblance to "yesterday's tomorrow": interplanetary travel as it had been visualized by Robert Heinlein and Chesley Bonestell, and computers on a 1960 level at best. It also fossilized society under a self-perpetuating class of political careerists that had eventually devolved into the one-person rule of the "Implementer of Correct Social Organization," as humans translated the title.

Thus the Rogovon discoverers of Kogurche had found a wealthy, intensely industrialized system stagnating under what was at its best a kind of Confucian statism. And it had been stagnating for a long time. That last part made the discovery even more unsettling to the Lokaron than Earth had been, for they had to ask themselves what they would have found (or, perhaps, been found by) if Korgurche had continued developing instead of locking itself into an artificial stasis.

Nevertheless, the commercial possibilities were obvious, once the Rogovon had forced the system open by means similar to those used by the Tizathon on EFP-controlled Earth (but rather less subtle, as was the Rogovon way). Not many non-Rogovon interests among the Lokaron had become involved at first, for it was too far from their normal areas of operation. It was, however, in precisely the region where humans, newly released from the dead hand of the EFP, were beginning to expand. Rivalry would have been inevitable even if a legacy of poisonous hate hadn't already existed.

Then, in the midst of complex negotiations for concessions, the reigning Implementer had been assassinated, throwing the Kogurche society—already dissolving in a flood of new technology—into chaos. In such a setting, the human-Rogovon rivalry had grown increasingly cutthroat. In retrospect, the only surprise was that the conflict had festered for nine more years before erupting into open war in 2066.

Afterward, the peace settlement brokered by the other Lokaron powers had made Kogurche a recognized human sphere of influence, and the Implementer now hosted a human "resident advisor" appointed by the CNE. But, to the disgust of humans of Franklin Valdes's persuasion, those same Lokaron powers had prevented the Rogovon or any other Lokaron from being excluded altogether. So intrigue simmered under the system's seemingly placid surface.

They emerged through a transition gate that had been built with human know-how and local Kogurin resources. Andrew chuckled to himself at the sight of Persath paying toll. Ahead lay the yellowish Sol-like Kogurche A. Off to starboard the dim Kogurche B, currently near perihelion, glowed ruddily. Perath wordlessly shaped a course in the latter's direction and made various adjustments to his communications panel. All the while, his eyes periodically flicked toward the detector readouts, as they had been doing since the discovery that they were being shadowed.

For a long time, Andrew and Rachel held their peace, reluctant to disturb their pilot. Finally Persath swiveled his seat around and faced them.

"As you have probably surmised, we are headed toward the region of space where Reislon is to be found, if indeed he is currently present in this system. I have activated an automatic signaling device, operating on a special frequency, with which he provided me in case I should find it necessary to contact him in an emergency."

"So we can only wait until he responds?" asked Rachel.

"Yes. But in the meantime, there is a development I find disturbing." The translator performed the difficult feat of making Perath sound slightly crestfallen. "In the course of making transition . . . well, I was busy, and I temporarily lost sight of the vessel that had been following us in overspace. And now . . . I find I cannot locate that vessel."

"Uh, maybe whoever they are just continued on in overspace and didn't come through the transition gate," Rachel offered.

"Rubbish!" snapped Persath. "Their course would make no sense unless they intended to make transition here, nor would the fact that they were following us."

"Then where are they?" asked Andrew in what he thought were eminently reasonable tones.

"I don't know." In his perplexity, Persath momentarily forgot to be irritable. "They should show on my normal-space scanners."

There seemed nothing more to be said on the subject,

and they settled in to await Reislon's acknowledgment of Persath's signal while nervously speculating as to the nature of the mysterious intruders. They had not long to wait. A flashing light on the comm panel brought Persath scurrying up to the control console, where he performed various cryptic manipulations in silence.

"Uh, what does he say, Persath?"

"Nothing. The signaling device is precisely that: it sends an almost infinitesimally brief squirt of data on its peculiar frequency, announcing one's presence. Reislon has no wish to actually engage in radio conversation that might be overheard, thus compromising himself and . . . his associates."

"Persath," said Andrew grimly, "there's a *lot* you're not telling me!"

"How does it feel?" Rachel was heard to mutter.

"What's the story on these associates?" Andrew persisted, ignoring her.

"All will become clear in good time." Persath placed both hands in front of his chest and tilted his head back, which Andrew recalled was the Lokaron equivalent of a human raising a hand palm-outward to forestall an anticipated outburst. "Suffice it to say that their presence in this system is not generally known—not known at all, in point of fact, any more than is Reislon's—and they are rather particular about radio silence. Therefore Reislon is coming out to rendezvous with us. A physical meeting is far safer, as it will take place in the gravitational borderlands between the two components of the Kogurche system, where there is nothing except the occasional robotic ore-carrier."

A glance at the nav plot showed Andrew that this was indeed the case. Their drive was pushing them outward from Kogurche A, which was falling astern, and into a hyperbolic course which, if carried beyond a certain point, would result in capture by the gravity of Kogurche B.

Further questioning extracted nothing from Persath, and they again had to draw on their depleted store of patience. Finally Persath cut the drive and went into a free-fall trajectory. Presently, a radar blip that Persath identified as Reislon's ship appeared, matched vectors, and began to maneuver alongside. When it came into visual range Andrew saw that it was smaller than their own craft and of an altogether different design—a purely space-to-space shuttle, with no need for streamlining of any kind. Persath, at the control console, carried out a brief, low conversation via short-range communicator; Andrew couldn't make out what he was saying, and his translator implant didn't pick up what was emerging from the console at all.

The new arrival extruded a short access tube that affixed itself magnetically to their starboard entry port with a muffled clang. The lock wheezed open and their ears popped as air pressures equalized. A Lokar dressed in a form-fitting light duty space suit stepped into the saloon.

To anyone familiar with the Lokaron, Reislon'Sygnath was clearly a transmitter and probably early middle-aged. But in his amazement, Andrew noticed none of that at first. He had automatically assumed that a Harathon agent would belong to the subspecies of that *gevah* and its offshoot Gev-Tizath—the "default Lokaron" type as far as humans were concerned. So he wasn't prepared for Reislon to be only a little over seven feet tall, less thin of build than the Harathon norm, and with skin that was not the standard light blue but rather a kind of greenish-blue, almost aquamarine . . .

Reislon, well acquainted with humans and their facial expressions, gave him a close-mouthed Lokaron smile. "You surmise correctly. I am a hybrid. The product of a Harathon primary male and a Rogovon transmitter, to be exact."

In his embarrassment, Andrew had nothing to say.

To humans, the most alien thing about the Lokaron, compared to which the external differences were merely cosmetic, was their three-sex reproductive pattern. The egg-producing transmitter—larger, stronger and traditionally the sexual aggressor—was impregnated by the primary male and subsequently implanted the fertilized egg in the female, whose only function was to give birth. Both stages of the process were accomplished using organs analogous to human male equipment, which had given rise among humans to no end of bad jokes about the transmitters. Direct intercourse between primary males and females was reproductively pointless and was regarded as a perverse vice.

Almost equally frowned upon was intercourse between transmitters and primary males of the various genetically engineered planetary subspecies into which the race, never given to terraforming, had differentiated itself. This could produce offspring—but the offspring, like those of Terran horses and donkeys, were sterile. (There were exceptions like the Harathon and the

Tizathon, which were essentially the same subspecies, but even in such cases social barriers existed.) In addition, for reasons that evidently made sense in terms of Lokaron biology, the offspring were almost always transmitters. Transmitters with nothing to transmit . . .

"The primary male," Reislon continued imperturbably, "was a member of a Harathon trade mission, seduced by a socially prominent Rogovon transmitter who, for reasons best known to himself, saw fit to subsequently have intercourse with a female."

Andrew nodded with understanding. Abortion was a nonissue for the Lokaron. A transmitter carrying a fertilized egg need only refrain from implanting that egg in a female, and it would die after a certain period. And the "females" were irrelevant to the nature of the offspring, which they merely carried. Even in present-day Lokaron society, they were hardly ever seen or mentioned.

"Rogovon society," Reislon went on, "was not particularly open to me." (A studied understatement, Andrew suspected.) "Afterward I departed for Gev-Harath and eventually found myself in the service of Hov-Korth. But that is enough about me. I imagine the presence of the two of you accounts for this unexpected visit. Is this true, Persath?"

"Indeed, indeed." Persath fussily performed belated introductions. "Captain Roark and Ms. Arnstein are both connected to the late Admiral Nathan Arnstein—the former as his chief of staff and the latter as his daughter."

"The late Admiral Arnstein?" Reislon's aspect grew expressionless. "I regret to learn that. I communicated with him less than a year ago. How did he die?"

"That is what we are trying to ascertain," Andrew lied, "as the CNE government is not being candid."

"But why come to me?"

"Because we have good reason to believe that the Black Wolf Society is somehow connected with his death."

Reislon's expressionlessness became absolute.

"I've told them everything, Reislon," said Persath quietly.

"I see." Reislon grew brisk. "And you were right to do so. This brings matters to a head. We must—"

The strident squeal of an alarm shattered the air.

Persath bounded up to the control bridge with Andrew just behind him. He slapped at various controls, and a harsh voice filled the saloon. "You will lay to and stand by to be boarded. Any attempt to uncouple your vessels will result in your destruction."

It took a second for Andrew to realize that he hadn't heard it through his translator implant. It had been a human voice, speaking English. A voice he somehow thought he ought to recognize.

He had no time to dwell on it, because at appreciably the same instant a radar blip flickered into existence on the screen—a very nearby blip that hadn't been there before, so nearby that it simultaneously appeared on the viewscreen, feebly reflecting the distant light of the two Kogurche suns.

"Where did it come from?" Rachel whispered.

"It must be the ship that was following us in overspace," said Persath. "But how has it approached so closely undetected?"

Andrew said nothing, but he suddenly recalled what

Svyatog'Korth had told him about the advanced stealth features the Harathon had briefly glimpsed in 2055, and his eyes met Reislon's in a moment of shared understanding.

Persath activated the magnification feature, and the intruder filled the screen. It was a lifting body, apparently a commercial vessel small enough to have surface-landing capability, but at least three times the size of their own ship. And it had been modified. Andrew's practiced eye recognized laser-weapon blisters—short-ranged ones, but quite adequate under the circumstances.

Reislon spoke to Persath. "Our two craft, besides being unarmed, are incapable of maneuvering while locked together. We are quite helpless. Do not attempt to resist." He seemed to be taking it very calmly.

"Very well." Persath spoke into the communicator. "Come ahead." Then, with a defiant flash of his usual asperity, he glared at the blank comm screen. "Who are you? Show yourself!"

The screen came to life. A human face looked out, wearing a tight smile of vindictive triumph.

It was the face of Amletto Leong.

CHAPTER NINE

THE HOSTILE SHIP remained watchfully on station in its matching orbit as it deployed an interorbital car—little more than a life-support bubble for two with a very low-powered drive unit. As it approached them, Andrew excused himself momentarily. When he returned, Rachel noted, but did not comment on, a small bulge under his pullover shirt at the small of his back.

The car maneuvered alongside and sealed itself to their port-side airlock, opposite Reislon's shuttle. Persath, with a great show of put-upon dignity, opened the lock and two figures emerged.

Both were dressed in the same sort of light-duty vacc suit that Reislon wore. It was standard garb for anyone riding a spacecraft as flimsy as the interorbital car: a form-fitting jumpsuit of flexible nanofabric with a slight bulge in the back holding a concentrated oxygen supply and short-term temperature-control unit. To become an emergency space suit, it was only necessary for the wearer to don gloves and pull over a hoodlike helmet made of a transparent version of the same nanofabric. That fabric had the additional virtue of automatically adjusting itself to whoever was wearing it, over a fairly wide range of sizes and forms and even races.

That was unnecessary in this case, for both of the boarders were human. One carried what Andrew recognized as a laser weapon about the size of a turn-of-the-century submachine gun—a lower-powered version of a military laser rifle, doubtless currently on its stun setting, which could be used safely inside a spacecraft. He obviously wanted to use it, as he looked at the greenish tinge of Reislon's skin with unconcealed loathing.

The other was Leong, armed with a commercial version of Andrew's gauss pistol—not as good, but it could kill you just as dead. He wore the same expression they had seen in the comm screen, but even more tightly controlled than before. The ingratiating functionary they had known on Tizath-Asor was nowhere to be found.

"Don't try anything foolish," he said without preamble. "I am in continuous communication with my ship." He tapped a standard earpiece communicator he wore. "If anything happens to us—which I doubt, because we will shoot you without hesitation if you make trouble—it is under orders to open fire."

Persath, indignant beyond fear, stepped up almost to the muzzle of the gauss pistol. He loomed over the diminutive Leong even more than he would over most humans. "What is the meaning of this outrage? I am informed that you are an employee of the CNE diplomatic service. The government of Gev-Tizath will hear of this hostile act! I shall protest strongly, yes, *strongly* to the—"

"Shut up!" snapped Leong. His fixed expression slipped, and what could be momentarily glimpsed behind it was ugly indeed. "As our prisoners, you're in no position to bluster."

"Yeah," the other man snarled. "Prisoners of *humans*! Get used to it!"

Leong irritably waved him to silence. "We primarily want you two for questioning," he said, indicating Persath and Reislon, "concerning the whereabouts of a certain . . . artifact." He turned to Andrew and Rachel. "You will have to come, too, as we can hardly let you go. Also, you may be able to provide useful information."

"You've already used us plenty," said Rachel expressionlessly, "letting us lead you to Resilon. But why is the CNE doing this?"

"Oh, we don't work for the damned gutless CNE," the laser-armed goon began.

"Quiet, you cretin!" rasped Leong.

"That's right, isn't it, Leong?" said Andrew. "Naval Intelligence might play it this way, but I doubt it. This is more the style of you people in the Black Wolf Society." Leong's expression told him his guess had hit home. He decided to risk another stab in the dark. "The only question in my mind is this: Are you also working for Admiral Valdes?"

For a moment, Andrew thought Leong was going to have a stroke. Then he smoothed out his features and apparently decided that dissembling was more trouble than it was worth under the circumstances. "As he's repeatedly stated, he isn't associated with us in any way. We do find much to agree with in his platform. We share his disgust with the CNE's groveling acceptance of the peace settlement that was forced on us by the Lokaron powers, robbing Earth of the full fruits of its victory. We're working toward the complete expulsion of the Rogovon interlopers from the Lupus frontier."

Using the profits from drugs and extortion and human trafficking, Andrew mentally finished for him. He considered saying it out loud in an attempt to provoke Leong into losing control, but decided it probably wouldn't have that effect. Leong's words might be those of a fanatic spouting doctrine—and the goon certainly took it that way, judging from his stupidly rapt expression—but to Andrew it had a strangely hollow quality, as though he was consciously trying to *seem* like a fanatic spouting doctrine. He confirmed the impression by dropping the oration as abruptly as he might have switched off a recording and turning businesslike.

"Now my ship will come alongside and we will commence transferring the four of you to it, after which your two ships will be destroyed, leaving no evidence. Afterwards—*what?*" Suddenly, Leong's attention was riveted on what he was hearing through his earpiece, and he swung around to look at the viewscreen, on which his ship still showed at full magnification.

Andrew at once saw what was happening. The laser blisters were swiveling in their mounts, turning away from Persath's ship toward some other target. Of course the laser beams were invisible in vacuum, but a sudden flash like that of heat lightning from off to the side suggested that they were being worked, and had hit something . . . an incoming missile, perhaps.

"Power up the drive and get out of here!" snapped Leong into his communicator. "We'll break this ship loose and try to escape." Then he turned back around, gauss pistol pointed at his prisoners. "Stun them!" he ordered the goon.

That worthy moved to comply, raising his laser weapon.

Up to this point, Reislon was the only one present who had not said a word. In fact, he had somehow made himself so perfectly ignorable that Andrew hadn't even thought of him as being silent—hadn't thought of him, period. Which made it all the more startling when he exploded out of his inconspicuousness, thrust out a hand, pointed at something behind the goon, and shouted, "*Look!*"

The goon turned his head to look (he would have been more than human if he had not), causing the laser weapon to swing out of line.

Reislon brought his outstretched arm down slightly, and raised the hand as a human would when making the *stop* gesture.

The six-digited Lokaron hand was different from the human version in many ways, just as the Lokaron skeletal structure in general differed. But raising it in the way Reislon had done exposed something analogous to the human "heel of the hand." Now he pointed it at the goon's direction and swept it horizontally across.

Andrew heard the sharp, vicious rapid-fire snapping sound as the tiny steel slivers of a gauss needler—a hundred of them in a single burst—broke the sound barrier. The long, thin needles were harmless against any sort of rigid barrier, but in living tissue they were lethally unstable. A stream of them sleeted across the goon's head, with no knock-back effect and the characteristic near-bloodlessness of instant death. He simply slumped to the deck.

Leong was already turning to bring his Gauss pistol to bear on Reislon. It gave Andrew a chance to reach behind him and pull out his M-3.

Leong saw him out of the corner of his eye and whirled back toward him . . . while Andrew was still in the act of clicking off his safety.

In what seemed like slow motion, Andrew watched Leong's muzzle come into line and knew himself for a dead man.

All at once they were bathed in a blinding glare as the viewscreen became a momentary sun.

A missile got past the lasers and the deflection shields, Andrew had time to think.

With a cry compounded of rage and despair, Leong turned to stare at the funeral pyre of his ship.

It gave Andrew the split second he needed.

He intended to use an autoburst to shoot Leong's gauss pistol out of his hand and take him alive (though doubtless minus the hand). But the wave front of expanding gas from the explosion reached them, rocking their ship and throwing off his aim. The first 3mm bullet shattered Leong's wrist, sending his pistol flying. But the rest of the burst slanted downward across Leong's abdomen, stitching a row of tiny holes. With a rasping moan, he sank to his knees and toppled over forward.

It had all happened too quickly for Rachel or Persath to even react. Now the former turned aside and looked like she was going to be sick, but mastered herself, while the latter still seemed marbled in shock.

Andrew turned to Reislon, who was critically examining the hole in the heel of his hand where the tiny flechettes had torn away a covering of artificial skin. Their eyes met. "It sometimes has its uses," said Reislon urbanely.

Surgically implanted weapons, operated by direct neural induction, were highly illegal on Earth. Among the Lokaron, a general distaste for implants in general made legal prohibition almost superfluous. But, Andrew reminded himself, Reislon was an atypical Lokar in many ways. He dismissed the matter from his mind and gestured at the viewscreen, where the white-hot debris was rapidly dissipating.

"Your associates?" he queried.

Reislon, an old hand with humans, nodded his head. "I would hardly have come here alone, without what you call backup."

Further explanation could wait, Andrew decided. He knelt beside Leong, who was still moaning softly, and turned him over. He seemed about to speak, but his mouth only produced a bloody foam. There was obviously no saving him, although he was taking his time about dying, considering his assortment of perforated vital organs.

"Leong," Andrew began—but then he staggered back with a nonverbal cry of horror, because before his eyes Leong began to *change*.

Leong's skin rippled and flowed in delicate patterns as it changed color and texture and became a purplish-white integument, too pale to be called lavender, repellently translucent. At the same time, his facial structure and entire body began to writhe and reshape. There was a creaking sound as the bone structure altered and foreshortened, the nanofabric of the suit contracting to keep pace with the change. Andrew also heard a grinding sound, but then realized it was his own teeth, in a rictus of shock.

A moan of agony finally escaped the small lipless orifice that was no longer a human mouth, rising to a kind of choked shriek that could never be produced by a human throat. The spray of froth was no longer the same shade of pink. The body went into a sudden violent convulsion and then lay still. It was dead, and the obscene transformation was over.

Behind him, Andrew heard a gagging followed by a splash. This time, Rachel was being sick. There was no other sound.

They all stared down at that which they had known as Amletto Leong. It was a biped less than five feet tall, slightly built even in proportion to its height, with arms almost as long as its legs. Those arms terminated in disproportionately large hands whose four spidery fingers were all mutually opposable. The face was dominated by huge golden-black eyes. There was no nose as such, only a small but complex orifice flush with the face, which tapered from a wide forehead to a tiny mouth and almost nonexistent chin. The head had an unpleasantly thin covering of white hairs or perhaps cilia. The pool of blood that was beginning to spread from under it was a kind of dark copper color.

Rachel wiped her mouth and pointed unsteadily at the thing. "What *is* that?" she whispered.

Andrew turned to the two Lokaron, whose race had explored a significant fraction of the galaxy. "Do you know . . . ?"

"No." Reislon's usual urbanity was in abeyance, but the translator conveyed calmness. "I have never heard of this species. Nor have I ever heard of *any* species which could alter its form in this manner."

"It's a myth among us," said Rachel. "Were-animals, usually wolves."

"We lack even such a myth. Incidentally, as you will have noted, the transformation did not overtake the other one." Actually they hadn't noted it, in their stupefaction. But in fact the goon's body was still as human as it had ever been.

"This requires study," said Reislon in a masterpiece of understatement. "Fortunately, we will soon have the facilities available." He indicted the viewscreen, where a ship was gliding into view. Andrew automatically classified it as what the CNE Navy called a frigate: a light combatant, the lightest capable of mounting its own transition engines (the lessons of the events of 2030 had not been ignored, and the Lokaron navies had begun mounting such engines on lighter vessels than cruisers), although heavier than the corvettes that were the heaviest capable of landing on and taking off from a planetary surface. It was not intended for fleet actions, but it was more than adequate for the kind of battle it had just fought. A vague familiarity made him feel he ought to be able to identify its class, but he wasn't exactly thinking straight at the moment.

"If you will," Reislon said to Persath, indicating the post-side passenger lock.

"Oh . . . yes. Of course." Persath gave what seemed to be a delayed-action shudder and came out of shock. He busied himself clearing the lock by disengaging the intership car and letting it drift off into infinity. In the meantime, Reislon went to the comm console and hailed the approaching ship. A face appeared on the comm screen.

Rachel gasped. Andrew didn't even do that. He had had too many shocks to his sensibilities already.

It was a Lokaron face, as expected. But it was a green-skinned face, and it was broader than the faces of humanity's Harathon and Tizathon associates, and it was . . . *Rogovon!* Andrew forced down the emotions that a face like that aroused in every human.

He turned and gave Reislon a long look. "Well, I see you finally decided which side to come down on."

CHAPTER TEN

"THIS," SAID REISLON, formally introducing the Rogovon transmitter they had seen in the comm screen, "is Borthru'Goron."

The newly arrived ship—which Andrew now recognized as a Rogovon *Potematu*-class frigate, an obsolescent prewar design—had maneuvered alongside and sealed its access tube to the port-side lock. Borthru had entered: a stereotypical Rogovon in ways besides his green skin, for he was less than seven feet tall and almost as broadly built as a human, in keeping with the almost one-Terran-g planet for which their subspecies had been gengineered. It was not a body type that the other Lokaron admired.

"And these," Reislon continued, "are Rachel Arnstein—"

"Arnstein?" Borthru cut in. His voice held the oddly

metallic-sounding quality that was one of the things setting the Rogovon apart from other Lokaron. "Would that be . . . ?"

"Yes." Rachel's voice rang with quiet defiance. "My father was Admiral Nathan Arnstein—a name I imagine is familiar to all Rogovon."

Andrew wondered if it was only his imagination that the hulking Lokar flinched just a bit.

"And I," he said before Reislon could continue, "am Captain Andrew Roark of the CNE Navy. I was formerly Admiral Arnstein's chief of staff, after previously serving under him in a number of capacities."

"Including, perhaps, the Battle of Upsilon Lupus?" Borthru asked mildly.

"I was executive officer of a battlecruiser there."

"Ah." Borthru's eyes seemed to darken to a deep gold, but his voice remained mild. "I have heard that there were inexplicable delays in acceptance of some of our ships' surrender signals there—fatal delays, in certain cases."

Andrew met those eyes unflinchingly. "I've heard that, too. I've also heard that Gev-Rogov had struck my world with a kinetic-kill weapon, intended as a preliminary to wiping it clean of all life, including my species."

They glared at each other for a silent heartbeat. It was Borthru's eyes that slid away.

"I cannot deny historical fact. Especially when the act in question was so very much in character for the regime we are trying to overthrow. It should come as no surprise to you, as your own history should teach you what totalitarian regimes are capable of."

"What?" Andrew blinked. "You mean you're not Rogovon Navy?"

"That's what I was about to explain, Andrew," said Reislon patiently. "I am associated with what you would term a revolutionary organization, whose rogue fleet is secretly based here in the outskirts of the Kogurche system, outside the jurisdiction of Gev-Rogov."

"Yes," Borthru exclaimed, and the translator registered bitterness. "We're sick of Gev-Rogov being a pariah among the other *gevahon*. It isn't just that they find us physically unappealing. It's our centralized, authoritarian government that's the real freak."

Andrew found himself nodding. "Yes. The governments of the other *gevahon* are so limited that they're barely governments at all by human standards. The ideologues who were running Earth when the Tizathon arrived never recovered from the shock!"

"You understand, then, why we want Gev-Rogov to become a normal *gevah*, instead of continuing to stagnate under a system that, as our defeat in the war showed, is as corrupt and incompetent as it is repressive." Borthru seemed to rein himself in. "I'm sorry. I didn't intend to burden you with a political speech."

Andrew turned to Reislon. "So this is where you went when you dropped from sight after the war."

"Yes, but I had been working with the revolutionary elements in Gev-Rogov even before the war."

"Are you aware that Svyatog'Korth thinks you were working for Gev-Rogov Intelligence at that time?"

"So does Gev-Rogov Intelligence, since I was pretending to do precisely that. It was thus that I was able to maintain very indirect lines of contact with the revolutionaries."

Andrew struggled to keep it all straight. "And *we* think you were working for the CNE during the same pre-war period, although as far as I know Svyatog isn't aware of it. Was *that* also a pretense?"

"Not at all. I passed some quite useful information on to your service and aided it in planting a certain amount of disinformation. You must understand, I never felt I was in any way betraying my employer, Hov-Korth, in any of this. My goal, a reformed Gev-Rogov integrated into mainstream Lokaron civilization, would be to the benefit of everyone, including Hov-Korth and, incidentally, Earth. Also, I was working to prevent the war." Reislon gave Borthru a sidelong glance. "This did not endear me to certain factions among the revolutionary underground."

"Yes." Borthru's bitterness was back in full force. "We were fools—children! We actually *wanted* a war, thinking that defeat would discredit and destabilize the regime, creating a power vacuum for us to fill. Reislon warned us that we were dreamers, and that the only result would be tightened repression. And he was right. Oh, there was some disorder at first, and a great deal of outrage over the regime's mishandling of the war. The government offered some concessions as a sop. But then, as soon as quiet had returned and the regime felt secure enough, they clamped down, rescinding all the reforms, and now things are worse than before."

Andrew considered this in light of what CNEN Intelligence knew, and it fit. After the war, despite all attempts at censorship, it had been clear that Gev-Rogov had been wracked by political upheavals, brutally suppressed.

"There were mutinies in the fleet," Borthru continued. "Some succeeded. Those whose ships had integral transition capability—including the one I led—escaped into over-space. We met at prearranged rendezvous points—we had had that much forethought at least—and decided that we needed to establish a base outside Gev-Rogov. The Kogurche system at first seemed an odd choice, but the more we thought about it, it was rather like . . . like . . ."

"Hiding in plain sight," Rachel suggested.

The translator evidently had a little trouble with that, as it often did with paradoxes, for Borthru paused perceptibly. "Yes. It had certain other advantages. It was as close to Gev-Rogov as we could safely get. It was easy to remain undetected in these unfrequented gravitational hinterlands between the two component suns. And once the treaty came into operation and allowed Lokaron—including Rogovon—access to Kogurche, we were able to pass unnoticed on the system's inhabited planets."

"I arranged my own disappearance at this point." Reislon picked up the thread. "I realized I would not be able to sustain the rather complex game I had been playing for much longer. And you were right, in a sense, Andrew. For all my high regard for Svyatog'Korth, honesty forced me to confront the fact that my first priority was and always had been the liberation of Gev-Rogov from the regime that had . . . mistreated me in my youth. Finally, I was disgusted by the failure of my efforts to prevent the war—a war I was more and more convinced was being promoted behind the scenes by the Black Wolf Society."

"Which doubtless was also behind this attack on you," Borthru said grimly.

"So it was. But . . . there is more." Reislon turned and led the way to a storage area with temperature controls that allowed it to be used as an improvised meat locker. While waiting for Borthru, they had loaded the two corpses into it, with Andrew's flesh crawling at the touch of "Leong," although he had retained enough presence of mind to notice that the body had seemed very light even for the short, slight human they had thought they'd known. Now Reislon opened it and slid out the tray on which the bodies lay. Borthru made a rustling sound that Andrew recognized as the Lokaron equivalent of a sharp indrawing of human breath.

"It gets worse," said Rachel. "On Tizath-Asor we knew this being as a human, working for the CNE embassy. He still appeared to be one when he showed up here and declared himself a member of the Black Wolf Society. And then, as he was dying, he somehow changed into . . . *this.*"

"What's more," Andrew put in, "he followed us here from Gev-Tizath in a ship using a form of cloaking technology more advanced than any we know—except that of certain ships briefly glimpsed by a Harathon vessel in the Sol system in 2055. Yes, Reislon, I know about that."

"I believe," said Persath carefully, "that this calls for further study."

"Agreed," said Borthru firmly. "Fortunately, we have the facilities for it."

✧ ✧ ✧

The three vessels proceeded in formation to the headquarters of the rogue Rogovon fleet. It appeared in the viewscreen as a sprawling junk sculpture, a madman's caricature of a space station, obviously added on to over the years with components surreptitiously brought to this system and bits and pieces of damaged or uselessly obsolete ships, each segment with its own artificial-gravity generators. Escher would have gone crazy trying to figure it out.

They disembarked in what must have passed for a central reception area, although it looked more like a deserted factory. After the one Tizath-Asor G they had been used to, a near-Terran gravity pull seemed almost burdensome. Persath didn't trouble to conceal the fact that he thought so.

Borthru and Reislon had been in almost constant communication with the station, and a fair-sized group awaited them. Andrew, who prided himself on his *savoir faire* among Lokaron, now realized it extended only to the "good guy" genotypes; he could not yet overcome his discomfort in the presence of so many Rogovon. But one member of the group stood out by reason of several departures from the stereotype. For one thing, he was short even for a Rogovon—only about six and a half feet—and less inclined than most Rogovon to what passed among the Lokaron for stockiness. Secondly, he was dressed, even in these surroundings, in the universal Lokaron semiformal attire of double-breasted tunic and sleeveless robe, suggesting an old-fashioned, shabby-genteel fustiness. Possibly accounting for the last, his old age was obvious even to a non-expert like Andrew. Borthru introduced him as Zhygon'Trogak, the revolutionaries' chief medical officer, head of research, and general polymath. He listened with avid interest to the story behind the two corpses.

"Exobiology is one of my interests," he told them, "including the study of humans. And we have fairly up-to-date biological sensors and other tools here." He took the bodies away, and Andrew and Rachel were assigned quarters where they waited with all the patience they could muster.

It was an awkward wait. The quarters were most charitably described as "functional," less charitably as "industrial-hideous," and they were not designed for human occupancy, least of all for privacy of humans of different genders. The two of them established a set of unspoken protocols for handling the problem, but the time still dragged.

Finally Zhygon reported his findings to a group consisting of the two humans, Reislon, Persath, Borthru, and a couple of members of the executive committee that governed the ragtag refugee community. "The human-appearing corpse is, in fact, indisputably human. The other is, obviously, something else. What that something is, I cannot say. The species is entirely unfamiliar."

"But," Rachel protested, "he *looked* human! We never suspected him of being anything else. He passed for human well enough to get a job with the CNE diplomatic service. For God's sake, he passed for human with a bunch of human chauvinists like the Black Wolf Society! How can that be possible? Shape-shifting like that is supposed to be a fantasy."

"That was what took me so long. Fortunately, I was

able to draw on a human analogue, which may make it easier for you to understand.

"Put very simply, this species—let us call them the Shape-Shifters for convenience—has a gland somewhat similar to the human pineal gland, producing a hormone similar to a more extreme form of pinearin. The result is something beyond the most extreme case of hyperpinealism. It affects the surface tension of the protoplasm's cells in such a way as to make the entire body plastic and malleable. And unlike hyperpinealism among humans, which is an allergic reaction, this is produced and controlled as a conscious act of will. Evidently the hormone also reroutes the sympathetic nervous system to the cerebral cortex, or its equivalent."

Andrew wasn't sure what to marvel at more: Zhygon's knowledge of human biochemistry, or the ability of the translator software to cope with all this.

"This ability must have limitations," Persath argued.

"Undoubtedly. First of all, while it may be able to arrange and shape its organs to resemble the imitated species, their function would remain closer to their own species."

"So their heartbeat might be slower or faster than a normal human heartbeat?" Rachel asked.

"Precisely," Persath continued. "More importantly, it must be able to affect the skeletal structure in a very limited way, so it can only assume the shape of a quadruped or a two-armed biped. Furthermore, there must be very definite limits on the degree to which density, and therefore size, can be varied. This is a small species, as sentients go. I am surprised it was able to assume the form of a human."

"Leong was a small man," Rachel said.

"No doubt. And if you had weighed him, he would have proven to be even lighter than he looked."

"Something else," said Andrew. "Leong was obviously of mixed ethnic background, sort of racially nondescript—an average human being. Maybe the Shape-Shifters find that easier than trying to convincingly reproduce a well-marked set of ethnic features." He wasn't sure how much this meant to the Rogovon, in whose eyes all humans probably looked alike. But in Reislon he thought to detect the body language of agreement.

"And," Rachel added, "on today's Earth there are more and more racially mixed people." A thought seemed to occur to her. "But how is it that they can speak English like they were born to it?"

"Oh, that must be relatively simple," Zhygon explained. "The technique of imprinting a new language on the speech centers by direct neural induction is well known. We Lokaron hardly ever use it because, as you may know, we find most such procedures to be vaguely distasteful, and because the ubiquity of translation devices renders it unnecessary."

"Still," Rachel speculated, "each infiltrator must be a unique work of art, as it were. Another Shape-Shifter, even if it could assume exactly the same human form, would bring its own personality to the . . . performance."

"Indubitably," Zhygon agreed. "I don't believe we have to worry about multiple copies of the same person."

"Question," interjected Reislon. "Captain Roark killed Leong with a gauss pistol. I should think that a Shape-Shifter in the state you have described would be able to ignore bullets."

"Except maybe *silver* bullets," Rachel muttered *sotto voce*.

"An astute observation, Reislon" said Zhygon. "And you are undoubtedly correct in the case of a *single* bullet, or perhaps even more than one. But the condition of the corpse made it clear that Captain Roark fired an entire autoburst, inflicting so much trauma to so many organs that it overloaded the capacity of the protoplasm to simply reconfigure itself."

"I thought he seemed to take an awfully long time to die, under the circumstances," said Andrew.

"So," mused Reislon, "we will find these beings very hard to kill, despite their seeming physical fragility. I doubt if any number of flechettes from my implanted weapon would have sufficed, given the extremely small diameter of the perforation they inflict."

"But why did he change back when he died?" Rachel wanted to know.

"I have a theory on that," said Zhygon, who seemed to have a lot of theories. "As I mentioned, the process is a conscious one—although after the initial transformation it must become more or less automatic and effortless, since they are obviously able to remain in their assumed forms for extended periods of time, and function normally while doing so. As death approaches and consciousness fades, the mind becomes incapable of sustaining it. If you had inflicted *instantaneous* death—which, as Reislon has deduced, would take some doing—I suspect the body would have been left frozen in its human form."

"But," argued Persath, "it could still be identified as nonhuman by genetic testing."

"Or even by a reasonably thorough scan with a hand-held medical sensor such as the one I performed," Zhygon agreed. "Only . . . it would never have occurred to anyone to perform such a scan."

After a few heartbeats, Andrew thought someone should break the general thoughtful silence. "Well," he said briskly, "what are we left with? What do we know about this race? Let's start with what we *don't* know: their name, their origin, their objectives. We do know that they have the ability to masquerade as humans—"

"And, we must assume, other four-limbed vertebrates as well," Persath interjected.

"—and have used that ability to infiltrate the Black Wolf Society."

"They may have come to dominate it," said Rachel. "You can add that to your list of things we don't know about them."

"If they've infiltrated it thoroughly," said Reislon, with the air of an expert in such matters, "then they've been active among humans for a while. These things take time."

"Longer than you think," said Zhygon. "I imagine this species has, courtesy of evolution, an almost instinctual ability to assume the forms of various animals on its planet or origin. But masquerading as an alien life form must be an acquired skill. It surely required a lengthy and extensive study of human physiology."

"Their superior stealth technology must have helped with that," said Andrew grimly. "We don't know what else they have that's technologically superior. Or how long they've been at this game of infiltration. Or what they've infiltrated besides the Black Wolf Society."

"The catalogue of our ignorance grows and grows," grumbled Persath.

"But we have one definite clue to build on, Persath. Remember when Leong, as I suppose we have to continue calling him, said he wanted you and Reislon for questioning about an artifact? I think we know what that artifact must be, don't we?"

"Yes," said Persath with a sidelong glance at Reislon. "I believe we do. For whatever reason, the Black Wolf Society—or at least the Shape-Shifters behind it—are very, very interested in the device brought back from Mars in 2055."

"And they must not know that the Imperial Temple of the Star Lords has it." Andrew nodded. "Otherwise they wouldn't have needed to go through this whole elaborate scheme—or they could have simply infiltrated the Temple."

"But *why* are they so interested in it?" Rachel sounded bewildered—understandably, Andrew thought.

"That's what we need to find out. It seems to be the only line of inquiry open to us." Andrew turned to Persath and Reislon. "We've got to go to the Sol system and—"

Borthru had said nothing for a long time. Now he cut in brusquely. "You use the word 'we' rather freely, Captain Roark. I remind you that our organization's purpose is the overthrow of the present regime in Gev-Rogov. And from what I have heard so far, this is an internal human problem." He gave the distinct impression that he did not lavish a great deal of concern on human problems.

"But these Shape-Shifters are a menace to us all," Rachel protested.

"Are they?" Borthru gave Zhygon a shrewd look. "You explained why these beings are barely able to masquerade as humans, and small humans at that. In your opinion, would they be able to convincingly assume the form of Lokaron?"

"I see no way," said the old scientist forthrightly. "Infants, perhaps. But what would be the point?"

"Just so," said Borthru with an air of self-satisfied triumph. "So you will understand, Captain, that we cannot divert any of our all-too-inadequate resources to aid in your quest, when these Shape-Shifters do not pose a threat to our race."

"I'm not sure I agree with that last," said Reslon with his trademark deceptive diffidence. "They are working through the Black Wolf Society, and may in fact have made it their tool. Its agenda is implicitly anti-Lokaron in general, and explicitly anti-Rogovon in particular."

"I've always thought you exaggerate that group's importance," Borthru argued. "And besides, if it's opposed to the present Gev-Rogov regime, then we and it may actually be . . . well, scarcely potential allies, but perhaps . . ."

"Fellow travelers," Rachel suggested archly.

"I doubt if xenophobes like the Black Wolf are interested in Rogovon internal political arrangements," cautioned Reislon. "You've admitted that you and others of your persuasion fell victim to wishful thinking before the war. Do not do so again. We can't afford it."

Borthru glared at him but had no reply. Reislon had been proved right too often.

"All we would need," Reislon resumed, "would be a

single small ship with integral transition capability, very heavily stealthed. We're not planning to fight any battles."

"Very well," Borthru conceded. "I suppose this does merit further investigation."

"We will also require a couple of technicians with the requisite equipment for studying this artifact."

"Yes, I can provide that," said Zhygon.

"One other thing, Zhygon," said Andrew. "The handheld medical sensor you referred to earlier . . . Could I trouble you for one, and a short course on how to use it?"

CHAPTER ELEVEN

THE *TROVYR* WAS A FRIGATE, like the *Potematu*-class that had rescued them, but of a different class. It was specialized for scouting and covert planetary insertions, so it deemphasized armament and defenses in favor of speed and cutting-edge stealth technology—or at least cutting-edge as of a few years ago, for like everything else the rebel Rogovon fleet had, it was prewar. Something else not emphasized was spaciousness of living accommodations. Things were decidedly cramped with four passengers aboard, especially given the requirement that the two humans be given separate quarters.

Borthru had insisted on taking command of it. (*Not* "she," as Andrew constantly had to remind himself. The Lokaron did not share humanity's habit of giving ships a gender.) At first Andrew was apprehensive at the prospect of a skipper whose heart wasn't really in the mission. But another nautical tradition that had never occurred to the Lokaron was that of treating a ship's captain as its absolute despot. Borthru deferred to Reislon in everything not involving the internal running of the ship.

They emerged from overspace more than a light-hour from Sol and well outside the plane of the ecliptic, then worked their way slowly sunward, minimizing their energy output. Such a small ship, so heavily stealthed, had little reason to fear detection, but Borthru insisted on caution and Reislon concurred. Andrew could see their point. The war had been over for seven years, but he wasn't sure a Rogovon warship caught in the solar system would be given an opportunity to explain its political alignment. This didn't stop Persath from grumbling about the crowded discomfort of the voyage, and Andrew could sympathize with that too.

They finally inserted themselves into a solar orbit trailing Earth. In free fall and effectively immune to detection, they discussed their plans. In particular, they would require inconspicuous planetside transportation.

"Will you solicit the aid of your Legislative Assemblyman Valdes?" asked Borthru, who by now had heard the entire story at length.

"No," said Andrew. "I don't entirely trust Valdes. There's only one person on Earth I'm absolutely certain I can trust. One *living* person," he added, to the puzzlement of his listeners. "And as luck would have it, she lives fairly close to where we need to go."

The ship's gig would hold four, and Reislon knew how to pilot it. Even more heavily stealthed than the frigate relative to its mass and energy signature, it had no trouble landing undetected on peacetime Earth's nightside in a thinly populated area. It settled with the noiselessness and flamelessness of reactionless drives onto an upland meadow in the Rockies. Only then did Andrew make a call by ordinary cell phone.

"Andy!" exclaimed Katy Doyle-Roark. "Where have you been? I've been worried sick, but I didn't want to risk making inquiries. I haven't heard from you since—"

"Mom, it's a long story. Right now, I need your help. Specifically, I need an air-car."

"Where are you?" was all she said. The concerned mother was abruptly gone, displaced by the woman who had been an undercover intelligence agent long ago.

"Not far from you—just a little higher up, to the west. I have a beacon you can home in on."

"All right." Katy had some fairly non-standard devices available to her, such as a small military-grade transponder.

"And just so you'll know what to expect, I'm in a ship's gig. A *Rogovon* ship's gig."

"All right," Katy repeated. She knew when questions had to wait.

By the time Katy arrived, dawn was breaking over the eastward ranges, casting a morning glow over the pine-clothed upper slopes of the surrounding mountains and the aspens below, beginning to show the first pale-green overlay of oncoming spring. The approaching air-car cleared the eastern escarpments, reflecting the dawn rays, and settled alongside the gig. Katy and Andrew exchanged a brief, hard hug in the thin air, still cold at these altitudes, before he introduced his companions.

"Mom, this is Rachel Arnstein, daughter of the late Admiral Arnstein. Like me, she's been trying to ascertain the circumstances of her father's death." His hope that his mother would take the hint and not blurt out the fact of Arnstein's suicide was not disappointed. She merely expressed her condolences in general terms. Rachel, for once, looked overawed in the presence of a living legend.

"And this," he continued, "is Reislon'Sygnath, formerly of Hov-Korth intelligence."

"I've heard stories about you," said Katy. She didn't turn a hair at Reislon's half-Rogovon appearance.

"And I about you and your late husband," said Reislon urbanely.

"And this," Andrew finished, "is Persath'Loven, a Tizathon scholar who has authored several highly regarded works on human studies." It never hurt to stroke Persath whenever possible.

"Yes, I've heard of your works." Andrew wasn't sure his mother was telling the truth, but Persath looked gratified. "I must say, Andy, you've certainly collected an *intriguing* group of companions."

"That's not the half of it. As I said, it's a long story. Let's go to your place before I try to tell it. Your air-car will hold me and Rachel and Persath. Reislon will wait here with the gig—maybe move it somewhere even more inconspicuous if he can find one."

"All right." Katy pulled up the hood of her coat against a gust of chill wind and visibly suppressed her curiosity. "I suppose the house *would* be more comfortable. Let's go."

". . . And that's the story," Andrew finished, hoarse

from so much talking, and took a pull on his Bourbon. They all found they needed drinks. Alcohol affected the Lokaron nervous system in much the same way as the human one, and Katy kept a supply of voleg for guests. But in his earlier days on Earth, Persath had acquired a taste for Scotch.

"Andy," said Katy at last, "this is quite a lot to adjust to. In particular, these Shape-Shifters are the ultimate counterintelligence nightmare."

"I know." He reached into a pocket and pulled out a datachip. "This has, among other things, pictures of the dead shape-shifter."

She waved it aside. "Oh, there will be time for that later. The question is, where do you go from here?"

"There's only one direction we can go, because we have only one lead: the fact that the Shape-Shifters are searching for what we might as well call the Cydonia artifact. They let me and Rachel lead them to Reislon, who they evidently thought was the one who knew."

Persath spoke up. "It is reassuring to know that they are fallible. All along it was *I* who had the information, and they knew where I could be found." Andrew knew Lokaron expressions well enough to have to smother a smile as Persath suddenly realized what might have happened to him if they *hadn't* been mistaken.

"Well," Rachel said, "the point is that we need to get access to this thing and find out what's so important about it."

"That's not all you need to do," said Katy in a voice that made them all look up. "You need to *steal* it." She smiled at their expressions. "Andy, you're not an intelligence specialist.

Steve White

I was. One of the fundamental truisms is that secrets can't be kept forever. If beings with the special abilities these have, and the Black Wolf Society to work through, want to find this out badly enough, sooner or later they will. And when they do, can you imagine a bunch of woo-woos like the Imperial Temple of the Star Lords being able to assure its security? No, it can't be left in their custody."

"Then whose custody?"

"If you had asked me that this time yesterday I would, of course, have said the CNE. But now . . . Christ! The Shape-Shifters may have infiltrated *anything*."

"Anything *human*," Rachel corrected. "If Zhygon knows what he's talking about, they can't infiltrate the Lokaron."

"That's right. So the only safe place is this secret Rogovon fleet." Katy shook her head. "I never dreamed I'd live to hear myself say something like that!"

"Politics makes strange bedfellows," Andrew quoted.

"So I've heard." Katy smiled reminiscently. "Your father used to say there were some well-known figures he suspected were pretty strange bedfellows even before they went into politics!" She turned serious again. "All right. What do you need?"

"I need to know the current leadership of the Imperial Temple of the Star Lords," said Persath.

"Easy enough." Katy led the way from the great room to her office and booted the computer. A brief search showed Persath what he wanted.

"A stroke of luck!" he exclaimed. "After almost eighteen years I was afraid there would be no one left in the hierarchy that I knew. But Arnold Waemhofer is now the

Steward, which is what they call their titular leader, who according to their doctrines is acting in the capacity of stewardship for the lost galactic empire until it returns."

"They must have gotten it from Tolkien," Rachel muttered to Andrew.

"In 2056 he was a relatively junior member of the group that showed me the artifact and the preserved body. He must he quite elderly now. But hopefully he will remember me."

A phone call resulted in a series of tedious delays as Persath was shunted through successive organizational levels. Finally the screen showed the face of a well-fed man with silvery gray hair and mild blue eyes in a good-natured face. He looked extremely well-preserved, doubtless by courtesy of Lokaron biotech. Andrew wondered if he appreciated the irony of that. His surprise at seeing a Lokaron face in the screen was obvious but he politely smoothed it out.

"Dr. Waemhofer," Persath began, "you probably don't remember me, but we met eighteen years ago. I am Persath'Loven."

Waemhofer beamed as individual recognition overcame alienness. "Why, my dear Persath, I had no idea you were on Earth again! Of course I remember you. We had many stimulating discussions then. We were gratified by the interest that you, a Lokar, showed in the revelations of the Imperial Temple."

"And I, in turn, was flattered by your willingness to share with me some of the highly confidential scientific evidence that proves the truth of those revelations."

"Ah . . . well . . . ahem! Yes . . ." Waemhofer seemed

to look around him nervously, as though in search of listeners.

"As you know," Persath soothed, "I fully lived up to my promise not to publish any mention of . . . that to which I just alluded, and which I will not identify now."

Waemhofer looked so relieved that Andrew expected him to break out a handkerchief and wipe off the sweat that had popped out on his smooth brow. "Indeed you did, Persath. We took a great risk by trusting you. But you justified our faith in your word of honor, and we are grateful for it."

"I'm glad to hear that, Arnold," said Persath, launching into the strategy they had worked out on the voyage, "for I am about to ask another favor of you."

"Yes?"

"First of all, let me assure you that I have continued to keep my promise—which, as you will recall, applied to the public media. However, I have privately shared the information of which we speak with—"

"*What?!*"

"Calm yourself, Arnold. To repeat, I acted on a strictly private and confidential basis, with people I know I can trust."

"But . . . but . . ."

Persath motioned Andrew and Rachel into the pickup. "Let me present Patrick Nolan and Sarah Rosenfeld, researchers from the colony planet Esperance, on the Sagittarius frontier. I made their acquaintance on a recent stopover at their planet."

Andrew spoke up. "Sir, Persath has sworn us to secrecy, and we have no intention of letting this go any further without your permission. But it may interest you to know that certain relics recently discovered in the Esperance system suggest that there may have been an outpost of the Empire there."

"This is the first I've heard of this," said Waemhofer, his interest piqued.

"Of course," said Rachel. "The evidence has been largely suppressed by powerful elements in the scientific establishment."

"Our enemies are everywhere," Waemhofer intoned with a nod.

"But fortunately the two of us knew of the Imperial Temple's teachings. So when we learned of the relics, we were able to put two and two together. Then we discussed it with Persath, for we knew of his interest in Earth's hidden past. That was when he told us what he knew." Rachel gave a smile that Andrew couldn't imagine the old duffer resisting. "We understand the importance of keeping the items which Persath has described to us secret, at least for the foreseeable future. But Patrick and I believe that if we are allowed to examine them with certain state-of-the-art Lokaron devices, we will be able to gather data that will prove the authenticity of the relics beyond any doubt and burst the cover-up wide open."

"But I can't possibly authorize any further compromising of the secret on my own! You have no conception of its transcendent importance—no one has, outside the Imperial Temple's innermost circles. Earth's future reunion with the Empire hangs by a thread! No, such a decision would require convening a full meeting of the Stewardship Council and—"

"Our time on Earth is very limited, Dr. Waemhofer," said Andrew. "If you could make an exception, we would be grateful. It would confirm Sarah and me in our growing faith in the Imperial Temple's teachings. And . . . it might well result in a new acceptance of those teachings among the people of Esperance."

Waemhofer's eyes lit up. The Imperial Temple had yet to make any headway among the growing human colonies.

"Er . . . how long would it take?"

"If what we are looking for is there to be found, finding it will take only a few minutes," Rachel assured him. "In fact, if you could let us in yourself, no one else would have to know."

"I fully vouch for their trustworthiness, Arnold," Persath put in.

"Well . . . I shouldn't, you know. But perhaps a brief viewing would do no harm. Persath, can you bring them to the High Shrine at midnight tomorrow?"

"I believe that can be easily be arranged. In fact, we're quite nearby."

"All right." Waemhofer seemed to overcome his jitters. "When you are half an hour out, call and use this extension." He read it off. "That will connect you with me directly. I'll make sure no one else is present." He gave another compulsive look around before signing off.

"I hate all this lying and deception," said Rachel. "And I *really* hate what we're going to be doing to him. He's just a harmless old eccentric."

"I know how you feel," Katy soothed her. "But it's necessary. There's just too much at stake here."

"And remember," Andrew added, "he won't come to any physical harm."

"I know. I wouldn't be a party to this otherwise. Still . . . am I the only one here who could use another drink?"

CHAPTER TWELVE

THE IMPERIAL TEMPLE of the Star Lords would have liked to build its High Shrine on the site of the Empire's original colony, from whence their doctrines held that humanity had spread across the globe. Alas, it now lay underwater, for the ever-eclectic Sebastian Gruber had brought in Atlantis along with so much else, attributing its sinking to the titanic forces unleashed in the Empire's final, cataclysmic war. It helped to no end when explaining away the embarrassing lack of the sort of archaeological evidence a prehistoric high-tech civilization would have been expected to leave.

So Gruber had done the next best thing and located it in the San Luis Valley, where the upper reaches of the Rio Grande flowed southward between the San Juan-La Garita Mountains and the Sangre de Christo range, from the vicinity of Saguache in southern Colorado down to Taos, New Mexico. Throughout its history, the valley had seemed to attract the macabre (several serial killers, including one cannibal), the bizarre (cattle mutilations), the supernatural (manifestations of both the Virgin Mary and the Devil), and, in the late twentieth century, UFOs. Gruber had tended to downplay the last, for little grey aliens had no place in his synthesis of sucker bait. But recently his successors had even worked them in, declaring that the Greys were a subject race of the resurgent Empire who had been assigned to scout out Earth and had returned a negative report after finding it in the throes of the Cold War. Anyway, there was something about the valley in general that tingled the spines of the gullible. So the High Shrine stood on a foothill of Marble Mountain, not far from the Caverna del Oro, entrance to a vast cavern system under the Sangre de Cristo holding one of the buried treasures with which the valley was (of course) reputed to abound.

The site's remoteness had made it a natural repository for treasured secrets. It had also encouraged Waemhofer to permit a surreptitious midnight visit.

The dramatic setting was lost on Andrew, Rachel, and Persath as they approached in Katy's air-car under the myriads of desert stars, homing in on a beacon Waemhofer had activated in response to their call. The minimal lights he had consented to turn on allowed only a ghostly glimpse of the building's eccentric six-sided design. Gruber had understood how a wealth of detailed description can lend a spurious air of reality, and he had by "astral clairvoyance" provided extensive information on Imperial civilization, ranging from architecture to costumery.

The latter was on display when they settled onto the landing pad and emerged, Andrew and Rachel each carrying a satchel containing tools. Waemhofer emerged to meet them. He apparently considered the occasion one of sufficient gravity to warrant his ceremonial vestments, in a color scheme ranging from electric blue to silver, with a white cape descending from flared shoulders. It occurred to Andrew that if anyone had ever written a science-fiction comic opera, this would have fitted right into the wardrobe.

"I'm taking an awful risk," he jittered as he hurriedly ushered them inside, through a doorway beneath a bas-relief of the Imperial symbol as described by Gruber: a spiral galaxy surmounted by a crown. They proceeded through a series of overdecorated halls. "You have no conception of the significance of what you are about to see."

"We realize that great events may be about to unfold," Andrew assured him.

"Yes! We are fortunate to be alive in these times. For it is now clear that what we once hardly dared hope is actual fact. Somewhere in the galaxy, the Empire has arisen from the ashes and purified itself, and is reaching out to its long-deserted children. Over a hundred years ago the Star Lords sent their faithful nonhuman servants ahead to investigate Earth. We were found unworthy in those dark days. But then the Imperial Temple arose, and from the beginning we sought to establish astral contact and let the Empire—if it still existed—know there were those on Earth who had rediscovered the truth and were keeping the faith. And we must have succeeded, for now the Star Lords have given this world a second chance. They themselves—*humans* from beyond the stars—are abroad in the solar system!"

"Persath told us how you recovered the body of one from a crashed ship on Mars," Rachel prompted.

"It is the most precious thing we possess," Waemhofer said quietly as he led them down several flights of stairs. "It conclusively proves that Imperial humans have been active in this system for at least the last twenty years. Surely you, my dear, will live to see the glorious day when the great ships descend from the sky and the Star Lords make themselves known to all. I may even live to see it."

"Persath also said you have a device recovered from that same crash," said Andrew.

"Indeed." Waemhofer became less rapturous but remained enthusiastic. "The fact that it survived unscathed amid the wreckage proves that it must be a product of the Empire's ancient technology. So does its . . . inexplicable capabilities."

"But you didn't test out those capabilities to the fullest?"

"No. We dared not, in our state of ignorance. And at any rate, all will be revealed when the Empire returns." They had reached the bottom of the stairs, to find themselves in a bare chamber of no great size, holding nothing but an elevator door. Waemhofer stepped in front of what Andrew recognized as an up-to-date ranged genetic scanner, and the door slid open. They descended into still lower levels, which had doubtless been hollowed out using Lokaron nanotech molecular disassemblers.

"Now perhaps you understand what a unique privilege it is to be allowed this viewing," he told them. "I consented to it out of my high regard for Persath, who has earned our trust."

Maybe you'll even put in a good word for him with the Empire, Andrew thought. By now he knew Persath's expressions well enough to recognize the Lokar's discomfort at the prospect of betraying that trust.

The elevator reached bottom. They emerged into a fairly long chamber filled with enclosed display cases. Most of them seemed to contain old manuscripts or artifacts from archaeological digs "proving" the Imperial Temple's dogmas. But at the far end was a door that required another genetic scan of Waemhofer before it would open. Within was a small chamber holding only two objects.

One was a pedestal with one of the enclosed display cases atop it, holding a metallic object no larger than a handbag. The comparison came instantly to mind because it had a handle, so featureless and utilitarian as to give no clue as to the nature of the hand for which it was intended. In front of the handle was a group of tiny holes. The surface was partly blackened with carbonization, but there was no other evidence of damage.

The other was a coffin-shaped container with a transparent plastic top. Inside it lay a body. Andrew heard a quick, unsteady indrawing of breath from Rachel as they stared down at what lay under the transparency. The body was a mass of charred horror, with what was left of the face frozen into a mask of agony. But it was unmistakably a human form.

Waemhofer indicated the device on the pedestal and spoke in what were, for him, matter-of-fact tones. "It's lighter than it looks. The fact that it is also practically indestructible is surely proof of a technology beyond our horizons."

Andrew wasn't so sure of that. He was reasonably sure that familiar technologies could produce something just as light and durable using molecularly aligned crystalline steel for the casing and packing the solid-state internal components in composite laminate materials. In fact, he knew of examples. Nevertheless, he put awe into his voice.

"Now I understand what a stroke of incredible good fortune it was that the crash on Mars was discovered by the Imperial Temple, and not by someone who would not have understood what it truly meant."

"I believe there was a Higher Power at work," said Waemhofer simply.

"I gather you know how to activate it. How does it work?"

"Flush with the underside of the handle is a tiny pad. When it is depressed, the holes on the surface light up. So the power source also survived the crash, although of course we have no way of knowing how much longer it will last. It is operated by covering the holes with one's fingers in a certain order, interrupting the beams of light. By trial and error our explorers on Mars produced a momentary effect which defied explanation, as if space itself was distorted. They naturally experimented no further. We demonstrated this for Persath."

"I remember it vividly," said the Lokar.

"I would like to perform scans with certain instruments," said Andrew, reaching into his satchel and withdrawing one. "Would it be possible to uncover the device?"

"Certainly." Waemhofer bent over it and snapped open a very basic mechanical latch—no more was required, after all the security they had already passed through—and the display case's lip rose.

"Thank you." Andrew stepped behind him, touched the device to the base of his spine, and pressed a firing stud.

Sonic stunners—a more humane alternative to the stun setting of laser weapons—used ultra-high frequency focused sound that affected the nervous system. Unfortunately, the difficulties of creating a unidirectional beam had defeated all attempts to make it a ranged weapon. On contact, though, it worked very well. Waemhofer went limp.

"I hate this," said Rachel, not for the first time, as she helped Andrew ease him to the floor.

"He'll awake in a few hours with no ill effects beyond a headache," Andrew reassured her.

"That, and a great deal of understandable disillusionment," said Persath. A complex of emotions was making him nervously irritable. "Let's take the artifact and go!"

"Right." Rachel lifted the device by its handle. "It really is lighter than it looks. Ready, Andrew?"

"In just a moment," said Andrew in a preoccupied voice. He had stepped over to the coffin-shaped capsule and was bending over it with an instrument he had taken from his satchel.

"Well?" snapped Persath, his nerves seemingly at the

breaking point. "Do you plan to take the body with us as well?"

"No," said Andrew, and something in his voice stopped both his companions in their tracks. "We don't need to. I know everything about it I need to know." He stood up and held out the instrument. It was the handheld medical sensor he had borrowed from Zhygon. His hand, like his voice, was steadier than he felt. "That is the body of a Shape-Shifter."

"*What?*" blurted Rachel. "But that's crazy! He would have transformed back into his natural shape when he died."

"Not if Zhygon knows what he's talking about. Remember, he theorized that sudden, instantaneous death, before the consciousness has had time to fragment, will leave the body locked into its current form. Only a prolonged death agony like Leong's gives enough time for the mind's control of the process to slip and the protoplasm to resume its natural form."

Rachel looked at the burned body with a new level of revulsion.

"Well," Persath broke the silence, "now we know why the Shape-Shifters want this device. It is, after all, their property."

"But why is it so very important to them?" Rachel wondered aloud.

"Maybe that will become apparent when we've found out what it is and what it does," said Andrew. "Let's get out of here."

Rachel handed the device to Persath, and she and Andrew each took Waemhofer under one arm. Together they lifted him partly upright and dragged him in front of the genetic scanner. The door slid open and, with some difficulty, they pulled him to the elevator and hoisted him up again, with the same result.

"Do we have to haul him any farther?" puffed Rachel.

"No," said Andrew, entering the elevator and motioning the others to follow. "Leave him here. He didn't have to get past any scanner that I could see when we came in through the main entrance. I'm counting on that."

They rode the elevator upward—Andrew had been careful to observe Waemhofer's manipulation of the controls—and ascended the stairs. They fled through one hallway after another, hoping that their recollection of the layout was accurate. There was no one about—Waemhofer, who had been bending the rules, had seen to that, as they had planned that he would—and they reached the main entrance without incident.

"All right, I think we're home free," said Andrew as he lifted the perfectly standard-looking latch.

It was, of course, precisely the wrong thing to say. An alarm screamed.

"Run for it!" yelled Andrew as he shoved the door open. They sprinted for the aircar, with Persath lagging behind under the burdens of age and Earth's gravity. Andrew strapped himself in and activated the transponder. The gig's location appeared as a blinking red light. As soon as Persath, emitting the thin whistling sounds of Lokaron gasps for breath, was inside, he flung the air-car aloft and into a north-northwestward course.

"Persath, call Reislon and tell him plans have changed. We're coming directly back to the gig. Tell him to have it ready for takeoff. Tell him also to get on the horn to Borthru and have him get started toward the rendezvous point immediately." Only then did he get out his cell phone and make a call of his own.

"Mom, we're not coming back to your house. We can't afford to remain on Earth a minute longer than we have to. We're leaving immediately on the gig. Your air-car will be there. You remember where it is?"

"Yes, yes, of course," Katy said impatiently. "Don't worry about the damned air-car. What's going on? Is there anything I can do to help?"

"No! I don't want you to endanger yourself by getting involved in this in any way. As far as anybody, including the IID, is concerned, you don't know I've been back on Earth."

"What are you not telling me, Andy?"

Andrew thought of the spurious human corpse. "We've learned things that you don't need to know," was all he said. It was enough.

"Where will you go?" she asked simply.

"Back to the rebel Rogovon fleet, I suppose. I can't think of anywhere else to go just now."

He needed no comm screen to see her somber expression in his mind's eye. "Andy, I've never been religious, so I won't tell you to go with God. But it's my belief that a very great deal is going with *you*. Take care. I love you."

"I love you, Mom."

After a time, he became aware of a gentle pressure on his shoulder. It was Rachel's hand.

They fled on through the night.

CHAPTER THIRTEEN

REISLON WAS READY FOR THEM. No sooner had they piled out of the air-car and into the gig than he activated the drive and lifted off from the darkling mountain meadow, ascending at the sharpest angle of attack of which the craft was capable.

"I gather all did not go as planned," he said dryly.

Andrew gave a succinct account, including the true nature of the Imperial Temple's treasured "human" corpse. "Sonic-stun victims can be revived ahead of schedule," he concluded. "Even now, Waemhofer is probably telling all. So we've got to get off Earth and into space as soon as possible."

"You have," Reislon pointed out. In the view-forward, the stars were appearing in even greater multitudes than were visible from the remote reaches of the Rockies, no longer twinkling but gleaming with the diamond-hard steadiness they showed in vacuum.

"*Over*space would be better still," said Andrew. "Especially since the Shape-Shifters' cloaking technology doesn't seem to be as effective there, for some reason. Did Borthru—?"

"Yes, he acknowledged my call and brought the ship to general quarters. *Trovyr* is now accelerating." Reislon indicated the nav plot.

The problem was that the frigate was trailing Earth in its orbit around the sun. So now it was accelerating into a hyperbolic solar orbit heading outward, to reach the region where they could make transition, and at the same time rendezvous with the gig, which after it escaped from Earth's gravity would begin to kill its velocity and, in effect, wait. It was a maneuver they had planned with inconspicuousness in mind. With reactionless drives it was possible, as it would not have been with rockets, however advanced.

Earth had fallen well behind by the time the maneuver was completed and they matched vectors. Reislon cradled the gig in *Trovyr*'s bay, and they all ran to join Borthru in the control room. As they ran, the acceleration warning sounded, and their weight jumped to what felt like one and a third Terran gravity. Persath staggered under what was, for him, slightly over 1.8 G. They helped him the rest of the way.

As they entered the control room, Andrew bade naval propriety be damned and shouted at Borthru. "You're going to kill Persath! At his age—"

"It is only because of his presence that I haven't

ordered a higher acceleration. We must get out to the transition limit—about the distance of Sol's asteroid belt—without delay, and this time we have Sol's gravity working against us, not for us. At the same time, we must work our way above this system's plane of the ecliptic lest we be detected."

"I think," said Reislon, "that we already have been."

They all followed his gaze to the sensor plot, where a subordinate was already turning to report to Borthru. He didn't need to. The purple dot—the standard color that Lokaron fleets used to denote "hostile"—was obvious in the tactical plot.

It was immediately clear that the ship was not coming from Earth. It had been stationed ahead of the mother planet in its orbit, and now it was accelerating outward on an intercept course.

"How did they find us so readily?" Rachel asked. "I mean, isn't this ship heavily stealthed?"

"There can be only one answer," said Reislon. "They knew exactly where to look." He studied the readouts. "The ship's mass indicates that it is a cruiser, of the heavy strike cruiser category. Of course, it is impossible as yet to determine its precise class."

"It hardly matters," said Andrew. "A frigate—even one optimized as a combat ship, which this one isn't— wouldn't have a prayer in Hell against a strike cruiser and the fighters it can deploy." In a corner of his mind, it occurred to him that he was coolly calculating the odds for a fight against a ship of his own service and his own race.

"Persath," said Borthru tightly, "please go to sick bay. They will be able to put you in a special acceleration bed."

"It's no use," said Andrew. He knew enough of the common Lokaron script to make some sense of the readouts, and the course projections were self-explanatory. "That ship is crewed by humans—young, trained, physically fit humans. They can stand higher Gs than even your Rogovon. Given the respective courses we're on, we can't evade them or outrun them."

"We can try," snapped Borthru.

But the hopelessness of it soon became apparent. Even with the ability to accelerate continuously, without the reaction-mass limitation that had crippled the last century's rockets, there were very finite limits to the extent that gravity and inertia, and the orbital courses around the Sun that they imposed, could be overcome. And whatever efforts Borthru made to wrench *Trovyr* into new courses, struggling steeply "uphill" against the gravity gradient, her pursuer could more than match them. The gap narrowed and narrowed until finally they received a signal.

"This is CNS *Broadsword*, calling the Rogovon frigate. You are in violation of Earth's approach limits without authorization. Kill your acceleration and prepare to be boarded. Otherwise you will be destroyed."

"How do they know this is a Rogovon ship?" Rachel whispered. Andrew had no answer.

"It would appear," said Reislon, "that we have two choices: surrender, or commit suicide by attempting to fight."

"Which is no choice at all," said Borthru heavily. "But before surrendering, should we jettison *this*?" He indicated the enigmatic device that Persath had brought aboard.

"No!" Andrew shook his head emphatically even

though he was sure the gesture would mean nothing to Borthru. "We can't throw away our only lead to the Shape-Shifters. And it's not as if we were surrendering to the Shape-Shifters, or to the Black Wolf Society, which must be considered effectively the same thing. This is the Confederated Nations Navy, for God's sake! With them we at least have a hope of getting a hearing."

"Agreed," said Reislon. "However, indulge my cautious habits and conceal the artifact until we know where we stand with our captors. I'm sure, Borthru, you can think of any number of places on this ship."

"We await your reply," came the human voice from the comm station.

Borthru sought to temporize. "We have two humans aboard."

"We are aware of that," was the cold reply after the slight time lag of light-speed communications.

Andrew stepped up to the communicator with its still-blank screen. "This is Captain Andrew Roark, CNEN. I wish to speak to your commanding officer—and see him, if possible."

After another delay as comm lasers crossed and recrossed space, the screen came to life. The man in it wore CNEN dark green with black and gold trim and the four-starburst insignia of a captain. Even in the screen, one could tell that he was a big man. His face was strong-featured and about as dark as African-Americans generally came.

"Jamel!" exclaimed Andrew, recognizing an old friend and classmate from the Academy, and a fellow veteran of Upsilon Lupus. "Jamel Taylor! I never expected to see *you* here."

Taylor's face showed no surprise, nor anything at all except grimness. "Well, I fully expected to see you. We know all about you, you see. But—" (a flash of pained bewilderment in the dark eyes) "—I never expected to find you a traitor!"

The Security personnel who swarmed aboard the unresisting *Trovyr* were no Black Wolf thugs. They were pros. A quick, efficient scan revealed Reislon's implanted gauss needler, and a device that emitted a focused electromagnetic pulse disabled it.

But they didn't find the Cydonia artifact. There was, Andrew realized, no way they could have known what to look for.

As soon as they reported the ship secured, Taylor came aboard. Andrew, Rachel, Persath, Reislon and Borthru awaited him in what would have been called the wardroom on a human warship, under the alert eyes and leveled M-3s of a Security detail. In the room's viewscreen, *Broadsword* could be seen, a watchful killing machine, its intricate massiveness lost in the distance.

Taylor strode into the room, his face like a dark storm cloud. Following him, and dwarfed by him, was a gaunt woman in severe civilian dress, with equally severe features and short iron-gray hair.

"This," said Taylor without preamble, "is Ms. Erica Kharazi. She is here as liaison and . . . advisor from the office of Legislative Assemblyman Valdes."

"Valdes?" Andrew exclaimed.

"Yes." Taylor gave him a look that held neither nostalgia nor friendship. "It's thanks to him that we know about you. He came to the Admiralty in confidence and explained how he had sponsored your and Ms. Arnstein's trip to Tizath-Asor. After you departed that planet without informing your contact, a Mr. Leong of our embassy, he knew you'd gone rogue."

"Leong? Listen, Jamel, Leong was—"

"Shut up!" snapped Kharazi in a voice that went with the rest of her. "It was thanks to Leong's quick thinking and initiative that we found out you were headed to the Kogurche system, and that there you made contact with Reislon'Sygnath, in whom we've been interested for a long time. We always knew he was a double agent, and now we know he's a *triple* agent."

"How, exactly, do you know that?" Rachel demanded. "Have you heard from Leong lately?"

"Assemblyman Valdes has many sources of information," said Kharazi with a tight smile. "It's true that Leong is believed dead. That will be another charge against you two, to add to the list."

"Jamel," said Andrew desperately, *"think!* Valdes hasn't got any magic interstellar radio. How could Leong have gotten any information to Valdes that would have enabled you to zero in on this ship the way you did? What kind of sources of information are we talking about?" Thinking to see a flicker of doubt on his old friend's face, he pressed what might possibly be his advantage. "You've got to listen to me. First of all, Leong was a member of the Black Wolf Society—"

"I told you to shut up!" screeched Kharazi.

"—and what's more, he was an alien, belonging to a species that can masquerade as humans. No, *transform*

into human semblance." Before the stunned silence in the
room could break, Andrew rushed on. "Jamel, you know
me. You know I'm not insane. And you also know I'm not
stupid—at least not stupid enough to invent a story this
implausible."

Taylor's face reflected his inner conflict. "Ms. Kharazi,
there are a number of seeming discrepancies in all this
about which I'm confused. I think we should investigate
them further."

Kharazi gave him an unpleasant look. "I advise against
wasting time that way, Captain. You already know what
you need to know: that these two, through their contact
Reislon'Sygnath, have sold out to Gev-Rogov—"

"We do not represent Gev-Rogov," Borthru broke
in. "In fact, we represent the opposition to the *gevah*'s
current regime."

"Of course," sneered Kharazi. "Gev-Rogov will say the
same thing about you. It's called 'plausible deniability,'
Captain Taylor. A child wouldn't be fooled by it, and
neither should you. The other thing you should investigate
is the theft these people have committed, and locate the
item they have stolen. You must use any and all means
necessary to get the truth out of them. This is no time for
squeamishness."

"There will be no torture used aboard my ship, Ms.
Kharazi. I'm aware that I'm under orders to consider your
advice—"

"Get it straight, Captain. You're under orders to *follow*
my advice. Remember, Assemblyman Valdes has *very*
high connections, inside and outside the Navy. And even
now he's in space, in his private vessel, and will probably

rendezvous with us later. You'd be wise to consider the impact your decisions may have on your career prospects, Captain."

Andrew felt a dull, dead hopelessness congeal in the pit of his stomach as he looked from one face to the other. And, in the way the mind has of seeking refuge at such moments by fleeing into irrelevancies, he couldn't help being struck by the physical contrast—comical at any other time—between Taylor and Kharazi, who was . . .

Small, and racially indistinguishable.

No. Don't be crazy. There are lots of people who are below average in size. And lots of people who are multiracial, especially on today's cosmopolitan Earth.

And yet . . . what other alternative have I? And what have I got to lose?

It all flashed through his mind in less than a second. At appreciably the same time, he caught Rachel's eye. They exchanged a look, and somehow he knew that she had had the same stunning thought, and that she knew what he was about to do.

An infinitesimal nod of her head confirmed it. Then, without further ado, she let her legs go limp under her and collapsed to the floor.

When a woman appears to faint, any men present, however well-trained and focused, are going to take notice. That wavering of attention gave Andrew his chance.

He lunged at the nearest Security guard on his left, grasping the man's right wrist and bringing it down across his knee. The M-3 dropped to the deck. Andrew scooped it up with his free right hand. It was set on semiautomatic, but with gauss weapons there was practically no delay between shots.

Oblivious to the pandemonium that had broken out, Andrew used the fractional second he had to squeeze off several shots. The characteristic snapping sound was almost as rapid-fire as on autoburst.

The first shot hit Kharazi in the heart. Blood welled up . . . but slowed immediately, and she stayed on her feet.

The other hypervelocity projectiles all whipped through the chest and abdomen. She sank to the deck.

Then the state of slowed time in which Andrew had been living was suddenly shattered by an explosion of sickening pain as someone punched him from behind in the kidney. Helpless with agony, he was forced to the floor, and both his arms were pulled up to the small of his back. He had already dropped the M-3, which he no longer needed.

He became aware that his fellow prisoners were going prone on the deck at the shouted orders of two Security guards, who were pointing their M-3s two-handed for emphasis. Another guard, presumably with medic training, was crouched over Kharazi. He looked up and shook his head.

"It's no use, sir," he told Taylor. "She's dying. They don't even have a sick bay for humans here. And even if they did . . . I can't understand why she's not already dead."

Taylor swung over to Andrew as the two guards holding Andrew's arms hauled him excruciatingly to his feet. He thrust his face to within inches of Andrew's. "You murdering bastard!" he grated.

"Sir! *Sir!*" The medic's voice rose to falsetto as he leaped to his feet and staggered backward from the obscenity he was witnessing.

Andrew could sympathize. It all came back to him as he watched: the horribly translucent lavender-white skin with its sprinkling of white hairs; the writhing and reconfiguring as the skeletal structure changed with a creaking sound that set the teeth on edge; the huge empty eyes . . .

Shock gripped the room. The guards could only stare in horror. Andrew heard one M-3 fall to the deck. Below the level of any of the senses, he could feel panicked horror rising very close to the surface.

Taylor's deep voice halted it.

"Release Captain Roark," he said heavily.

CHAPTER FOURTEEN

"BUT WHAT IF you had been wrong?" demanded Rachel as they hurried along the passageway deep in CNS *Broadsword*.

"Well," said Andrew, shrugging uncomfortably against the slightly ill-fitting uniform he had borrowed after going through the formality of reporting himself off leave to Taylor, "I suppose they would have executed me for murder after executing me for treason. Or," he added thoughtfully, "do you think maybe it would have been the other way around?"

"You're about as funny as pork barbeque at a bar mitzvah. And I must be as crazy as you are. I can't imagine what possessed me to help you with your little stunt."

"I never did get around to thanking you for that, did I? You did exactly the right thing."

She made a nonverbal sound of deep skepticism.

They arrived at their destination, a briefing room where others were already present or filing in: Reislon, Persath, Borthru, and Commander Huai Mei, *Broadsword*'s executive officer. This was hardly the first meeting the room had seen, as the two ships continued to coast outward from the Sun on their high-velocity hyperbolic orbit. The first had been for the purpose of revealing Kharazi's body to Huai and Taylor's other officers and, while they were still in a proper state of shock, recounting the entire story to them—accurately, except that Andrew had continued to withhold the fact of Admiral Arnstein's suicide. Afterward had come the process, through the usual military educational trickle-down method, of disseminating the facts of their situation to the cruiser's crew after requiring full medical scans under the guise that some type of toxin may have been released by the captured vessel. This had gone fairly smoothly. This was not the day of fighting sail, when crews had consisted of press-ganged gutter scrapings, nor even the more recent naval eras when crews had included unwilling draftees. Space crew were intelligent, educated people; they had to be.

"Attention on deck!" rapped a master-at-arms at the hatchway. Everyone rose as Taylor entered. Andrew had carefully briefed the three Lokaron on such points of human naval etiquette.

"As you were," Taylor said gruffly , taking his place at the head of the table. "We all know by now the facts of the . . . extraordinary situation in which we find ourselves. Now we must decide what to do next. Most especially, what to do in connection with *that*." He indicated the

Cydonia artifact, which sat in the center of the table, enveloped in its flesh-crawling aura of mystery. "Fortunately, we have some leeway, as we're still in free fall and I haven't communicated any reports as yet."

"There is a new factor to take into account," said Reislon. "We must assume that Legislative Assemblyman Valdes is in league with the Shape-Shifters."

Even after what had happened aboard *Trovyr*, it was shocking to hear it put into words. Huai shook her head. She wore a Chinese flag shoulder patch—the CNEN had a policy of encouraging personnel exchanges among its national components—but her English was almost unaccented. "I simply can't believe that of Admiral Valdes," she said, using Valdes's military title as most Navy people still did. "Maybe they've made a dupe of him, infiltrated his political organization—"

"Perhaps you're right, Commander," said Reislon. "But even if you are, it makes no practical difference. Either way, we cannot afford to trust him. Which means in turn that we don't know who we *can* afford to trust in the CNE Navy or government. Remember, he has very high connections."

Huai's expression of resentful incredulity was unchanged, but she had no rejoinder to make.

"So," said Persath, "it appears that we're back where we started. All we have to work with is this device. We need to ascertain its capabilities and purpose. I propose that we take it to Tizath-Asor. At the risk of seeming immodesty, I can say without fear of contradiction that my research establishment there is amply equipped and staffed for such an investigation."

"It is also undoubtedly under close observation by the Shape-Shifters," Reislon reminded him. "As you'll recall, they had infiltrated the CNE embassy there. And now that they know of your role in all this, their cloaked ships must be patrolling the orbital approaches."

Persath made a sound that must have been an inarticulate splutter, for the translator was silent. The possibility of his privacy being violated had obviously never occurred to him.

"No," Reislon continued, "I fear we must revert to the course of action we were pursuing before we . . . encountered Captain Taylor and his command. We must return to Kogurche, and the Rogovon rebel base there."

Huai glanced sideways at Borthru. The rogue Rogovon starship captain had, by prior agreement with his companions, kept silent and as inconspicuous as possible, for his was a face that humans had, for over four decades, identified as the face of the enemy.

"Are you sure?" asked Huai. Without waiting for an answer, she turned to Taylor. "I don't like it, Captain."

"I don't, either," said Taylor with equal forthrightness. "And I'm open to alternatives. I can't think of any myself."

"Remember," Rachel urged, "that's one place where we don't have to worry about Shape-Shifter infiltration, since everybody there is Lokaron."

Of a sort, said Huai's expression as she glanced again at Borthru.

For the first time, Borthru spoke up. "I would remind you of something everyone seems to have forgotten: the highly advanced cloaking technology the Shape-Shifters possess. For all any of us know, this ship may be under observation even as we speak." He gave a closed-mouthed Lokaron smile at the CNEN officers' visible reaction. "Admittedly, Persath was able to detect the vessel following him from Tizath-Asor to Kogurche in overspace, which may indicate that the technology is less effective in that domain . . . or it may simply mean that they felt no need to conceal themselves from his yacht, as they undoubtedly would from your cruiser." His expression hardened. "The point of all this is that by letting you come to our base, we would be running a risk of compromising its location. I have been given a wide range of discretion, and I am willing to run the risk in the interest of solidarity against a common threat." He laid a heavy emphasis, which might have held an element of irony, on the last five words as he gazed levelly at Huai.

"You must understand our reluctance in dealing with the Rogovon," Taylor rumbled.

"I understand why you hate and fear Gev-Rogov," said Borthru bluntly. "Do not deny it. You have a right to. What *you* must understand is that some of us are trying to change Gev-Rogov into something neither you nor anyone else will have to hate and fear."

"I've dealt with Borthru's people," said Andrew, using the word *people* without the slightest hesitancy. "I've found them trustworthy. And Jamel . . . I too was at Upsilon Lupus."

"So you were." Taylor wore a look of brooding concentration for a few heartbeats. "All right. Is there any further discussion? If not, we will make transition as soon as we reach the gravitational limit and then shape an overspace course for Kogurche."

"Just two points," said Andrew. "First, I have an idea

that may help alleviate Borthru's entirely legitimate concerns, and perhaps also provide us with additional sources of information. I got the germ of the idea when we were in Persath's ship being followed." He proceeded, in very rough outline, to lay out his plan.

"Hmmm," Taylor ruminated. "It has definite possibilities. And we all know that CNEN officers have a wide range of latitude in dealing with smugglers—which, officially, is all we know we're looking at here. I can think of a few refinements, but . . . yes . . ."

"I concur," said Borthru.

With all CNEN personnel certified as human, the cruiser, accompanied by *Trovyr*, plunged on toward the outer Solar system.

When they neared the inner fringes of the asteroid belt, human and Lokaron pilots relinquished control to their ships' synchronized computers and both ships performed a simultaneous transition into overspace. Reislon lay in an improvised Lokaron-compatible acceleration couch in *Broadsword*'s control room and watched along with Andrew and Rachel as a polychromatic tunnel seemed to recede astern and the indescribable surge of transition seemed to pull them through a hole in reality. Persath was in sick bay, out of caution.

Almost immediately, a blip appeared on the sensor screen.

"Well," Andrew heard himself say, "I guess this settles the question. They can cloak themselves in normal space, but something about the characteristics of overspace prevents it."

The blip promptly settled into a course following theirs. It could, of course, do so in perfect safety despite the cruiser's firepower. Ships in overspace could detect each other's energy output by special sensors, at least at short ranges. (The range limitation had defeated all attempts to create a faster-than-light interstellar communications network using buoys in overspace signaling to each other by a kind of Morse code.) But they could not interact physically, or even communicate normally, due to the still poorly understood physics of energy transfer in overspace. All combat must take place in normal space.

"So it does. And I see no need for delay in setting your plan in motion." Taylor turned to his intraship communicator and spoke a brief order to the chief engineer. *Broadsword*'s power plant put out a momentary energy pulse, meaningless and barely noticeable to anyone who wasn't looking for it and didn't know its significance. Borthru did. Aboard *Broadsword* and *Trovyr*, a brief simultaneous countdown began.

At a prearranged instant, the cruiser engaged its transition engine, while *Trovyr* continued on in overspace toward Kogurche.

Transition from overspace involved the usual surging sensation, but the visual manifestation was different in this starless realm. The tunnel through which they were seemingly pulled was not a light show here, but a series of waves of various shades of black. Of course that made no sense, but everyone who had ever experienced it had described it that way.

Andrew tried to imagine what was flashing through the head of the skipper of the ship following them, who found himself forced into making a snap decision. The frigate's uninterrupted course must be disturbing. But his attention was naturally focused on the great strike cruiser, and he would lose it beyond all hope of recovery if he did not follow it back into normal space, where he could cloak himself from its sensors. Andrew's plan depended on his decision.

Abruptly, transition was over and they were back among the innumerable stars of normal space. Even their brief time in overspace had taken them far beyond the Oort Cloud, and Sol was merely a zero-magnitude star astern, lost in the stellar multitudes.

"Now we'll see if they—" Taylor began.

Before he could finish, lights at the sensor station flashed with confirmation of the gravitational flux that meant a ship had made transition—a ship that could not be detected.

That emergence into normal space was close to them—practically in their laps, in terms of the usual distances with which spacefarers were accustomed to deal. The very brief interval between their own commencement of transition and the enemy commander's decision had brought his ship flashing closer to them in overspace before he initiated transition. The result was a dramatic narrowing of the range in normal space once they were both there. That, too, had been an element of Andrew's plan.

They were still too far away to use shipboard laser weapons, which despite certain artificial-gravity-based tricks that extended their range were still basically chained to the diameter of their focusing optics—and engineering practicalities imposed definite limits on those. But Taylor rapped out a pair of orders. The first caused the cruiser to begin decelerating, so as to bring the still-accelerating ship behind them into even closer proximity. The second resulted in a salvo from the cruiser's missile launchers, whose crews had been at general quarters since before transition. The missiles—essentially miniature unmanned spacecraft with overpowered reactionless drives that burned themselves out as they produced accelerations whose g-forces would have reduced any life forms to protoplasmic mush—streaked aft.

Their target, now that it was in normal space, was cloaked beyond any possibility of ordinary targeting. But the location of its transition emergence, combined with its last observed velocity, gave the computers something to get their figurative teeth into, allowing a reasonable prediction of where it ought to be.

It was on that point in space that the missile storm converged.

CHAPTER FIFTEEN

IT WAS ONLY THE IMPOSSIBILITY of precise targeting solutions that enabled the cloaked ship to survive even momentarily. The cruiser's missiles detonated simultaneously, their warheads energizing nuclear-pumped X-ray lasers that poured an inferno of concentrated energy into the volume of space their invisible target was projected to occupy. Most undoubtedly missed. But it immediately became apparent that the ones that hadn't had sufficed to disable the cloaking system. The stranger lay revealed: a commercial ship almost the size of a naval frigate, with some obvious modifications, doubtless related to the fact that someone with a great deal of money had retrofitted it with an integral-transition engine.

It was also obvious to their sensors that the stranger's deflection shield had overloaded and failed. The ship lay naked as well as visible. Sensibly, her skipper was making no attempt to run or evade. Taylor wasted no more missiles. Instead, he brought his command into range of shipboard lasers and launched a squadron of fighters for added emphasis. The little two-seat craft, whose crews were chosen for (among other things) acceleration tolerance, were intended to get in close to enemy ships, where deflection shields' space-distorting properties were less of a problem, and deliver precision strikes with small missiles whose limited range requirements enabled them to carry disproportionately large warheads. Andrew could never look at such a fighter without remembering the Lokaron one his parents had ridden on an insane suicide run in 2030, as a result of which Earth had lived.

They began to receive frantic calls. Taylor quite properly ignored them until, in his own good time, he hailed the stranger.

"This is CNS *Broadsword*. Yow will match vectors with us and, on our signal, go into free fall and prepare to be boarded. Failure to obey this order will result in your destruction, as will any attempt at flight. Now, identify yourself."

The face that appeared on the comm screen was that of a lean dark-haired man in need of a shave. In the background, damage-control work was in progress as a man with a chemical extinguisher put out a series of electrical fires where controls had shorted out.

"This is private vessel *City of Osaka*, Zoltan da Silva commanding. And we surrender, damn you! You've got us. Why don't you just finish us?"

"We have no intention of finishing you as long as you

behave," Taylor purred deeply. "In fact, after putting a prize crew aboard your ship, we intend to bring you, personally, aboard *Broadsword*. We have a few questions to ask."

Taylor awaited the prisoner in the office portion of his day cabin, seated behind a desk. Andrew sat unobtrusively beside the desk to his left, with Rachel behind him.

In person, Zoltan da Silva was no less surly-looking than he had appeared on the screen. Two Security guards ushered him in and stood him directly in front of the desk, then stationed themselves watchfully beside the hatch.

"Now, then," Taylor began, "why was the Black Wolf Society interested in following my ship?"

"The Black Wolf Society?" The prisoner gave a truculent sneer. "That's just a myth invented to justify harassing small private merchants who aren't linked up with the big cartels that are hand in glove with the government! It's all part of a conspiracy to squeeze out—"

"Stow it," Taylor cut him off dispassionately. "All right. What was a private merchant doing following us? And what was he doing with a ship equipped with an integral-transition engine . . . and a stealth system beyond state of the art?"

"We weren't following you! We just happened to be going the same way. And we had an emergency that caused us to have to drop out of overspace, and then you attacked us, and—"

At that moment, a buzzer sounded. Taylor pressed a button to signal "Enter." Reislon came through the hatch, carrying the Cydonia artifact. He set it down on the desk and moved to stand behind Taylor.

For an instant, da Silva's eyes widened and a shiver ran through him. But only for an instant. Then his *persona* reasserted itself as though with a clang.

"Why are you so interested in this thing?" asked Taylor mildly.

"Who's interested in it? I've just never seen one, that's all. Besides, I was surprised to see a Lokar aboard your ship—especially one who almost looks Rogovon."

"Were you? And you still haven't answered the question about your ship's . . . special equipment."

Da Silva turned to bluster. "Am I under arrest? If so, I refuse to answer your goddamned questions until I've seen a lawyer. I've got rights!"

"No you don't," said Andrew, speaking for the first time and standing up, arms folded. "*Humans* have rights."

The bluster rose a few decibels. "Who the hell are you? And what do you mean by—"

"We know what you are," said Andrew in a tightly controlled voice.

With unnatural abruptness, the tack changed to one of wheedling. "Hey, Captain, look . . . All right, I admit I'm mixed up with the Black Wolf. My business is a little irregular, you see. I suppose you'd probably call me a smuggler. I prefer free trader. That's why I need what you call special equipment. The Black Wolf Society was able to supply it—they've got some stuff that isn't generally available, you see. But I never—"

"It's no good," said Andrew, unfolding his arms and revealing a small instrument in his left hand that had been concealed behind his right elbow. "You may not be familiar with this model—it's Rogovon—but you know a med sensor when you see it. I've had it under the ledge of the desk, performing a scan on you while you've been talking. It confirmed what I was already pretty sure of. I've seen enough Shape-Shifters in human form by now to have a sense of the signs."

"Who *is* this nut, Captain?" Da Silva's bluster was back, but in a forceless sort of way. "What's this crazy nonsense he's talking?"

Andrew sighed and drew his M-3. "You want to do this the hard way? I can put a single bullet through your chest, and we can watch you not die from it. Or, even more definitively, I can go to full auto and destroy too many of your vital organs for your reconfiguring ability to handle, and we'll watch you die slowly, during which process you'll become unable to sustain the human semblance. I've seen that happen twice to you Shape-Shifters."

For an eternal moment, their eyes locked. Then, too abruptly for the change to be noticed, Da Silva sloughed off his assumed personality like a cloak.

"Actually," he said in a conversational tone, "our name for ourselves is Kappainu, as nearly as a human voice box can produce the sound."

There are things so outrageous that, even when one is absolutely certain of them, it is still a shock to hear them openly acknowledged. It is even worse when the acknowledgment is almost casual. Several heartbeats passed before Andrew was able to speak and break the stunned silence.

"There are a great many questions—a *very* great many questions—that we want to ask you, beginning with words like *who* and *where* and *why*. But we have to start somewhere. So . . . what should we call you?"

"Oh, you may as well continue using Zoltan da Silva. You wouldn't be able to pronounce my true name correctly, any more than I can pronounce your language properly when in my natural form. The vocal apparatus is too different. For that reason—and also the inconvenience and discomfort involved in a transformation—I will retain my present form."

Zhygon was right, Andrew mentally filed away. *After the initial transformation, the mental effort required to sustain it must become pretty much automatic.* "All right. Next question: What is this object on the desk, and why are you so interested in it?"

Da Silva shook his (her? its?) head in an altogether humanlike gesture. "No. I won't answer any of your questions here."

"You're not exactly in a position to refuse."

"No? As you've pointed out, you can kill me. But that won't get you any answers."

"We have ways of getting them," said Taylor darkly.

"Do you? You'll find that none of your truth drugs work on me, due to differences in body chemistry. And as for torture . . . well, as you've deduced, we are very resistant to physical traumas that aren't extreme enough to kill us. But aside from that, we're basically a very fragile species—our nervous system will take very little abuse. I don't believe you'd be able to torture me without killing me and therefore learning nothing."

"I would be willing to try," said Reislon. Even through the medium of the translator his voice was chilling. "But there is another method: imprisonment under conditions of sensory deprivation. I don't think you could stand up under that for long."

"Probably not. But you would have no way of verifying the truthfulness of my answers."

"Still," Rachel spoke up, "I'm sure you'd just as soon avoid it. And . . . if I recall your exact words, you said you wouldn't answer any of our questions *here*."

"You are very alert, Ms. Arnstein. Yes, I have every intention of telling you what you want to know—but only on my own terms, which involve going to the locale where I can demonstrate this device."

"Fine," said Taylor. "Let's go."

"No. I don't trust you. I have no intention of allowing this cruiser, with its firepower, into the region to which I am referring. I will take you, Commodore Roark." (In a certain corner of his mind, Andrew managed to be amused by the use of the traditional "courtesy promotion" extended to anyone with the rank of captain aboard a ship commanded by someone else, who alone could be addressed by the sacrosanct title.) "And you, Ms. Arnstein. We will use *City of Osaka*'s gig. I can perform all nonautomated piloting functions."

"Either you're insane," said Taylor, "or you think we are."

"You can follow in your cruiser, Captain, just out of range of your ship-to-ship laser weapons, with no fighters deployed. If anything untoward happens, you'll be able to obliterate me immediately thereafter."

"Along with Captain Roark and Ms. Arnstein. They'd be your hostages."

"My entire crew is in your hands, Captain. You'll have more hostages than I will."

"I'm willing to chance it, Jamel," said Andrew.

"So am I," added Rachel.

"I can't put you at risk, Ms. Arnstein," Taylor protested. "You're a civilian."

"I'm here of my own free will, Captain Taylor. You're not responsible for me or in authority over me."

"Actually, Ms. Arnstein, I am. As long as you're on this ship, you're under military jurisdiction."

"I think she's earned the right to decide for herself, Jamel," said Andrew. "Anyway, remember that I'll be armed and he won't be. I ought to be able to control the situation."

"I would also like to go, Captain," said Reislon, "as a representative of Borthru and his organization, who seem to have become partners in this enterprise. There will be room for me—barely—in the gig. And I, too, am armed." His implanted gauss needler had been reactivated, as a gesture of trust. It wasn't lethal against the shape-shifters, but it had proven it could be useful.

"I have no objection," said Da Silva.

Taylor glared. "If I tried really, really hard, I *might* be able to think of something I care about less than your objections or lack of them." He turned contemptuously away and addressed Andrew. "All right. Against my better judgment I'm going to allow this. Just remember, Andy, you're in command of this crazy little expedition, with full enforcement powers. Remember also that *Broadsword* will be shadowing you."

"One other thing," said Reislon with a smile. "Don't tell Persath about this." The old Lokar was still in sick bay, having been shaken up by the maneuvering involved in the trap they'd sprung on *City of Osaka*. "He would insist on going, out of sheer curiosity."

A very short, precisely calculated overspace hop brought the two ships back to a point within the outer solar system, closer in than the orbits of Neptune and the demoted one-time planet Pluto but well outside the plane of the ecliptic. ("Above," in the arbitrary terms of the nav plot.) Their exact destination was a set of coordinates provided by Da Silva, who said it was in an orbital position trailing their mysterious objective.

The gig detached and accelerated ahead. *Broadsword* and *City of Osaka* followed, just barely outside the range at which the former's shipboard laser weapons could have promptly reduced the gig to a rarefied gas. If Da Silva was disturbed by Taylor's very literal-minded interpretation of his terms, he gave no sign.

In the course of the voyage, Andrew and Rachel tried various tactics to draw out their pilot/prisoner. None had the slightest effect. They eventually resigned themselves to the fact that Da Silva was only going to share information in his own good time. Reislon seemed to accept that from the outset, as though recognizing a fellow professional.

Finally there came a time when Da Silva cut the gig's drive and turned to the Cydonia artifact, which he had resolutely refused to discuss. "I must now perform certain operations with this device. It is, to some extent, voice-activated, so it will be necessary for me to give commands in my own language, within the limitations of my present form."

"Go ahead," said Andrew. "But just remember that *Broadsword* is out there." He let his hand rest on the grip of his M-3 for additional emphasis.

Without comment, Da Silva proceeded to activate the photonic controls and manipulate them too rapidly to follow, in a meaningless flickering and flashing of tiny lights. He then spoke in an equally meaningless series of sounds, in a language clearly never intended for a human throat. Something about it sent a chill sliding along Andrew's spine. Then came more fiddling with the controls, after which a few of the little lights continued to glow steadily. Nothing happened, as the gig coasted on in free fall.

"Well?" said Andrew, his voice brittle with a sense of anticlimax.

"Be patient." Was there, quivering beneath Da Silva's expressionlessness, a kind of gloating anticipation? Andrew's hand closed on the M-3's grip.

Rachel was the first to sense it. "Andy! What—?"

There was an indescribable sensation of gravitational flux and sensory wavering, almost too brief to register. And then the universe of stars, including the tiny, distant sun, was gone, and they were in blackness. Dead ahead, filling most of the view screen, was a titanic space habitat, oblately spheroidal and festooned with weapon blisters and instrument pods.

They were shaken out of their stunned immobility by a shudder whose origin Andrew recognized. Remote applications of artificial-gravity technology—"tractor beams" as they were called, to the prissy disapproval of the purists—were inherently impractical beyond very short ranges. But that was precisely the range at which the impossible space station had somehow materialized. The gig was in the grip of such a beam . . . and no sooner was it gripped than a sideways jerk sent all of them, including Da Silva, slewing sideways in their seats.

Andrew righted himself, drawing his M-3 and aiming it at the center of Da Silva's face, which now wore an unmistakable smile of triumph. He wanted nothing more than to wipe out that smile with an autoburst. But he needed answers.

"What happened? Where are we? Where did that space station come from?"

"All will be made clear. For now, all you need to know is that we are totally invisible and undetectable to your cruiser."

Andrew gave a shaky laugh. "Is this an application of your cloaking device? You yourself found out how much good that does against weapon fire. And *Broadsword* knew exactly where we were and what our course was at the time we vanished."

"You have surely noted the lack of incoming laser fire. No, this is something else—which, as I say, will be explained. In the meantime, it goes without saying that resistance is useless. I might also add that my comrades will not take kindly to any harm done to me, or any attempt to use me as a hostage."

"He's right," said Rachel dully.

"Yes," agreed Reislon, slowly lowering the arm that held his weapon implant.

Andrew could not disagree. He holstered his M-3 and watched as they were drawn into the space station. A docking bay seemed to engulf them as they slipped through an atmosphere screen and were deposited on the deck of a hangar so vast as to induce vertigo.

"Shall we?" smirked Da Silva, extending his hand. Andrew surrendered his M-3. "And," he added to Reislon, "I know you won't try anything foolish. Besides which, you are aware that we are effectively impervious to the extremely small-caliber needles your implanted weapon fires." He opened the hatch, and they emerged from the gig. A squad of armed guards appeared, wearing nondescript light-duty space dress and armed with what appeared to be laser weapons, doubtless on a stun setting. For the first time they saw living, active Shape-Shifters— no, Andrew mentally corrected, Kappainu—*au naturel.*

There was something unpleasantly insectlike about the way the diminutive beings moved, and beneath the translucent pale-lavender skin whatever they used for blood could be seen to circulate. Andrew had never had a problem with aliens *per se*, but there was something about these things that made his gorge rise.

Da Silva had a short conversation with the leader of the security detail. The language had sounded, and continued to sound, strange as pronounced by him. But the sounds produced by the Kappainu vocal apparatus were positively eerie. Da Silva turned back to the prisoners.

"The leader of our operations on Earth recently arrived here. He is still in human form and wishes to interview you. Come."

They departed the hangar and proceeded through a series of passageways. Andrew and, to an even greater extent, Reislon, had to crouch to avoid head injuries. Nevertheless, Andrew's eyes were in constant motion as he observed fixtures, machinery, controls, and all the rest with the same attention he had already given to the hangar deck and the guards' gear.

Ascending a couple of flights of steps, they left the areas that were starkly functional and entered precincts where decoration, following esthetic precepts Andrew's mind could not grasp, was in evidence. *The executive level*, he thought. *Some things are universal.* They came to a final door, behind which iridescent hangings parted for them as they entered a chamber so large as to constitute ostentation in a space habitat—Reislon could even stand up straight. Two of the guards accompanied them in and took up station flanking the entry.

Between two doorways in the opposite wall was a long, low desk—so low that it must have been uncomfortable for the human figure behind it, who was bending even lower to peer at a display screen. He abruptly switched it off, raised his head, and smiled at them.

Rachel gave a small shriek, immediately choked into silence.

Afterward, when he had the leisure to look back over his reaction, Andrew realized that he hadn't really been all that surprised that the face was that of Franklin Ivanovitch Valdes y Kurita, Rear Admiral CNEN (ret.) and Legislative Assemblyman.

CHAPTER SIXTEEN

VALDES—or whatever his true name was—stood up with apparent relief and sat on the desk. "I'll retain this semblance. It facilitates communication with you, and, as you've undoubtedly deduced by now, after the initial transformation the mental effort becomes automatic and effortless. Besides . . . after all these years, I've come to actually enjoy the human form."

"I hope you continue to enjoy it," said Andrew, "in the brief time remaining to you before CNS *Broadsword* locates this rather large station and proceeds to reduce it to space junk unless you release us and surrender."

"Not a bad bluff, Captain." Andrew could have sworn that Valdes's expression held something like pity. "But you're thinking in terms of our ships' cloaking system. It employs a field that channels radiation of various wavelengths—including that of visible light—around it. This station uses a more advanced approach, too energy-intensive to be practical for mobile installations. Without going into the technical details—in which I'm not a specialist anyway—it is a combined spinoff of the cloaking system and the artificial-gravity technology used to produce deflection shields. Instead of channeling the radiation, it *absorbs* it on one side and recreates it on the other. The area within the field—actually a pair of near-concentric fields with variable, harmonic properties—is effectively nonexistent as observed externally. The device which unfortunately was aboard one of our ships that crashed on Mars in 2055—we call it the 'access link'—is able, by means of dimensional distortion, to detect the field from outside and communicate through it. By the way, we observe the outside universe by means of remote sensor-equipped buoys with their own access links. Even now, they are observing and reporting on your cruiser."

"Which," said Reislon thoughtfully, "explains why you have been so very concerned with recovering the device. It might have fallen into the hands of competent scientific investigators, rather than that ridiculous pseudo-religious cult. Research into it might have eventually led the humans to the right conclusions. After which they could have located your base. Would this have a connection with the brief sighting of your ships in this system by the Harathon just after the access link was lost?"

"Yes. We were searching for it so frantically that we let our usual precautions slip. It was an understandable lapse, given the gravity of the situation. The access link is the only way the field can be detected. All our ships carry them—although," Valdes added casually, "any time a ship carrying human Black Wolf personnel is forced to use one, they have to be eliminated. *City of Osaka*, for example, has one, concealed where no one would ever look for it or guess its function. Otherwise, the only way the field can be penetrated is if a material object blunders through it. And as soon as we had gravitically captured your gig, we shifted the station, including you—perhaps you noticed the sensation—away from the gig's vector. *Broadsword* is even now searching along that vector, to no effect. Your Captain Taylor is very persistent."

"All right," said Andrew doggedly. "So you're extremely well-hidden. But you're forgetting something. Captain Taylor knows about you Kappainu now. If he can't find us, he'll go back to Earth with evidence that can't be ignored, however hard you try to use your influence to suppress it."

"True. It will therefore be necessary to destroy *Broadsword*. Even as we speak, this station, inside its field, is being maneuvered back into a position across *Broadsword*'s course—a process which takes a good deal of time, as we are not very maneuverable—so that the 'blundering through' I mentioned earlier will occur. *Broadsword* will then find herself in the same position you just did—and will be destroyed."

Andrew laughed scornfully. "I know this is a damned big space station, and obviously armed. But *Broadsword* is a Confederated Nations Navy strike cruiser! Not a single consideration went into her design except efficiency as a fighting machine. But of course you know all about that . . . Admiral."

"Granted. But our hangar decks house a number of

armed ships, which we are now deploying inside the field. They are admittedly no match for *Broadsword*, at least not individually, and probably not even collectively. But their combined firepower, added to the station's, against a ship that is stunned by surprise . . ." Valdes let the sentence trail off.

"You're forgetting *City of Osaka*. Her prize crew also know the truth."

"Fortunately, Captain Taylor is keeping her in very close formation with *Broadsword*. She too will be destroyed."

"But your own crew is still aboard her, as prisoners!" Rachel cried.

Valdes's expression was puzzled, as though he honestly couldn't see the relevance. "But they are only humans. Da Silva, here, was the only one of us aboard her." His voice took on a tone of mocking irony. "It is unfortunate that we must take these measures to maintain secrecy. After all, as will soon become clear, we are the best friends the human race has ever had!"

"What in God's name do you mean by that?" demanded Rachel.

"Especially," Reislon interjected, "considering the rather extraordinary lengths you have taken to conceal yourselves from your human 'friends' here in the outer Solar system."

"Speaking of which," said Andrew, "I've been observing things carefully since the moment we came aboard this station. I've reached certain conclusions about your technology."

"Oh?"

"Nothing I've seen here looks any more advanced than what we've got, if that. And it's certainly not as advanced as cutting-edge Lokaron stuff. Yet your ships' cloaking system—let alone the system you've described for this station—is beyond anything any of us have. Why this discrepancy?"

"The discrepancy is actually a matter of divergent paths of development, which reflect differences between our race's psychology and both of yours. Technology, after all, is merely the servant of deep-seated predispositions. In order for you to understand, I must give you some background."

Please do. Andrew found himself wondering why Valdes was telling them all this. Maybe, after decades of unrelieved subterfuge, he had a pent-up need for frankness. That wouldn't have been a plausible reason if Valdes had been human . . . but he had, after all, alluded to fundamental psychological differences. Maybe this was one of them.

"Our race, as you are aware, is a physically feeble one, and we arose on a planet with great numbers of very formidable predators. Before we became toolmakers, our only advantage was our protean physical nature. It was our tool for species survival. This shaped our evolution. We are biologically programmed to seek concealment— hence the path our technology has taken—and work through others rather than directly.

"Some time ago we achieved space flight. We were horrified to discover that we had emerged into a galaxy dominated by the Lokaron. Our home system is not far, as interstellar distances go, from a frontier of Lokaron space.

Fortunately, the main currents of Lokaron expansion have been on other frontiers. But it is only a matter of time before they discover us. This danger must be eliminated."

Beside him, Andrew sensed Reislon stiffening at the off-hand tone of Valdes's last sentence.

"But," Andrew surmised, "you found that your good old time-honored techniques didn't work. You can't masquerade as Lokaron, due to their size."

"Actually, there's more to it than that—certain fundamental differences of biochemistry. But you're quite correct, as far as you go. We cannot infiltrate the Lokaron. We can, however, infiltrate humanity, which has now become a player in the Lokaron interstellar order. So our strategy is obvious: we will use the human race as our instrument." Valdes flashed his most charming politician's smile. "We intend to make humanity the galaxy's dominant race!"

For a space Valdes visibly relished the stunned silence he had created.

"And how will you accomplish this?" Andrew finally managed to ask.

"We've been at it for a while. Our operations in the Sol system began not long after the Lokaron discovered you."

"So you were somehow behind the Eaglemen, with their anti-Lokaron agenda?"

"Oh, no, we had nothing to do with them. At that time, we were still observing and infiltrating with great caution, without taking any overt action. You see, we are extremely thorough—"

"And cowardly."

"If you insist on putting it that way," said Valdes evenly.

"We *were* involved in the Jihadist insurgency of 2039. Our original plan had been to use radical Islam as our instrument for unifying Earth and expelling the Lokaron. We still think it has real possibilities—and it's so perfectly controllable! We'll continue our efforts to cultivate it and make it the dominant force in human culture. But we acted prematurely. The insurgency failed, and for now we've resigned ourselves to working within the Confederated Nations of Earth. It at least can be influenced—"

"For which purpose you infiltrated and now control the Black Wolf Society?" queried Reislon.

Valdes laughed heartily. "You couldn't be more wrong. We *created* the Black Wolf Society in 2043 to serve as our human front. Our in-depth studies of human history had shown us how useful a criminal organization with a nationalist or racist agenda can be. The early Sicilian Mafia, the Chinese White Lotus Lodge, the Japanese Black Dragon Society . . . yes, we followed our historical models very closely. By now, the Black Wolf controls more of Earth's vice and illegal activities than anyone realizes—and is wealthier than you imagine."

"I think I might be able to imagine," said Andrew, recalling *City of Osaka* and her modifications.

"This, however, is merely incidental. It is how we fund the Black Wolf's real purpose: to promote human expansionism and militarism. It was through the Black Wolf that we instigated the war with Gev-Rogov."

"By assassinating the Implementer of the Kogurche system," Reislon stated rather than asked, with an air of vindication.

"That, coupled with a long-term campaign of subtly

molding CNE attitudes through influence on the media. This was not too difficult—the human hatred of Gev-Rogov was already there. We've merely intensified it, making it even more useful."

"You," breathed Rachel, "are madder than the March Hare."

"In addition to being an essential element of our plan in itself," Valdes continued, ignoring her, "the war opened up additional advantages. We had certain valuable intelligence sources inside Gev-Rogov. We offered our services to Admiral Arnstein on a clandestine basis. He refused at first, but gradually came around. There were, after all, historical precedents. In World War II, for example, the Allies accepted help from the Mafia during the Italian campaign, and from its Corsican equivalent during the landings in the south of France."

Andrew heard Rachel draw in her breath with a hiss. He dared not look at her.

"After the war, this enabled us, through the Black Wolf Society, to blackmail him into advancing my career—getting me into the Strategic College, for example. Eventually, though, we slightly overplayed our hand. We upped the ante on the blackmail, pressuring him to declare his support for my candidacy. This, apparently, was his sticking point."

Reislon spoke up. "Was this, by any chance, around the same time, earlier this year, when I used circuitous routes to convey my suspicions about the Black Wolf Society to him?"

"Yes. The timing was unfortunate. The strain of his guilt had gradually worn him down. After hearing from you, he contacted Persath and then, seeing no way out, committed suicide."

"No," Rachel whispered, shaking her head frantically. "No, you lying piece of filth! He was murdered under mysterious circumstances. You told us that yourself."

"Oh, that was a lie to persuade you to lead us to Reislon, through Persath. Captain Roark here is in a better position to verify your father's suicide than anyone else. He was the one who discovered the body. He thought I didn't know that he knew I was lying, and he pretended to believe me for reasons of his own. But he's known the truth all along."

"What?" Rachel turned and stared at him.

"Rachel," Andrew began—and then stopped short, halted by what he saw in her changeable light eyes. They had turned to pure ice, so cold that the chill entered into his own soul. He had never known a human face could contain so much contempt.

"But the Human-Rogovon war was only the first step," Valdes resumed, dismissing the digression concerning Admiral Arnstein. "We can now proceed with the next step, without the distraction of trying to recover the lost access key. I will be elected president-general of the CNE. Admiral Arnstein's endorsement would have been helpful, but it is not essential. For one thing, the Black Wolf Society can provide clandestine campaign funding as well as performing such tasks as voter intimidation and occasional 'accidents' to inconvenient individuals. Shortly after my election, I will announce, to general amazement, that I've concluded humanity has bitten off more than it can chew in the Lupus/Sagittarius frontier."

An incredulous laugh escaped Andrew. "How do you suppose your adoring followers will react to such a reversal of all the jingoist rhetoric they've been lapping up for years?"

"It won't matter. Before anyone can recover from the shock, I'll offer to turn various exclusive concessions we got under the treaty over to Hov-Korth and the other *hovahon* of Gev-Harath. They, of course, won't be able to resist such a bait.

"Gev-Rogov will go out of its mind with rage. It regarded that frontier as its sphere of influence until the war with the CNE forced it to reluctantly accept the human presence there. But humanity, which neither the Rogovon nor any other Lokaron can even now bring themselves to take altogether seriously, is one thing: Gev-Harath is another. It's already the richest and most powerful *gevah* of them all. Gev-Rogov will go to war with Gev-Harath to prevent the transfer. And the lesser Lokaron powers will join them for balance-of-power reasons, not wanting Gev-Harath's preeminence to turn into outright domination."

"But the Lokaron don't fight wars," Rachel said, shaking her head as though to clear it of the horror of the truth of her father's death. "Not *real* ones," she amended. "Sure, they've fought lots of small, limited conflicts on the frontiers, but never a general all-out war among the *gevahon*."

"True. They've always avoided that, with their limited, decentralized governments and their constantly expanding frontier where there was room for everyone. For that very reason, they've come to regard a suicidal total war as unthinkable. As your own history shows, people who think that way are all the more likely to blunder into such a war."

Without realizing what it will mean, thought Andrew with a mental nod, recalling Europe before World War I. He was certain that the Lokaron had no real conception of a high-intensity war fought with today's military technology. He wasn't sure he did.

"We will keep the CNE neutral in the war," Valdes continued, "while working behind the scenes to encourage it to take some adroit pickings from the Lokaron wreckage. At the same time, we'll manipulate things—through loans and other assistance to the weaker side at any given moment, for example—to keep the war as long-lasting and wasting as possible before the coalition led by Gev-Rogov finally wins a Pyrrhic victory. The victory will grow even more Pyrrhic afterward, as Gev-Rogov cements its hegemony over its erstwhile allies in a series of aftershock wars of the sort that always follow such a conflict. The end result will be an exhausted Gev-Rogov exercising a characteristically ham-handed imperium over the ruins of the Lokaron civilization.

"In contrast, the CNE will remain internally strong— and, in fact, enriched by war profiteering and enlarged by its acquisitions. And at every point its interests will clash with those of the moribund Rogovon empire. Instigating a conflict probably won't even require much manipulation by us. Given the heritage of hate, war will be inevitable. Its outcome will be equally inevitable: a universal human empire."

"Controlled from behind the scenes by you Kappainu," Andrew added.

"Of course. But does it really matter? Humans won't know it. They can enjoy the fruits of imperialism in blissful ignorance."

"But we don't *want* an empire!" blurted Rachel. "We've gotten that kind of thing out of our systems. The Earth First Party was the last hurrah of the Totalitarian Era. We've learned that what governs best really *is* what governs least. This diabolical scheme of yours can't possibly succeed."

"I assure you that it can. Every phase of the plan has been subjected to a rigorous mathematical analysis. All contingencies and variables have been considered."

"Except one," Reislon pointed out. "Your projections are based on the assumption that Gev-Rogov will continue to be ruled by its present centralized, brain-dead regime, whose actions are of course perfectly predictable."

"Yes, that is a necessary precondition. Therefore the elements seeking to overthrow it must be thwarted. That is why learning that you have been working with them, and now capturing you, have been highly desirable fringe benefits of this operation."

Da Silva spoke up in tones of self-congratulation. "I didn't dare be too obvious and insist on your presence in *City of Osaka*'s gig. Besides, I knew it was unnecessary, because you'd want to come."

Reislon regarded the two Kappainu. "You evidently know quite a lot about me. But there is one thing you don't know. It concerns that same gig, which is now under guard on one of your hangar decks."

"Yes?" inquired Valdes impatiently.

"I booby-trapped it."

✯✯ ✯ ✯✯
CHAPTER SEVENTEEN
✯✯ ✯ ✯✯

THERE WAS NO QUESTION but that Reislon had everyone's undivided attention. Andrew and Rachel simply stared, while Valdes turned a look of angry inquiry on Da Silva.

"He's bluffing!" the latter protested with the indignation of the wronged underling. "The gig was scanned as it entered the hangar deck, in accordance with standard procedure."

"The device is inert and effectively undetectable by a routine scan," said Reislon easily. "It can, with difficulty, be detected after it is activated—which I did as we were leaving the gig. But I doubt if you can do so before it reaches the end of the countdown it has already commenced. And even if you do, any tampering will cause it to detonate immediately and do your station considerable damage."

"Have the gig launched on autopilot and sent outside the station's deflection shield," Valdes ordered Da Silva.

"I would advise against it," Reislon cautioned, "as any such attempt will also result in immediate detonation."

Valdes turned to Andrew. His earlier emotionless smugness was in abeyance. "Do you know of this?"

"He doesn't," Resilon answered for him. And, in an aside to Andrew: "I saw no reason to bother you with things you didn't need to know." Andrew could only gawk.

"I still say this is a bluff," Da Silva insisted.

"Are you willing to gamble on that?" Reislon asked Valdes. "Especially when you don't need to. You see, I'm perfectly willing to deactivate it . . . on one condition."

Valdes' eyes narrowed. "Yes?"

"When you destroy *Broadsword*, you must not destroy *City of Osaka*. Instead, capture it—which shouldn't be difficult, given the damage it has sustained and the inadequacy of the prize crew—and use it to transport me to the rebel Rogovon base in the Kogurche system."

As though from a great distance, across an abyss of shock and rage, Andrew heard himself begin to speak. "You miserable—"

"Name-calling serves no purpose. And you have no grounds for accusing me of dishonesty, nor any right to feel betrayed. I have never made any attempt to conceal the fact that my primary loyalty is to Gev-Rogov. I want to see it revolutionized so it can attain its potential instead of continuing to stagnate. This must be my primary concern."

"But," said Andrew, thinking frantically and speaking to Valdes as much as to Reislon, "you've just heard that they want to keep Gev-Rogov just the way it is, to avoid upsetting their master plan."

"True." Reislon turned back to Valdes. "If you agree to my conditions, I in turn will undertake to influence a new regime in Gev-Rogov in the direction you want."

Valdes looked as stunned as Andrew felt. "You mean . . . influence it to go to war with Gev-Harath on schedule?"

"Precisely."

"But . . . why would you, a self-proclaimed Rogovon loyalist, be willing to do that? You've heard me describe what we intend for the ultimate fate of Gev-Rogov to be."

"Yes, I've heard your plan—and, on reflection, I believe I want to further it. Because, you see, I think you're wrong in one important particular: Gev-Rogov, not the CNE, will emerge as the ultimate victor."

Rachel looked like she had passed beyond shock into a kind of emotional dead zone. Andrew could only stare at Reislon, and all he could see was the greenish coloring, and all he could feel was what that shade had caused humans to feel since before his birth. Only the laser weapons trained on him kept him motionless.

"Congratulations," he said with a calmness that surprised him. "You've now become a *quadruple* agent."

Valdes shook his head in perplexity. "If you turn out to be right, then our plan will have failed. So why should I agree to this?"

Reislon gave a Lokaron smile. "Because you think I'm *wrong*. If you really believe in your own plan, you should welcome this chance to have me unintentionally working for you. In any event, I suggest you not wait too long to make your decision." He brushed a finger over an area of skin on the underside of his right wrist, and the imprinted circuits of what Andrew guessed was a timepiece glowed to life. He gave Valdes a significant look. Da Silva began to look jittery.

Valdes appeared to consider. In fact, he seemed to put on a great show of it before finally nodding. "Very well. I agree to your terms."

Rachel suddenly swung on Reislon and spoke wildly. "Damn you, if you're supposed to be so smart, can't you see he's just pretending to agree? The moment you've deactivated your bomb, he'll—" Her voice ended in a gasp of pain as one of the guards reversed his laser weapon and used its butt to strike her on the back of the head, sending her staggering forward onto her hands and knees, moaning.

Before Andrew could act, he saw—through the reddish mist that filmed the world in his eyes—the guard bring the weapon back around and point it at his midriff. He held himself in check with a shivering effort.

"Enough of this." Valdes touched a communicator button on his desk and began to speak in his native language as well as his human form permitted. *Reporting to his superior*, Andrew guessed. An individual who spent almost all his time on Earth, among humans, wouldn't be able to function as the ultimate Kappainu boss in the solar system. That individual must reside here, at their secret base. The short conversation ended, and Valdes turned back to Reislon. "Very well. Let us proceed to the hangar bay, where you can do whatever is needful."

"One additional point. I will require Captain Roark's

assistance. As commander of the gig, he alone has access to certain code-locked instruments I will need."

What in God's name is he talking about? thought Andrew blankly. He started to open his mouth. Then Reislon's eyes met his.

That eye-contact lasted for only a fraction of a second, before Reislon hastily looked away. But all at once, Andrew knew that he must play along.

"Why should I cooperate with you, you half-Rogovon mongrel bastard?" he spat, hoping he wasn't overdoing truculence.

"You will cooperate with him," Valdes stated firmly and gave a peremptory jerk of his head. Da Silva and one of the guards hauled Rachel to her feet, one grasping each arm, while the other guard kept Reislon and Andrew covered with his weapon. Valdes led the way, reversing the route they had come before, until they reached the cavernous hangar bay where the gig rested with its hatch still open, dwarfed by the ships that rested on the extensive deck. Beyond the atmosphere curtain lay starless blackness, with the universe of stars as invisible to them as they were to it.

"All right," said Valdes to Reislon and Andrew. "Go aboard and do whatever you need to do. One of the guards will accompany you. Ms. Arnstein will remain here with us as a form of insurance."

Reislon led the way up the short ramp the gig had extended to the deck, followed by the guard. Andrew brought up the rear, casting anxious looks over his shoulder at Rachel, even though he was fairly sure what he'd see if he met her eyes.

The gig was a standard design. There was no airlock, only a hatch suitable for fastening to a larger ship. Within the passenger cabin, there was barely space to move around among the acceleration seats—human-designed ones, so Reislon had been decidedly uncomfortable. Now he wedged himself awkwardly in and proceeded to do something. The guard behind him made it impossible for Andrew to see what that something was, or to get all the way through the hatch.

Suddenly, with a flashing of lights and a whir of power, the gig came to life.

This is impossible, flashed through Andrew's brain. *There's a checklist to be run through! There's a sequence! There's—*

Then he had no leisure to further catalogue all the things that weren't right, for Reislon swung around with remarkable agility in the cramped space, raised the arm that held the weapon implant—and therefore was necessarily heavier than the other one—and brought it viciously down on the guard's head. There was a sickening sound, and it immediately became obvious that the Kappainu were as fragile as they looked.

Reislon shoved the unconscious form out the hatch. As it tumbled out, it collided with Andrew, causing him to stagger halfway through the hatch, whose frame he grasped to steady himself.

Reislon called to him to get inside. The translator rendered it as a yell.

At the same moment, the guard on the hangar deck outside aimed his laser weapon at Andrew, who was still trying to get his balance—and even if he hadn't been, he had a realistic appreciation of his chance of dodging a beam that struck at the speed of light.

Rachel, breaking away from Da Silva, tackled the guard, grabbing his weapon and wrenching it aside, while wrestling him to the floor. It flashed through Andrew's mind that a young human woman—even a slender, not especially athletic one—was probably at least as strong as the Kappainu. But then Valdes and Da Silva both grappled her from behind and dragged her, kicking and clawing, off the guard. They must, Andrew assumed, want her for whatever hostage value she might possess, for future contingencies.

Andrew prepared to launch himself down the ramp at them.

At that instant, with a rise in the volume of the power-whine, the gig lurched as it lifted off the deck, tumbling Andrew back inside just before the hatch clanged shut.

"Strap in!" snapped Reislon as he brought the gig around and gunned it toward the atmosphere curtain. That field of pressure-gravity was impervious to molecules in a gaseous state, but would pass a solid object moving no faster than a brisk walk. Andrew, as he flung himself into a seat, was certain Reislon must be exceeding that limit. But before he could shout at the Lokar to slow down, they were through the curtain and Reislon applied full power.

Andrew wondered if the gravity beam that had reeled them through the hangar bay was strong enough to over-power the gig's engines in a straight game of tug. In the event, he didn't have to find out. The beam was not currently activated—there was no reason for it to be—and before its stunned operators could bring it on line the straining gig was beyond its limited range. The same, Andrew decided, must be true of the station's laser weapons; he kept expecting to die in an inferno of coherent energy, but he continued to live as the gig fled at an acceleration that pressed him back into the seat. He wondered how Reislon was holding up under it, jammed uncomfortably into a seat designed for humans.

Then, with the same lack of warning they had experienced before, they were suddenly among the blazing hordes of stars. Astern, where the Kappainu space station had loomed a second before, nothing could be seen.

Andrew realized he had been holding his breath for a long while. He released it with a *whoosh*. "Reislon—!" he gasped.

The Lokar looked shaken up, but spoke in his usual calm way—altogether too calm for Andrew's taste. "Yes, I know I owe you an explanation. I did not, of course, actually plant a bomb aboard this gig. I did, however, rig special override circuitry which allows instantaneous powering-up and activation of all systems—a panic button in your parlance. It has its uses in emergency situations, though naturally, such a brute-force approach carries a cost. This gig's electrical systems will need to be overhauled before—"

"Damn you, Reislon! *You left Rachel back there!*"

"What would you have had me do? I would naturally have preferred to get all three of us away. But a hopeless rescue attempt would have had no effect but to prevent the escape I had maneuvered for so carefully. And *none* of us would have escaped with the priceless knowledge of Kappainu capabilities and intentions that we now possess.

"But even that is secondary. The important thing—no, the essential thing—is to warn Captain Taylor of the trap being laid. I have already activated a homing beacon; we should be able to establish contact with him shortly, and *City of Osaka* will be able to get clear."

"*City of Osaka*? You mean *Broadsword*, don't you?"

"I mean *City of Osaka*. *Broadsword*'s survival, like Ms. Arnstein's escape, is of course desirable. But remember what Valdes said: *City of Osaka* has a concealed access key, like the Cydonia artifact that we've now lost. It *must* get to Kogurche, so Zhygon can examine it and, if possible, reverse-engineer it."

Andrew drew a breath. "Reislon, I'm just glad that you are—I think—on our side."

CHAPTER EIGHTEEN

AS REISLON HAD FORETOLD, it took very little time to establish contact with *Broadsword*. Taylor's bewildered face appeared on the comm screen.

"Andy! What in the hell happened to you? Where have you been? What—?"

"Jamel, there isn't time for a full explanation. This is urgent. The Kappainu have their base out here, and it's undetectable—it might as well be in a private universe of its own as far as any outside sensors, including the Mark One Eyeball, are concerned. It can be moved, very clumsily, and they're now maneuvering it across your projected course so you'll enter its surrounding field like we did and be taken by surprise. You've got to take evasive action at once."

Taylor visibly forced himself to defer further questions.

He turned aside and gave a series of orders. Evasive action was easier said than done for spacecraft, with their inherent lack of maneuverability, but reactionless drives made it less impractical than it once had been. "All right. Done," he told Andrew.

"Good. Next—and this is just as urgent—you need to detach *City of Osaka* from *Broadsword* and have her set a course away from you and away from the area where this gig just seemed to appear out of nowhere, to rendezvous with us. And tell the prize crew we'll be docking with her."

"What? I need for you to report back here. Why do you want to rendezvous with *City of Osaka*?"

"It's a long story—longer than we have time for. Briefly, we were captured and escaped—at least Reislon and I did. Rachel . . . Ms. Arnstein is still a prisoner. And we lost the Cydonia artifact."

"You *what*?"

"But there's another one concealed somewhere aboard *City of Osaka*. It's called an access key, by the way, and it's the only means by which the Kappainu base can be detected and communicated with. We've *got* to get it to the Rogovon rebels at Kogurche so Zhygon, the scientist we told you about, can study it."

Once again, Taylor clamped self-control down on his raging curiosity and spoke to his communications officer. "Raise *City of Osaka*. Tell Lieutenant Morales she's to break formation and apply a lateral vector of—" he thought briefly and rattled off figures "—and await Captain Roark, who's approaching in a gig." Andrew, looking at the gig's rudimentary nav plot, saw that the orders were being carried out. Then Taylor turned back to him. "All right. Done. But, Andy, do you really need to go to Kogurche? With the evidence you and Reislon now have, surely we can blow this wide open, let everyone on Earth know that—"

"Jamel, there *really* isn't time for this. You just have to take my word that we can't afford to risk trusting anyone connected with the CNE. You have no idea how deep this infiltration runs."

"But—"

"Jamel, listen to me: *Valdes is a Kappainu.*"

Taylor's face was a study in stunned incredulity. "No . . . no, you're wrong. You've *got* to be wrong! This is too crazy."

"He's there, I tell you, on the Kappainu space station. We talked with him. He told us their plan. They want to rule the galaxy—by proxy, because that's their way of doing things and because they're cowards. But, as we already know, they can't use the Lokaron. So they're going to use *us* instead. The human race is going to be their puppet. They're going to engineer a fratricidal general war among the Lokaron, leaving only a crippled Gev-Rogov which humanity—led by President-General Valdes—will finish off and pick up the pieces. Oh, I'm sure it will be all streaming banners and glittering uniforms and monumental architecture and rousing military parades—I'll bet they'll mine Albert Speer for stylistic inspiration for the grand and glorious Human Empire. And from behind the stage scenery, aliens will be controlling us for their own purposes, in which our welfare plays no part. Who knows? Maybe they'll eventually feel secure enough to cut the crap and dispense with us altogether."

As Andrew talked, Taylor's features gradually stiffened into a dark gray mask. When he finally spoke, his voice was very controlled. "You're in possession of knowledge that is just as important as the access key—is that what you called it?—aboard *City of Osaka*. This makes it doubly essential that you get away. But I see that you're approaching rendezvous."

Andrew glanced at the nav plot and then at the view screen, and saw that it was so. The frigate-sized hull of *City of Osaka* was gliding into view. Neither Andrew nor Reislon was familiar with the gig's docking conventions, but those were almost entirely computerized. As the gig maneuvered itself toward the concavity of its docking berth, Andrew concluded another hurried consultation with Taylor.

"All right, Andy, I've ordered Lieutenant Morales to turn command of *City of Osaka* over to you, and to be ready for transition as soon as you and Reislon are aboard. You'll find she's very competent. When you've completed transition, *Broadsword* will follow and—*what?*" Taylor's head turned aside, and Andrew could hear the cry of "*Incoming!*" and the loudspeakers blaring "General quarters!"

"Jamel, what's happening?" demanded Andrew as the gig rose into position and the clamps that held it began to descend from above.

"We're under attack," was Taylor's terse reply. "The hostile ships are in cloak, but the fact that weapons fire is originating from them partially reveals their locations. We're returning fire. Make transition fast! We'll follow. And now . . . I'm a little busy." He signed off just as the gig completed its docking procedure and the hatch opened. Andrew emerged to find a CNEN officer—young, female, Hispanic-looking, compactly built—awaiting him on the docking berth's tiny deck.

"Lieutenant Morales, sir. I've been ordered to—"

"Yes. You stand relieved, Lieutenant. You're now my X.O. And now let's get the hell up to the control room and get this ship out of here!"

As he made his way through the ship with Reislon and his new executive officer, Andrew reflected that what was happening wasn't the Kappainu's style. It must show their desperation. Seeing the failure of their ploy to trap *Broadsword* and *City of Osaka,* they had launched their warcraft in an entirely out-of-character direct attack. He knew nothing about the capabilities of those warcraft, but he was willing to bet that only their cloaking technology gave even a group of them any chance whatsoever against a CNEN strike cruiser.

It might be enough.

He pounded into the control room, where members of the prize crew were frantically at work. He gestured Morales's "Attention on deck!" to silence and threw himself into the captain's chair.

"Get me a tactical plot," he ordered Morales. "And where do we stand on our countdown to transition?"

"Just about there, sir."

Andrew studied the tac plot that wakened to life on a holographically projected display screen in midair before his eyes. It immediately became apparent that Taylor's orders, and Morales's execution of them, had achieved what Andrew had intended. *City of Osaka* was headed outward, with *Broadsword* interposed between her and the region of space where the Kappainu base had its ghostly existence, and from which the attackers were swarming. The plot showed those attackers' deduced locations, computer-projected from the origins of the beams and missiles that were stabbing at *Broadsword*. The latter, and her deployed fighters, were returning fire—not without effect, judging from analysis of the debris and the diminished volume of hostile fire, for a couple of the inferred hostile icons were flickering. Andrew wished the status board Jamel Taylor must be intently watching could be downloaded to him so he could see how much damage *Broadsword* was taking.

"Raise Captain Taylor," he commanded. When Taylor's face appeared in the comm screen there was no visible damage in the background, but the entire image shuddered with a near miss, and the damage-control klaxons could be heard in the background.

"Jamel," he began without ceremony, "we're about ready to make transition. Start you own sequence and follow us."

"Negative." Taylor's voice matched his face, which was a mask of dark iron. "We'll stay here and cover your withdrawal. I don't think you'll get away otherwise. Look at your tac plot."

Andrew did. Many of the missiles streaking from the cloaked attackers were now following courses that ignored *Broadsword*. Some of those attacking ships' inferred courses also began to change.

"You see, Andy," said Taylor, and his tone gentled. "They get it. *City of Osaka* is the ship that matters, carrying an access key and your knowledge. You've *got* to get to Kogurche. CNS *Broadsword* has just become expendable."

"Jamel—"

"Signing off. Good luck." The comm screen went blank.

"Approaching final countdown to transition, sir," reported Morales.

Andrew barely heard her. He stared at the tac plot.

Broadsword, foregoing self-defense, concentrated her laser fire on the Kappainu missiles targeting *City of Osaka*, leaving her fighters to frantically seek out the enemy ships. Some of those missiles began to flicker and go out . . . but not all of them. Three came inexorably on, narrowing the gap as Andrew watched with horrified fascination.

City of Osaka's only armament was a pair of antimissile lasers. What made such laser installations practical was a focusing application of artificial gravity that extended their range beyond that of the bomb-pumped lasers of missile warheads. But these were light versions, and the margin was a narrow one. They both concentrated on one of the missiles at a time. They caught one and then another. But then the third icon flashed stroboscopically, denoting detonation.

At that instant, while the nuclear-pumped X-ray laser flashed across space, the stars in the view-forward began to stream aft.

The space-distorting effect of transition, combined with the ship's deflection shield, made the hit a glancing one. Nevertheless, the explosive energy-release shook the ship, and for an instant the control room was a hell of concussion and noise.

But then the streaming tunnel of multicolored light was past, and they were in the blackness of overspace, with the deck steady as the ship's artificial gravity resumed its mastery.

"Set a course for the Kogurche system, Lieutenant," Andrew ordered as reports began to come in. There were no injuries, and hull integrity was holding.

"Already done, sir," said Morales with what Andrew was beginning to recognize as her customary crispness.

"Excellent." Only then did Andrew let himself lean back, close his eyes, and tell himself, over and over, that when he'd last seen her *Broadsword* still lived.

He also reminded himself that the same was true of Rachel Arnstein . . . who now despised him.

He finally turned to Morales. "I'm sorry I didn't have a chance to get to know you before this rather abrupt change of command, Lieutenant—Alana, isn't it? But I assume that you, like all of *Broadsword*'s personnel, were briefed on the situation as we now know it to exist, including the existence of the Kappainu and their special capabilities."

"Yes, sir. I don't mind saying that some of it was difficult to accept."

"Well, I and Reislon'Sygnath here have been their captives, and we've learned things you're going to find even harder to swallow. You and the rest of the prize crew are also probably going to be taken aback at the nature of the allies we're going to Kogurche to contact. In short, we have a lot to talk about. But at the moment, exhaustion is finally starting to catch up with me. So for now I'll turn the con over to you and—"

"Sir!" Something in Morales's voice made Andrew disregard her unheard-of interruption of the captain. She was staring at the overspace scanner screen. He followed her gaze, and the fatigue toxins seemed to drain out of him as he saw the two red blips that had appeared aft.

"We are being followed," said Reislon unnecessarily.

The voyage to Kogurche gave them time to organize a stem-to-stern search for *City of Osaka*'s access key. It was barely enough time, for the thing was so fiendishly hidden that for a while Andrew entertained the possibility that Valdes had been lying for some unfathomable alien reason. But it finally turned up, so embedded in the ship's navigational instrumentation that they didn't dare risk trying to extract it while en route.

At least the problem gave them something to think about besides the Kappainu ships shadowing them.

Repeating the trick *Broadsword* had played was, of course, out of the question. *City of Osaka*, with her two pathetic point-defense lasers, was no strike cruiser. If she suddenly transitioned out of overspace, her pursuers would simply follow her into normal space, where she would be at their doubtless extremely limited mercy.

"Of course," said Andrew as he, Reislon, and Alana Morales sat glumly at a wardroom table discussing the hopelessness of that option, "if we did so somewhere short of Kogurche, at least we wouldn't be revealing to them the location of the Rogovon rebel fleet."

Morales's dark eyes flashed. She had been told

everything and had more or less adjusted to the fact that there were Rogovon who must be treated as allies, but there *were* limits. She glanced at Reislon, then immediately looked away, but not before the Lokar noticed.

"Actually," said Reislon evenly, "I would advise against that. This ship's destruction or capture would simply mean that everything we've learned so far would go for naught and the Kappainu would be free to proceed with their plans, with all that implies for both our races—including the Rogovon revolutionary movement. No, our only alternative is to stay the course, in the hope that help will be waiting in the Kogurche system. Remember, Borthru proceeded directly there in *Trovyr*, and has presumably been there for some time."

"Very well," Andrew decided. "We'll make transition in a region that's not right on top of your people's base but close enough to it to offer some hope that it's being patrolled. And we'll start broadcasting a distress signal on their special band as soon as we're in normal space."

They came out of overspace in the gravitational hinterlands between the two Kogurche suns. Their pursuers appeared astern, at a range so short as to earn Andrew's grudging respect for their precision.

"They're not even bothering to cloak themselves," said Morales.

Why should they? thought Andrew. Aloud: "Get the distress signal out."

"Already done, sir." Morales, Andrew decided, should set that to music.

"They also are not troubling with a surrender demand," said Reislon as missiles, launched at extreme range, appeared on the tactical plot.

"Evasive action," Andrew ordered. There wasn't much else he could do, as they were already at general quarters. So he studied the sensor readouts on the Kappainu warships, which he had never had a chance to observe uncloaked before. They were no more than frigate-sized, which came as no surprise; the hidden Kappainu space station, huge as it was, could hardly have accommodated anything larger in significant numbers. So they wouldn't be carrying fighters. They were actually less massive than *City of Osaka* . . . but they were warriors and it was a drone.

Still, he didn't think much of their tactics. He himself would have waited and gotten in closer before launching missiles—assuming that the Kappainu could endure extended high accelerations, which they probably could since the artificial gravity in their station had seemed to be roughly Earth normal. The missiles' lengthy flight time allowed his defensive lasers plenty of time for targeting solutions, and they did themselves proud once the missiles came within their limited range.

But it was not enough. Some missiles got close enough to detonate. *City of Osaka*'s deflection shields could not cope with that concentration of directed energy, and she shuddered and lurched under repeated hits.

"The lasers' fire-control electronics are fried, sir," Morales reported calmly. "And the deflection shields—"

"I see, Lieutenant," said Andrew. *No way out*, he forced himself not to add as he stared at the two scarlet blips of their tormentors, which would now undoubtedly close to the range of ship-to-ship lasers rather than wasting any more missiles . . .

And as he watched, those blips went out.

"What—?" he heard Morales gasp.

"It appears," said Reislon from his ill-fitting acceleration couch, "that they have gone into cloak and ceased all weapon fire, which would reveal their position."

"And I see why," said Andrew as an entire formation of blips began to appear on the outer edges of the scanner screen.

"They could still have gotten us, sir," said Morales. "They had time, just barely, before those ships could come in range—"

"—And obliterate them," Andrew finished for her. "Yes, they could have done it . . . if they'd been willing to sacrifice themselves. But, as I'm coming to understand, that's not the Kappainu way. Which," he concluded thoughtfully, "is what may save us yet."

"We're being hailed, sir," said the communication officer. And the screen came to life, revealing a Lokaron face of the green-skinned, relatively thick-featured variety.

"Borthru!" Andrew exclaimed.

Off to the side, Morales sighed, "I never thought I'd be so glad to see a face like that."

CHAPTER NINETEEN

"HOW DID YOU LOCATE US SO QUICKLY?" Andrew asked as Borthru's ships formed a protective englobement around *City of Osaka*, just in case. "Not that I'm complaining, mind you."

"When *Broadsword* failed to follow us here, we feared the worst," Borthru explained. "We have been conducting intensive patrolling ever since. Some among us have been arguing for its discontinuance, saying all hope is gone. It is fortunate that you arrived no later than you did. But where is *Broadsword*?"

"She may or may not be following us, so please keep up your patrols for now. I'll explain why later. We have a *lot* of news, most of which you won't like—so much that I don't want to have to repeat it all twice. For now, let me just tell you that we have a device like the Cydonia artifact aboard this ship, but that it's going to require Zhygon and his team to get it out."

"I'll signal ahead. And now, let us proceed to the base. I'll do my best to contain my curiosity until our arrival." Borthru signed off.

"All right, X.O., make formation with our allies," Andrew told Morales.

"Aye, aye, sir." The young lieutenant's unease was palpable as she cast glances at the Rogovon ships in the viewscreen, but she carried out her orders with her usual emotionless efficiency.

Andrew drew her aside and spoke privately. "Alana, when we arrive at our destination a Rogovon scientist named Zhygon'Trogak and his assistants are going to come aboard and extract the access key. You will cooperate with them to the fullest. Understand?"

"Yes, sir."

"Good. Now, we're going to be docking at a space habitat, or collection of habitats, full of Rogovon. I imagine you and your crew will be most comfortable remaining on this ship during our stay."

Morales's lips quirked upward in the closest thing to a smile he had yet seen on her. "That's one way to put it, sir."

"All right. Here's something to occupy your time. I want you to start working on your human prisoners—the original Black Wolf crew. Take them one at a time, as is standard interrogation technique. Show them the evidence that they've been pawns of aliens and see if you can turn any of them. Some of them may have information we can use."

"Aye, aye, sir. Of course, you realize I'm not an Intelligence specialist."

"No, but as I've found out, you're damned intelligent. Close enough."

Andrew had never realized how comforting Rachel's presence had been when he had first been among the Rogovon revolutionaries. It had prevented him from being the only human around, as he now was as he sat at a conference table otherwise occupied by Borthru, Zhygon, three of the principal leaders of the revolutionary coalition . . . and Reislon, who barely even seemed like an alien any more.

He was hoarse from talking for hours. Fortunately, one of the few luxury items the revolutionaries possessed was coffee—a lucrative export item for Earth, for caffeine, like alcohol, affected the Lokaron and human nervous systems similarly. He appreciated their generosity in letting him keep himself awake with it as he and Reislon recounted the entire, incredible story. He doubted his Rogovon listeners would have believed him without Reislon's corroboration.

Now there was an appalled silence. Andrew started to reach for his awkward Lokaron-designed coffee cup again, but thought better of it. It wouldn't do to have to ask to be excused at some crucial point in the discussion.

Kostov'Zhythog, who appeared to be *primus inter pares* in the revolutionary leadership, finally broke the silence. He was a transmitter, as were his colleagues Vrontu'Torath and Gorova'Suvak, which was no surprise; the Rogovon were considered socially backward by the other Lokaron, and even their radicals had old-fashioned attitudes concerning gender roles. He also showed all the indicia of old age. But he had listened alertly. Now he shook himself in a way that Andrew recognized as a characteristic bit of Lokaron body language, denoting a wish to wake up from a nightmare known to be real.

"So," Kostov said heavily, "this is to be the destiny of Gev-Rogov: the instigator of a war that will bring all the Lokaron societies—including, in the end, itself—down in ruins, leaving a rubble heap ruled by these Kappainu, acting through—" He glanced at Andrew and stopped himself short of saying something tactless.

"But the Kappainu may be wrong," said Gorova'Suvak, leader of a moderate faction and a vacillator by nature. "Maybe their plan will fail in the long run."

"In the short run, however, it calls for our movement's failure," Reislon reminded him.

"Which makes your organization and we humans natural allies," Andrew added.

"But we can't trust the CNE government," declared Vrontu'Torath. He headed a hard-line faction, and Andrew had found him the toughest nut to crack. "It has obviously been infiltrated, we don't know how deeply. And even if it hadn't been, it wouldn't trust *us*."

"Probably true," Andrew admitted. "Which is why I don't propose that we involve the CNE. And it goes without saying that you can't approach the Gev-Rogov government. So . . . I suggest that we deal with the problem ourselves."

For a moment, Andrew permitted himself to savor the sensation of, for once, having left even Reislon thunderstruck. Then he hurried on before his listeners could recover.

"The Kappainu space station is in the dark outer reaches of the Sol system where their invisibility technology is practically redundant. Even without it, they'd be noticed only by a wild chance, especially considering that they're well outside the plane of the ecliptic, which is all anyone ever pays attention to. Entirely consistent with their psychology, of course—they're hyper-cautious by nature. But in this case their caution is self-defeating. Your fleet can go there and make transition from overspace unobserved. The CNE doesn't even have to know about the operation."

Vrontu made noises that the translator ignored, before finally managing to form words. "But what if we fail? You're asking us to risk our carefully husbanded military resources on a mission that has nothing to do with our organization's reason for existence: the liberation of Gev-Rogov. No, our duty is to Gev-Rogov, not to humans!"

"I remind you," said Reislon, "that the Kappainu are committed to keeping the present regime in place in Gev-Rogov. It is integral to their plan. We will never succeed in overthrowing it unless their power is broken."

"Reislon is right," said Borthru abruptly. "This is our fight, too. And besides . . . it has been altogether too long since we have been offered a bold plan of action." He turned to Andrew and gave a classic Lokaron smile—the smile of a race of omnivores tending to a more carnivorous orientation than that of *Homo sapiens*. Then he faced his political leaders again. "It's too bad that we had to have it offered to us by a human. But that's our fault, not his."

There was an uneasy silence. Andrew knew the pitfalls of trying to deduce the political nuances of nonhumans, but he sensed that in this assemblage Borthru spoke for the younger Rogovon military officers among the revolutionaries, who had been kept straining at the leash for too long.

Gorova, ever the voice of caution, spoke hesitantly. "But even if we break them in the Sol system, they may just fall back to their home system—regarding whose location we have no clue—and try again."

"Still," Borthru urged, "it would be a major setback for them. They would have to start over from scratch, rebuilding a structure of infiltration that took decades. This would give us time to carry out *our* plans. After the revolution, with a new Rogovon regime that knows all about them, their scheme will no longer be viable."

"At the same time," Reislon mused, "it would be highly desirable to obtain more facts about them—notably the location of their home planet—so we could attack the problem at its source."

"Yes." Andrew spoke decisively, for Reislon had given him an opening. "Also, we need irrefutable evidence to persuade the CNE government to adopt all-out antiKappainu security measures: biological scans of all its personnel, and so forth. I therefore propose that we not destroy the station—at least not until we've had a chance to penetrate it. Also," he continued, trying to make it sound like an afterthought, "they have a human prisoner, whose testimony would be useful."

"Ah, yes, Ms. Arnstein," said Reislon. Andrew knew what a Lokaron smile looked like, but this was the first time he had seen one being smoothed out. "Yes, I suppose it would be desirable to recover her alive . . . for debriefing."

"Er . . . ahem . . . yes, precisely. Debriefing."

"But," demanded Vrontu, on whom the byplay was lost, "how can we penetrate the station?"

"I have an idea for that. Remember, we have an access key and therefore can detect the station and communicate with it. Zhygon, you've had time to study the thing. Can you replicate it?"

"Yes," said the old scientist unequivocally. "In reverse-engineering an unfamiliar device, knowing exactly what it is intended to do is half the battle. It also helps that, as you have pointed out, the overall Kappainu technology is no more advanced than ours; this is just an application of it that has never occurred to us. Our facilities here are up to producing a fair quantity of comparable units—not as compact and elegant as the original, but quite functional, and adapted to installation on our ships. The greatest problem was figuring out the controls by trial and error."

"Can you rig an auxiliary control board for the one from *City of Osaka* that will be usable by humans?"

"I should think so, with the help of your technicians."

"Good." Andrew turned back to the others. "So your ships will be able to detect the station. And as I've explained, the cloaking system their ships use is relatively elementary; detecting *them* should be easy. Knowing them, I suspect that finding out that they're in full view of their enemies will shatter their morale."

"You still haven't explained how you think it will be possible to simply walk into the station," Vrontu persisted.

"What makes it possible is that we have a ship—*City*

of Osaka—of a type used by the Black Wolf Society, whose human personnel they are accustomed to employing. Also . . . I have an officer who should be able to play a useful role."

"Sit down, X.O.," said Andrew as Lieutenant Morales entered his cabin aboard *City of Osaka*.

"Thank you, sir." She lowered her compact body—no more than five feet two but well-proportioned for its height—into a chair. She looked more Castilian than anything else, but with a hint of high Indian cheekbones and a slightly dusky skin tone that suggested African genes.

"So, how is it going with our guests?"

"Difficult, sir. It seems the Black Wolf Society has a very strict code of silence, and even my promises of protection against vengeance haven't budged most of them. And they think what we've told them about the Black Wolf being under the control of shape-shifting aliens is an elaborate lie. There are a few, however, who've revealed flexibility, and I've made some progress with them—thanks to Zhygon."

"Zhygon?" Andrew's eyebrows rose.

"Yes, sir. He's kept the body of 'Amletto Leong' in cryo suspension. He let us show it to the ones we thought might be open to influence. It made an impression. But there's only one of them I really think is worth any further effort. And he'd be a good catch; he was pretty high-ranking and was involved with communications."

"I'm *very* glad to hear that. You see, I have a plan, for which it sounds like he can be very useful. And so can you."

"Me, sir?"

"I believe so. But first, let me ask you something. Did Da Silva, the Kappainu captain of this ship, ever see you while we had him as a prisoner?"

"No, sir." Morales was obviously puzzled by the question. "He was brought aboard *Broadsword* just before I was sent over with the prize crew. We never met."

"Good." Andrew leaned forward and spoke carefully. "Alana, I'm sure you're already aware that you happen to bear a certain physical resemblance to the type of human form that the Kappainu assume when they shape-shift."

"Yes, sir. That was one of the things that Captain Taylor explained to us aboard *Broadsword* before we left the Sol system. Some of my so-called friends kidded me about it. Thank God for medical scanners!"

Andrew's expression stayed serious. "Well, this is why you can be uniquely useful—if, and only if, you choose to. You see, my plan is this." He proceeded to set forth his idea, and her part in it, concluding: "I want you to understand, Alana, that this is strictly on a volunteer basis—a *real* volunteer basis, by which I mean that if you say no, this conversation never took place. I cannot order you to hazard yourself on a long chance like this."

"Actually, sir, it's worse than a long chance. With all due respect, it's crazy as hell." She gave an ear-to-ear smile that made her almost unrecognizable. "I think I like it."

"You know, Lieutenant, you remind me of stories my mother used to tell me about a friend of hers named Ada Rivera, who was one of those killed in 2030. If the name sounds familiar, there are streets named after her today." Andrew stood up, not trusting himself to say anything more. "And now, let's go and talk to this potential Black Wolf defector of yours."

Rory Gallivan was a raffishly handsome man in his thirties, a classic Black Irish type with startlingly blue eyes under his dark brows. His appearance was appropriate, for he came from a long line of IRA men. His father had been the last of them, though, for even in his grandfather's time the organization—and its Orange opposite number—had been growing increasingly irrelevant after the Belfast Accords that had set in motion the process of eventual reintegration of Ulster into the Republic. The remaining hard-liners had tried to sabotage it, but everyone saw them more and more clearly as mad dogs for whom terrorism had become an end in itself—the only way of life they knew. Several years before Rory's birth, the CNE had seen the peace process to completion. By then his grandfather had died of sheer, festering bitterness and his father had departed for the greener pastures of organized crime—greener than ever, now that they were nourished with the proceeds of interstellar smuggling.

But by the time Rory Gallivan had been of an age to follow in the paternal footsteps, the industry's small entrepreneurs were gradually being squeezed out by the Black Wolf Society, which had been born only three years after himself. He had inherited his father's sense for the direction the wind was blowing and had joined the new umbrella organization, which didn't react well to holdouts.

"Yes," he explained to Andrew and Morales, sitting across a table from them in an insouciant pose, right ankle on left knee. "If a man doesn't have a proper regard for his own skin, he can hardly expect anyone else to, now can he?" Andrew wondered if he worked at cultivating his engaging brogue.

"It appears that you rose fast in the organization," said Morales. "In fact, you were second in command to Da Silva."

"Aye, that I was. Indeed, I was a confidant of Da Silva, as I suppose we must still call him." Gallivan gave his head a shake of bogus disillusionment. "I always *knew* there was something just a mite queer about that spalpeen!"

Andrew leaned forward on his elbows and smiled coldly. "Gallivan, I'm three-quarters Irish myself. So you can save the blarney for the tourists. We're here to try and work out a way you can help us and thereby earn our help in avoiding the justice you so richly deserve. Now, then. I understand that Da Silva entrusted you with certain emergency communication protocols. Correct?"

"Yes, Captain," said Gallivan in something more closely resembling Standard English. "If Da Silva was dead or disabled, I was to bring *City of Osaka* to a certain region of the outer Sol system and implement those protocols."

"Which," Andrew surmised, "would have triggered an emergency activation of the access key, about which you knew nothing, and sent out a prerecorded message." His smile grew even colder. "It's pretty clear what this was all about. I seem to recall reading somewhere that cowardice and miserliness go together. The Kappainu didn't want to lose their ship even if Da Silva, the only member of their race aboard, was dead. So you would have brought it home to them . . . after which you and all the other human crew members, having seen their space station, would have been killed to maintain security."

"So I've come to understand, Captain." Gallivan's blue eyes grew icy. "That's why I'm willing to listen to any program you may see fit to propose."

"All right. Here's the plan." Andrew spoke for several minutes. Gallivan's jaw sank lower and lower as he listened. When Andrew was done, he swallowed hard.

"Do you recall what I said earlier about a certain regard for one's skin, Captain? It appears that you and this lovely Spanish lady have very little for yours—which is regrettable in her case, at least—and even less for mine."

"Should that surprise you?"

"Not at all. But surely you must understand that I'll require a bit more inducement if I'm to play the role you're asking of me."

"You're in no position to be bargaining," said Morales, on whom the charm of the Western Isles was clearly wasted.

"Such as?" Andrew queried, shushing her.

"Over the years, I've been a very saving man, Captain. I've even saved certain sums my right to which the Black Wolf Society might question."

"I'll say this for you," said Andrew, smiling in spite of himself. "You're a very bold embezzler, if nothing else."

Gallivan gave a wince of misunderstood innocence before resuming. "I've found it prudent to place my savings in certain numbered Swiss bank accounts. Now, I realize that's not the assurance it was a hundred years ago. But if you can promise me that I'll have a full pardon for my prior activities, and that my assets will be untouched . . ."

"Gallivan, you know perfectly well that I'm not empowered to commit the CNE to any amnesties. But for some unaccountable reason, I like you. And the smuggling you've been doing is probably the least repulsive facet of the Black Wolf's business. So you have my word that if you cooperate with us, and we get back to Earth alive, I'll be the strongest advocate you could wish for. That's all I can promise."

"You're an honest man, Captain. I'm somewhat lacking in experience of dealing with honest men. All right. I'm with you." He extended a hand. After only the barest hesitation, Andrew took it.

"Very well. We'll get you moved into relatively comfortable quarters and shortly commence some detailed pre-mission briefing."

As they stood up to leave, Alana Morales turned back to Gallivan and spoke, as though it were an afterthought. "Oh, by the way, one other thing. This is going to involve the two of us working together on the same ship for a time. If you step out of line just once, I'll personally crush your balls with pliers. Understood?"

"Yes, Lieutenant." The brogue was barely perceptible.

CHAPTER TWENTY

THEY EMERGED INTO NORMAL SPACE in the effectively sunless realm just inside the orbit of Neptune, fairly close to the region where computer simulations indicated the Kappainu station's orbit could by now have taken it, but not so close that even multiple transitions could be detected by grav scan.

The Rogovon task force didn't really qualify as such, but Andrew couldn't complain about the percentage of their combat strength the rebels had been willing to commit. There were none of the strike cruisers and even larger battlecruisers that were the capital ships of space, but there were five cruisers of smaller classes, and a number of frigates of the transition engine-bearing classes, some of which had originally been designed as scouts but were now modified with additional weaponry. All had been fitted with Zhygon's improvised access keys. Borthru commanded them all from the cruiser *Krondython*. But the whole array was backup for one frigate-sized converted merchantman.

Borthru was clearly not a happy camper, hanging well back out of probable sensor range. "Why don't we follow you more closely, so we can provide support when necessary?" he grumbled from *City of Osaka*'s comm screen. "After all, we're concealed by the maximum countermeasures our technology can manage."

"We've been through this before," Reislon reminded him. "The Kappainu are the masters of stealth technology, so we don't dare assume they're any less advanced in penetrating other people's stealth."

"That's right," agreed Andrew. "Just wait for us to reappear and signal you, and then move in quickly to give us covering fire while we're on our way back to you."

"If you are," Borthru corrected with no good grace. But he subsided with only a little more pessimistic grumbling, and *City of Osaka* surged ahead, seeking out the Kappainu's hiding place.

Andrew examined the access key. Zhygon had, as promised, set up a crude but human-usable control panel for the thing, complete with readouts. As an additional flourish, he had discovered that use of the protocols Gallivan had been given would not only activate the device but also link its communication function into the ship's ordinary electronics. An ingenious arrangement . . . and a very useful one for their present purposes.

Andrew turned to Gallivan. "Now remember, you're not supposed to know anything except what Da Silva told you. You're just bringing this ship to the region of space he specified and following instructions."

"Rest assured, Captain, acting's in my blood. I'll act surprised in all the right places."

"See that you do," said Morales darkly, letting her hand rest on her M-3.

Gallivan winced and began to key in the coded signal.

The lights of the access key's original Kappainu controls at once winked to life, to Andrew's relief. Using Zhygon's auxiliary controls, he activated the device's detection function. Presently, a telltale awoke on Zhygon's board, showing the station's heading and distance.

Andrew addressed Gallivan again. "Remember—"

"I don't know it's there." There was faint film of sweat on the ex-Black Wolf man's brow as his signal continued to go out.

With startling abruptness, the comm screen lit up. The face it revealed was, to all appearances, human . . . and seemed puzzled.

Gallivan acted appropriately thunderstruck. "Who the Devil are you? And where are you?"

"Never mind! Who are *you*?"

"Why, this is *City of Osaka*, and it's First Officer Gallivan you're addressing. I'm reporting in as instructed, using the emergency protocols I was given, so a bit more civility might be in order."

"*City of Osaka*?" The face goggled. "Stand by while I . . . Just stand by!" The screen went blank.

Gallivan looked pleased with himself. "It seems we've set a cat among the pigeons."

"Quiet!" Morales hissed.

The screen reawakened, and Gallivan did a quite creditable simulation of astonishment. "Why, saints preserve us! It's *you!* Where are you broadcasting from?"

"That can wait," snapped Zoltan da Silva. "How did you get here? *City of Osaka* was captured, and it left the solar system."

"Ah, well, that's a rather long story. Yes, we could tell the ship was departing in some haste—there seemed to be a fine set-to in progress, although they told us prisoners nothing. But when the ship reached its destination, which we later learned was the Kogurche system, we were able to turn on the prize crew and overpower them, at the cost of some losses. Barely had we taken the ship back when an array of ships appeared and began hailing us—Rogovon they were, of all things! As soon as they realized who was in control of *City of Osaka*, they demanded our surrender. We were hardly in a position to refuse. Then they assigned one of their ships to escort us to some kind of base."

Andrew imagined what was going on behind Da Silva's expression of intense concentration. He would know about the Rogovon flotilla from the report of the two Kappainu ships that had pursued *City of Osaka* to Kogurche and then fled at the approach of that flotilla. He must assume that the prisoners' successful rebellion had come just after that.

"This still doesn't explain what you're doing back here in the Solar system," he pointed out.

"Ah, well, perhaps you've heard the old adage about the luck of the Irish. Another Black Wolf ship showed up."

"Another Black Wolf ship?"

"Aye—and rather better armed than ours, which was

fortunate. She disposed of the Rogovon ship that was shepherding us, but was fatally damaged herself. We were able to rescue some of her survivors, including the captain. She wanted to come to Sol anyway, and we were more than happy to provide transportation. And so here I am, as you instructed me."

"Hmm . . . good work, Rory. I'd be very interested in talking to this captain. But first, a question. When you took the ship back, did you take Captain Roark and his Lokaron friend Reislon'Sygnath alive?"

"Alas, we did not. If the truth be known, we decided that the taking of prisoners was a luxury we could not afford."

"That's unfortunate, Rory! I had a great deal I wanted to ask them, as did my superiors." Da Silva gave a sideways glance. Andrew guessed he was making eye contact with Valdes, standing outside the pickup where his well-known face couldn't be seen by Gallivan, who, like all the Kappainu's unwitting human minions, wasn't supposed to know of his involvement. Valdes must have said something, for Da Silva's expression changed. Andrew guessed that Valdes had reminded him that he and Reislon could have warned Gallivan of what lay in store for him when he returned *City of Osaka* to the Sol system. "Well, perhaps it's for the best after all. But you were about to introduce me to your guest . . ."

"At once!" With a flourish, Gallivan motioned Morales into the pickup, where she faced Da Silva.

This was the crucial moment. Their hopes were based on several assumptions. First, that Da Silva and Valdes wouldn't know all the members of their race currently masquerading as humans, or be *au courant* with all their activities. Second, that the Kappainu didn't have some kind of covert recognition signal to give each other in situations like this, when the presence of Black Wolf humans required them to speak circumspectly and in English. And third, that under these circumstances Morales's appearance, aided by judicious hints, would suffice to convince them that she was one of their own.

"Alana Morales," she announced without preamble. "I was sent to Kogurche to investigate the . . . matters with which we're concerned there. I obtained important information, which I was about to bring to your superiors here, when I happened to encounter *City of Osaka* and her escort."

"It's unfortunate about your ship," Da Silva commiserated.

"Yes. But at least I'm bringing this one back to you, with . . . that which it contains." She looked Da Silva in the eyes, wordlessly reminding him of the access key.

"Yes . . . yes, that is *very* important. But as to this information you bring?"

"Obviously, I'm not in a position to speak freely about it here." Morales glanced significantly in Gallivan's direction, then back to Da Silva.

"No, of course you're not. Well, come ahead. You know what to do . . . But no." *He must*, Andrew thought, *have suddenly recalled that the access key can't be used in the presence of the human crew.* "No," Da Silva repeated. "We'll simply continue to use the emergency protocols. I'll download navigational directions to your ship's computer. They'll bring you to . . . where you need to come. Gallivan, implement the instructions and don't bother asking questions. Don't be surprised by what you see. And stand by to be taken in tow by a tractor beam. Don't worry—everything will be made clear." He bestowed a grim smile on Morales and signed off.

Morales leaned on a console, limp with the release of accumulated tension.

"Well done, Alana," said Andrew, releasing his breath. The Kappainu might have intended to simply flood the ship's interior with lethal gas, or otherwise summarily dispose of the inconvenient human Black Wolf crew, but now Morales's presence would preclude that.

"Aye—a bravura performance indeed," said Gallivan with a grin. "Are you sure you're not part Irish?"

Morales smiled, before remembering who was speaking. "*Absolutely* sure," she said with a glare that didn't quite come off.

They followed the navigational instructions they had been given, decelerating to almost nothing and going into free fall at the designated instant, while Andrew resumed worrying. The success of their initial deception had only brought them face-to-face with a whole new set of problems. One was the awkward absence of *City of Osaka*'s original Black Wolf crew, all of whom except Gallivan had been left in the Kogurche system. The prize crew could be explained as Morales's fellow survivors. But they would have to act before Da Silva had time to notice the absence of *any* familiar faces.

Andrew was still thinking about it when they entered the Kappainu space station's region of invisibility. He was prepared for the unnatural sensations of passage, and for the sudden appearance of the Brobdingnagian structure dead ahead. His companions weren't.

"Holy Mary, mother of God!" gasped Gallivan. Morales murmured something in Spanish.

Andrew shook Gallivan out of his stunned immobility. "Start frantically signaling! It's what they'll expect you to do, although they probably won't bother to acknowledge."

His prediction proved accurate as the communicator remained silent. They felt the characteristic jar as the tractor beam took hold and began to haul them in.

Andrew considered ordering a futile effort to break free and escape, simply to keep Gallivan in character, but decided against it—the weapons the station was training on them would have been obvious to anyone. So he watched with renewed tension as the station grew closer. The last time he had been here, the Kappainu had deposited the gig he had ridden on a hangar deck. But there might not be room for the near frigate-sized *City of Osaka*, in which case they would park the ship alongside the station . . . and all bets would be off.

But the maw of the docking bay gradually surrounded them and they slid through the atmosphere screen into the hangar. Andrew ordered himself not to go weak with relief and studied the vast interior space. It seemed even larger than it had before, when it had held a number of the Kappainu warships. Now it was nearly empty. He had no idea what the warships' absence portended; it might or might not be good news from the standpoint of Borthru's force, but it left ample room for *City of Osaka*, and for that at least he was profoundly grateful.

The gravitic hands holding their ship lowered it to the

deck with scarcely a bump. At once, two files of Kappainu guards hurried out to cover the egress ports with their carbine-sized handheld laser weapons. There was still no attempt at communication.

"I think they assume you've taken charge, Alana," said Andrew.

"Don't keep them waiting," Gallivan added grimly. "Lead forth your prisoners."

They all went down to the main personnel port. Morales emerged first, followed by Gallivan and the all but two prize crew. Andrew and Reislon remained concealed inside the port, each to one side. Andrew peered surreptitiously out, not certain what to expect in the next few seconds but sure that the Kappainu would not simply open fire on the humans as long as they were behind Morales.

His heart sank as he saw Zoltan da Silva emerge from the rank of guards and advance to the ramp.

Morales stopped halfway down the ramp. Da Silva halted at its foot and addressed her in a string of syllables that Andrew recognized as the Kappainu language as mispronounced by a human-configured throat.

Morales stood, unable to speak.

Da Silva frowned and spoke again, more peremptorily than before. As he did, he seemed to glance at the file of humans behind Morales—perhaps noticing that Gallivan's was the only familiar face among them—and his frown deepened.

Morales' paralysis broke. "Ah . . . I regret that I suffer from a rare condition which makes it impossible for me to pronounce any but a human language while in this—"

Without warning, Da Silva screamed an order to the guards. Simultaneously, he drew a laser pistol from his belt and fired at Morales.

She was drawing her M-3 and twisting desperately to her right side as he fired. She screamed as the coherent energy glanced searingly against her upper left arm.

"NO!" roared Gallivan He flung himself forward, pushed her down, and grabbed the M-3 she had half drawn. Fortunately, she had already set the weapon for autoburst fire. It blasted Da Silva's head apart.

All this took less than a second. The Kappainu guards were still bringing their carbine-sized laser weapons into line, and the prize crew were still going prone on the ramp.

"FIRE!" Andrew roared into his wrist communicator to the two crewmen who had not accompanied Morales but were manning *City of Osaka*'s two point-defense lasers. They already had their orders from him, based on his recollection of the hangar deck's layout.

X-ray laser weapons could be produced without the need to detonate a fusion bomb by using a free-electron laser to ionize carbon material, the resultant plasma undergoing a population inversion and giving off coherent x-rays. They were ideal for space combat, where nothing less was energetic enough across the distances involved. They were never intended for use in atmosphere, which absorbs X-rays and therefore reduces their range to almost nothing. But "almost nothing" was precisely the range involved within the hangar bay.

These lasers were small weapons of their kind, comparable to the antiaircraft guns mounted by the previous century's wet-navy ships. But within an enclosed space—even one of this size—the crackling roar as tunnels of vacuum were drilled through air was deafening. The air grew thunderous with ozone, and the heat of energy exchange made it almost unbreatheable. One of the gunners sent a rapid-fire series of X-ray pulses down the line of guards, who simply exploded into pinkish-gray mist at the touch of energies beyond any ever intended for antipersonnel use.

The other laser fired at the glassed-in control mezzanine that overhung the hangar bay. It exploded outward in a sheet of flame and a shower of debris. Andrew hoped those controls had included the only ones by which the atmosphere screen could be turned off, leaving the hangar bay in vacuum as a tornado of air sucked them all out into space. It was not an unreasonable hope; deactivating such screens was, for obvious reasons, made almost impossible to do by accident and difficult enough to do on purpose.

Andrew, drenched with sweat, ran down the ramp to where Morales lay. Gallivan, using a knife Andrew hadn't even known he was carrying, was cutting open her left sleeve to expose the ugly laser burn. Reislon came immediately behind.

"I thought this might be useful," the Lokar remarked as he applied pain-deadening antiradiation salve from a tube in a first-aid kit, then slapped on a seal that restored the light-duty vac suit's integrity.

"Kozlowski!" Andrew shouted to a first-class petty officer. "Get the weapons distributed to everyone. You, and the rest of Section One, will come with me and Reislon. Lieutenant Davis, you stay here with the rest and guard the ship—and set up our little surprise. Now get Lieutenant Morales inside to sick bay."

"Like hell." Morales struggled to her feet, swaying in the ovenlike heat. Gallivan helped her upright. She resisted . . . but, Andrew thought, not too hard. "I'm coming, Captain."

"As am I," said Gallivan.

"God damn it, this is no time for goddamned insubordination! I could have both of you shot!"

Even in this hellish time and place, Gallivan's grin was infectious and his brogue was back in full force. "Sure now, Captain, darlin', you'll not be reducing your already none-too-numerous following by two?"

"I can handle an M-3, Captain," said Morales quietly. "And I won't slow you up."

"I've got no time to argue," sighed Andrew. Kozlowski was passing out bandoliers of grenades and a choice of weapons. Reislon picked a Rogovon flamer, which fired a devastating but short-ranged discharge of superheated plasma—ideal for combat inside a space habitat if one wasn't overly concerned with damage to property or bystanders. Andrew took an M-15A gauss submachine gun, firing hypervelocity 3mm bullets like the M-3's, only more of them. "Do you know how to use one of these?" he demanded of Gallivan.

"I'm not unacquainted with it."

"All right. Let's go!"

He led the way at a run toward the hatchway he remembered, and hoped he could remember the rest of the route he had taken before.

✸ ✸ ✸
CHAPTER TWENTY-ONE
✸ ✸ ✸

THEY ADVANCED RAPIDLY through the passageways Andrew recalled, occasionally pausing to clear side-passages and compartments of resistance with grenades tossed through doorways followed by bursts of automatic fire. Reislon withheld use of his flamer; its fuel supply was limited, besides which the resistance they encountered was too light to require such a terror weapon.

Andrew was certain that in a human military installation—or, he was almost equally certain, a Lokaron one—they would have had to fight their way through determined if improvised defenses while counterattackers worked their way around, through the maze of passageways, to flank the intruders. But the Kappainu, heirs to the genes of a million years' worth of ancestors who had survived by concealment, subterfuge, and indirection, were ill-prepared to cope with a direct, brutal assault by enemies who knew their secrets. Andrew was counting on it, for it was the only thing that gave his plan even a hope of success. So far the theory seemed to be panning out; as often as not, any Kappainu they spotted were simply running away.

"Now remember," Andrew cautioned the others as they trotted along in the half-crouching gait everyone except Morales had to adopt in these Kappainu-scaled passageways, "our primary objective is to take Valdes alive but our secondary objective is to rescue Ms. Arnstein. He'll be the clinching proof we need."

"But what if he's shifted back to his natural form?" asked Morales. She had been as good as her promise to uncomplainingly keep up with them, although the pain-lines were visible on her face. "We won't even be able to tell him apart from the other Kappainu."

"Then we're pretty much fucked," said Andrew forthrightly. "But I've consistently gotten the impression that a volitional shape-shift, in either direction, takes a bit of time and effort for them, which is why the ones masquerading as humans prefer to keep on doing so even when they're here and don't need to. It's one of the things I'm counting on." *One of the many,* he didn't add.

Then they reached the steps Andrew remembered and ascended to the more spacious and ornamented precincts above. They were almost suspiciously empty. Then they were through the hangings and into the chamber where Valdes had interviewed his prisoners. It too was empty.

"Secure this compartment," Andrew ordered, and

men moved to cover the two doors Andrew remembered in the opposite wall. He was just telling himself that something didn't seem right when a roar of explosions came through the doorway they had just entered. Kozlowski acknowledged something on his wrist communicator. "Rear guard's under attack, Skipper. They're coming in here—they've lost two men, and they can't hold."

At that moment the opposite doors opened and Kappainu rushed in—only to be ripped apart by M-15A fire from the two point men. Morales ordered men forward to secure the doors. They used the standard tactics—grenades, then poorly aimed blasts of automatic fire—after which no more Kappainu came through.

Grenades don't seem to be a favorite Kappainu weapon, thought Andrew. *They're probably not used to combat in this kind of environment. Thank God for that.*

In fact, this doesn't seem to be a particularly well-executed counterattack in general. But, he amended as he saw the remains of his rear guard scurry through the entrance, turning around to fire through the doorway at their pursuers, *it seems to be good enough to have trapped us in here.*

These split-second reflections had barely flashed through his mind before he barked an order at Morales. "Lieutenant, we've got to push on ahead. It's our only chance."

"Aye aye, sir. Uh . . . which door?"

And there was the rub. Andrew thought fleetingly of "The Lady and the Tiger," then shouted, "The right-hand one!" for no particular reason. "Reislon, see if you can slow down the ones behind us."

The Lokar stepped back to the ingress door and fired a gout of superheated plasma flame. From down the passageway came the eerie sound of what Andrew assumed was Kappainu screaming as the hangings and any nearby flammable plastic ignited. The two men of the rear guard fired follow-up bursts for good measure, then they all sprinted to the door Andrew had indicated. Grenades and another roaring flame-discharge from Reislon's terror weapon cleared away any Kappainu who might have been waiting on the other side.

"Go!" Andrew yelled. Kozlowski motioned the point men through the door. He, Andrew, Morales, Gallivan, and the others followed them as quickly as they could squeeze through the door into the hellish heat of the blackened, devastated chamber beyond.

Dehydration will be the death of us yet, thought some imp in the shielded depths of Andrew's mind.

Then there was no time for inner gallows humor, for they were through and into a chamber beyond—and into an inferno of fire from Kappainu behind an improvised barricade of piled furniture. One of the point men died before the barricade was cleared using some of their diminishing stock of grenades—they dared not use Reislon's flamer in a small enclosed space holding any of their own people.

After that it became a timeless hell as they fought their way through one compartment after another. The Kappainu might be physically feeble, but they were nightmarishly hard to kill. It even grew hand-to-hand—Andrew once glimpsed Gallivan plunging his knife into a Kappainu and then gutting the being before his protoplasm could simply reconfigure the wound out of existence. Another time he saw Morales thrust the muzzle of her M-3 into a Kappainu's mouth before firing a burst that shattered the flimsy-looking alien head. But in the midst of horror he forced his mind—one segment of it, anyway—to focus on memorizing the layout of the passageways they were traversing.

It didn't last. The Kappainu could not stand up under this kind of fighting. They scattered, and all at once Andrew and the half-dozen or so who still followed him found themselves in the clear.

They had broken into what was clearly a control center, oblong in shape, the side walls a mass of instrumentation and consoles. But Andrew had no eyes for any of that. At the far end were figures. One was a human female, tall and slender, her left arm pulled up behind her in what was obviously a painful hold by a short, compact male who, Andrew knew, was only seemingly human. For a split second her eyes and Andrew's locked.

"Rachel," he gasped, then shouted at his followers, "Hold your fire!" He advanced slowly. "Let her go, Valdes."

Valdes brought up his right hand from behind his captive. It held a laser pistol—Earth manufacture, Andrew automatically noted—whose muzzle he instantly pressed against her head. "One more step and her brain is deep-fried."

Andrew halted but didn't drop his M-15A. Out of the corner of his eye, he saw that Morales had Valdes covered with her M-3. "We're taking you with us, Valdes," he said evenly. "If Ms. Arnstein is released unharmed, we'll be as nice about it as possible."

"Otherwise . . ." What Gallivan put into that one word would have chilled the blood of anyone who knew humans half as well as Andrew thought Valdes surely must.

"No, you're not taking me, Roark. I'm leaving through that hatchway a few feet behind me. After which, you're welcome to Ms. Arnstein—I'll push her back through the hatch as I'm going out. The hatch is heavily armored, by the way—nothing you've got will be able to break it open so you can follow me."

Andrew risked a small step forward, betting that Valdes wouldn't throw away his shield lightly. "You know, we're really trying to do you a favor. If you stay here, you'll die along with everyone else on this station. Even as we speak, my people back in the hangar bay are planting a nuclear device—"

"Oh, come on, Roark! *That* ploy again? Reislon used it before, but this time—"

"This time, knowing precisely what we were getting into, wouldn't we have been stupid *not* to do it? It's no bluff now. We brought a bomb with a very short detonation sequence, which we plan to initiate just as our ship departs." Looking closely, Andrew saw that the Kappainu simulation of the human body was perfect right down to the ability to sweat.

"You're lying! But just in case you aren't . . . I think I'll keep Ms. Arnstein with me, after all. You won't blow up the station with her aboard it."

"Are you sure of that?" Andrew dared not meet Rachel's eyes.

"Besides," Valdes went on, "blowing it up wouldn't do you as much good as you think. You may have noticed that the hangar decks are largely empty. That's because our warships are almost all deployed. We've been doing extensive patrolling ever since *Broadsword* escaped." Andrew forced himself not to let his relief show and hoped everyone else was doing the same. "I'm sure you didn't come here unsupported, but any stealthed Rogovon rebel forces will find themselves in difficulties as soon as you lead us to them by rendezvousing with them."

"That won't do you, personally, much good," Andrew pointed out.

"Oh, I was planning to depart anyway, aboard my personal ship. Legislative Assemblyman Valdes's junket in the outer solar system is due to end shortly. I'll simply advance my schedule . . . leaving Ms. Arnstein here, of course. And now . . ." Valdes began to back away toward the hatch, carefully keeping Rachel positioned so as to make it impossible for Andrew or Morales to risk a head shot.

In doing so, he left himself open to Reislon, who could hardly do any precision shooting with his flamer.

With a single motion, the Lokar dropped the flamer to the deck with a clang and brought up his left arm. With a crackling snap, a burst of slivers from his implanted needler whipped past Rachel's cheek at a distance of millimeters and through Valdes's laser pistol and the hand holding it.

The Kappainu's hand didn't even have time to bleed before reconfiguring itself around the tiny holes. But it startled him, and the laser pistol was knocked out of line before he could press the firing stud.

Rachel broke free and brought an elbow back into

Valdes's midriff. At the same instant, Morales sprang forward like a leopard, dropping her M-3 so as to use her good arm to grip his right wrist and wrench the laser pistol from it. Together, the two women wrestled him to the deck.

Andrew touched the human-seeming forehead with the muzzle of his M-15A. "If you try to transform back into your natural shape, I'll destroy your brain. We happen to know that instantaneous death halts the process and leaves you in human form." Valdes only glared.

Andrew noted a trickle of blood from a hairline cut on Rachel's cheek. "You took an awful chance with that shot," he remarked to Reislon.

"My weapon implant incorporates a neural targeting feature that projects crosshairs directly onto my optic nerve," the Lokar explained. "It's quite accurate."

"I'm glad you risked it," said Rachel. "Thank you. Thank you all." For an instant her eyes met Andrew's, and what he saw caused warmth to seep back into his soul.

"Let's get back to the ship," he said gruffly.

"First," said Gallivan, "we might want to make certain our friend here can't raise an alarm about our little surprise package." With his knife he cut two strips from Valdes's sleeve. One he used as a gag, the other to tie Valdes's wrists behind him. While he worked, Andrew spoke into his wrist communicator to Lieutenant Davis, in charge at the ship.

"The hangar bay is still secured, sir," reported the very young officer in a commendably steady voice. "They've got all the exits—including the one you went through— blocked off, and they've tried a couple of probing attacks, but not very hard. Maybe they're afraid we'll use the ship's lasers again if they succeed in breaking in."

"Sit tight and prepare for immediate departure—and for activation of the detonation sequence. We're on our way. Out." Andrew turned to what was left of Section One. "All right. Let's go. Reislon, bring up the rear. On your way out, use your flamer's last fuel on this control center."

They returned the way they had come, through devastated compartments and passageways, seeing few Kappainu. Valdes's hostage value proved sufficient to get them past those few without resistance. Then they were nearing the hangar bay, and Andrew could see the Kappainu barricade ahead.

Andrew grabbed Valdes by one upper arm and shoved him forward while holding his M-15A to his head. "Attention!" he yelled. "We have Valdes. If we are fired on, he dies!"

He didn't really have any reasonable hope that any of the Kappainu up ahead understood English. But apparently his tone and the sight of Valdes were enough. The Kappainu parted for them, and they stepped over the barricade warily. Just ahead was the open hatchway with the hangar bay beyond it.

Just about there, Andrew thought, trying not to let relief weaken him.

"Watch him," Andrew ordered and stepped up toward the hatch, activating his wrist communicator. "Hold your fire," he ordered Davis. "It's us. We're coming through."

Someone uttered an exclamation behind him. He swung around just in time to see Valdes wrench his gag off with his free hands.

So they can vary the size of their wrists and hands just enough to slip out of bonds, flashed through his mind in some tiny fraction of a second.

Valdes yelled something in his own language as he lunged back toward the barricade. Andrew suspected a rough translation would be: *"Stop them! They've planted a bomb!"*

Morales lunged, grabbing awkwardly with her left arm. With unerring viciousness, Valdes punched her where the patch showed she had been wounded. With a strangled gasp of pain she staggered backward, dropping her M-3. Valdes scooped it up and swung it toward her.

Gallivan flung himself forward, pushing her down out of the line of fire, just in time to take the hypervelocity bullet meant for her. It struck his inner right thigh just below the groin, and he collapsed to the deck just as Valdes turned and sprinted back toward the barricade, where the Kappainu were standing in indecision, hesitant to use their weapons with him in the line of fire.

Rachel, who had been standing frozen, broke into a run and took Gallivan under the left shoulder. Morales took him under the right, and together they helped him hobble toward the hatch.

At that instant, Valdes cleared the barricade and an insanely short-range firefight erupted. Kozlowski took a laser beam full in the face and dropped like a poleaxed steer. The others sprayed the barricade with their M-15As, sending the surviving Kappainu crouching for cover.

"Move!" Andrew yelled. "Get to the ship."

With a final blast of fire to keep the Kappainu down, they made for the hatch and emerged into the vastness of the hangar deck. With sudden inspiration, Andrew shouted, "Lieutenant Davis, use the shipboard lasers on the hatchway!" He did *not* shout it into the wrist communicator; it was for Valdes's benefit. *That ought to get them moving back, away from the hatch,* he told himself, *unless Valdes figures out that we can't really do it until we're clear of the hatch ourselves.*

The ploy seemed to be working. There was no pursuit from the hatch as they crossed the hangar deck toward *City of Osaka* at the best speed they could manage.

"Leave me and run," Gallivan grated in his pain.

"Shut up," snapped Morales.

Davis's men closed in around them as they neared the ramp, covering their rear. Davis himself waited at the top of the ramp. He helped with Gallivan as they piled in.

"Is the bomb—?" Andrew began.

"Yes, sir," Davis assured him. "We found the best hiding place for it we could. It's in the—"

"Never mind! Start the detonation sequence now. And give the hatch we came through a hit with one of the lasers. Then get us out of here."

Davis spoke an order into the intercom as he headed for the control room. The ship trembled with the shock of abruptly heated air as the unique crack assaulted their ears. Andrew hoped the Kappainu, up to and especially Valdes, were just inside the hatch, but he wasn't counting on it.

Andrew knelt beside Gallivan while Reislon applied his first-aid kit with the assistance of the medical corpsman who was the closest thing to a doctor the prize crew had. "The bullet must have just missed the femoral artery," said the latter, "or you would already have bled to death."

The Irishman looked down toward his groin. "Fortunately," he said tightly, forcing his words past his pain, "it also just missed something else."

"Lie still," Andrew said. "You'll be all right."

"Of course I will." Gallivan somehow managed a roguish grin at Morales and Rachel. "How could it be otherwise, with not one but two lovely angels of mercy?"

"I've got to get to the control room," said Morales. For an instant her eyes and Gallivan's held each other.

"I'll stay with him," Rachel told her.

"Get him to sick bay and strap him in for acceleration," Andrew ordered. "Alana, you belong there, too. But come with me."

Davis was nearing the end of the takeoff checklist and sounding the acceleration warning when Andrew, Morales and Reislon ran into the control room. Assuming the captain's chair, Andrew ordered a final laser blast as they lifted off the hangar deck and slid through the atmosphere screen and into the featureless blackness beyond.

"Now straight outward—*fast!*" Andrew ordered. "Never mind about our heading for now."

He wasn't concerned with the station's tractor beam, which the ship's drive could overcome. But he was coldly certain that the only way to avoid annihilation by the station's laser weapons was to get *City of Osaka* through their field of fire in very little time. Acceleration hit them.

But the laser fire was oddly uncoordinated, not the time-on-target salvo Andrew had feared. The ship's deflection shield was able to handle it. He wondered if the command center Reislon had incinerated had contained crucial elements of the targeting cybernetics. Whatever the reason, he was in no mood to complain.

Then the station was no longer visible astern, and the stars appeared.

CHAPTER TWENTY-TWO

CITY OF OSAKA **FLED OUTWARD,** broadcasting its signal to Borthru, who presumably had already detected the ship's emergence from the Kappainu station's zone of nullity. Andrew ordered the acceleration cut to one gee—more was not needed, when their objective was to rendezvous with the Rogovon rebels. He also ordered Morales to join Gallivan in sick bay. She obeyed with less resistance than he had expected.

Just after she departed, Rachel made her way up to the control room. She really had no business there, but Andrew was disinclined to stand on regulations. *Maybe she needs to be here*, he thought. *Maybe I need for her to be here.*

"Strap in," he told her expressionlessly. "We may be in for some rough maneuvering if those warships Valdes mentioned come after us."

"Right," she acknowledged in a tone as neutral as his. She settled into the acceleration couch beside his, which Morales had vacated, and their eyes met warily. They both knew they had much to say to each other, but this was hardly the time or the place.

"It's too bad Valdes got away," she finally said as though seeking a safe conversation opener.

"Yes. Especially since, if he lived through our last laser blast, they're now searching the hangar area frantically for our bomb."

"Didn't you say it had a short detonation sequence?"

"Yes, but we couldn't make it *too* short, because we weren't able to foresee the exact circumstances of our departure. We had to allow ourselves ample time to get clear." Andrew glanced at the chronometer. "Still—"

"Incoming!" yelled the rating manning the sensor station.

All at once the display board Zhygon had hooked up to the access key began to flash as the device detected the Kappainu fighting ships. It was set up to feed data directly to the tactical plot, and red "hostile" icons began to appear . . . all too many of them. Missiles were streaking ahead of them, grimly seeking *City of Osaka*.

"Captain," called the comm rating just as Andrew was ordering evasive action, "Borthru acknowledges. They're—"

"I see them," said Andrew as the green icons began to flash into existence. Then he turned back to Rachel, who was staring at him with the round eyes of someone who had never been in a space battle before, and resumed where he had left off. "Still, assuming that they haven't found the bomb and disarmed it or, more likely, sent it out into space, it should be just about—"

All at once, the control room was bathed in a white glare from the view-aft.

"—now."

The generator for the station's invisibility field must have survived the blast for some fraction of a second, because the nuclear explosion was already in progress when it became visible. So it was even more startlingly abrupt than such things normally are. One millisecond there were the serene star fields against their black velvet backdrop; the next there was a new, temporary sun that dazzled the eyes of anyone who happened to be looking at the view-aft at that moment. A rapidly expanding and dissipating cloud of glowing debris surrounded it, for the Kappainu space station had been too massive to be simply vaporized. There were even some fairly substantial chunks, which was one reason they hadn't dared to cut their escape too fine.

Rachel slumped down into her acceleration couch, weak with reaction. There was a scattering of cheers. Andrew did not join them, to Rachel's evident surprise. His face remained unrelievedly grim as he studied the tac plot. Rachel looked over his shoulder. He knew she didn't understand all the supplemental data displays, but the crawling color-coded icons were self-explanatory.

City of Osaka was forging ahead along the orbit the Kappainu station had formerly followed around the distant sun. As they watched, its point defense lasers dealt with all but one of the missiles, and the deflection shield held off the survivor's bomb-pumped laser. No more missile-icons had separated from the scarlet icons of the enemy ships, whose crews were doubtless stunned by the cataclysmic destruction of their base and further rattled by the appearance of Borthru's force.

That paralysis, Andrew was coldly certain, would not last.

The two formations of icons crept toward each other in the tac plot. Both were equally slaves to the same orbital mechanics as *City of Osaka*. The red one swept forward and outward from a point of origin slightly sunward of the space station's former location. The green ones converged inward. But they both followed courses that would shortly bring them together in a maelstrom of techno-annihilation.

And in between, the tiny white icon of *City of Osaka* was on course to be ground between the upper and nether millstones.

"Mister Davis," Andrew suddenly rapped out, "we've got to get out of here. Apply a vector tangent to our present course that will take us in a sunward direction. It's our best avenue for getting out of the battle that's about to commence."

Rachel looked at the tac plot and then at Andrew. He gave her what he hoped was a reassuring look, for he knew her background had not prepared her for this. Her early hero worship of her father had been overrun by her parents' divorce, when her mother had taken her into a world where the military mind-set was neither understood nor admired. She was still conflicted, and out of her element in this control room. But what she saw in Andrew's face seemed to embolden her to speak up.

"Uh, Andy, not that I know anything about it, but is there really going to *be* a battle? I mean, now that their base is gone, won't the Kappainu ships just make transition into overspace—which I know they can do, 'way out here—and go home? Or am I just being naïve?"

"No, you're not. I imagine that's exactly what they'd like to be doing. But they don't dare. If they did, Borthru could go into overspace and follow them. And then we'd know the location of their home system—and they must be *really* afraid of that. No, before they can go home they have to destroy every ship in a position to observe them."

"Including this one," she said evenly.

"That's why I'm taking us out of the line of fire. This ship has got no business in the battle that's about to begin. And for a while, at least, the Kappainu are going to be otherwise occupied."

Rachel stared, clearly mesmerized, as the red and green icons continued on their convergent courses, the green ones spawning a scattering of offspring as Borthru's cruisers launched their fighters. Before the antagonists interpenetrated, the space between them began to be crisscrossed by missile salvos. Those tiny icons began to flash bewilderingly as they were destroyed by defensive fire or else got through and detonated as was their destiny. Then the opposing forces slid together into the range of their shipboard lasers, and any attempt at formations dissolved into a brutal melee. Ship-icons began to flicker and die in the ravening hell of directed-energy fire.

"Can Borthru win?" Rachel breathed.

"Maybe," said Andrew without looking up at her. "He's heavily outnumbered, but his five cruisers are bigger than anything the Kappainu have got. And it's clear from the tactical analysis that he's taking advantage of that."

"Clear to some people, maybe," muttered Rachel, obviously bewildered and appalled by the prettily colored light show of death she was watching.

"He's deployed his frigates and the cruisers' fighters outward in a kind of umbrella," Andrew explained. "They're trying to sort of herd the Kappainu inward, into the concentrated fire of the cruisers, which he's keeping close together so they can datalink without appreciable time lag. The Kappainu don't seem to have been able to work out a very effective counter to his strategy."

"Why not?"

"Well, they've probably grown so dependent on their cloaking technology that they're having trouble dealing with enemies who can detect them. I wonder if they may also be overdependent on central control from their late, unlamented space station, and now find themselves on their own. And on top of all that, the Kappainu lack experience in space combat—not their style. The Rogovon, on the other hand, do have experience, thanks to—"

"—Their war with us."

"Right." Andrew finally looked up and met Rachel's eyes. "They're not likely to forget the lessons your father taught them."

"With help from a lot of others," Rachel added. "Including, as I recall, you."

Andrew did not trust himself to reply, for he could not let the moment last—he had too much to think about. So he contented himself with a wordless smile before turning his attention back to the display and the readouts.

Rachel watched, too. But since it all meant less to her, it captivated her attention less totally than Andrew's.

Thus it was that she was the first to notice the tiny red icon in a portion of the plot remote from the battle.

"Andy," she said hesitantly, "I don't want to bother you, but isn't this a hostile ship?"

His eyes followed her pointing finger, and he stiffened.

"Mister Davis!" he snapped. "Verify the tac display return at—" He rattled off coordinates.

Davis went to the sensor station, then turned to Andrew, his young face flushed with excitement. "It checks, sir. That's an unidentified and presumably hostile ship on a sunward course compatible with having departed the space station just before it blew."

Rachel held Andrew's eyes. "Didn't Valdes say something about—"

"—His private ship," Andrew nodded. "Mister Davis, change course immediately. We will pursue that ship."

"Sir?" Davis's voice rose to a squeak and broke.

"You heard me. I believe that's Valdes, running away. He thinks we're too distracted to notice him—and he knows Borthru is fighting for his life and can't detach a ship to follow him home even if he *is* noticed. But *we* can follow him!"

"But what can we do to him, with no ship-to-ship weapons . . . sir?"

For a manic instant, Andrew was reminded of the old chestnut about a dog chasing a car: What would he do with it if he caught it? But, he told himself, it wasn't applicable here.

"We don't need to fight him," Reislon explained to Davis. "All we need to do is follow him in overspace to his destination, then turn around and come back—and we'll know the location of the Kappainu home system!"

Andrew could almost see the proverbial lightbulb going on in midair above Davis's head. "And now, Lieutenant, I'll be obliged if you carry out your orders."

"Aye, aye, sir!" Davis wrenched *City of Osaka* into a tight course change to follow the red icon on the nav plot, which seemed to be shaping a flat hyperbolic course that, if continued indefinitely, would pass Sol at a distance of about one astronomical unit.

"Why is Valdes heading across the inner solar system?" asked Rachel in her now-accustomed state of bewilderment.

"I suppose his destination is some star somewhere on the far side of Sol from here, and he might as well be headed in the right course when he makes transition," said Andrew. But in fact he felt puzzled himself.

"Captain," Davis spoke up. "I've been analyzing the sensor readings on that ship—specifically, the mass readings. And it's a pretty small ship, less than corvette-sized. Furthermore, the acceleration it's pulling suggests a drive whose mass requirements would . . . well, sir, the bottom line is, that ship can't possibly mount an integral transition engine."

"Will its course take it to any of Sol's transition gates?" Andrew demanded.

"Negative, sir," said Davis after a brief check. "Nowhere close to them."

Andrew thought furiously and stared at the nav plot. *Funny*, he thought as he studied Valdes's projected course. *It's almost as though he's . . .*

"Lieutenant," he ordered, "put the planetary orbits on the nav plot and have the computer project the position of Earth at the time the hostile ship will be at its closest approach to Sol."

"Aye, aye, sir. I'll speed both of them up." The scarlet icon zoomed ahead on its course, like a bead sliding along a string. At the same time, a tiny circle representing Earth swung around Sol on its orbital path. The two came together and intersected.

"It can't be coincidence," Andrew thought aloud, "especially since Valdes is coming in from outside the plane of the ecliptic, making it in effect an interception in three dimensions."

"He's not fleeing from the solar system at all!" blurted Davis.

"No," said a new voice. "He's going back to Earth."

Andrew swung around. "Damn it, Lieutenant Morales, I ordered you to sick bay!"

"The corpsman declared me fit to return to duty, Captain."

"I'll just bet he did! You bullied him into it. But now that you're here, I suppose you may as well stay. And you're absolutely right. Legislative Assemblyman Valdes is going to resume his career without a break."

"But he *can't!*" protested Rachel. "Not now, after what's happened."

"Why not? Nobody back on Earth knows what's happened. He'll reestablish himself in his 'Valdes' persona, after which it will be his word against ours—and guess who'll win."

"But Andy," Rachel persisted, "it won't be just our word. We'll have the med scanners—"

"Come on! Do you really think we'll get a chance to use them? And even if we did, he'd be able to suppress the results, given the power he'll be able to bring to bear and the inherent implausibility of our story." Andrew shook his head. "No. He'll be back in place and the Kappainu can resume their grand plan. The loss of their base in the Sol system will be inconvenient but not catastrophic."

"But if Borthru succeeds in wiping out their forces—"

"Even if he does—and we can't count on it—do you really believe the CNE will listen to Rogovon? *Any* Rogovon? No, the human race will still be ripe for use as the Kappainu's dupes!" For an instant, looking at Andrew's face, Rachel thought he was in physical pain. Then his features cleared, leaving nothing but determination.

"Mister Davis," he said, "belay my previous order to simply follow that ship. We will pursue and overtake it. We've got to stop Valdes from reaching Earth."

"But Captain," asked Morales, "*how?*"

And there was the rub. Unbidden and unwelcome, the dog-and-car joke came back to gibe at Andrew, because now it had become all too relevant.

"I don't know." It was something a skipper was never supposed to say, but Andrew found he couldn't lie to these people, not after what he and they had been through together. "We'll just have to improvise, and do whatever seems indicated." He didn't need to add that that *whatever* might involve their own deaths. Nor did anyone else bring it up. They simply muttered "Aye, aye, sir," and turned to their duties. Rachel said nothing.

"I'm sorry you're caught up in this," Andrew told her.

"Don't be. I asked for it. And I couldn't be going through it with better people."

But it soon became apparent that they weren't going to be able to overhaul their quarry. He had too much of a head start, and Davis had been right about the strength of his drive, for he was capable of practically equaling *City of Osaka*'s sustained acceleration. It was a stern chase that could not succeed.

"What does the computer say, X.O.?" Andrew demanded after a while.

"It says, 'almost,' sir," Morales reported quietly.

"Thank you." Andrew glared at the nav plot, oblivious to the occasional reports of the battle they had left behind, whose outcome was still in doubt. He focused on his ship's green icon, as though he could somehow will more speed into it. It was frustrating—no, maddening—to be crawling like this across the Solar system's mere billions of kilometers in normal space. In overspace, *City of Osaka* could leap the light-years . . .

Abruptly, it hit him.

"X.O.," he heard himself saying before the idea was even fully formed, "cut the drive immediately. And prepare for transition into overspace."

"Sir?" Morales looked up with a blank look that

everyone in earshot shared. "But . . . where are we going? I thought we were pursuing Valdes to Earth."

"We are. Let me finish! We will remain in overspace just long enough to get us to a point as close to Sol as transition can be safely performed. We will then perform a second transition, reentering normal space. This will get us to within roughly an AU of Earth practically instantaneously, leaving Valdes eating our dust!"

The facial expressions were no longer blank. They now covered a spectrum from incredulity to consternation. Andrew understood why. The very characteristics of overspace that made it so useful for traversing the interstellar abysses did not make it amenable to fine-tuning. Even the almost immeasurably brief hop into overspace involved in *Broadsword*'s capture of *City of Osaka* had carried them far beyond the outermost confines of the solar system. Now he was proposing such a hop within the system, something no one had ever attempted.

Davis tried to speak a couple of times before succeeding. "Sir, we can't possibly calculate such a short time in overspace with any preciseness!"

"And," Morales continued for him, "if we end up making transition back into normal space closer to Sol than the two-AU safety limit—"

"—Our transition engine will be permanently wrecked, with the possibility of some collateral damage to the ship. Yes, I know. I also know that it's as much as a naval officer's career is worth to let that happen. But right at the moment that's not my primary concern. Now carry out your orders!"

"But, Captain," Morales persisted, and Andrew had to

respect her guts, "what if we come out of overspace and find that we've overshot Earth? We'd have no hope of killing our velocity and coming back around in any reasonable length of time. The orbital mechanics—"

"That's precisely why I want you to aim for a spot *outside* the two AU limit. That at least minimizes the chance that whatever error creeps in will carry us beyond Earth—or so close to Earth that we wouldn't be able to kill our residual velocity in time to be captured by it, which would be just as bad. Otherwise, I would have ordered you to try for a transition *within* the limit, closer to Earth, and to hell with the transition engine. I don't really expect we'll be needing it again, whatever happens. Do you?"

"No, sir, probably not," Morales admitted. "Especially considering that Valdes doesn't have one in the first place. Which, in turn, means he won't be able to try this trick himself even if he wants to."

"This is a bold plan, Captain Roark," said Reislon. "I just hope it isn't a reckless one."

"A human military theoretician named Clausewitz once made a remark to the effect that a plan which succeeds is bold and one which fails is reckless."

The Lokar gave a smile that Andrew interpreted with some confidence as rueful. "You have me. That is indeed the distinction."

Andrew turned back to Morales and Davis. "So, without any further argument, can we please get busy and make sure this plan turns out to be one of the *bold* ones?" He made his absolute best effort at doing pompous indignation. "This is without a doubt the most disrespectful, insubordinate, undisciplined, and generally scurvy crew of pirates in the entire CNEN!"

"Yes, *sir!*" said Morales, holding a fierce smile tremblingly in check.

"Thank *you*, sir!" added Davis, his absurdly young face flushed with pride.

They and the rest of the control room crew went to work in a mood resembling exaltation. Davis fed the problem into the computer and reported to Andrew. "It may just barely be possible, sir. There's just enough time for the transition engine to reset itself between the first and second transitions. This is going to be the shortest overspace trip ever attempted."

"And what's the shortest up until now?"

"The one we did in *Broadsword*, sir."

"Well, then, we'll break our own record. And as soon as we're back in normal space, don't wait for orders: commence deceleration immediately."

As the countdown began, Andrew noticed that, without his being aware of it, his left hand and Rachel's right had found each other and clasped. He looked at her, and judging from her expression, she hadn't noticed it, either.

"Once again," he began awkwardly, "I'm sorry—"

"And once again, forget it. Hey, I'm going to be in on the setting of a new record!"

Before he could think of a reply, the indescribable gravitational surge took them, pulling them through a hole in the space-time continuum, and the kaleidoscopic tunnel of light began to flow past.

CHAPTER TWENTY-THREE

ANDREW HAD NEVER EXPERIENCED anything like it before. Neither had anyone else in the entire history of interstellar travel.

There was no appreciable pause after the strange pulling-rather-than-pushing sensation of being sucked through a hole in space-time; no time for the utter blackness of overspace to register on their optic nerves. With nauseating abruptness the entire experience reversed itself, and the tunnel of light was flowing forward rather than aft, and then dissolved into the star swarms of normal space . . . and, smaller than seen from Earth but nevertheless inarguably a sun rather than a star, the yellow-white glare of Sol. Dead ahead was a tiny blue dot.

At that instant, from deep belowdecks, there came a sickening noise as metal and crystal ruptured. The ship shuddered, and a smell of acrid smoke invaded the control room. The damage-control klaxon began to whoop.

"Sir," called Morales, "it's—"

"—The transition engine," finished Andrew in a voice as shaken as hers. "I know. But we were prepared to accept the possibility of its destruction." He ran an eye over various readouts and saw to his relief that all essential systems, including the drive, seemed to have retained their integrity.

Through it all, Davis kept his head and activated the drive, applying a braking thrust to kill their velocity relative to Earth. So as a final assault on their sensibilities, deceleration pressed them down into their couches.

Andrew looked anxiously at Rachel, even less prepared by experience for this than the rest of them. She appeared somewhat sick, but managed a tremulous smile.

"Are you all right," he demanded.

"Sure." Her smile firmed up. "Hey, if you could simulate that for an amusement park ride, people would pay money to do it."

"Let's patent it and get rich." He gave her hand a quick squeeze, then turned to his officers and began receiving reports.

They had come fairly close to their intended distance from Sol of two astronomical units—1.67 AU, to be exact. Coming in as they were, on an Earthward course at almost a seventy-degree angle to the plane of the ecliptic, and given that Earth was currently on their side of Sol on its orbital path, this put them less than one AU from their destination. A quick calculation showed that this gave a reasonably comfortable margin for matching Earth's orbit, for they hadn't had time to build up too much velocity before they had made their unprecedented double transition. Andrew ordered the deceleration lessened, and normal weight returned as the ship's artificial gravity resumed control.

"All right," Andrew next demanded, "how long will it take us to get to Earth? Just roughly," he hastened to add. "No decimal places."

"Given the optimum scenario of maintaining our present velocity as long as possible, with rapid high-G deceleration in the last stages, slightly less than three standard days, sir," Davis reported crisply.

"And how long will it take Valdes?"

"He's started from about three AUs inside the orbital radius of Neptune, about twenty-seven AUs from here. Based on his last observed vector, and assuming that he plans to follow the standard procedure of accelerating at one g to the midpoint of a very flat hyperbola and then flipping and decelerating the rest of the way . . . about twenty-four days. Of course, sir, he can render that assumption invalid by increasing his acceleration. If, for example, he maintains one and a half g—"

"From the impression I got of the Kappainu during my captivity," Rachel cut in, "I don't think they're physically capable of that, at least not over the long haul."

"Still," Andrew ruminated, "I prefer to err on the side of caution—"

"We've all noticed that, sir," Morales deadpanned. Rachel smothered a laugh.

"—and therefore I'm going to assume that we have a margin of two weeks rather than three," Andrew continued with a *pro forma* glare at both women. "That still gives us time to arrange a welcome for him, even though we're up against the same old problem of not being able to go through regular channels. We'll have to work covertly."

"But," asked Rachel, "won't our transition from overspace have been observed, this close to Earth?"

"The possibility exists," Andrew admitted. "But I doubt it. The sensors that can detect it are very specialized, and they're directional in nature. They have to be looking for the transition in the region where it occurs. And remember, we're well above the plane of the ecliptic, in a region of space that nobody normally pays attention to, at least in peacetime. That should also help us approach Earth undetected."

"As should the fact that this ship, while it lacks the full panoply of Kappainu cloaking technology, is very stealthy by any other standards," Reislon added. "But . . . what do we do when we get there? As you have pointed out, we cannot publicly announce our presence."

"No, we can't. So we're in the same position we were in when we landed on Earth last time. There's only one person on the planet we know for certain we can trust."

In the end, they made a more cautious approach to Earth than Davis had projected, partly to further minimize their chances of being detected and partly because the CPO who served as the prize crew's engineering officer was dourly insistent on babying the drive after the wrenching shakeup it had gotten when the transition engine had self-destructed. It gnawed a little more time away from their head start over Valdes.

It also added to the time Andrew and Rachel were together in the same ship.

They were almost never alone. But there came a time when Andrew stepped into *City of Osaka*'s tiny observation deck and saw her standing, straight and slender, silhouetted against the star clouds, staring out at the steadily growing blue planet ahead.

Afterward, he was certain he would have yielded to cowardice and slipped back out unnoticed had she not heard him and turned her head. "Oh," she said. "Hello."

"Hello." With no other alternative, he stepped all the way into the almost intimately small space.

For a moment they said nothing. Small talk seemed out of the question. Andrew took the plunge.

"I lied to you," he said without preamble. "I had my reasons. Maybe not good enough reasons, but I had them. I was trying to play Valdes, who I thought didn't know how much I knew. And you were there. And after that—"

"I understand why you did it." Her tone was unreadable.

"No, you don't, not altogether. There was another reason. I was afraid the truth would hurt you badly. I couldn't face the thought of that."

There was a long silence, then she turned back to gaze at the heavens. "Is it true that you were the one who discovered my father's body?" she asked without looking at him.

"Yes."

"I won't ask you how he killed himself. I don't think I want to know. I don't think I'm ready for that just yet."

"Then I won't tell you. But I will say this: his death was quick—instantaneous, in fact—and therefore practically painless."

"Was it? Physically, maybe. But I've always thought suicide must surely be the most horrible way to die, because of the utter despair that precedes it. It's beyond my imagination: such unrelieved hopelessness that the basic survival urge switches off. I've been thinking about this a lot, you see." She abruptly turned to face him, and her eyes would not let his go. "The Black Wolf Society drove my father to that. Which means the Kappainu did. I want them to hurt."

"We've already hurt them," Andrew pointed out, recalling the nuclear fireball where the Kappainu space station had been.

"Not enough. I want your promise that they'll hurt more before this is over."

"They'll hurt. *I'll* make them hurt. That's how I'll pay the debt I owe you."

"It is enough." Her eyes continued to hold his, but the embrace warmed.

For the first time since that impulsive moment just before they had recklessly flung themselves into and out of overspace, their hands found each other. Wordlessly, for no words were required, they turned and left the observation deck to the unfeeling stars.

As Reislon had intimated, *City of Osaka* was a smugglers' ship and therefore heavily stealthed. So was her gig, given the uses to which the Black Wolf Society had put it.

They left Davis in acting command of the ship in its trailing orbit and took the gig down. Besides Andrew, it held Rachel, Reislon, Morales and Rory Gallivan, suffering from no worse than a slight limp by grace of Lokaron-derived tissue-regeneration technology, and as insouciant as ever. He acted as pilot, being the most familiar with the gig. Andrew felt a certain déjà vu as they passed the terminator into Earth's night side and descended over the darkened Rockies.

They were less cautious than last time, when they had felt no special time pressure. Andrew called ahead from high altitude, and instead of finding a secluded mountain meadow, Gallivan landed the gig on the barely adequate level area on the aspen-clothed foot of the familiar mountain, within walking distance of the stone-and-timber house and shielded from view only by the crags above and its own ability to camouflage itself. An elderly but vigorous woman was already on the way out from the house to meet them, carrying a lamp. Spring was now well-advanced and the starry night wasn't too chilly.

"I somehow knew I'd see you again, Andy," she said as they embraced. "I was certain of it."

"I'm glad you were so sure, Mom. There were times when I wasn't." Andrew motioned the others forward into the lamplight. "You've already met Rachel Arnstein and Reislon'Sygnath. Let me introduce Lieutenant Alana Morales, executive officer of the ship of which I'm currently in command." Morales simply stared, round-eyed and open-mouthed, at Katy Doyle-Roark. "And this is Rory Gallivan, a . . . er, a civilian consultant."

"Now then, Captain, let's not be havin' your mother

on . . . especially when she's so great a lady as this, and of Irish descent to boot." Gallivan gave Katy a small bow. "The truth of the matter is, you see before you a former member of the Black Wolf Society who has seen the error of his ways."

Morales rolled her eyes heavenward.

Katy gave him a cool regard. "I'm gratified to learn of your repentance, Mr. Gallivan. I don't doubt that you're now a credit to the Emerald Isle." She turned to her son. "I said it before and I'll say it again, Andy: you do have a way of acquiring *interesting* associates whenever I let you out of my sight."

"Especially if you define 'associates' broadly enough to include the Kappainu," said Andrew grimly.

"The . . . ?"

"That's the Shape-Shifters' name for themselves. It's the least important of the things we've learned about them. The most important, at the moment, is that one of them is Legislative Assemblyman Valdes."

Katy came out of shock more quickly than Andrew would have thought possible. "I think," she said calmly, "that we'd better get inside so you can tell me everything. I also think we'll probably need drinks."

"A great Irish lady indeed," murmured Gallivan. Morales jabbed him in his bad thigh.

As it turned out, the drink they needed most was coffee. None of them got any sleep, for there was too much to tell.

"And so," Andrew concluded, "as near as we can figure it, Valdes will be here in not more than three weeks, possibly two. We've got to somehow stop him, and *City of Osaka* is all we've got to do it with."

"It may be more than just him you have to deal with," his mother reminded him. "You left the battle between the Kappainu and your Rogovon allies behind. You have no way of knowing who won it. If the Kappainu did, then presumably some of them will be coming in just behind him in their cloaked ships, to give him backup."

"On the other hand," Reislon continued the thought, "if Borthru won, he won't be able to help us. Recognizably Rogovon warships would hardly be welcome in Earth's skies."

"Don't you think I've considered all this?" Andrew's misery was palpable.

"You can't do it by yourselves," Katy stated bluntly. "You've got to get help."

"Yes—but where?"

"I can only think of one place. And it happens that you're in luck. Svyatog'Korth has been gone, but now he's back on Earth."

"Svyatog?"

"That's right. You know that *his* organization can't have been infiltrated. And from what you've told me of the Kappainu's plan for the Lokaron—including Gev-Harath—he has a stake in this too, whether he knows it or not." Katy glanced out the window. Dawn was breaking over the Rockies. "Being on the east coast, he may even be awake." She stood up stiffly and moved toward the phone, heedless of the awe-struck stares from Morales and Gallivan.

"But . . . but Mom, you can't just ring up the executive director of Hov-Korth!"

"Just watch me."

Katy used a special, secured line that took her directly to a level where she had only a couple of layers of underlings to wade through before reaching Svyatog's private secretary. "I regret that the executive director is unavailable," that worthy declared. "He has only just arisen and will be occupied throughout the day with important business." The translator faithfully reproduced the faint, sneering stress the Lokar laid on the word *important*, as though underlining Katy's comparative lack of that quality. "I suggest you try again another time."

Andrew decided the time for discretion was past. He leaned into the pickup. "This is Captain Andrew Roark. Tell him that Reislon'Sygnath is with me and wishes to resume a conversation that was interrupted ten years ago on the subject of the Black Wolf Society and the threat it poses to Hov-Korth and the rest of Gev-Harath. And . . . tell him we'll wait."

CHAPTER TWENTY-FOUR

AFTER WHAT SEEMED LIKE mere seconds, Svyatog'Korth's face appeared on the screen, wearing a flustered look that Andrew had never imagined he would see on it.

"Good morning, sir," Andrew said politely. "I'm sorry to have to bother you so early, but I'm calling regarding matters of the highest—one might say transcendent—importance." Receiving no reaction from Svyatog, he pressed on. "As you may recall, when we last spoke you told me about an intelligence agent who had worked for Hov-Korth during and before the war."

"I recall very well. At the time, you allowed me to believe that you had never heard of that agent's existence, much less his name."

"I regret that I wasn't able to be altogether candid

with you. In fact, my father's upload had told me about Reislon'Sygnath. Among other things, he told me Reislon had been working with CNEN Intelligence." Only a human as familiar with the Lokaron as Andrew would have recognized the instantly suppressed look of surprise on Svyatog's blue face. "The only thing you told me that I didn't already know was that you believed he had also been working for Gev-Rogov."

"You haven't explained the reason for your lack of candor."

"The upload insisted on it." It occurred to Andrew that it sounded silly if you put it that way. "Reislon's connection with us has never been declassified, you see."

"Then why are you telling me now?"

"Because humans and Lokaron now face a common threat that requires us to communicate in an atmosphere of mutual trust. If that requires the breaking of certain rules, so be it."

"In your judgment."

"My judgment, and that of my mother—which I know you trust—and also that of Reislon'Sygnath. I'm going to let you talk to him now."

Reislon stepped into the pickup. The two alien faces were unreadable.

"It's been a long time, Reislon," Svyatog finally said.

"Indeed. I regretted the necessity of departing from your service without explanation."

"Perhaps you are now in a position to explain."

"I am. First of all, Captain Roark spoke with great preciseness when he said you believed I had been working for Gev-Rogov. It was necessary to give that impression, if

I was to convince Rogovon intelligence of the same thing. In fact I was, and still am, working for the revolutionary movement seeking the overthrow of the Gev-Rogov regime. It was in that movement's interest that I sought to avert the war, which effort in turn caused me to cooperate with CNE intelligence."

"Your games were even more complex than I had supposed."

"Complex, perhaps, but never inimical to the interests of Gev-Harath. In fact, what we wish to establish in Gev-Rogov is a regime with which Hov-Korth and the other *hovahon* of Gev-Harath could do business."

"That is an outcome to which we would not be averse," said Svyatog in a carefully neutral voice.

"Which is why I am presuming to ask for your help now. I would not expect you to commit yourself simply for the benefit of the movement. But we have learned of the existence of a threat, not just to ourselves, but also to Gev-Harath and, in fact, to all of Lokaron civilization."

"From the Black Wolf Society?" Svyatog's skepticism was palpable through the medium of the translator.

"From that which lurks behind it. When I warned you against it, I never imagined the full extent of the truth. The Black Wolf Society is only a tool of an unsuspected alien race—an instrument for making a tool of the CNE itself. And that, in turn, will be a means to the end of the destruction of the Lokaron interstellar order."

Svyatog leaned forward. "Perhaps you had better tell me the details."

"No. It's a long story, and a seemingly fantastic one. We'll need to present evidence or you won't take us seriously."

"I might, if Katy vouches for you. And this is a secure line."

"There is no such thing as absolutely secure communications—you know that. No, we need to meet with you in person."

"And that presents problems," said Andrew, reentering the conversation. "Our presence here on Earth isn't generally known, and at least for now it has to remain that way. We came here in a heavily stealthed ship that is now in a trailing orbital position, and landed in a gig, which we naturally can't take over to the East Coast. And we can't use public transportation; Reislon would be too conspicuous."

"Are you suggesting that I should come to meet you?"

"In normal times, I wouldn't dream of such a thing. But the times have ceased to be normal. Reislon isn't exaggerating the scope of the threat we all face. And you're the only one we can turn to for help."

Katy spoke up. "It's true, Svyatog. And without going into details I will tell you this much: Legislative Assemblyman Valdes is involved."

Svyatog's expression grew shuttered—out of habit, Andrew thought, for of necessity he always maintained a posture of scrupulous neutrality in human internal politics. But it was easy to imagine what he thought of Valdes' human-chauvinist campaign bombast, and the probable consequences to Hov-Korth of a Valdes president-generalcy.

"Perhaps," Andrew prompted, "you could take your private suborbital transport to Denver and obtain an air-car there."

"No," said the Lokar after a moment's thought. "That would attract too much attention. I can, however, invent a plausible excuse to depart on my private space vessel three or four days from now, and its crew is completely trustworthy. Return to your ship and put it into a distant parking orbit around Earth, the exact elements of which I will communicate to you presently using this line. I will rendezvous with it by homing in on your transponder, Katy. Please understand: I make no advance commitments, except that whatever you tell me will be held in confidence."

"Thank you, Svyatog," said Katy. "Now, more than ever, I'm in your debt."

"You, Katy? Never." Two pairs of aging eyes, of as many different species, met in a moment's communion that held memories Andrew could only dimly imagine. And then the screen was blank.

"Well," said Andrew, "after he sends us those orbital elements, we'd better get back to *City of Osaka*. Mom, could you just let us catch up on a little sleep and a little food before we leave?"

"What are you talking about?" Katy sounded genuinely puzzled. "I'm coming too."

"You're *what*?"

"What's the matter, dear? Doesn't your gig have room for one more?"

"Yes. But . . . but . . . but you *can't*!"

"Of course I can. In fact, I have to. That military-grade transponder is a very special piece of equipment. I can't trust it to just anybody, you know."

"I *think* I can manage it!"

"I'm not so sure. And besides, when you're telling your story to Svyatog you'll need me there to vouch for your sanity. I'll just cross my fingers."

Andrew desperately sought for an appeal that might work. "You realize, of course, that having to bring you back here before we head out into deep space would expose us to unnecessary risks and possibly jeopardize the mission."

"Who said anything about bringing me back?"

Andrew took a deep breath. "Mom, this is crazy. You're—"

"A woman? I notice you've got a couple of those along already."

"That's not the issue! Both of them are young enough to be your granddaughters!"

"It's true that I'm an old bat—so old that it's been a good many years since I had any excitement." Katy abruptly turned serious. "Besides, Andy, the last time I watched you head out, thinking I'd probably never see you again, I promised myself it would be the last time." The moment passed, and she smiled again. "If it would make you feel any better, go down to the basement and clear it with you father's upload."

"What's the use? I know what *he'd* say." Andrew turned frantically to his companions, seeking help and finding no signs of it. Gallivan, in particular, looked infuriatingly entertained.

Svyatog's private spaceship, the *Korcentyr*, reminded Andrew of Persath'Loven's yacht, only more so. Much more so.

The resemblance lay in the sleek, rakish lines of a vessel designed for rapid atmospheric transit, enhanced by the elegant design (orange and dark burgundy, in this case) that decorated its surface. But the effect was on an altogether larger scale, for *Korcentyr* was almost the size of a naval corvette. This made it considerably smaller than *City of Osaka*, and it had no integral transition engine— any more than did *City of Osaka* at the present time, Andrew thought ruefully—nor did it need one, for any places the executive director of Hov-Korth would wish to go were certain to be accessible via transition gates.

Another feature of *Korcentyr* became apparent when the two ships rendezvoused in orbit. There was none of the usual careful jockeying that preceded the connection of passenger-access tubes to access ports, for a tractor beam pulled the two ships together into a gentle kiss. Andrew had never heard of such a small ship mounting the device, which normally required a massive generator, and he could only suppose that the Lokaron of Gev-Harath, always on the technological cutting edge, had succeeded in miniaturizing it.

Svyatog came aboard *City of Osaka* alone—doubtless to the consternation of his security guards, Andrew thought. They conducted him to the conference room just aft of the control room and launched into a carefully prepared presentation. They had no Kappainu corpse to display, but the ship's database held extensive electronic documentation of their story. That story, beginning with Andrew and Rachel's meeting with Persath and subsequent journey to Kogurche and continuing up to the destruction of the Kappainu base and their desperate in-system overspace jump to head off Valdes, took quite a while to tell. Svyatog sat through it with remarkably few interruptions. Afterwards the old Lokar brooded for a full minute in a silence that no one felt inclined to break.

"The Kappainu plan," Svyatog finally said, "assumes that the *hovahon* of Gev-Harath will behave as predicted and jump at the bait that Valdes, as president-general, dangles before them, thus provoking the general Lokaron war. Now that I am aware of their intentions, this assumption is no longer necessarily valid. I am not entirely without influence."

Andrew managed to keep a straight face at this staggering understatement. "I've thought of that, sir. And it's quite possible that you would be able to deflect Gev-Harath's course enough to throw a monkey wrench into the scheme." Presumably the translator could handle that. "But that would leave humanity under their control, with Valdes still ensconced as president-general—"

"—And the Black Wolf Society still exerting influence and pressure," Rachel finished for him grimly.

"True. But that would be an internal human problem."

"Also a problem for Gev-Harath, to some extent, for Valdes would hardly be as favorably disposed as the present government," Katy pointed out.

"And in the meantime," Reislon urged, "they would continue to work to prop up the status quo in Gev-Rogov, which is hardly in your best interests."

"Besides," Andrew added, "with Earth under their thumbs, they would be in a position to regroup and start over and try something else—something we *wouldn't* know about—to subvert the Lokaron powers. Wouldn't it be better to abort their plan now, while we still have the advantage of knowing what that plan is?"

"These are all cogent arguments," Svyatog admitted. "But I am still not clear on what, precisely, you want me to do."

"Help us stop Valdes before he reaches Earth. This ship is unarmed except with a couple of light point-defense lasers. We need something with ship-to-ship firepower."

"That I cannot offer you." Svyatog smiled at Katy. "Forty-four years ago there happened to be a Harathon navy cruiser here in the Sol system when we needed it. We can hardly expect that kind of good fortune twice. No, all we have is my ship . . . and it is entirely unarmed."

Alana Morales spoke up. "But your ship does have a tractor-beam generator. And we know Valdes's ship is a relatively small one—less than corvette-sized, probably smaller than yours. If both our ships intercept him and yours locks on to him . . ."

"You can haul him in so close that even our lasers can put holes in him!" exclaimed Gallivan. He whooped laughter and gave Morales's shoulders a quick squeeze. "Darlin', I always knew you were a pirate at heart! Anne Bonny to the life, with a touch of Grace O'Malley!"

Morales's glare somehow lacked conviction.

"It might actually work," said Andrew slowly. He led the way into the control room, absently muttering "As you were" to Davis, and set up the problem on the nav plot, displaying Earth's orbit and Valdes's projected course approaching it. The difficulty was too obvious to require verbalization. They couldn't simply head out to meet Valdes;

the ships would flash past each other at a tremendous relative velocity.

"We're going to have to position ourselves out here," said Andrew, indicating a region along Valdes' route. "Then be ready to start back inward toward Earth when our sensors show that Valdes has reached the point at which we can intercept him and match vectors."

"That first step—getting out there into position—is going to be the hard part," said Morales. "We'll be struggling against our own residual orbital velocity around Sol. Swimming against the tide, as you might say."

"Just so." Andrew knew that the maneuver, which would have been laughably out of the question with old-fashioned rockets, would be difficult enough even with today's reactionless drives. And it was depressingly certain that it would allow no time to talk his mother into returning to Earth and take her there. "Mister Davis, feed the problem into the computer. Assume continuous 1.5 g acceleration." Then he remembered Katy and Reislon. "No, make that one g. I want to know how much time we've got."

"Less than you may think." It was Gallivan's voice: flat, cold, and without a trace of banter. He pointed to the display, which showed the returns from the long-range sensors, hooked into the access key and focused narrowly on Valdes's projected course to maximize their range. A scarlet icon had winked into life at the outermost limit of detection, headed Earthward.

"He must have nearly killed himself, piling on the gees," Rachel breathed. "How soon will he be here?"

Andrew did a quick calculation. "About a week. We had hoped for two. Mister Davis, include this new factor in your nav problem and tell me how soon we have to start out."

"Can we even do it?" Morales wondered aloud.

"No, we can't," said Davis after a moment. "But using your original figure of 1.5 G, it's just barely possible—if we head out within two hours."

"Two hours? But that won't give time to return Svyatog to Earth!" And, Andrew thought with a sick sense of defeat, it would have been hopeless anyway: 1.5 Terran G was slightly over two Harath-Asor gees.

"My ship, as you may have noted, is a luxury model," said Svyatog. "It has compensating internal gravity fields to reduce apparent acceleration. I can accommodate Reislon and your mother aboard *Korcentyr*."

"You mean *you're* going? *Personally?*"

"There appears to be no other alternative."

Katy's grin banished decades from her face. "Just like old times, isn't it, Svyatog?"

CHAPTER TWENTY-FIVE

WALKING CAREFULLY under his half-again-normal weight, Andrew went to the nav tank and stood over it, gazing at the three-dimensional plot. Nothing had changed. He hadn't really expected that it would have.

The relevant portion of Earth's orbit around Sol showed as a curving string-light along which the icon of the mother planet slid in a counterclockwise direction. Above the plane defined by that orbit, Valdes's course extended down at a seventy-degree angle from the right to intersect the orbit at the point where Earth would be at the time of the intersection. And farther to the right, off to the side of that course's scarlet thread, were the two tiny green icons of *City of Osaka* and *Korcentyr*, still working their way into position.

Merely reaching Earth's escape velocity would have

sent them outward in the plane of the ecliptic on a parabolic orbit. Instead, they had boosted "upward," above that plane, and fought to overcome the intrinsic eighteen-plus miles per second that Earth had imparted to them. Soon the untiring exertions of their reactionless drives would send them curving back, and they would be back to normal weight, at least for a time.

He felt rather than heard Rachel join him. She had held up uncomplainingly under the acceleration, with the often surprising resilience of young human females. But her lack of naval experience made her even less able than the rest of them to cope with the gnawing uncertainties of what awaited them.

"Surely he can detect us," she said nervously.

"Probably. But not necessarily. Remember, that's a very small ship, with a powerful drive taking up space. We don't know what he's got in the way of sensors. In fact, we don't know anything at all about what he's got."

"Including weapons."

It was, of course, the great imponderable. "We've gone over that," Andrew reminded her. "We have no hard information, but it's difficult to believe that a ship that small could have even as much as this one, or that its deflection screens could be as strong as ours or *Korcentyr*'s. In fact, if the ship is supposed to suit Valdes's official role, you wouldn't expect it to be armed at all."

"I hope you're right, especially considering that *Korcentyr* definitely isn't." Then, as she saw Andrew's wince of worry and belatedly remembered who Svyatog's ship was carrying: "Oh, I'm sorry. I shouldn't have—"

"That's all right." He took a last look, then sighed and

squared his unnaturally heavy shoulders. "We'll know the answers to all of this soon enough."

The interception turned out to involve less trouble than Andrew had feared. Their quarry attempted a certain amount of evasive action, but he was severely limited in what he could do if he wanted to stay on course to be captured by Earth. If he simply accelerated on his present course, he would flash past Earth and continue sunward on a flat hyperbola from which he would probably take many weeks to struggle back even with today's drives . . . which was fine with Andrew, for it would give them the leisure to devise new strategies. And besides, Legislative Assemblyman and front-running president-general candidate Valdes was expected back at a particular time.

"So we've got the bugger where we want him!" exulted Gallivan as they observed a nav plot that could now be reduced to the tactical scale as they closed in.

"If I didn't know it was useless," said Morales, "I'd tell you not to get cocky. Remember, this is going to involve some extremely delicate coordination. *Korcentyr* doesn't have an access key, so Svyatog is going to be dependent on our ability to pierce Valdes's cloaking field."

"Ah, but thanks to the good Lieutenant Davis's efforts, we can download our sensor readings directly to *Korcentyr*, rather than having some poor sod—most likely me, if you had your way!—sit at the communicator and read them off."

"Which is why this ought to work," said Andrew, "as long as everyone carries out my orders. *All* my orders," he added firmly, with a significant glance at Gallivan. "Don't forget, the optimal outcome is to take Valdes alive, for questioning and for living evidence."

"Also," Rachel opined, "his ship was based on the space station, and they wouldn't have allowed Black Wolf humans there. So his crew must be all Kappainu."

"Right," Andrew nodded. "So we're going to give him a chance to surrender. Understood?"

They all muttered agreement, with varying degrees of enthusiasm.

Valdes's ship proved to be even smaller than they had expected, visibly smaller than *Korcentyr*. And their theories about it panned out: it was unarmed and mounted only the most minimal civilian-model deflection shields. After a certain amount of seemingly half-hearted evasive maneuvering, it was seized by *Korcentyr*'s tractor beam. From *City of Osaka*'s control room, Andrew watched it being reeled in.

This is going too smoothly, he thought.

"Very well," said Valdes in response to their hail. He seemed oddly calm. "I surrender. I appear to have no choice—especially inasmuch as *Broadsword* will surely be headed in-system soon, if it isn't already."

Andrew half rose, all his resolve to be coolly distant forgotten. "*Broadsword*?"

"Yes, that's right; you wouldn't know, would you?" Valdes smiled his campaign smile. "While I was en route toward Earth, *Broadsword* appeared and intervened in the battle. She must have been waiting and observing that region of space, and seen the explosion of our station. At any event, she made it possible for your Rogovon allies to wipe out our mobile forces."

"I can imagine," said Andrew. Jamel Taylor's strike cruiser must have been like a tiger among jackals.

"So," Valdes continued urbanely, "my only hope was to get to Earth and reentrench myself. But now I see that I have failed and have no more cards to play. So I will give myself up to your Lokaron confederates." Valdes signed off, seemingly leaving his strangely composed expression on the screen like the smile of the Cheshire Cat.

Svyatog's face appeared. Katy was visible in the background. "I will bring him aboard as soon as we've brought our respective passenger ports together."

"Right. Signing off." Andrew turned to the viewscreen and watched Valdes's ship gradually approach *Korcentyr*.

"I don't like this," Andrew muttered. "He's giving up too easily."

"What else can he do?" asked Rachel. "Do you expect him to blow up his ship and *Korcentyr* with it when they come in contact? Somehow that doesn't seem consistent with Kappainu psychology."

"No, it doesn't," Andrew admitted. "I don't expect that." But he continued to stare, brooding, at the viewscreen.

Abruptly, he stood up. "I'm going over to *Korcentyr*. X.O., you have the conn. Have them break out the gig."

"You'll be wanting me to pilot the gig, Captain," Gallivan stated rather than asked.

"I'll come, too," said Rachel.

"No!" Andrew didn't know the source of his premonition,

but he was in no doubt as to its strength. "For once I'm going to put my foot down. Stay here. Please."

She started to speak, but something she saw in his face stopped her. She simply nodded. Their eyes held each other for a moment. Then, with a gesture to Gallivan to follow him, he was gone.

It wasn't far, as *City of Osaka* was holding position within the effective antiship range of her point-defense lasers. But Gallivan took the gig on a curving course, partly to stay well outside those lasers' field of fire and partly to come around to *Korcentyr*'s starboard access port, on the opposite side from the one toward which Valdes's ship was being drawn. Gazing out the gig's transparent canopy, Andrew watched the two ships gently touch.

Maybe I'm just getting worked up over nothing, he told himself.

They glided around *Korcentyr*'s stern. As Gallivan began his approach to the starboard side, it occurred to Andrew that Svyatog wasn't expecting him. "Raise *Korcentyr*," he ordered.

Gallivan activated the communicator. No sound came, and the small screen remained black. He tried it again, frowning. "Odd. They're not responding."

Suddenly, with a burst of static, the gig's interior was filled with a confused cacophony of panicky sounds: scuffling, and several voices trying to talk at once, among which Andrew could make out his mother's. Then Valdes's shout rose above all of them, silencing them.

"I said shut up! And everyone keep your hands where I can see them—especially you, with your weapon implant! I won't hesitate to use this flamer again."

Andrew, his mind trapped in nightmare, leaned forward against his straps. "Get the video!"

Gallivan raised a cautioning finger. "Valdes clearly doesn't know the audio is on. Somebody—Reislon, I'll wager—contrived to turn it on, in send-only mode, so we can listen. Let's not give that advantage away."

Andrew nodded slowly, forcing a semblance of calm on himself. It was hard—very hard. Especially when Katy's was the next identifiable voice.

"What do you expect to gain by this?" she asked. "Your ship—and this one, for that matter—are still covered by *City of Osaka*'s weapons."

"Which they'll hardly use with you and the executive director of Hov-Korth aboard. I couldn't have asked for more valuable hostages."

"To what end?" asked Svyatog, as Andrew's translator rendered the Lokaron sounds coming from the communicator grille. "To force them to let you resume your course for Earth? At this short range, they can undoubtedly disable the drives of both ships without killing us. Then you will find yourself in a deadlock—and *City of Osaka* can afford to simply wait you out."

"You're wrong!" The triumph in Valdes's voice rose to almost manic intensity. "Did you really think we had *all* our mobile assets in the outer system? We keep two cloaked ships on permanent station near Earth. I summoned them while en route. They have had to overcome unfavorable orbital elements, but they should be arriving at any time now. They will dispose of *City of Osaka*." A trace of mockery entered the flawlessly human voice. "Don't worry: they won't destroy this ship as long as I am aboard.

And now, I suggest we all settle in to await their arrival."
The communicator subsided into silence.

"Captain," Gallivan half whispered and half rasped, "I
think I can bring us up against *Korcentyr*'s starboard
access port and attach us magnetically without him noticing. I don't think that's exactly where his attention is
focused at present."

"But what good will that do us? We can't get in unless
he opens the port for us."

Gallivan grinned fiercely. "Captain, the press of events
has perhaps prevented me from being entirely forthcoming with you—as was always my intention!—about the
capabilities of *City of Osaka*. The truth of the matter is, in
the course of her . . . former occupation, it was sometimes
necessary to enter another ship from the outside without
help from the inside. That is especially true of this gig,
which of course has no air lock but merely a port that can
fasten to that of a larger vessel."

"Get to the point, damn you!"

"Ah . . . well . . ." Gallivan fumbled under the instrument console and brought forth an object roughly the size
and shape of a deep pie plate. "Shaped charge," he
explained with uncharacteristic succinctness. "With magnetic clamps to attach it to the inside of our hatch."

"But if we blow their hatch inward, how do we know
what the effect in there will be?"

"We don't, Captain. I can't guarantee the safety of any
of them . . . including your mother. But what choice have
we?"

"None." Andrew drew a deep breath. "Do it. And be
prepared to rush in there the instant it blows. Surprise is

the only thing that's going to give us a chance." He drew his M-3 and charged it . . . and then remembered something. "But you're unarmed."

"Valdes doesn't know that." Gallivan grinned and then sobered with the speed of a leprechaun. "It's as I said, Captain: What choice have we? Your mother's in there."

Andrew said nothing. He lacked the words. "I'll go first," was all he could finally manage.

As the gig moved slowly toward its goal, the silence from the communicator was broken by a rapid-fire spate of Kappainu words in Valdes's voice. *He must,* Andrew thought, *be talking into a hand communicator to the crew of his ship.* Then Valdes spoke in English, for the benefit of his prisoners.

"All right. My two warships are approaching. You—go very slowly to this ship's communicator and raise your other ship. I'm going to tell them that if they value the lives of my hostages, they'll allow my private vessel to depart."

"Quick," Andrew hissed. "Disconnect! We can't let him know we've been listening all along." But Gallivan had thought of it himself; his hand was already slapping the switch.

The down side, of course, was that they no longer knew what was happening aboard *Korcentyr.* But Valdes must have done as he had intended, for on the far side of *Korcentyr* they could see his ship break free and begin to drift away.

Then Gallivan brought the gig up against the starboard access port with a precise delicacy Andrew would never have thought possible without the assistance of a tractor beam. He activated the magnetic seal. Then he hefted the limpet charge and met Andrew's eyes. Andrew nodded, and Gallivan affixed it to the hatch of the gig, which of course had no air lock. Then he unceremoniously pushed Andrew down behind their acceleration couches.

"It is, as I say, a shaped charge," he said with an apologetic look. "Still—"

Inside the restricted interior space of the gig, the blast was ear-shattering, and the concussion shook them with teeth-rattling force. Coughing his lungs clear of the acrid smoke that filled the gig, Andrew launched himself at the shattered hatch, with Gallivan close behind. They shoved aside the wreckage, and were inside *Korcentyr*.

Andrew was prepared for the abrupt transition from zero G into *Korcentyr*'s internal artificial-gravity field. At least it was only one Harath-Asor G. He hit the deck as weight descended on him, rolled, and sprang upright.

With senses seemingly speeded up to such a pitch that the rest of the universe was stationary, he took in the chaotic scene.

His drop-and-roll had taken him through the small entry port into the central saloon. Several Lokaron, including Svyatog and Reislon, were still flinching away from the blast that had ripped *Korcentyr* open. So was Katy. So was Valdes, who held in both hands a plasma flamer pistol, the smallest weapon of its type that could be engineered, and only by sacrificing almost everything to miniaturization, leaving it practically useless as a battlefield weapon. *I'd wondered how he managed to sneak something like that aboard,* thought Andrew in his state of suspended time. *Still, Svyatog's security sucks.* But at the moment, the point was that the pistol was devastating in a confined space like this . . . and that Valdes had somehow kept it trained on his hostages.

Andrew leveled his M-3. "Drop it, Valdes."

"No!" Valdes was wild-eyed. "I'll kill them all. You don't dare try a shot!"

For a couple of eternal heartbeats, the motionless tableau held.

Andrew let his eyes stray toward the hostages. They met his mother's. She smiled.

All at once, she launched herself at Valdes.

Her rush naturally had little speed and less force. But its sheer unexpectedness, combined with the Kappainu's physical weakness, allowed her to throw Valdes off balance as she clutched feebly at his gun arm. As they grappled, Andrew still couldn't risk firing.

With a convulsion of desperate strength, Valdes flung her off him. She spun away, and her head struck a bulkhead. She dropped to the deck.

At the same instant, Gallivan sprang. Valdes, still trying to restore his balance, fired wildly.

The blinding gush of superheated plasma stabbed out, brushing against Gallivan's left arm. He fell, screaming and beating frantically at his burning sleeve. The plasma beam went on to incinerate the head of one of Svyatog's crewmen.

But Valdes was now in the clear. Andrew fired on full automatic, bringing the stream of hypervelocity bullets from crotch up to mid-breast. Valdes collapsed with a shriek that had very little that was human about it, his tissues trying in vain to reconfigure themselves around the massive simultaneous trauma to so many vital organs.

He began to change.

Andrew became a robot with no purpose save to rush to the communicator and raise *City of Osaka*. He spoke emotionlessly. "Lieutenant Morales, this is the Captain. The situation is under control here. Destroy Valdes's ship immediately. You have two incoming stealthed ships." He had intended to use Valdes as a hostage when the Kappainu warships arrived, but that hope, like so much else, was gone. Receiving Morales's acknowledgment, he permitted himself to turn around and see . . . but not to feel. Not yet.

Reislon had used a first-aid kit to sedate Gallivan and was applying anti-burn salve to his blackened, crisped arm. There was nothing to be done for the Lokaron crewman, whose head was little more than a charred stump. Svyatog was on the deck beside Katy. He looked up at Andrew and shook his head slowly. It was unnecessary. Andrew could see the side of her head, which had crunched into the bulkhead temple first.

Moving in a strange universe of unreality, Andrew turned and looked down at Valdes. The Kappainu's screams had subsided to a moan, and his features were writhing and reconfiguring in the repulsive way Andrew had seen before.

"There's something I've always wondered about," he said conversationally. He pointed his M-3 and destroyed Valdes's brain. Death was instantaneous. The transformation stopped, incomplete, leaving a thing on the deck that was half human and half Kappainu—an obscene travesty of nature, beyond the capability of the most depraved mind to conceive. The indescribable face was frozen in a mask of agony.

For a while, silence reigned. The communicator broke it. It was Morales.

"Valdes's ship is out of action, sir," she reported. In the viewscreen, Andrew could see the small craft receding sunward in free fall, clearly lifeless, streaming air and trailing clouds of glowing debris. "But we've detected two approaching ships, on an intercept vector that we can't avoid. They're not bothering to cloak themselves, but the sensor readings are compatible with—"

"—Kappainu warships. And we're all out of options. I'd hoped we'd have Valdes as a hostage, but he's dead."

In the comm screen, Morales's face was a battlefield where propriety struggled and lost. "Uh, Captain . . . is Rory . . . I mean Mr. Gallivan . . . ?"

"He's badly injured, but he'll live." Andrew's lips quirked in a ghastly parody of a smile. "For a little while."

Morales's expression matched his. "I see what you mean, sir."

"It has been an honor to serve with you, Alana."

"And with you, Captain."

Rachel's face appeared beside Morales's in the screen. Given the total absence of privacy, all Andrew could say was, "I'm sorry."

"You're always saying that when it isn't necessary." Her smile brought a trace of warmth creeping back into Andrew's soul.

Morales turned to receive a report, then faced the pickup expressionlessly. "They've commenced launching missiles, sir."

Andrew glanced at Svyatog, who turned to his surviving crewmen. "Take evasive action. We'll split up and do the same." His eyes locked with Rachel's. *What can it matter now, what I say or who hears it?* He started to open his mouth.

From somewhere in *City of Osaka*'s control room came a shout loud enough to be picked up by the communicator. Morales spun around, stared, then faced Andrew again. "Sir, we have fighters coming in at an incredible velocity. They must have been launched from a ship moving at—"

"*Broadsword!*" whooped Andrew. "It's got to be." He turned to the viewscreen and looked in the direction from which the Kappainu ships were approaching. Lines of flashes began to appear, as though fireflies were winking on in formation. He recognized what he was seeing at a distance: spreads of the small nuclear warheads of fighter-launched missiles.

"Sir," said Morales, visibly struggling to maintain formality, "we're being hailed by *Broadsword.*"

"Patch him in to this ship, on a split screen." There was a perceptible time lag.

It took a moment before Andrew even recognized Jamel Taylor. He had never imagined his friend could look so haggard. He knew the signs of a man who had spent too long under dangerously high acceleration. "Andy, we got here as quickly as we could. I launched all my fighters a while back, to save time."

"Plenty of time, Jamel," said Andrew with a weary smile. "Ample time. I don't suppose any of the Rogovon ships came with you?"

"No. That didn't seem like such a good idea. But Borthru is aboard."

"Give him my best," said Andrew, reflecting that

the Lokar, Rogovon or no, must be half dead from the sustained g-forces.

"And now," Taylor continued, "we've built up too much velocity to kill anytime soon. We're going to have to flash past you—and Earth, for that matter—and loop back around."

"That's all right, Jamel." Andrew looked at the viewscreen. A larger flash than the others erupted, then another—the funeral pyres of the Kappainu ships. "Thanks to your fighter pilots, I think we can take over from here. Signing off." Taylor's image vanished, leaving those of the two women in *City of Osaka*'s control room.

"Lieutenant Morales," he said briskly, "please bring these ships together at *Korcentyr*'s port access hatch so I can come back aboard. The gig is slightly out of commission." He turned around. Unnoticed by him, Svyatog had had Gallivan and the corpses removed—all three corpses, including his mother's.

All at once, everything he had been suppressing overflowed and burst the barriers he had erected. He slumped down on the console, burying his face in his arms. His shoulders began to heave. Neither Svyatog nor any of the other Lokaron saw fit to disturb him.

CHAPTER TWENTY-SIX

THE FACILITY LAY DEEP in a mountain not far from Geneva, under what appeared to be an inconspicuous ski chalet. No one except Confederated Nations personnel with the highest security clearance knew of its existence. Fewer still had ever actually been inside it. No nonhumans had, until now.

Svyatog'Korth, Reislon'Sygnath and Borthru'Goron sat on one side of a long conference table with Andrew, Rachel, and Jamel Taylor. Across the table were only three humans . . . but very important ones.

Savitri Gupta, president-general of the CNE, closed the folder she had been reading with a decisive snap. She glanced to her right at Admiral Bruno Hoffman, Chief of Naval Operations, and to her left at Ilya Trofimovitch Tulenko, director of the CNE's Security and Investigations Bureau.

The three of them, along with certain highly cleared staffers and technical experts, had by now heard the entire story and seen its electronic documentation. They had also seen the Kappainu corpse that had been Erica Kharazi, and the half-human horror that was still recognizable—just barely—as Franklin Ivanovitch Valdes y Kurita. At the sight of that last, Gupta had excused herself, gagging, to return a few minutes later with restored composure but with an ashy undertone to her normal duskiness. Now she turned to Hoffman, tapped the folder, and spoke briskly.

"Admiral, I approve the plan for performing medical scans on all military personnel. But I must emphasize the importance of doing it quietly, without attracting media attention."

"I understand, Madam President-General. That's why we're going to be doing it in stages, each with its own rationalization. One 'disease outbreak' here, another 'public health emergency' there . . ."

"Yes. So I gather." Gupta turned to Tulenko. "And I want this program extended to all CNE government employees, starting with those in the most sensitive positions."

"A detailed plan will shortly be ready for your perusal, Madam President-General. Of course, this involves additional complications, some of them of a political nature. For example, the members of the Legislative Assembly—"

"Understood. But it must be done. And I insist that I myself be the first."

"Actually, Madam President-General, I've already taken the liberty of having scans unobtrusively performed

on everyone who has entered this facility, including you
. . . and, of course, myself."

For an instant, Gupta's eyes flashed dark fire. Then
her glare subsided, and she even permitted herself a tiny
smile.

"But," Tulenko continued, "there are limits to the
SIB's capabilities and scope. Some of those restrictions
are legal in nature."

"And they will be observed to the letter," Gupta stated
firmly. "The Confederated Nations is dedicated to a belief
in limited government. We're going to live by it."

"Of course, Madam President-General. And at any rate,
there are practical limitations as well. Simply put, we will
never be able to scan the entire population of this planet."

A glum silence settled over the room. "Yes," Gupta
finally acknowledged. "That is the problem. There can be
no absolute guarantees."

"Actually," said Reislon, "that is not the only problem,
nor even the greatest one. At the risk of being what I
believe you humans call the 'skeleton at the feast,' I must
remind you that we have no live Kappainu prisoners to
interrogate, and no captured ships to comb for astrogational
data. In short, we have no way of locating their home
planet. So they have a safe haven wherein to lick their
wounds and devise new plans. There was nothing of use
recovered from the debris of the Kappainu Station and
ships."

"Perhaps the scanning programs will net us some
prisoners," Tulenko argued. "And of course we're going to
start taking the Black Wolf Society a lot more seriously,
which should open up some new avenues of investigation."

"I doubt if any Kappainu you are able to capture will be in possession of any useful astronomical data, given their racial penchant for caution and concealment. And no human Black Wolf people will know anything useful."

"It seems," said Rachel, "that from now on, even more than ever, the price of freedom is going to be eternal vigilance."

"And," said Gupta, "it will be harder than ever because that vigilance is going to have to be maintained in secret, without Earth's people ever knowing how they're being protected, or what they're being protected from." She turned to the three Lokaron across the table. "As you've probably learned by now, shape-shifters appear in many human cultures as legends of supernatural evil. If it became generally known that *actual* shape-shifters have been at large among us, manipulating us, and that the government can't guarantee that they aren't *still* among us . . . well, the result would be panic and hysteria. It won't mean anything to you Lokaron when I say it would be like the seventeenth century witch-hunting mentality come back. But take my word for it: society would splinter. No. The secret must be kept. No one except the highest placed can be allowed to know the facts about what has happened."

"Including the fact of my father's suicide?" asked Rachel levelly.

"That's right, Ms Arnstein. As you've learned since your return to Earth, he has been interred, covered with honors. Which is as it should be. He deserved no less of the CNE. No clouds from his very last days should be allowed to shadow his glory."

"Thank you," Rachel whispered.

"For the same reason," Gupta continued with a look of cold disgust, "it has already been announced that Legislative Assemblyman Valdes was lost in a tragic accident in the course of his return from a fact-finding tour in the outer system, with no remains recovered."

Rachel's expression grew hard. "Yes. I've heard some of the eulogizing in the media. Including yours."

"Do you think I enjoyed making that pro forma speech? You don't understand the difficulties of my position, given the political realities!" Gupta halted, as though suddenly realizing what she sounded like, and took a deep breath. "All right. I don't like it any better than you do. But it has to be." She turned again to the three Lokaron, and to Svyatog in particular. "In order to keep the secret from the human populace, I must implore you to keep it secret as well. If it becomes general knowledge in Lokaron societies—especially in Gev-Harath—it will get back, given the free-trade relationship which now exists, and which we all wish to see maintained."

"Certainly," said Svyatog. "As you know, the *hovahon* are not unaccustomed to keeping secrets from the governments of the *gevahon*." He politely ignored Gupta's visibly mixed emotions: philosophical disapproval versus practical relief. "And in the meantime, I—meaning Hov-Korth—will be alert to any signs of a resurgence of the threat."

"And," Borthru put in, "the movement I represent can abort any attempt by the Kappainu to revive their scheme in its original form, if we succeed in replacing the present regime in Gev-Rogov with one which will be aware of their existence and will not react as they predict."

"Yes," said Svyatog. "And, just incidentally, Hov-Korth would undoubtedly find you easier to do business with. We will provide you with has much covert aid as possible."

"So will the CNE," said Gupta. "But I'm reassured by your use of the word 'covert'. I must emphasize again the paramount importance of secrecy."

Andrew spoke for the first time. "So my mother's death . . . ?"

"Will be attributed to natural causes, quite plausible given her age." Compassion overlaid the sternness in Gupta's face, but the sternness was still unmistakably there. "Likewise, the fatalities among *Broadsword*'s crew will be explained as accidents. The recommendations you and Captain Taylor have made for Lieutenant Morales and others will be acted on, but they'll never be able to wear their decorations, and the citations will never be declassified. Neither will *Broadsword*'s log. Her personnel will be sworn to secrecy and provided with a full cover story for what they've been doing . . . and made aware of the criminal penalties for security breaches. The theft of the Cydonia artifact from the Imperial Temple of the Star Lords will simply be an unsolved crime, in which Persath'Loven was an innocent dupe of the two thieves Patrick Nolan and Sarah Rosenfeld. To sum up: *none of this ever happened.*"

The last notes of the bagpipes were gone, drifting away on the breeze. All the various dignitaries had departed, leaving four figures, two human and two Lokaron, standing at a freshly dug grave alongside another that was only slightly less fresh.

The last time Andrew had been at Arlington National Cemetery—seemingly a lifetime ago—it had been a harsh winter day. Now it was late spring, and Washington's cherry blossoms were past, but the stultifying heat and humidity of summer still lay mercifully in the future. It was a perfect day.

"I thought the president-general's address was most moving," said Svyatog.

"Yes," Andrew acknowledged. There had been quite a lot to say about Katy Doyle-Roark, even without that which could not be said. "I want to thank the two of you for coming."

"You know perfectly well I would never have missed it," Svyatog reproved. "Reislon and Borthru were only sorry they had to send their regrets, having already departed for Kogurche."

"Nor would I," said Persath'Loven. "Even though I must now return to Tizath'Asor and resume my researches. Important, yes, *important* questions can be answered now that I have an access key to work with."

"And those answers may be quite useful if we have to deal with the Kappainu again in the future," Svyatog pointed out.

"Yes, yes. The practical applications can't be ignored, I suppose. But the theoretical considerations are what really matter." He turned to go. But then, for an instant, his fussiness wavered as he glanced at the newer grave. "I only met your mother once. I wish I could have known her better. Good-bye."

"I too must leave," said Svyatog. But he hesitated, gazing at the graves. "Our rituals in connection with the dead are different. But this ceremony, like the one for your father this past winter, spoke to me on a level that transcends all our differences." An amused tone crept into the translator. "Doubtless it is because of my own advanced age. Soon enough I will have a great deal in common with them indeed."

"Don't talk like that, Svyatog!" said Andrew. He looked at the graves, then at the old Lokar, and attempted lightness. "When you go, the Age of Heroes will be well and truly over."

Svyatog looked down from his great height and gazed deeply into Andrew's eyes. "No, it won't," he said succinctly. And then he was gone.

After a moment, Rachel broke the silence. "Have you heard anything more about Rory?" she asked, making conversation.

"You mean aside from the fact that his record has been wiped clean? No, I know what you mean. He's convalescing well, and already providing Tulenko with lots of valuable information on the Black Wolf Society. He'll be all right . . . at least if Alana Morales has anything to do with it!" They both chuckled at the unfathomable workings of fate. Then Rachel sobered and looked at the rise of ground beyond which lay another grave of recent vintage. They had visited it the day before.

"I feel almost guilty," she said suddenly. "When they buried my father they rattled off his entire life, with all his accomplishments but with the dark things at the end left out. Your mother, though . . . what she did at the very end couldn't be told either."

"I don't think she really would have minded.

Remember, she was a spook in her day. More often than not, in that line of business, the fact that nobody ever knows you did your job simply means you did it right. She understood that."

"I never knew her much better than Persath did. Like him, I wish I'd gotten to know her better."

"You still can, you know."

Rachel gave Andrew a sharp regard. "What on Earth are you talking about?"

"I know that sounds odd. It has to do with a present Svyatog gave my family a while back. You see . . . Listen, are you free to take a little trip out to Colorado?"

Rachel put on her best demure look. "Why . . . yes, I suppose so."

"Good. We'll go to my parents' place and I'll take you down into the basement—"

"The *basement*?"

"Right." Andrew smiled—the first full-blooded smile she had seen on his face in far too long. "In fact, there's somebody down there I'd like you to meet."

GLOSSARY

CNE—Confederated Nations of Earth; a loose world government formed after the overthrow of the Earth First Party in 2030.

CNEN—Confederated Nations of Earth Navy; the CNE's space fleet and principal military service.

Corvette—Small space warship, the largest capable of landing on a planetary surface.

Cruiser—The primary combatant ship of space navies, typically carrying a complement of fighter craft. The largest variety, the "strike cruiser," is the true "capital ship" of space. Until recent years, cruisers were the only warships capable of performing transition (q.v.) independently of transition gates.

Frigate—A warship smaller than a cruiser. In recent times there has been a trend toward equipping frigates with integral transition engines.

Gevahon (singular "gevah")—Lokaron interstellar "nations," normally with limited, decentralized governments. Each gevah comprises a subspecies gengineered for colonization of a particular planetary environment.

Gev-Harath—The richest and most powerful of the Lokaron gevahon; on friendly terms with Earth since 2030.

Gev-Lokarath—The Lokaron gevah centered on the race's original homeworld and inhabited by its original, unmodified genotype. Tends to look down on the other gevahon, which in turn regard it with a kind of overcompensated inferiority complex.

Gev-Rogov—Lokaron gevah, large and powerful but in somewhat bad odor with the other gevahon because its subspecies (more divergent from the original genotype than most) is regarded as physically unappealing, and because its centralized, authoritarian governmental system is repugnant to Lokaron norms. The object of bitter human hatred since 2030.

Gev-Tizath—Lokaron gevah, originally a secondary colony of Gev-Harath and inhabited by essentially the same subspecies. Home of the original Lokaron discoverers of Earth, with which it is now on good terms. Regarded as a bumptious newcomer by the older-established gevahon.

Gig—A small craft carried by a large spaceship that cannot itself land on a planetary surface.

Harath-Asor—Capital planet of Gev-Harath (q.v.).

Hovahon (singular "hovah")—Lokaron megacorporations which wield the real power within the gevahon (q.v.).

Hov-Korth—The wealthiest hovah of Gev-Harath (q.v.); a close trading partner of Earth, with which it has enjoyed a special relationship since 2030.

Lokaron (singular "Lokar")—Nonhuman race, similar in many biochemical respects to humanity but with numerous differences, most notably a three-gender reproductive pattern. The most widespread, advanced, and powerful race in the known galaxy, differentiated into subspecies originally gengineered as colonists for various planets, each with its own politically sovereign gevah.

Overspace—A dimension congruent with normal space, in which points corresponding to points in normal space are vastly closer together. This makes it possible to evade relativistic limitations and effectively exceed the speed of light.

Tizath-Asor—Capital planet of Gev-Tizath (q.v.).

Transition—Convenience label for the act of entering or departing from overspace (q.v.) by creating a multi-dimensional "tunnel" in the space-time continuum, by means of either a ship's own internal "transition engine" (typical of warships and exploration ships) or external "transition gates" (which make interstellar commerce economically viable).

Upload—A digital copy of a brain's memories, which can be run as a self-aware computer program. Cutting-edge technology even for the Lokaron.

The Following is an excerpt from:

CAPTAIN VORPATRIL'S ALLIANCE

LOIS McMASTER BUJOLD

Available from Baen Books
November 2012
hardcover

CHAPTER ONE

Ivan's door buzzer sounded at close to Komarran midnight, just when he was unwinding enough from lingering jump lag, his screwed-up diurnal rhythm, and the day's labors to consider sleep. He growled under his breath and trod unwillingly to answer it.

His instincts proved correct when he saw who waited in the aperture.

"Oh, God. Byerly Vorrutyer. Go away."

"Hi, Ivan," said Byerly smoothly, ignoring Ivan's anti-greeting. "May I come in?"

Ivan took about a second to consider the, at best, complicated possibilities Byerly usually trailed in his wake, and said simply, "No." But he'd hesitated too long. Byerly slipped inside. Ivan sighed, letting the door slide closed and seal. So far from home, it was good to see a familiar face — just not By's. *Next time, use the security screen, and pretend not to be here, eh?*

Byerly padded swiftly across the small but choice living

quarters of Ivan's downtown Solstice luxury flat, rentals by the week. Ivan had picked it out for its potential proximity to Solstice nightlife, which, alas, he had so far not had a chance to sample. Pausing at the broad glass doors to the balcony, Byerly dimmed the polarization on the seductive view of the glittering lights of the capital city. Dome, Ivan corrected his thought to Komarran nomenclature, as the arcology existed under a hodgepodge of seals to keep the toxic planetary atmosphere out and the breathable one in. Byerly pulled the drapes as well, and turned back to the room.

Yielding to a curiosity he knew he would regret, Ivan asked, "What the hell are you doing on Komarr, By? Isn't this off your usual beat?"

Byerly grimaced. "Working."

Indeed, an experienced observer, which Ivan unfortunately was, could detect a distinct strain around By's eyes, along with the redness from drink and perhaps recreational chemicals. Byerly cultivated the authentic look of a Barrayaran high Vor town clown given over to a life of dissolution and idle vice by actually living it, ninety percent of the time. The other ten percent, and most of his hidden income, came from his work as an informer for Imperial Security. And ninety percent of that was just more dissolution and vice, except for having to turn in reports at the end. The residue, Ivan had to concede, could get dicey.

Ratting out your friends to ImpSec for money, Ivan had once heckled By, to which By had shrugged and replied, *And the greater glory of the Imperium. Don't forget that.*

Ivan wondered which it was tonight.

In reflexive response to the manners drilled into him in his youth, Ivan offered, "Something to drink? Beer, wine? Something stronger?" He contemplated By's boneless flop onto his living room couch. "Coffee?"

"Just water. Please. I need to clear my head, and then I need to sleep."

Ivan went to his tidy kitchenette and filled a tumbler. As he handed it to his unwelcome guest, By said, "And what are you doing in Solstice, Ivan?"

"Working."

By's open hand invited him to expand.

Ivan sat across from him and said, "Trailing my boss, who is here for an Ops conference with his assorted counterparts and underlings. Efficiently combined with the annual Komarr Fleet inspections. All the excitement of a tax inventory, except in dress uniform." Belatedly, Ivan realized By had to already know all this. He'd found Ivan, hadn't he? Because By's random social calls, weren't.

"Still working for Admiral Desplains?"

"Yep. Aide-de-camp, secretary, personal assistant, general dogsbody, whatever he needs. I aim to make myself indispensable."

"And still ducking promotion, are you, Captain Vorpatril?"

"Yes. And succeeding, no thanks to you."

By smirked. "They say that at Imperial Service Headquarters, the captains bring the coffee."

"That's right. And I like it that way." Ivan only wished it were true. It seemed barely months ago, though it was over a year, that the latest flare-up of tensions with

Barrayar's most traditional enemy, the Cetagandan Empire, had pinned Ivan to military headquarters 26.7 hours a Barrayaran day for weeks on end, sweating out all the most horrific possibilities. Designing death in detail. War had been averted through non-traditional diplomacy, mostly on the part of Barrayaran emperor Gregor's weaseliest Imperial Auditor and, to give credit where it was due, his wife.

That time. There was always a next time.

Ivan studied Byerly, who was only a few years older than himself. They shared the same brown eyes, dark hair, and olive skin common to Barrayar's somewhat inbred military caste, or aristocracy, whatever one wanted to call it, and, indeed, common to most Barrayarans. By was shorter and slighter than Ivan's six-foot-one, broad-shouldered fitness, but then, he didn't have a Desplains riding him to keep up the recruiting-poster appearance expected of an officer serving at Imperial Headquarters. Granted, when they weren't squinting from the dissolution, By's eyes had the startling beauty that distinguished his famous, or infamous, clan, to which Ivan was connected by a few twigs in his own family tree. That was the problem with being Vor. You ended up related to all sorts of people you'd rather not be. And they all felt free to call on you for favors.

"What do you want, Byerly?"

"So direct! You'll never become a diplomat that way, Ivan."

"I once spent a year as assistant military attaché to the Barrayaran Embassy on Earth. It was as much diplomacy as I cared for. Get to the point, By. I want to go to bed. And by the looks of you, so do you."

By let his eyes widen. "Why Ivan! Was that an invitation? I'm so thrilled!"

"Someday," Ivan growled, "I might say yes to that old line, just to watch you have a coronary."

By spread his hand over his heart, and intoned wistfully, "And so I might." He drained his water and gave over the vamping, the face so often arranged in a vague smarminess firming intently in a way Ivan always found a touch disturbing. "Actually, I have a little task to ask of you."

"Figured."

"It's quite in your line. I may even be said to be doing you a good turn, who knows. I'd like you to pick up a girl."

"No," said Ivan, only in part to see what By would say next.

"Come, come. You pick up girls all the time."

"Not on your recommendations. What's the catch?"

Byerly made a face. "So suspicious, Ivan!"

"Yeah."

By shrugged, conceding the point. "Unfortunately, I'm not entirely sure. And my duties with, if I may say it, the unusually unpleasant people I am presently accompanying—"

Spying on, Ivan translated this without difficulty. And the company By kept was usually unpleasant, in Ivan's opinion. *Unusually* unpleasant implied . . . what?

"— leave me little opportunity to check her out. But they have an inexplicable interest in her. Which I suspect is not friendly. It worries me, Ivan, I must say." He added after a moment, "She's quite well-looking, I assure you. You need have no fear on that score."

Ivan frowned, stung. "Are you implying I'd refuse to supply assistance to a homely girl?"

Byerly sat back, eyebrows flicking up. "To your credit, I actually don't believe that's the case. But it will add a certain convincing verisimilitude for the outside observer." He pulled a small plastic flimsy from his jacket and handed it across.

The background was too fuzzed to make out, but the picture showed a striking young woman striding down a sidewalk. Apparent age could be anything between twenty and thirty standard-years, though that was no certain clue as to real age. Tumbling black hair, bright eyes, skin glowing an interesting cinnamon brown against a cream tank top. Decided nose, determined chin; either the natural face she was born with, or the work of a real artist, because it certainly didn't bear the stamped-from-the-same-mold blandness of the usual body sculpture, a biological ideal that lost its appeal with repetition. Long legs in tan trousers that hugged in all the right places. A nicely full figure. *Nicely* full. If the face was natural, might the other prominent features be, too? With weakening reluctance, Ivan said, "Who is she?"

"Supposedly, a Komarran citizen named Nanja Brindis, lately moved to Solstice from Olbia Dome."

"Supposedly?"

"I have reason to suspect that might be a recent cover identity. She did move here about two months ago, it does seem."

"So who is she really?"

"It would be a fine thing if you could find that out."

"If she's hiding her identity for a good reason, she's

hardly going to tell me." Ivan hesitated. "Is it a good reason?"

"I suspect it's a very good reason. And I also suspect she is not a professional at the game."

"This is all pretty vague, Byerly. May I remind you, my security clearance is higher than yours."

"Probably." Byerly blinked in doubt. "But then there is that pesky need-to-know rule."

"I'm not sticking my head into one of your dodgy meat grinders — *again* — unless I know as much as you know. At *least*."

Byerly flung up his well-manicured hands in faux-surrender. "The people I'm with seem to have got themselves involved in a complex smuggling operation. Rather over their heads."

"Komarr local space is a major trade nexus. The place is lousy with smugglers. As long as the transients don't try to offload their goods within the Imperium, in which case Imperial Customs deals sharply with 'em, they get ignored. And the Komarran trade fleets police their own."

"That's two out of three."

Ivan's head came up. "The only thing left is the Imperial fleet."

"Just so."

"Crap, Byerly, if there was even a hint of that sort of thing going on, Service Security would swoop in. Damned hard."

"But even Service Security needs to know where and when to swoop. I am doing, as it were, a preliminary pre-swoop survey. Not only because mistakes are embarrassing, especially if they involve accusations of Vor scions with arrogant and powerful relatives, but because they tip off the real crims, who then promptly escape one's tediously set net. And you've no idea how tedious that can get."

"Mm," said Ivan. "And once military personnel get involved with, they think, simple civilian crime, they become vulnerable to more treasonous blackmail."

By bared his teeth. "I'm so pleased you keep up. One of your saving graces."

"I've had practice." Ivan hissed alarm. "Desplains should know about this."

"Desplains will know about it, in due course. In the meanwhile, try to remember you *don't* know." Byerly paused. "That caution is cancelled, of course, should my dead body turn up in a lewd and compromising position in some ditch outside the dome in the next few days."

"Think it might?"

"The stakes are very high. And not just the money."

"So how's this girl connected, again?"

Byerly sighed. "She's not with my crew. She's definitely not with the non-Barrayarans they're dealing with, though it's not outside the realm of reason that she could be a defector. And she's not what she pretends to be. What's left, I am forced to leave to you to find out, because I can't risk coming here again, and I'm not going to have time in the next few days for side-issues."

Ivan said slowly, "You think she's in danger of her life?" Because why else would By bother to set even a side-friend on this side-issue? By didn't make his living through charity.

But he did make his living through a weird sort of loyalty. And, somewhere underneath the persiflage, camouflage, and just plain flage, he was high Vor of the highest . . .

"Let's just say, you would gratify me by staying alert. I should not care to explain any accidents that might befall you to your lady mother."

Ivan allowed the concern with a rueful nod. "So where am I to find this so-called girl?"

"I am fairly certain she's a real girl, Ivan."

"You think? With you, one never knows." He eyed By dryly, and By had the grace to squirm just a bit, in acknowledgement of his cousin Dono née Donna of lamented memory. Donna, that is. Count Dono Vorrutyer was all too vivid a presence, on the Vorbarr Sultana political scene.

By dodged the diversion and, so to speak, soldiered on, though the idea of By in any branch of the Service made Ivan wince in imagination. "She works as a packing clerk at a place called Swift Shipping. Here's her home address, too — which was unlisted, by the way, so unless you can devise a convincing reason for turning up there, probably better to run into her coming into or out of work. I don't gather she does much partying. Make friends, Ivan. Before tomorrow night, by preference." He rubbed his face, pressing his hands to his eyes. "Actually—by tomorrow night without fail."

Ivan accepted the contact data with misgivings. By stretched, rose a bit creakily to his feet, and made his way to the door. "Adieu, dear friend, adieu. Sweet dreams, and may angels guard your repose. Possibly angels with clouds of dark curls, sun-kissed skin, and bosoms like heavenly pillows."

"Dry up."

By grinned over his shoulder, waved without turning around, and blew out.

Ivan returned to his couch, sat with a thump, and picked up the flimsy, studying it cautiously. At least By was right about the heavenly pillows. What else was he right about? Ivan had an unsettling premonition that he was going to find out.

Tej was conscious of the customer from the moment he walked in the door, ten minutes before closing. When she'd started this job a month ago, in the hopes of stretching her and Rish's dwindling resources, she'd been hyperaware of all customers who entered the shop. A job that exposed her directly and continuously to the public was not a good choice, she'd realized almost at once, but it had been the entry-level position she could get with the limited fake references she commanded. A promotion to the back office was mentioned, so she'd hung grimly on. It was being slow in opening up, though, and she'd wondered if her boss was stringing her along. In the meanwhile, her jagged nerves had slowly grown habituated. Till now.

He was tall for a local. Quite good looking, too, but in a way that fell short of sculpted or gengineered perfections. His skin was Komarran-pale, set off by a long-sleeved, dark blue knit shirt. Gray multi-pocketed sleeveless jacket worn open over it, indeterminate blue trousers. Shoes very shiny yet not new, in a conservative, masculine style that seemed familiar but, annoyingly, eluded recognition.

He carried a large bag, and despite the time noodled around looking at the displays. Her co-clerk Dotte took the next customer, she finished with her own, and the fellow glanced up and stepped to the counter, smiling.

"Hi, there" — with difficulty, he dragged his gaze from her chest to her face — "Nanja."

It didn't take that long to scan her nametag. *Slow reader, are you? Why, yes, I get a lot of those.* Tej returned the smile with the minimum professional courtesy due a customer who hadn't, actually, done anything really obnoxious yet.

He hoisted his bag to the counter and withdrew a large, asymmetrical, and astonishingly ugly ceramic vase. She guessed the design was supposed to be abstract, but it was more as if a party of eye-searing polka dots had all gotten falling-down drunk.

"I would like this packed and shipped to Miles Vorkosigan, Vorkosigan House, Vorbarr Sultana."

She almost asked, *What dome?* but the unfamiliar accent clicked in before she could make that mistake. The man was not Komarran at all, but a Barrayaran. They didn't get many Barrayarans in this quiet, low-rent neighborhood. Even a generation after the conquest, the conquerors tended to cluster in their own enclaves, or in the central areas devoted to the planetary government and off-world businesses, or out near the civilian or military shuttleports.

"Is there a street address? Scanner code?"

"No, just use the scanner code for the planet and city. Once it gets that far, it'll find him."

Surely it would cost this man far more to ship this . . .

object to a planet five wormhole jumps away than it was worth. She wondered if she was obliged to point this out. "Regular or premium service? There's a stiff price difference, but I have to tell you, express won't really get there much faster." It all went on the same jumpship, after all.

"Is it more likely to arrive intact with premium?"

"No, sir, it will be packed just the same. There are regulations for anything that goes by jumpship."

"Right-oh, regular it is."

"Extra insurance?" she said doubtfully. "There's a base coverage that comes with the service." She named the amount, and he allowed as it would do. It was in truth considerably less than the shipping charges.

"You pack it yourself? Can I watch?"

She glanced at the digital hour display over the door. The task would run her past closing time, but customers were fussy about breakables. She sighed and turned to the foamer. He stood on tiptoe and watched over the counter as she carefully positioned the vase—a glimpse of its underside revealed a sale tag with four markdowns— closed the door, and turned on the machine. A brief hiss, a moment of watching the indicator lights wink hypnotically, and the door popped back open, releasing a pungent whiff that stunned her sense of smell and masked every other scent in the shop. She bent and removed the neat block of flexifoam. It was an aesthetic improvement.

Ivan Vorpatril, read the name on his credit chit. Also with a Vorbarr Sultana home address. Not just a Barrayaran, then, but one of those Vor-people, the conquerors' arrogant privileged class. Even her father had been wary of — she cut the thought short.

"Do you wish to include a note?"

"Naw, I think it'll be self-explanatory. His wife's a gardener, see. She's always looking for something to stuff her poisonous plants into." He watched her slide the foam block into its outer container and affix the label, adding after a moment, "I'm new in town. Yourself?"

"I've been here a while," she said neutrally.

"Really? I could do with a native guide."

Dotte closed out the scanners and turned off the lights as a broad hint to the laggard customer. And, bless her, lingered by the door to see Tej safely free of the shop and him. Tej gestured him out ahead of her, and the door locked behind them all.

The oldest human habitation on the surface of Komarr, Solstice Dome had a peculiar layout, to Tej's eye. The aging initial installations resembled the space stations she'd grown up in, with their labyrinths of corridors. The very latest sections were laid out with separate, street-linked buildings, but under vast, soaring, transparent domes that mimicked the open sky the residents hoped to have some-day, when the atmospheric terraforming was complete. Middling areas, like this one, fell between, with much less technologically ambitious domes that still gave glimpses of an outside where no one ventured without a breath mask. The passage that Swift Shipping fronted was more street than corridor, anyway, too broad for the persistent customer to easily obstruct her.

"Off work now, huh?" he inquired ingenuously, with a boyish smile. He was a bit old for boyish smiles.

"Yes, I'm going home." Tej wished she could go home, really home. Yet how much of what she'd known as home still existed, even if she could be magically transported there in a blink? *No, don't think those thoughts.* The tension headache, and heartache, were too exhausting to bear.

"I wish I could go home," said the man, Vorpatril, in unconscious echo of her thought. "But I'm stuck here for a while. Say, can I buy you a drink?"

"No, thank you."

"Dinner?"

"No."

He waggled his eyebrows, cheerfully. "Ice cream? All women like ice cream, in my experience."

"No!"

"Walk you home? Or in the park. Or somewhere. I think they have rowboats to rent in that lake park I passed. That'd make a nice place to talk."

"Certainly not!" Ought she to invent a waiting spouse or lover? She linked arms with Dotte, pinching her in silent warning. "Let's go to the bubble car stop now, Dotte."

Dotte gave her a surprised look, knowing perfectly well that Tej — Nanja, as she knew her — always walked home to her nearby flat. But she obediently turned away and led off. Vorpatril followed, not giving up. He slipped around in front, grinned some more, and tried, "What about a puppy?"

Dotte snorted a laugh, which didn't help.

"A kitten?"

They were far enough from Swift Shipping now that

customer politeness rules no longer applied, Tej decided. She snarled at him, "Go away. Or I'll find a street patroller."

He opened his hands in apparent surrender, watching with a doleful expression as they marched past. "A pony . . . ?" he called after them, as if in one last spasm of hope.

Dotte looked back over her shoulder as they approached the bubble-car station. Tej looked straight ahead.

"I think you're crazy, Nanja," said Dotte, trudging with her up the pedestrian ramp. "I'd have taken him up on that drink in a heartbeat. Or any of the rest of the menu, though I supposed I'd have to draw the line at the pony. It wouldn't fit in my flat."

"I thought you were married."

"Yes, but I'm not *blind*."

"Dotte, customers try to pick me up at least twice a week."

"But they aren't usually that incredibly cute. Or taller than you."

"What's that have to do with anything?" said Tej, irritated. "My mother was a head taller than my father, and they did fine." She clamped her jaw shut. *Not so fine now*.

She parted company with Dotte at the platform, but did board a bubble car. She rode to a random destination about ten minutes away, then disembarked and took another car back to a different stop on the other side of her neighborhood, just in case the man was still lingering out there, stalker-like, at the first one. She strode off briskly.

Almost home, she started to relax, until she looked up

and spotted Vorpatril lounging on the steps to her
building entrance.

She slowed her steps to a dawdle, pretending not to
have noticed him yet, raised her wristcom to her lips, and
spoke a keyword. Rish's voice answered at once.

"Tej? You're late. I was getting worried."

"I'm fine, I'm right outside, but I'm being followed."

The voice went sharp. "Can you go roundabout and
shake him off?"

"Already tried that. He got ahead of me somehow."

"Oh. Not good."

"Especially as I never gave him my address."

A brief silence. "Very not good. Can you stall him a
minute, then get him to follow you into the foyer?"

"Probably."

"I'll take care of him there. Don't panic, sweetling."

"I'm not." She left the channel open on send-only, so
that Rish could follow the play. She took her time closing
the last few dozen meters, and came to a wary halt at the
bottom of her steps.

"Hi, Nanja!" Vorpatril waved amiably, without getting
up, looming, or lunging for her.

"How did you find this place?" she asked, not amiably.

"Would you believe dumb luck?"

"No."

"Ah. Pity." He scratched his chin in apparent thought.
"We could go somewhere and talk about it. You can pick
where, if you like."

She simulated a long hesitation, while calculating the
time needed for Rish to get downstairs. Just about . . .
now. "All right. Let's go inside."

His brows shot up, but then his smile widened. "Sounds great. Sure!"

He rose and politely waited while she fished her remote out of her pocket and coded open the front entrance. As the seal-door hissed aside, he followed her into the small lift-tube foyer. A female figure sat on the bench opposite the tubes, hands hidden in her vest as if chilly, voluminous patterned shawl hiding her bent head.

A slender gloved hand flashed out, aiming a very businesslike stunner.

"Look out!" Vorpatril cried, and, to Tej's bewilderment, lurched to try to shove her behind him. Uselessly, as it only cleared the target for Rish. The stun beam kneecapped him neatly, and he fell, Tej supposed, the way a tree was said to, not that she'd ever witnessed a tree do such a thing. Most of the trees she'd seen before she'd fetched up on Komarr had lived in tubs, and did not engage in such vigorous behavior. In any case, he crashed to the tiles with a vague thrashing of upper branches and a loud *plonk* as his head hit. "Owww . . ." he moaned piteously.

The quiet buzz of the stunner had not carried far; no one popped out of their first floor flat door to investigate either that or the thump, alarming as the latter had seemed to Tej.

"Search him," Rish instructed tersely. "I'll cover you." She stood just out of reach of his long but no doubt tingling arms, aiming the stunner at his head. He eyed it woozily.

Tej knelt and began going through his pockets. His athletic appearance was not a façade; his body felt quite fit, beneath her probing fingers.

"Oh," he mumbled after a moment. "You two are *t'gether*. Thass all right, then . . ."

The first thing Tej's patting hand found was a small flimsy, tucked into his breast pocket. Featuring a still scan of her. A chill washed through her.

She seized his well-shaved jaw, stared into his eyes, demanded tightly: "Are you a hired killer?"

Still weirdly dilated from the stun nimbus, his eyes were not tracking quite in unison. He appeared to have to think this question over. "Well . . . in a *sense* . . ."

Abandoning interrogation in favor of physical evidence, Tej extracted the wallet he'd flashed earlier, a door remote much like her own, and a slender stunner hidden in an inner pocket. No more lethal weaponry surfaced.

"Let me see that," said Rish, and Tej obediently handed up the stunner. "Who is this meat really?"

"Hey, I c'n answer that," their victim mumbled, but fell prudently silent again as she jerked her aim back at him.

The top item in the wallet was the credit chit. Beneath it was a disquietingly official-looking security card with a heavy coding strip identifying the man further as one *Captain Ivan X. Vorpatril, Barrayaran Imperial Service, Operations, Vorbarr Sultana*. Another mentioned such titles as *Aide-de-Camp to Admiral Desplains, Chief of Operations*, with a complicated building address featuring lots of alphanumeric strings. There was also a strange little stack of tiny rectangles of heavy paper, reading only *Lord Ivan Xav Vorpatril*, nothing else. The fine, black, raised lettering bumped under her curious fingertips. She passed them all up for Rish's inspection.

On sudden impulse, she drew off one of his polished

shoes, which made him twitch in a scrambled reflex, and looked inside. *Military* issue shoes, aha, that explained their unusual style. 12 Ds, though she couldn't think of a reason for that to be important, except that they fit the rest of his proportions.

"Barrayaran military stunner, personally coded grip," Rish reported. She frowned at the handful of IDs. "These all look quite authentic."

"Assure you, they are," their prisoner put in earnestly from the floor. "Damn. By never mentioned any lethal blue-faced ladies, t' ratfink. Izzat . . . makeup?"

Tej murmured in uncertainty, "I suppose the best cappers would look authentic. Nice to know they're taking me seriously enough not to send cut-rate rental meat."

"Capper," wheezed Vorpatril — was that his real name? "Thass Jacksonian slang, innit? For a contract killer. You expectin' one? That 'splains a lot . . ."

"Rish," Tej said, a sinking feeling beginning in her stomach, "do you think he could really be a Barrayaran officer? Oh, no, what do we do with him if he *is*?"

Rish glanced uneasily at the outside door. "We can't stay here. Someone else could come in or out at any moment. Better get him upstairs."

Their prisoner did not cry out or try to struggle as they womanhandled his limp, heavy body into the lift tube, up three flights, and down the corridor to the corner flat. As they dragged him inside, he remarked to the air, "Hey, made it inside her door on t' first date! Are things lookin' up for Ma Vorpatril's boy, or what?"

"This is not a date, you idiot," Tej snapped at him.

To her annoyance, his smile inexplicably broadened.

Unnerved by the warm glance, she dumped him down hard in the middle of the living room floor.

"But it could be," he went on. ". . . To a fellow of certain special tastes, that is. Bit of a waste that I'm not one of 'em, but hey, I can be flexible. Was never quite sure about m'cousin Miles, though. Amazons all the way for him. Compensating, I always thought . . ."

"Do you ever give up?" Tej demanded.

"Not until you laugh," he answered gravely. "First rule of picking up girls, y'know; she laughs, you live." He added after a moment, "Sorry I triggered your, um, triggers back there. I'm not attacking you."

"Dead right you're not," said Rish, scowling. She tossed shawl, vest, and gloves onto the couch, and dug out her stunner again.

Vorpatril's mouth gaped as he stared up at her.

A black tank top and loose trousers did not hide lapis lazuli-blue skin shot with metallic gold veins, platinum blond pelt of hair, pointed blue ears framing the fine skull and jaw — to Tej, who had known her companion and odd-sister for her whole life, she was just *Rish*, but there were good reasons she'd kept to the flat, out of sight, ever since they'd come to Komarr.

"Thass no makeup! Izzat . . . body mod, or genetic construct?" their prisoner asked, still wide-eyed.

Tej stiffened. Barrayarans were reputed to be unpleasantly prejudiced against genetic variance, whether accidental or designed. Perhaps dangerously so.

"'Cause if you did it to yourself, thass one thing, but if somebody did it *to* you, thass . . . thass just *wrong*."

"I am grateful for my existence and pleased with my

appearance," Rish told him, her sharp tone underscored by a jab of her stunner. "*Your* ignorant opinion is entirely irrelevant."

"Very boorish, too," Tej put in, offended on Rish's behalf. Was she not one of the Baronne's own Jewels?

He managed a little apologetic flip of his hands — stun wearing off already? "No, no, 's gorgeous, ma'am, really. Took me by surprise, is all."

He seemed sincere. He hadn't been expecting Rish. Wouldn't a capper or even hired meat have been better briefed? That, and his bizarre attempt to protect her in the foyer, and all the rest, were adding to her queasy fear that she'd just made a serious mistake, one with consequences as lethal, if more roundabout, as if he'd been a real capper.

Tej knelt to strip off his wristcom, which was clunky and unfashionable.

"Right, but please don't fool with that," he sighed. He sounded more resigned than resistant. "Tends to melt down if other people try to access it. And they make issuing a replacement the most unbelievable pain in the ass. On purpose, I think."

Rish examined it. "Also military." She set it gingerly aside on the nearby lamp table beside the rest of his possessions.

How many details had to point in the same direction before one decided they pointed true? *Depends on how costly it is to be mistaken, maybe?* "Do we have any fast-penta left?" Tej asked Rish.

The blue woman shook her head, her gold ear-bangles flashing. "Not since that stop on Pol Station."

"I could go out and try to get some . . ." Here, the truth drug was illegal in private hands, being reserved to the authorities. Tej was fairly sure that worked about as well as it did anywhere.

"Not by yourself, at this hour," said Rish, in her *and no backtalk* voice. Her gaze down at the man grew more thoughtful. "There's always good old-fashioned torture . . ."

"Hey!" Vorpatril objected, still working his jaw against the stun numbness. "There's always good old-fashioned *asking politely*, didja ever think of that?"

"It would be bound," said Tej to Rish, primly overriding his interjection, "to make too much noise. Especially at this time of night. You know how we can hear Ser and Sera Palmi carrying on, next door."

"Houseless grubbers," muttered Rish. Which was rude, but then, she'd also had her sleep impeded by the amorous neighbors. Anyway, Tej wasn't sure but that she and Rish qualified as Houseless, too, now. And grubbers as well.

And that was another weird thing. The man wasn't yelling for help, either. She tried to decide if a capper, even one who'd had the tables so turned upon him, would have the nerve to bluff his way out past an influx of local police. Vorpatril did not seem to be lacking in nerve. Or else, against all the evidence, he didn't think he had reason to fear them. Mystifying.

"We'd better tie him up before the stun wears off," said Tej, watching his tremors ease. "Or else stun him again."

He did not even try to resist this process. Tej, a little concerned for that pale skin, vetoed the harsh plastic rope from the kitchen stores that Rish unearthed, and pulled out her soft scarves, at least for his wrists. She still let Rish tug them plenty tight.

"This is all very well for tonight," said Vorpatril, observing closely, "especially if you break out t' feathers — do you have any feathers? because I don't like that ice cube thing — but I have to tell you, there's going to be a problem come morning. See, back home, if I didn't show up for work on time after a night on the town, nobody would panic right off. But this is Komarr. After forty years, assimilation into the Imperium's going pretty well, they say, but there's no denying it got off to a bad start. Still folks out there with grudges. Any Barrayaran soldier disappears in the domes, Service Security takes it up seriously, and quick, too. Which, um . . . I'm thinking might not be too welcome to you, if they track me to your door."

His comment was uncomfortably shrewd. "Does anyone know where you are?"

Rish answered for him: "Whoever gave him your picture and address does."

"Oh. Yes." Tej winced. "Who *did* give you my picture?"

"Mm, mutual acquaintance? Well, maybe not too mutual—he didn't seem to know much about you. But he did seem to think you were in some kind of danger." Vorpatril looked down rather ironically at the bindings now securing him to a kitchen chair, dragged out to the living room for the purpose. "It seems you think so, too."

Tej stared at him in disbelief. "Are you saying someone sent *you* to *me* as a *bodyguard*?"

He appeared affronted by her rising tones. "Why not?"

"Aside from the fact that the two of us took you down without even getting winded?" said Rish.

"You did too get winded. Dragging me up here. Anyway, I don't hit girls. Generally. Well, there was that time with Delia Koudelka when I was twelve, but she hit me first, and it really hurt, too. Her mama and mine were inclined to be merciful, but Uncle Aral wasn't — gave me a permanent twitch on the subject, let me tell you."

"Shut. *Up*," said Rish, driven to twitch a bit herself. "Nothing about him makes sense!"

"Unless he's telling the truth," said Tej slowly.

"Even if he's telling the truth, he's blithering," said Rish. "Our dinner is getting cold. Come on, eat, then we'll figure out what to do with him."

With reluctance, Tej allowed herself to be drawn into the kitchen. A glance over her shoulder elicited a look of hope from the man, which faded disconsolately as she didn't turn back. She heard his trailing mutter: "Hell, maybe I should've *started* with ponies . . ."

— end excerpt —
from *Captain Vorpatril's Alliance*
available in hardcover,
November 2012, from Baen Books

The Following is an excerpt from:

SUNSET
OF THE
GODS

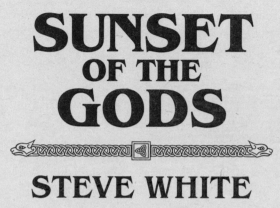

STEVE WHITE

Available from Baen Books
July 2012
Trade Paperback

CHAPTER ONE

EVEN ON OLD EARTH, nothing was forever unchanging, as Jason Thanou had better reason than most to know—not even on the island of Corfu, however much it might seem to drift down the centuries in a bubble of suspended time, lost in its own placid beauty.

For example, the Paliokastritsa Monastery had long ago ceased to be a monastery, and the golden and silver vessels were no longer brought there every August from the village Strinillas for the festival of the Transfiguration of Jesus Christ, by a road which had led laboriously up the monastery's hill between tall oak trees and through the smell of sage and rosemary. Now aircars swooped up to the summit, and the monastery had been converted into a resort, bringing visitors from all around Earth and far beyond it, who stared at the ancient chambers, a few of those visitors at least trying to comprehend what must have been felt by the cenobites who had lived out their lives of total commitment under the mosaic gaze of Christ Pantocrator.

They came, of course, for the incomparable location. From the monastery balcony, one could look out on the endlessness of Homer's wine-dark sea. Northward and southward stretched the coast, its beaches broken into a succession of coves by ridges clothed in olive and cypress trees and culminating in gigantic steep rocks like the one that the local people would still tell you was the petrified ship the Phaecians, once rulers of this island, had sent to bear Odysseus home to Ithaca and his faithful Penelope.

Now Jason stood on that balcony and wondered, not for the first time, what he was doing here.

He could have taken his richly deserved R&R in Australia, where the Temporal Regulatory Authority's great displacer stage was located . . . or, for that matter, anywhere on Earth. Or he could have gone directly back to his homeworld of Hesperia—his fondest desire, as he had been telling everyone who would listen. Instead he had come back to Greece . . . but only to this northwesternmost fringe of it, as though hesitating at the threshold of sights he had seen mere weeks ago. Weeks, that is, in terms of his own stream of consciousness, but four thousand years ago as the rest of the universe measured the passage of time.

There were places in Greece to which he was not yet prepared to go, and things on which he was not yet prepared to look. Not Crete, for example, and the ruins of Knossos, whose original grandeur he had seen before the frescoes had been painted. Not Athens, with its archaeological museum which held the golden death-mask Heinrich Schliemann had called the Mask of Agamemnon, although Jason knew whose face it *really* was, for he had known that face when it was young and beardless. Certainly not Santorini, whose cataclysmic volcanic death he had witnessed in 1628 B.C. And most assuredly not Mycenae with its grave circles, for he knew to whom some of those bones belonged—and one female skeleton in particular. . . .

Unconsciously, his hand strayed as it so often did to his pocket and withdrew a small plastic case. As always, his guts clenched with apprehension as he opened it. Yes, the tiny metallic sphere, no larger than a small pea, was still there. He closed the case with an annoyed snap. He had seen the curious glances the compulsive habit had drawn from his fellow resort guests. The general curiosity had intensified when word had spread that he was a time traveler, around whose latest expedition into the past clustered some very odd rumors.

"Is it still there?" asked a familiar voice from behind him, speaking with the precise, consciously archaic diction Earth's intelligentsia liked to affect.

A sigh escaped Jason. "Yes, as you already know," he said before turning around to confront a gaunt, elderly man, darkly clad in a style of expensive fustiness—the uniform of Earth's academic establishment. "And what brings the Grand High Muckety-Muck of the Temporal Regulatory Authority here?"

Kyle Rutherford smiled and stroked his gray Vandyke. "What kind of attitude is that? I'd hoped to catch you before your departure for. . . . Oh, you know: that home planet of yours."

"Hesperia," Jason said through clenched teeth. "Psi 5 Aurigae III. As you are perfectly well aware," he added, although he knew better than to expect anyone of Rutherford's ilk to admit to being able to tell one colonial system from another. Knowledge of that sort was just so inexpressibly, crashingly vulgar in their rarefied world of arcane erudition. "And now that you've gotten all the irritating affectations out of your system, answer the question. *Why* were you so eager to catch me?"

"Well," said Rutherford, all innocence, "I naturally wanted to know if your convalescence is complete. I gather it is."

Jason gave a grudgingly civil nod. In earlier eras, what he had been through—breaking a foot, then being forced to walk on it for miles over Crete's mountainous terrain, and then having it traumatized anew—would have left him with a permanent limp at least. Nowadays, it was a matter of removing the affected portions and regenerating them. It had taken a certain amount of practice to break in the new segments, but no one seeing Jason now would have guessed he had ever been injured, much less that he had received that injury struggling ashore on the ruined shores of Crete after riding a tsunami.

The scars to his soul were something else.

"So," he heard Rutherford saying, "I imagine you plan to be returning to, ah, Hesperia without too much more ado, and resume your commission with the Colonial Rangers there."

"That's right. Those 'special circumstances' you invoked don't exactly apply any longer, do they?" Rutherford's expression told Jason that he was correct. He was free of the reactivation clause that had brought him unwillingly out of his early retirement from the Temporal Service, the Authority's enforcement arm. He excelled himself (so he thought) by not rubbing it in. Feeling indulgent, he even made an effort to be conciliatory. "Anyway, you're not going to need me—or anybody else—again for any expeditions into the remote past in this part of the world, are you?"

"Well . . . that's not altogether true."

"What?" Jason took a deep breath. "Look, Kyle, I'm only too well aware that the governing council of the Authority consists of snobbish, pompous, fatheaded old pedants." (*Like you*, he sternly commanded himself not to add.) "But surely not even they can be so stupid! Our expedition revealed that the Teloi aliens were active—dominant, in fact—on Earth in proto-historical times, when they had established themselves as 'gods' with the help of their advanced technology. The sights and sounds on my recorder implant corroborate my testimony beyond any possibility of a doubt. And even without that. . . ." Jason's hand strayed involuntarily toward his pocket before he could halt it.

"Rest assured that no one questions your findings, and that there are no plans to send any expeditions back to periods earlier than the Santorini explosion." Rutherford pursed his mouth. "The expense of such remote temporal displacements is ruinous anyway, given the energy expenditure required. You have no idea—"

"Actually, I do," Jason cut in rudely.

"Ahem! Yes, of course I realize you are not entirely unacquainted with these matters. Well, at any rate the council, despite your lack of respect for its members—

which you've never made any attempt to conceal—is quite capable of seeing the potential hazards of any extratemporal intervention that might come in conflict with the Teloi. The consequences are incalculable, in fact."

"Then what *are* you talking about?"

"We are intensely interested in the role played in subsequent history by those Teloi who were *not* trapped in their artificial pocket universe when its dimensional interface device was destroyed—or 'imprisoned in Tartarus' as the later Greeks had it. The 'New Gods,' as I believe they were called."

"Also known as the Olympians," Jason nodded, remembering the face of Zeus.

"And by various other names elsewhere, all across the Indo-European zone," added Rutherford with a nod of his own. "They were worshiped, under their various names, for a very long time, well into recorded history, although naturally their actual manifestations grew less frequent. And as you learned, the Teloi had very long lifespans, although they could of course die from violence."

"So you want to look in on times when those 'manifestations' were believed to have taken place? Like the gods fighting for the two sides in the Trojan War?"

"The Trojan War. . . ." For a moment, Rutherford's face glowed with a fervor little less ecstatic than that which had once raised the stones of the monastery. Then the glow died and he shook his head sadly. "No. We cannot send an expedition back to observe an historic event unless we can pinpoint exactly when it took place. Dendrochronology and the distribution of wind-blown volcanic ash enabled us to narrow the Santorini explosion to autumn of 1628 B.C. But after all these centuries there is still no consensus as to the date of the Trojan War. It is pretty generally agreed that Eratosthenes' dating of 1184 B.C. is worthless, based as it was on an arbitrary length assigned to the generations in the genealogies of the Dorian royal families of Sparta. On the other hand—"

"Kyle. . . ."

"—the Parian Marble gave a precise date of June 5, 1209 B.C. for the sack, but it was based on astronomical computations which were even more questionable. Other calculations—"

"*Kyle.*"

"—were as early as 1334 B.C. in Doulis of Samos, or as late as 1135 B.C. in Ephorus, whereas—"

"*KYLE!*"

"Oh . . . yes, where was I? Well, suffice it to say that even the Classical Greeks couldn't agree on the date, and modern scholarship has done no better. Estimates range from 1250 to 1180 B.C., and are therefore effectively useless for our purposes. The same problem applies to the voyage of the Argonauts, the war of the Seven against Thebes and other events remembered in the Greek myths. And, to repeat, the gods tended not to put in appearances in the full light of history. There is one exception, however." Rutherford paused portentously. "The Battle of Marathon."

"Huh?" All at once, Jason's interest awoke. It momentarily took his mind off the irritation he felt, as usual, around Rutherford. "You mean the one where the Athenians defeated the Persians? But that was much later—490 B.C., wasn't it?"

"August or September of 490 B.C., most probably the

former," Rutherford nodded approvingly. The faint note of surprise underlying the approval made it less than altogether flattering. "By that period, it is difficult to know just how widespread *literal* belief in the Olympian gods was. And yet contemporary Greeks seem to have been firmly convinced that Pan—a minor god whose name is the root of the English 'panic'—intervened actively on behalf of the Athenians."

"I never encountered, or heard of, a Teloi who went by that name," said Jason dubiously.

"I know. Another difficulty is that Pan—unlike most Greek gods, who were visualized as idealized humans—was a hybrid figure with the legs and horns of a goat and exceptionally large . . . er, male sexual equipment."

"That doesn't sound like the Teloi," said Jason, recalling seven-to-eight-foot-tall humanoids with hair like a shimmering alloy of gold and silver, their pale-skinned faces long, narrow and sharp-featured, with huge oblique eyes under brows which, like their high cheekbones, tilted upward. Those eyes' strangely opaque blue irises seemed to leak their color into the pale-blue "whites." The overall impression hovered uneasily between exotic beauty and disturbing alienness.

"Nevertheless," said Rutherford, "the matter is unquestionably worth looking into. And, aside from the definite timeframe involved, there are numerous other benefits. For one thing, the more recent date will result in a lesser energy requirement for the displacement."

"Well, yes. 490 B.C. is only—" (Jason did the mental arithmetic without the help of his computer implant) "—twenty-eight hundred and seventy years ago. Still, that's one hell of an 'only!' Compared to any expedition you'd ever sent out before ours—"

"Too true. But the importance of investigating Teloi involvement in historical times is such that we have been able to obtain authorization. It also helped that the Battle of Marathon is so inherently interesting. It was, after all, crucial to the survival of Western civilization. And there are a number of unanswered questions about it, quite aside from the Teloi. So we can kill two birds with one stone, as people say."

"Still, I don't imagine you'll be able to send a very large party." The titanic energy expenditure required for displacement was tied to two factors: the mass to be displaced, and the temporal "distance" it was to be sent into the past. This was why Jason had taken only two companions with him to the Bronze Age, by far the longest displacement ever attempted. Since the trade-off was inescapable, the Authority was constantly looking into ways to reduce the total energy requirement, and the researchers were ceaselessly holding out hope of eventual success, but to date the problem remained intractable. This, aside from sheer caution, was why no large items of equipment were ever sent back in time. Sending human bodies—with their clothing, and any items they could wear or carry on their persons, for reasons related to the esoteric physics of time travel—was expensive enough.

"True, the party will have to be a small one. But the appropriation is comparable to that for your last expedition. So we can send four people." Rutherford took on the aspect of one bestowing a great gift. "We want you—"

"—To be the mission leader," Jason finished for him.

"Even though this time you have to *ask* me to do it," he couldn't resist adding, for all his growing interest.

Rutherford spoke with what was clearly a great, if not supreme, effort. "I am aware that we have had our differences. And I own that I may have been a trifle high-handed on the last occasion. But surely you of all people, as discoverer of the Teloi element in the human past, can see the importance of investigating it further."

"Maybe. But why do you need me, specifically, to investigate it?"

"I should think it would be obvious. You are the nearest thing we have to a surviving Teloi expert." Jason was silent, as this was undeniable. Rutherford pressed his advantage. "Also, there is the perennial problem of inconspicuousness." Rutherford gazed at Jason, who knew he was gazing at wavy brown black hair, dark brown eyes, light-olive skin and straight features.

Jason, despite his name, was no more "ethnically pure" than any other inhabitant of Hesperia or any other colony world. But by some fluke, the Hellenic contribution to his genes had reemerged to such an extent that he could pass as a Greek in any era of history. It also helped that he stood less than six feet, and therefore was not freakishly tall by most historical standards. It had always made him valuable to the Temporal Regulatory Authority, which was legally interdicted from using genetic nanoviruses to tailor its agents' appearance to fit various milieus in Earth's less-cosmopolitan past. The nightmare rule of the Transhuman movement had placed that sort of thing as far beyond the pale of acceptability as the Nazis had once placed anti-Semitism.

"If we were sending an expedition to northern Europe," Rutherford persisted, "I'd use Lundberg. Or to pre-Columbian America, Cardones. But for this part of Earth, you are the only suitable choice currently available, or at least the only one with your—" (another risibly obvious effort at being ingratiating) "—undeniable talents."

Jason turned around, leaned on the parapet, and looked out over the breathtaking panorama once again. "Are you sure you really want me? After my latest display of those 'talents.'"

Rutherford's face took on a compassionate expression he would never have permitted himself if Jason had been looking. "I understand. Up till now, you have taken understandable pride in never having lost a single member of any expedition you have led. And this time you returned from the past alone. But that was due to extraordinary and utterly unforeseeable circumstances. No one dreamed you would encounter what you did in the remote past. And no one blames you."

"But aside from that, aren't you afraid I might be just a little too . . . close to this?" Once again, Jason clenched his fist to prevent his hand from straying to his pocket.

Rutherford smiled, noticing the gesture. "If anything, I should think that what you know of Dr. Sadaka-Ramirez's fate would make you even *more* interested."

Deirdre, thought Jason, recalling his last glimpse of those green eyes as she had faded into the past. *Deirdre, from whom it is practically a statistical certainty that I myself am descended.*

He turned back to face Rutherford. "Well, I don't suppose it can do any harm to meet the other people you have lined up."

— end excerpt —
from *Sunset of the Gods*
available in trade paperback,
July 2012, from Baen Books

PRAISE FOR
STEVE WHITE

"Exciting extraterrestrial battle scenes served up with a measure of thought and science."—*Kliatt*

"White offers fast action and historically informed world-building."—*Publishers Weekly*

"White perfectly blends background information, technical and historical details, vivid battle scenes and well-written characters. . . . a great package."—*Starlog*

SAINT ANTHONY'S FIRE
978-1-4391-3329-3 • $7.99 • PB
Elizabethan England is menaced by Spanish forces armed with powerful weapons provided by aliens from another dimensional world. Only if the source of the weapons, somewhere in the Americas, can be found is there hope for England—and the world.

BLOOD OF THE HEROES
1-4165-2143-7 • $7.99 • PB
Jason Thanoi of the Temporal Regulatory Authority was nursemaiding an academic mission to ancient Greece to view one of the biggest volcanoes at the dawn of human history. He and his charges were about to find that there was more to those old legends of gods and heroes than anyone had imagined. . .

FORGE OF THE TITANS
0-7434-9895-X • * $7.99 • PB
The old gods—actually extra-dimensional aliens with awesome powers—have returned, requesting human help against the evil Titans. But, judging from mythology, how much can you actually trust a god?

EAGLE AGAINST THE STARS
0-671-57846-4 • $6.99 • PB

WOLF AMONG THE STARS
978-1-4516-3754-0 • $25.00 • HC

One burned-out secret agent against the new alien masters of Earth.

PRINCE OF SUNSET
0-671-87869-7 • $6.99 • PB

Basil, Sonja and Torval, recent graduates of the Imperial Deep Space Fleet Academy, were looking forward to their future. But with a dying Empire and a rebellion threatening to engulf the galaxy in war, only they and powerful dragon-like beings held the key to stave off utter destruction.

And don't miss White's bestselling collaborations with David Weber:

THE STARS AT WAR
0-7434-8841-5 • $25.00 • HC

Crusade and *In Death Ground* in one large volume.

THE STARS AT WAR II
0-7434-9912-3 • $27.00 • HC

The Shiva Option and *Insurrection* (revised version) in one large mega-volume.

Exodus
with Shirley Meier
1-4165-2098-8 $26.00 HC
1-4165-5561-7 $7.99 PB

The sequel to *The Stars at War II*. Decades of peace have let the four races of the alliance grow complacent–dangerously so. From a dying planet, aliens have arrived in city-sized ships, looking for new worlds, inhabited or not.

Extremis
with Charles E. Gannon
978-1-4391-3433-7 • $24.00 • HC

Invaders fleeing an exploded home star plan to conquer the galactic region already occupied by humans and their allies, unless the alliance seen in the *NY Times* bestseller *The Shiva Option* can stop them.

Available in bookstores everywhere.
Order e-books online at our secure, easy to use website:
www.baen.com

"SPACE OPERA IS ALIVE AND WELL"*

And *NY Times* Bestseller
DAVID WEBER
is the New Reigning King of the Spaceways!

HONOR HARRINGTON NOVELS:

On Basilisk Station pb • 0-7434-3571-0 • $7.99
"... an outstanding blend of military/technical writing balanced by supderb character development and an excellent degree of human drama ... very highly recommended."— *Wilson Library Bulletin*

The Honor of the Queen pb • 0-7434-3572-9 • $7.99
"Honor fights her way with fists, brains, and tactical genius through a tangle of politics, battles and cultural differences. Although battered she ends this book with her honor, and the Queen's, intact."—*Kliatt*

The Short Victorious War pb • 0-7434-3573-7 • $7.99
"This remarkable story will appeal to readers interested in warfare, science, and technology of the future or just in interpersonal relationships, and important part of the story. Gratifying, especially to female readers, is the total equality of the sexes!"—*Kliatt*

Field of Dishonor pb • 0-7434-3574-5 • $7.99
"Great stuff...compelling combat combined with engaging characters for a great space opera adventure."—*Locus*

* *Starlog*

Flag in Exile   pb • 0-7434-3575-3 • $7.99

"Packs enough punch to smash a starship to smithereens." —*Publishers Weekly*

Honor Among Enemies   hc • 0-671-87723-2 • $21.00
                                 pb • 0-671-87783-6 • $7.99

"Star Wars as it might have been written by C.S. Forester . . . fast-paced entertainment." —*Booklist*

In Enemy Hands   hc • 0-671-87793-3 • $22.00
                                 pb • 0-671-57770-0 • $7.99

After being ambushed, Honor finds herself aboard an enemy cruiser, bound for her scheduled execution. But one lesson Honor has never learned is how to give up!

Echoes of Honor   hc • 0-671-87892-1 • $24.00
                                 pb • 0-671-57833-2 • $7.99

"Brilliant! Brilliant! Brilliant!"—Anne McCaffrey

Ashes of Victory   hc • 0-671-57854-5 • $25.00
                                 pb • 0-671-31977-9 • $7.99

Honor has escaped from the prison planet called Hell and returned to the Manticoran Alliance, to the heart of a furnace of new weapons, new strategies, new tactics, spies, diplomacy, and assassination.

War of Honor   hc • 0-7434-3545-1 • $26.00
                                 pb • 0-7434-7167-9 • $7.99

No one wanted another war. Neither the Republic of Haven, nor Manticore—and certainly not Honor Harrington. Unfortunately, what they wanted didn't matter.

At All Costs   hc • 1-4165-0911-9 • $26.00
                                 pb • 1-4165-4414-3 • $7.99

The war with the Republic of Haven has resumed. . . disastrously for the Star Kingdom of Manticore. The alternative to victory is total defeat, yet this time the cost of victory will be agonizingly high.

Mission of Honor   hc • 978-1-4391-3361-3 • $27.00

pb • 978-1-4391-3451-1 • $7.99

The unstoppable juggernaut of the mighty Solarian League is on a collision course with Manticore, and billions of casualties may be just over the horizon. But Manticore's enemies may not have thought of everything—if everything Honor Harrington loves is going down to destruction, it won't be going alone.

A Rising Thunder   hc • 978-1-4516-3806-6 • $26.00

The survival of Manticore is at stake as Honor must battle not only the powerful Solarian League, but also the secret puppetmasters who plan to pick up all the pieces after galactic civilization is shattered..

HONORVERSE VOLUMES:

Crown of Slaves (with Eric Flint)   pb • 0-7434-9899-2 • $7.99

Torch of Freedom (with Eric Flint)   hc • 1-4391-3305-0 • $26.00

pb • 978-1-4391-3408-5 • $8.99

Sent on a mission to keep Erewhon from breaking with Manticore, the Star Kingdom's most able agent and the Queen's niece may not even be able to escape with their lives....

The Shadow of Saganami   hc • 0-7434-8852-0 • $26.00

pb • 1-4165-0929-1 • $7.99

Storm from the Shadows   hc • 1-4165-9147-8 • $27.00

pb • 1-4391-3354-9 • $8.99

A new generation of officers, trained by Honor Harrington, are ready to hit the front lines as war erupts again.

A Beautiful Friendship   hc • 978-1-4516-3747-2 • $18.99

"A stellar introduction to a new YA science-fiction series."
—*Booklist* starred review

ANTHOLOGIES EDITED BY DAVID WEBER:

More Than Honor	pb • 0-671-87857-3 •	$7.99
Worlds of Honor	pb • 0-671-57855-3 •	$7.99
Changer of Worlds	pb • 0-7434-3520-6 •	$7.99
The Service of the Sword	pb • 0-7434-8836-9 •	$7.99
In Fire Forged	hc • 978-1-4391-3414-6 •	$26.00

THE DAHAK SERIES:

Mutineers' Moon	pb • 0-671-72085-6 •	$7.99
The Armageddon Inheritance	pb • 0-671-72197-6 •	$7.99
Heirs of Empire	pb • 0-671-87707-0 •	$7.99
Empire from the Ashes	trade pb • 1-4165-0993-X •	$16.00

Contains *Mutineers' Moon, The Armageddon Inheritance* and *Heirs of Empire* in one volume.

THE BAHZELL SAGA:

Oath of Swords	trade pb • 1-4165-2086-4 •	$15.00
	pb • 0-671-87642-2 •	$7.99
The War God's Own	hc • 0-671-87873-5 •	$22.00
	pb • 0-671-57792-1 •	$7.99
Wind Rider's Oath	hc • 0-7434-8821-0 •	$26.00
	pb • 1-4165-0895-3 •	$7.99

Bahzell Bahnakson of the hradani is no knight in shining armor and doesn't want to deal with anybody else's problems, let alone the War God's. The War God thinks otherwise.

BOLO VOLUMES:

Bolo!	hc • 0-7434-9872-0 •	$25.00
	pb • 1-4165-2062-7 •	$7.99

Keith Laumer's popular saga of the Bolos continues.

Old Soldiers	pb • 1-4165-2104-6 •	$7.99

A new Bolo novel.

OTHER NOVELS:

The Excalibur Alternative hc • 0-671-31860-8 • $21.00

pb • 0-7434-3584-2 • $7.99

An English knight and an alien dragon join forces to overthrow the alien slavers who captured them. Set in the world of David Drake's *Ranks of Bronze*.

In Fury Born pb • 1-4165-2131-3 • $7.99

A greatly expanded new version of *Path of the Fury*, with almost twice the original wordage.

1633 with Eric Flint hc • 0-7434-3542-7 • $26.00

pb • 0-7434-7155-5 • $7.99

1634: The Baltic War with Eric Flint pb • 1-4165-5588-9 • $7.99

American freedom and justice versus the tyrannies of the 17th century. Set in Flint's *1632* universe.

THE STARFIRE SERIES
WITH STEVE WHITE:

The Stars at War I hc • 0-7434-8841-5 • $25.00

Rewritten *Insurrection* and *In Death Ground* in one massive volume.

The Stars at War II hc • 0-7434-9912-3 • $27.00

The Shiva Option and *Crusade* in one massive volume.

PRINCE ROGER NOVELS
WITH JOHN RINGO:

March Upcountry pb • 0-7434-3538-9 • $7.99

March to the Sea pb • 0-7434-3580-X • $7.99

March to the Stars pb • 0-7434-8818-0 • $7.99

We Few pb • 1-4165-2084-8 • $7.99

"This is as good as military sf gets." —*Booklist*

Available in bookstores everywhere.
Or order ebooks online at www.baen.com.